Roots of the Wicked

By:

Keta Kendric

Keta Kendric/Hot Pen Publishing, LLC
P.O. Box 55060
Virginia Beach, VA 23471

Cover: Steamy Designs
Editing: A. L. Barron and Tam Jernigan

ISBN: 978-1-7332914-1-5/Roots of the Wicked

Contents

Dedication

To readers and fellow authors. The love and support you have shined on me during my writing journey have filled my heart and uplifted my spirit. I can't say thank you enough to express the true depth of my gratitude.

Synopsis

Jax Saint-Pierre is dedicated to building the success of her business and living life the way she mapped it. That is, until driven and charismatic Chase Taylorson stands firmly in her path with his arrogant charm. He was the first man to make her consider changing her strict no-relationship rule, but with her wicked past, she keeps him at a distance for his own good.

Chase Taylorson is the head of a billion-dollar empire. All it takes is one chance encounter with Jax Saint-Pierre to blow up his well-organized world. Independent and feisty, she demands he check his ego at the door, forget his entitled ways, and bury his coveted bachelor status in the sand. Jax assumed he had the perfect life, but will soon come to realize, even the privileged are tethered to wicked roots.

Warning
This book contains explicit language, strong sexual content, and triggers that may be offensive to some readers. If you are easily offended or triggered this may not be the book for you.

Note
Despite the title of this book, it is not dark romance. Although it contains hard subject matter, this book is not this author's usual book where bodies are dropping, and blood is spilling. Like Sankofa, this book is more about the journey of two individuals who have to glance into their pasts in order to see a way to their future. This book does contain a lot of explicit sex and drama though.

Chapter One

Chase

In and out of focus, my hazy gaze spanned the length of a small, pale arm resting on my chest. A curtain of thick black hair kept the face hidden, the length stretching across my body. The rumpled bed, the scent of sex still lingering in the air, and my dry mouth offered hints of how my night had gone.

I squeezed my eyes tight in an attempt to recall any time before this moment, with this woman, but only snatches of memories revealed themselves. I eased up, doing my best to avoid rousing her laying naked and half atop me. The sheets had pooled below the curve of her bare ass. Her blue panties were slung across the tilted lampshade on the bedside table, the rest of our clothes spread across the floor in discarded heaps.

A sigh of relief eased my mind at the sight of the used condom, stuck to my thigh. I mouthed a silent prayer; grateful I had been lucid enough to use protection. Once I successfully navigated my way from beneath the woman and out of the bed, I snatched some Kleenex from the box that had fallen to the floor. A touch of shame gripped me while I cleaned myself and folded the condom into the wad of tissue.

A glance over my shoulder showed the woman sound asleep. Grabbing my phone, I dragged my wrinkled clothes off the floor before heading into the bathroom. Condom flushed, bladder relieved, I washed my hands and avoided my reflection in the mirror.

A splash of cold water over my face did nothing to break apart the thick layers of fog still clouding my mind. I dried my hands and face with a fresh towel, before I swiped the shiny surface of my phone. Travis Holmes, my assistant, answered on the first ring.

"Good morning boss."

"Where am I? There is a long-haired brunette with me. Is she authorized?"

My mind called up choppy pieces of the previous night. I had attended some type of social function before I ended up here.

This wasn't my first time waking up in a hotel room with a strange woman I couldn't recall meeting in any capacity. I slipped my feet into my pants, figuring my boxers were still in bed with the woman.

"You attended the Mayor's Charity benefit for breast cancer awareness, and Paul, *your driver*, drove you to the Ritz-Carlton afterward."

I didn't miss the note of sarcasm in his tone. Travis had worked for me long enough to have earned every bit of the sassiness he dished out.

"You called me last night, *right before* the event to book you a room. Oh, and the woman's authorized."

He paused, no doubt reviewing my schedule for today.

Authorized meant the woman had signed a nondisclosure agreement that prevented her from speaking to the media about our time together. This was my life. I was one of the richest people in the country, but my personal life was a hazard zone of impulsive decisions.

I was revered as a well put-together billionaire business mogul. One of America's most sought-after bachelors and financial guru to the stars. However, the world saw only what it wanted to see. Through camera lenses, televised and written interviews, and the word of the stars that I worked with, I had the perfect life.

The media had turned me into a larger-than-life character, but half the time I didn't even feel human. I was a robot. One who smiled for the cameras and maintained the image built for me. Sit here, wear this, recommend that, date her, go there, and smile. My days were filled with work and tight schedules, performing to intrigue a large-scale audience.

Truth was, I was the loneliest person in the world. The ruthless women I met had turned me into a cynic who no longer cared about an endearing relationship. Alcohol fueled one-night stands with women that appealed as only a means to satisfy my sexual needs, suited me just fine.

The media casted me as the man that had it all, charm, good looks, and wealth, but emotionally, I was starved. My heart wept to be tethered to something meaningful. It was too bad I had yet to figure out what that something was, or how to attain it.

I made every attempt not to complain out loud or appear ungrateful as the media publicity had been the catalyst for me reaching my billionaire's status. It had also earned me appearances on television shows and cameos in blockbuster movies. I was a businessman who had A-list celebrities on his personal call list. I swallowed the self-pity I rarely allowed to surface and pushed on.

"How busy am I today?" I asked Travis.

"In an hour, you have breakfast with Randolph Eubanks, Chairman of the Board at Barents Technologies. At nine, you have your bi-weekly staff meeting. Then, a meeting with Mr. Tim Ware, editor of Impress Magazine, to discuss your upcoming photo spread and interview." Travis sighed. "Should I keep going?"

"No."

I gripped my aching head, my temples throbbing against my fingertips.

"Can you ensure Miss—?"

I couldn't recall the name of the woman I had just slept with hours ago.

"I'll make sure Ms. Delaney gets home okay," Travis finished for me. "And Paul is already waiting for you downstairs."

"Thanks," I said before hanging up. I threw on my shirt and eased out of the bathroom. On my way out, I retrieved my wallet from the bedside table, slipped into my shoes, and crept silently across the room.

In addition to my missing boxers, I was also leaving my overcoat. The cold of January would only nip at me for a few seconds, because Paul would have the car warm and ready. The last thing I wanted was to face the woman I couldn't remember, nor could I recall her face. She along with my missing clothes were hidden among the broken fragments of a memory nearly faded away.

How much longer would I be able to maintain this lifestyle before my mind imploded? Better yet, how much longer before my lonely heart turned cold?

Chapter Two

Chase

Months later.

If the briefing notes sitting on the table in front of me went up in flames, I wouldn't have noticed. The moment *she* captured my attention, it ignited a tingling spike in my pulse that sent my eyes chasing her movements.

Mingling bodies obstructed my view, but my determined focus kept her in my line of sight. My gaze trailed her body, sweeping the smooth brown surface of her skin before stopping on her face.

Frozen, I found myself captured by her untamed beauty. Based on the way she threw her head back and laughed at something someone had said, it became obvious she was acquainted with my staff.

Who was she?

Why didn't I know her?

Why had she been brought into my meeting?

I wasn't the only one in the room observing the intriguing woman either. Members of my staff gravitated in her direction. Several of them buzzed around her at once, their faces animated with excitement, as the atmosphere shifted from sluggish to energetic.

Douglas, my tight-lipped senior analyst, and even Travis, my openly gay assistant, had been yanked into *her* world. She was approachable, engaging, and projected a strength of confidence I hardly saw in people anymore.

Her neatly arched brows highlighted her sparkling eyes with lashes so long, I swore with one bat of her eyes, she could bring the strongest man to his knees. Her prominent features boasted a rich dark-honey complexion sought after by most sun worshippers.

A spark against the light caught my eye and stretched my focus. *A nose piercing?* Surprisingly, the tiny diamond didn't take away from her distracting beauty. My eyes narrowly glimpsed the start of a wicked tattoo peeking from the side of her neck.

Her hair was pulled into a big bun high on the top of her head, the style adding a touch of elegance as much as it opened a doorway to her lovely face. She possessed a treasure trove of interesting features that gripped my attention with an unyielding hold.

My lips hitched into a smile while taking in the contours of her body, her size a nice full medium that left images of her sexy silhouette swimming in my head. Her body demanded a lifetime of attention that I was willing to give.

The group conversated boisterously, but their spirited discussions escaped me. The aroma of the steaming food we enjoyed at these meetings wafted around the room as it usually did, but today, the bounty did not affect me, because all I craved now was a whiff of her.

Fascinated, I was unable to look away. She lit the air around her, pulling people in, gifting their senses with purpose. I waved Travis over.

"Who is that?" I feigned nonchalance, but he eyed me with a knowing expression.

The woman didn't appear to be dressed for the boardroom, wearing boyfriend jeans and a ripped white T-shirt that showed off her indigo tank underneath. Her clothing choice suggested that she instead was ready for a night out on the town, rather than a stuffy meeting with executives.

"That's Jax Saint-Pierre." Travis lifted his brow as though asking, *shouldn't you know her already?* The name resonated slightly before realization set in.

Jax Saint-Pierre is a woman? I assumed Jax Saint-Pierre, *a man*, ran the company which negotiated an IT contract with my company.

I had taken control of my father's multimillion dollar investment company five years ago and turned it into a billion-dollar empire. As the CEO of Swift Capital, I should've been acquainted with her before now. My staff sang the praises of her skills every chance they got. She expertly solved our computer issues and kept our network purring like a kitten.

New Generation was the company that had been recommended to set up our new network. They had been instrumental in pinpointing the root causes that had allowed our network to become vulnerable to hackers. Firewall breaches, and weak credentials had cost us millions. Jax had proposed the idea of us keeping her company on, under contract, to manage our network.

The pitch couldn't have been an easy feat because the chances of getting hired by Swift Capital wasn't an easy task. The candidate background checks, the qualifications, and experience required, intimidated most and left us selecting the best of the best to join our company. New Generation was chosen because of their previous work with Lexifour, another titan in the investment arena, and Northwest Global, a dominating force in the marketing world.

I snapped my fingers in Travis's direction to regain his attention before she walked out.

"Introduce us," I urged. The team must have assumed we had already been acquainted, otherwise, we would have been formally introduced already.

Travis stood across the table from me but was close enough to the exit to reach out and grab her attention. His lips hovered near her ear, I hoped, convincing her to return. When she turned away from the door, she scanned the clock above my head before her eyes fell to mine.

I was rewarded with a snapshot of a full-frontal view and realized I had missed the tiny circular barbell through the right corner of her bottom lip. How many piercings did she have? I never liked facial piercings, especially not on a woman. However, on *this* woman, they made sense.

Finally, I was able to see her free and clear without interruption and had to pause at the full force of her radiant beauty. Shaking off the trance, I forced myself to stand, reach across the table, and take the hand she offered.

This was the first time I found myself stunned by a woman's presence.

Chapter Three

Jax

My resistance to the light tug on my arm was downplayed with a fake smile. One of Swift Capital's executives was determined to Geek Squad me into their meeting to provide answers to their never-ending technical questions.

Curious male eyes found me the moment I crossed the threshold of the door. After a short round of small talk, I was ushered to one of their laptops sitting in front of the empty seats that most of them hadn't taken yet.

Even the handsome man sitting behind the table stared. He sat while others stood socializing and enjoying refreshments. Although I typed into the laptop, an unwavering connection kept pulling my attention from the group tossing IT questions at me.

"The issue is actually an easy fix. The only thing I found was that you hadn't properly added your certificates," I told the man whose computer I sat behind, but my mind was on the one who kept flirting with my curiosity.

Chase Taylorson?

He dropped his gaze as soon as mine zeroed in on his. Chase's face graced the covers of every money magazine I had come across. He was all over the Internet too. Although his company employed their own in-house network administrators, my company took care of their network engineering concerns.

At twenty-nine, Chase fell into our country's young billionaire's club, and was stamped one of the most sought-after bachelors. He had rarely been seen with the same woman twice since assuming the role as CEO of Swift Capital. He kept the media in an uproar as they angled for stories of his personal life, but he'd only ever disclosed the business side.

Those Internet and magazine photos didn't hold a candle to Chase in person though. He was as hot as dripping wax from a flaming candle and even managed to make glasses look sexy.

Popular blogs gossiped he had found a way to keep the details of his love life hidden from the public. Some presumed he was too busy raking in billions and had no interest in fostering a long-term relationship. Of course, he was labeled gay a time or two as well.

A tech question interrupted my mental reel of Chase's history. I responded while continuing to rectify the problem at hand.

"Yes. Something as simple as doing a green shutdown can solve that issue. All you need is the newest software updates. If that doesn't work, put in a trouble ticket, and one of the administrators can help you."

Another question followed, which was expected whenever technical support showed up unexpectantly. It appeared the group would hang on to their concerns until they saw you in person.

"It sounds like we may have to replace your thin client. No worries though, it should be an easy fix," I said, solving another issue, all while sneaking peeks at Chase, who I'd caught sneaking looks in my direction.

One of the execs off to my left leaned into his neighbor, firing off rapid Spanish. Unaware I was fluent in the language, I easily translated one telling the other, what he wouldn't give to get me in his bed.

My late mother, Danella Ramos, was an Afro-Venezuelan, born and raised in Venezuela, before her family relocated to the US when she was a teen. My mother had communicated in Spanish as much as she did in English. My Haitian father, Alexander Saint-Pierre, made sure I learned French, expanding my multilingual resume. Due to my parents, I was double dipped in chocolate and had a cultural history I was proud of.

After explaining to the group the difference between a network engineer, and a network administrator, I pointed at the clock on the wall above Chase's head.

"Your meeting will start soon, and I have another appointment to attend," I stated, hoping they got the hint. Swift Capital paid me for my network services, so I didn't mind answering their questions all day long, but I wanted no part in their meeting.

"*Yes!*"

I celebrated in silence when my feet edged closer to the exit. I was fully aware that some of the men had interest other than the IT services I provided, and I didn't intend to stick around feeding the flames of their dirty desires.

My eyes slammed shut, when I was stopped in my fast-moving tracks by the light stroke of a hand on my arm. It was Travis, Chase's assistant. He was who I often interacted with on Chase's behalf, if, or when any issue came up.

"Jax. A moment please."

When I glanced up, his face was set with determination, letting me know my escape attempt was over.

"I would like to introduce you to Mr. Taylorson."

The smile I forced was a shaky one.

"I'm sure Mr. Taylorson has more important things to do." Truth of the matter was, I didn't want to get closer. Although I wasn't one to shy away from something or someone I was interested in, I knew that being attracted to someone like Chase Taylorson was trouble, with a capital T.

"Please, Jax. It will only take a minute."

His begging eyes softened my hesitancy.

I turned back into the office of chatty executives, who, based on the wall clock should be starting their meeting in a few minutes. The lively murmurs around the room lowered as I approached the table, and I wasn't sure if it was because of me.

A few lingering steps led me back into the room where Travis stopped me, opposite the table as Mr. Taylorson. He didn't sit in the traditional place at the head of the table like most CEOs. Instead, he sat in the middle of the opposite side, facing the exit I had failed to escape through. An energetic view of the city sat behind him displayed through a wall of windows.

He drew me in, his pull on my senses unnervingly strong, despite the hesitancy I clung to. The moment our eyes connected, the sound around me dwindled, and every other soul in the room turned into shadows in the background. The air grew thicker, like feathery kisses against my skin. Each breath I drew boomed loud in my ears. My senses were going haywire, and I hadn't even shaken his hand yet.

He stood and reached across the table before taking my hand, his gaze imprisoning mine. His chiseled jawline and his dark handsomeness were a feast for my eyes. Cleanshaven, dark-haired, and olive-skinned, he was the kind of good-looking that stopped a woman in her tracks, made married women stray, and turned single women into side-pieces.

"Chase Taylorson, meet Jax Saint-Pierre." Travis' voice carried light, like he talked from a distance although he stood next to me.

"Chase, nice to meet you," I said.

His outstretched hand wrapped around mine and although my intent was to downplay my attraction, I believe I'd failed.

I noticed the way his right brow shot up after I addressed him so informally, calling him by his first name. I wasn't immune to letting a little puerility sneak out when I was met with situations I wasn't accustomed to confronting, namely Chase.

His warm hand continued to grip mine in a hold so tight, my gaze shot to our connection. A quick glimpse of a tattoo flashed when his sleeve inched up, making my brows hike with intrigue.

"Jax, nice to meet you. Have a seat please?" The edgy timbre in his tone insinuated this was a command rather than a request. He had taken my lead on the informal greeting, addressing me as Jax.

The group was set to start their meeting, so why was he asking me to sit in? I wanted no part of this corporate, boring-ass shit that excited them, just as they didn't want to know the intricacies of my work.

"It's time for your meeting. Don't let me disrupt your timetable."

Travis strolled away like he knew I was going to take the seat. In my peripheral, I spotted him talking to the group huddled near the table of food. Chase leaned toward me; his light-green eyes intense. Hypnotically powerful, they sparkled as yellow and brown flecks danced over a sea of brilliantly canvased green. His voice broke me out of the trance.

"Please, have a seat. They won't start this meeting until I'm ready."

Well hell, that settled it. If there was one thing I didn't like, it was being told to do something I didn't want to do. It made my other personality come out. The one who would have enjoyed using Chase's tie for a choke collar, while planting a five-inch heel so deep in his back, it scraped his spine.

Only because he'd captured my interest, did I take the seat as directed, checking him out as much as he checked me out. His gaze traveled along my hands folded in front of me on the table and zipped up my chest until our eyes reconnected.

A sliver of a smile danced across his eyes but avoided his lips. His lips were so sexy it made me speculate if he'd dished out money for them.

"I'm sure you've heard it before, and I apologize for being presumptuous, but I assumed you were a man."

"I get that often, but I'm not offended by it. The mistake works in my favor. Having the world believe I'm a man, in a male-dominated job gives me an advantage."

A small smile softened his features. Having the world believe I was a man also kept people from digging deeper into my personal life. I purposely used my male sounding nickname as my business name. My past was rooted in enough wickedness that I preferred hiding behind the fake male persona.

"Also, I must compliment you on your services to my company. My staff openly brags about your technical skills and expertise."

"Thank you."

I wasn't expecting his compliment. However, his pensive expression gave me the impression that it was more than a compliment? He let his gaze settle on me for a moment. His eyes fell to my piercings, lingered on my lips, and traced across my neck before returning to mine.

"I understand you have contracts with other companies. Would you consider working exclusively for Swift Capital?"

His job offer blew me away, forcing me to hide the fast-moving shot of energy coursing through me.

"As much as I appreciate your offer, I enjoy the freedom of being able to freelance and choose my clients. I wouldn't have the freedom to expand my skills in the ever-changing conditions of the open market."

Although he attempted to hide it, my comments caused his face to twitch with surprise before a smile glided across his sexy lips.

"I felt inclined to ask, although I was certain from the moment I saw you, you weren't easy…easily persuaded. However, I'm certain I can change your mind."

Well, fuck. It sounded like he was flirting with me and it was starting to turn me on, especially since I noticed how attractive he was up close. The whole tall, dark, and handsome with a nerdy vibe must have been created by him. He laid one of his hands out, palm up, preparing to present his next statement to me.

"Consider you, and your staff having your own wing in this building with access to state-of-the-art equipment, rights to manage the development and beta-testing of new software systems, and opportunities to take classes and obtain advanced skills paid for by Swift Capital. I would make it, so you don't need the open market. The market will come seeking you. It is an excellent opportunity to take your business to the next level. Take my offer Jax. You should be concentrating on developing new technologies, not fishing around in the open market."

My smile slipped. How the hell was he going to sit there and tell me what I should be concentrating on?

Jax, remember where you are at and who you're talking to, the little voice in my head warned.

Chase was attempting to make it impossible for me to say no. However, his underlying tone implied he wasn't used to hearing that word.

"Chase, may I be frank?"

"Please."

"I'm sure you can tell by my appearance, that not only am I not easy, but I don't like being told what to do. It's one of the reasons I work for myself and do my job well. Personally, I prefer to stay behind the scenes, and peek my head out only when it's necessary. Your offer is tempting, but I'd like the opportunity to think about it for the sake of my employees. I would also like to point out that I prefer to achieve *my* goals at *my* pace and on *my* own accord."

Another smile surfaced but was brushed away by the defiance that sharpened his gaze.

"Something we have in common," he added. He adjusted his glasses, pushing them up his nose, which enhanced the intensity of his already penetrating gaze. "In front of the cameras, I play my role, use my acting voice, but behind them, I despise being told what to do, even if it's for my own good. I give commands and expect them to be followed and, although I may come off as arrogant to some, my commands usually lead to both parties getting what they want."

Chase was flirting with me so smoothly, I found myself edging closer for more. The billionaire wasn't who he let on to be for the public's eye, the sharp businessmen that could turn pennies into millions.

This was the side of himself Chase hid from the public, the few parts I was arrogant enough to believe he had reserved for only me. Those delicious parts were also the very reason I needed to stay clear of him.

I was bold enough to be a danger to myself, but my employees and responsibilities kept me tame. My contract with Swift Capital was more important than my need to satisfy my personal interest.

I sprang up, feigning a stern expression before reaching across the table.

"Nice to meet you, Chase."

My gaze landed on our hands because he didn't let go right away.

"Let me walk you out," he offered, before loosening his grip and starting around the table. Why the hell was this man so determined to keep me in his presence?

He came around the long table and stood at my side. No one uttered a word when he held the glass door open and followed me out.

We walked side by side in silence as charged currents guided our movements. His closeness caused an unnamed tingle to sizzle on my skin as my mind fought to absorb the enormity of him. The raw energy flowed into me and licked at my blood before it pushed through my veins, an introduction of a different kind. One that had nothing to do with our minds, but everything to do with our bodies.

"Mind if I ride down with you? I can use the break." His tone was so low, deep, and husky it vibrated against my exposed skin, adding a little extra spice to the tingle already there. My gaze followed his finger to the down arrow he pressed, and I found his eyes waiting on mine when I lifted my head.

"No, I don't mind," I finally replied, taking in his tall, fit body. He was mountainous, at least six-four, and I noticed his dark suit made him appear leaner than he was. His hair was slicked back and tapered around his face and neckline. At close view, his body was manly, full, cut... *Leave it alone, Jax.*

Riveting silence gripped us as we waited on the elevator. Why did it feel like the billionaire was stalking me? I've had my share of men checking me out to the point of creepy, but this was something else. I was caressed in waves of warmth that sent ripples along my skin, and rained desire down on me. Chase could touch me without his hands.

When I met his stare again, I smiled, but the probing glint in his eyes was plucking at more than my sexual desire. He was doing things with his eyes most men wished they could do with their tongues.

The *ding* of the elevator's arrival dragged my attention away from him. I stepped inside, hit the button that would take us to ground level, and backed myself against the wall. When Chase stepped in, he didn't stand beside me as I assumed he would. He stepped straight ahead and into my personal space.

He towered above my five-six frame, but his gaze managed to sweep and outline my figure before he took my hand. His thumb swept across the thorny vine tattooed on the back of my hand. Did he know his boldness was turning me on? The fact that he was my boss was a dwindling memory as my lust had been set loose.

His free hand slipped up the side of my neck, sending a chill racing over my fevered skin. His soft stroke and the warm press of his hand around mine, kept me in place. With keen intensity, he examined my vine tattoo, stroking my neck with a light touch. He leaned in so close his warm breath feathered over my skin.

Although most of the tattoo was covered by my top, he traced the portion on my hand. He continued to trace it up my arm until he reconnected with the part visible on my neck. It occurred to me that he hadn't just been talking to me at the table, he was studying me like I had been studying him.

His domineering behavior had my impulses revved, and my heart thumped a chaotic beat to keep pace with the tone we had set. Anyone else would have gotten a knee to the fucking balls for touching me like this. I didn't know what the hell it was about Chase, but his daring touch kept me in line as I enjoyed the feel of his hands on me.

"There is something I have been dying to know," he stated, allowing his bold cockiness to come out and mingle with his heated tone. Again, his fingers slid across the tattoo on my neck, at the same time his thumb pressed into the tattoo branching the span of the back of my hand.

"How much of your body does this tattoo cover?"

My words floated above my tongue, and I held them there because it was smart not to let this go any further. I stared at him with a devious smirk. There was no damn way I could let this man know, a man who I had barely shared a conversation with, that he had me on the verge of hitting stop on the elevator, so I could shove my pussy in his face.

Chase's touch set off sparks within me, that I had yet to experience with anyone else. He was enjoying indulgences that I'd never before allowed. He was bold, confident, and didn't appear bothered by my dominating nature.

My tongue slid across my lips, wetting them, tasting the desire blazing through my blood.

"No one has gotten the full view and, believe me, it's more than a tattoo. It's art, precious and untainted by undeserving eyes. Truth is, Chase"—I inched closer making the little space we had between us smaller — "I've never found anyone interesting enough to share it with."

He leaned in, his hand tightening around mine, as his other held firm against my neck, adding just enough pressure to fuel my desire.

"I'm going to be the first." The determination set in his expression and his tone made me aware that he believed every word he spoke.

My nipples tightened into aching peaks while my pussy quivered, leaking wetness into my panties.

He spoke with an authoritative edge. Almost like he stated an unspoken truth. No one had seen my full tattoo because it was for me. I would dim the lights, take off only what was necessary, used blindfolds, you name it. I took control, all of it, only allowing my lovers to see what I wanted them to see.

I didn't respond to Chase's arrogant comment because he had managed to get me so turned on my fevered mind was chanting, *fuck him, fuck him, fuck him.* All I could do was glance up at him, as I fought to contain images of fucking him across the table of the boardroom we'd just left.

Contrary to what I assumed, his history in the media and his smart appearance, led me to believe he was soft and easily influenced. My assumption was dead ass wrong. He was hot as fuck and dripped the kind of sin I liked dipping into.

He was like the beautiful darkness that bent light, the shiny edge of a razor before it cuts, the flare of a flame before it burned. I wanted to breathe in his darkness, get nicked by his sharp edges, and get licked by the heat of his flames.

Jax! My inner voice was calling, but I was ignoring her ass. I wanted to play with this fire.

I twisted my wrist from his tight grip and pulled apart the cufflink at his wrist. The ping of it hitting the floor echoed in the small space but didn't break our intense connection.

"You first. How far does your tattoo go?" I raked my nails across the area at his wrist, letting him know I had spotted his ink. My action caused him to hiss in a shot of air, but his gaze never wavered when he reached up to finger his tie.

When he unfastened the top button on his shirt, the *ding* followed by the elevator door opening snatched us from the engulfing heat of our fantasy. Was he planning to take off his shirt to show me his tattoo? I guess I'll never know, but I'd be damned if I wasn't curious.

People didn't wait until we exited before they piled into the elevator. Chase turned and placed a firm hand on the elevator door so I could exit, his caressing gaze keeping me inflamed.

"It was nice meeting you Jax," he said. Chase kept the elevator door open, knowing full well no one would say a thing about being held up.

"You too Chase."

Without looking back, I strutted away with a soaking wet pussy, and the knowledge that Chase Taylorson, was nothing like he presented himself to the rest of the world. Like Clark Kent, I think the glasses were a prop to help hide his true nature.

The June heat outside had nothing on him. Chase had me so fucking hot and worked up, my damn titties were dripping sweat like I was strolling through the Mohave in black leather. I thrived on control, and he was the first man I'd met who could make me lose it.

I sensed his eyes on me as I marched closer to the spinning golden glass doors, wanting to sever our connection and be released onto Fifth Avenue. I focused on the view of the busy New York City street, eager to be swallowed by the crush of swirling bodies, the noise of honking horns, roaring engines, and the scent of excitement mixed with fumes of every kind.

It took great effort, but I used every part of me to aid in my refusal to look back. Too stubborn to give Chase the satisfaction of seeing how he affected me. He was smart, there was no denying that, but he was a powerhouse of masculinity hidden under those suits and glasses. I knew it as well as I knew information technology. This was our beginning, if Chase had anything to say about it.

Chapter Four

Chase

The next day, my secretary Kimberly, stood behind her desk with her arms folded over her chest when I walked in. Her stressed face and stiff posture slowed my stride.

"Good morning Mr. Taylorson."

"Good morning Kim. Is everything okay?"

"No sir. Your brother's here. He bullied his way into your office about ten minutes ago. I'm so sorry sir, but I didn't want to make a scene and call security."

A glance at my watch showed it was seven in the morning, and I was willing to bet Blake's breakfast had been a liquid one.

"It's okay Kim. You have no reason to be sorry. The next time he tries this, you have my permission to cause a scene and call security." She nodded, but I didn't miss the smirk on her face.

Blake had shown up on several occasions talking down to the staff, ordering them around, and causing his own scene. His last act had been particularly bad, as one of the employees had recorded him in a drunken rage, shouting, and knocking things off employee's desk.

He had ranted nonstop about me stealing his role as CEO of Swift Capital. The video had gone viral and painted him as the troubled brother that I was forced to deal with. The incident caused an even bigger rift between us as he blamed me for the recording and sharing the video on social media.

The sight of Blake, sitting in my office, behind my desk, made me want to turn around and start my day over.

"Hey brother," he spoke when I walked in, his tone filled with contempt.

"Blake," I greeted, walking up to my desk. "Out of the chair," I ordered, hating the fact that he had access to the building, much less into my office. However, any push or resistance on my part made him that much more destructive in his behavior.

Blake was older than me by two years, but you would never know it based on his conduct. Multiple DUI's, gambling, caught in the act of cheating on his wife multiple times. He'd been campaigning for a job as CEO of this investment firm when he had zero control over his own finances. After gaining access to his twenty-million-dollar trust fund at twenty-five, he had eaten through it in less than three years.

I imagined having his younger brother cast him in shadow was a hard pill for him to swallow. Instead of making an effort to get himself together, he wallowed in self-pity and chose to blame everyone else for the mistakes he made.

He stood in a rush, marching away from my seat and rounding my desk. My intent was to take a moment and brainstorm my plans for me and Jax, but Blake was infringing on the little free time I had. He'd been to rehab for alcoholism five times that I was aware of. What was the allotted number before one accepted defeat?

I was at a loss as to how to help him. According to Blake, my attempts were labelled as nothing more than opportunities for me to make him look bad.

"I couldn't get you on the phone, so I figured I would come and see you in person. I won't take up much of your time. I need to borrow one of your houses. If I don't get away from our father, he is going to drive me crazy. Fucking treats me like I'm ten."

"Maybe because you act like you're ten." I replied.

"I don't need shit from you too. Can I use one of your houses or not? It's not like you can live in all of them at the same time."

"No."

"Are you serious?! You have four houses and a penthouse last I counted, and you're telling me *no*. You hate me that much?"

"You know that I don't hate you, Blake. The last time I allowed you to stay in one of my homes, you nearly burned it down. Over a hundred thousand in damages. I ended up having to sell it for less than I paid for it."

His nostrils flared as anger seeped from his pores. "It's not like you can't afford it. I'm your *brother*, you're supposed to have my back."

Since I had assumed the role of CEO, he had taken it on himself to sabotage many of my efforts to make this company money in his failed attempts to gain control. However, our troubles ran much deeper than him wanting control of the company.

Even as kids, when he would mess up, our father would replace him with me. Blake saw me as the favorite son he had always wanted to be. Over time, the resentment he harbored, seemed to escalate his self-destructive behavior. He and his wife, Tonya lived in our family home with our father because every house he'd owned had been lost in some manner.

He took a belligerent stance on the opposite side of my desk. "I'm only going to ask one more time. Can I use a house or not?"

"I'm only going to tell you, one more time, no."

Blake swung an angry hand across my desk, taking out a stack of paperwork before he stormed out. I closed my eyes, concentrating on keeping myself seated, so I didn't go after him to knock some sense into him.

The last thing I needed was a viral video of me beating the daylights out of my *troubled* brother. If this was how my day was starting, I could only hope that it got better from here.

***

A week has gone by since my short encounter with Jadzia "Jax" Saint-Pierre. She had sent me hunting for any information I could find on her. Thankfully, being the CEO had its advantages. Rhonda, in Human Resources, didn't bat an eye when I requested Jax's file.

Images of her that I had memorized from our first and only meeting, tempted me, and I found myself spacing out when I should have been paying attention during briefings and conversations. The luxurious feel of her skin and that enticing mouth. If I concentrated hard enough, I could practically feel my dick pushing past her lips and sliding over her tongue.

She was a triple-threat, smart, beautiful, and from what I had learned, hardworking. Meeting her had stirred up raw sexual desires, but there was also an undercurrent of emotions she had motivated that left me anxious to see her again.

I'd had to stop myself from calling her several times after stalking her company's website. New Generation was a boutique IT company, set up around businesses needing specialized IT support. Jax had launched the company six years ago. Despite her company being small, she and her engineers handled an impressive client list. It was a list I wasn't supposed to have, but when you are worth billions, you could get *almost* anything you wanted.

As I scrolled through her website once again, I noticed she was the only one without a posted picture. I snooped enough to discover that she didn't have any social media pages, which was an anomaly in this day and age.

How long was it going to be before I saw her again? A simple computer issue didn't guarantee she would be the one to handle the problem. For her to show up, the problem needed to be a substantial one. One our in-house team wasn't equipped to handle.

I regretted that I hadn't taken a more aggressive interest in her and her company until now. Unfortunately, it had not been necessary as she usually met with my assistant. Her name and company logo were on multiple documents that had come across my desk, but it never occurred to me to request a face-to-face with her.

Had she stirred a spark of romance within me? The notion of it was a foreign entity that threw my thought pattern into disarray. Why else would I have such an urgent need to see her again when I could handpick whoever I wanted?

I was forced to go through the process of conducting pre-screenings of the women I dated and having them sign non-disclosure agreements, before we could even have a cup of coffee together. This process took the fun out of dating, but as someone with the amount of wealth I had built, I wasn't left with many other dating options.

Before employing necessary measures to protect myself from gossip, women had no problem leaking my personal business to the media for money. In those instances, I was forced to fork over handsome sums of money to media outlets. Even paying to have them delete scandalous photos of me. A couple of my one-night stands had also made outrageous attempts to steal my used condoms.

It didn't matter how powerful I was in business; I was no match for a woman on a quest to snag a rich husband. I had quickly learned the lessons of the world where wealth, power, and sex collided.

Jax was the one woman, a diamond among dust, who made me want to try my hand at traditional dating again. She made me want to know everything about her. Snooping into her background, I learned she valued her privacy as much as I coveted mine, but she wasn't totally unavailable. *The New Wave Annual Technology Convention* was coming up, and I was determined to attend this year, as I learned Jax attended every year. I phoned my secretary.

"I'll set it up for you right away," Kim replied to the request I'd been contemplating all day. "I'll have to reschedule your golf game with Mr. Timberlake."

"That will be fine."

"Yes, sir." She replied before hanging up.

Now that the convention was being booked, the torturous two-week wait to see Jax again was underway.

Chapter Five

Jax

I lifted my phone to my ear after it rang once, but my mind remained on the proposal I was writing for a new contract I was in the process of securing.

"Yes." I answered, pinning the phone between my neck and shoulder.

"You have a visitor," Lulu, one of my engineers informed me.

What was she talking about? We rarely had visitors because we went to most of our clients.

"Who is it?" I asked, but she didn't have to provide an answer, because Chase stood at my door. My phone fell into the cradle just as she was saying his name. Everything about him screamed sexy as he filled up the space around him.

"Umm, what are you doing here Chase?"

"Hello Jax. I was in the neighborhood and just thought I would stop by and say hi."

Bullshit!

After the elevator scene, one of us was destined to give in to the fiery temptations that had been stirred. I cast my glance around him to see if a camera crew had followed him in.

"Don't worry, my driver has become a pro at shaking the media. I made sure they didn't follow me."

Drinking in the dark smoothness of his features couldn't be helped because his sex appeal had its own zip code. He casually leaned against the door frame, impeccably dressed in dark gray slacks, and a light blue silk button up, as his suit jacket lay draped over his arm.

"What are you doing here?" I repeated my question.

"I made you an offer, you never gave me a reply."

The daring gleam in his eyes was hard to miss. Was he talking about the job offer he proposed or me? Truthfully, he could have been talking about both, but the amount of hot passion he bought with him into my office space, was as potent as the sight of him.

"It's only been five days. How long do I have to think about it?"

He finally stepped in, placing his jacket across the back of the chair in front of me, and held his tie in place as he stepped around the chair and sat down. His body filled the black guest chair, making it appear small as he stretched his long legs out before him.

"For you, there is no time limit, but I tend to be impatient when it comes to getting what I want."

Now, I *knew* he wasn't talking about the job. I didn't think he cared if I took it or not. He was interested in me and showing up at my office had proven it.

"So, how is it that I haven't run into you for eight months. I'm aware that there's work you can do remotely, but how often do you visit Swift Capital?"

My eyes narrowed and lingered on him before I answered. "I don't get out to Swift but once or twice a month, and during those times, I'm usually running tests and conducting inspections to make certain my engineers are doing good work. Most times, I'm here securing more business, writing proposals, or doing background work that keeps the company going."

He studied the interior of my office, taking in the tight space. My desk and chair, the chair he sat in, the framed picture

of a dark-purple flowery clematis vine hanging on the wall behind me, and a large table of computer equipment that took up
a third of my office. There were no spectacular views permeat-
ing the area, but it was stylized with modern contemporary
furnishings and made me feel at home.

"Before now, I had only seen you once by chance, but I've
heard good things about you, your company, and your impec-
cable work ethic."

"Thank you," I said. An odd silence sat between us; my
mind plunged in an unusual state of uncertainty of where to take
the conversation.

"You've been asking about me? May I ask why?" I knew
why but wanted to hear him admit it first.

"Yes, I have. You're an intriguing mystery I'd like to
solve."

His direct words left me dazed. I could hear myself breathing. The obscene amount of burning passion between us filled
the room and threatened to suffocate me. We sat in the moment,
allowing the vibrant flow of our connection to sink in.

"Are you dating anyone Jax?"

He didn't beat around the bush, an aspect of him that I
appreciated, although it threw me off.

"I've been contemplating someone. However, I have certain rules where it concerns dating. My number one rule is to
not make it a long-term investment."

He didn't need to know I had stepped away from dating
for the last six months in an attempt to get to know myself better. Mainly to figure out my need for absolute control.

Curiosity flashed in his focused gaze as he waited for me
to elaborate.

"I don't do long-term relationships, and rarely do I go out
on second dates. I say this now to make sure my expectations
on dating are made clear."

"Why?" he asked. "You're beautiful, interesting, and hardworking based on what little I know about you. Why deny someone the opportunity to get to know you?"

My reasons were too personal to share, so I chose to ignore his question.

"Thanks for the compliment, but I don't have the patience to share myself with someone."

His forehead crinkled. "Aren't you curious to at least try? What if you're missing out on someone that could make you happy?"

Why was he so interested? Sexual chemistry was one thing, but he appeared interested in more than a whiff of my pussy. After everything that I had read about Chase, his reaction was strange.

"My job brings me joy and happiness Chase. In my opinion, I'm doing my dates a favor by cutting them loose. My controlling nature is not something that most will abide long-term."

The determined set in his expression clearly said he was already dismissing everything I was telling him.

"Sometimes, all it takes is the right person who is willing to abide by your rules, but one who also has enough strength to show you a different way."

His intriguing words caused me to lean forward and tuck my palms under my chin.

"Are you the person that's supposed to show me a different way?"

"Of course, I am." He answered swiftly and with total confidence.

After a deep sigh, I dropped my head into my palm and scratched it, attempting to find a way to deter him from making a mistake.

"Since you've taken an interest in my work ethic, is there anything I may not have considered that will help improve Swift Capital?" I prayed the swift subject change would make him aware that I no longer wished to talk about relationships.

A teasing smile rested on his lips as he measured my words. Thankfully, he decided to play along. We maintained a casual business conversation until he stood, picked up his jacket and prepared to leave.

He edged up to my desk, his commanding height leaning over me was as potent as a full-body caress.

"Do me a favor Jax. Consider allowing yourself to accept something different. It won't hurt unless you allow it to."

I didn't answer, but our gazes held until he turned and walked out.

Once he was out of sight, I exhaled. His nearness caused me to acknowledge desires I'd never felt before. My body craved his touch. My mind desired his challenge. Even my damn spirit acted like it wanted to get involved.

Chase had everything going for him, leading me to wonder if he could show me that something different he'd mentioned, but I already know my battle to change wouldn't be easy. Was that why I was fighting so hard to turn him away? What if there was a chance for me to have more, release my demons, and stop denying myself?

Chapter Six

Chase

My anxiousness to see Jax again had worn me down, despite me pouring a decent amount of effort into my wait. It wasn't that I hadn't met ambitious, assertive women before, or ones that mirrored my drive-in business, it was definitely something else that drew me to her.

All girls or women had to know was my last name, and they would hunt me down, like I was a rare diamond on legs. Not Jax. I had never had to chase a woman. Not even when I was a skinny, pimply teenager. Jax had left me at the elevator the first time we met and appeared ready to shove me out of her office the second time.

There was no doubt about it, I had piqued her interest, but she hadn't made any efforts to call or seek me out. Her dismissal enticed me to pursue her with the same ferocity in which I had taken control of Swift Capital.

Her impression led me to believe that she was as noncommittal as me, and it would make our fling, when we had it, scorching hot, fast moving, and lust fueled. A smile tickled my lips thinking of the sinful things we'd do together. Passion stirring kisses, clothes ripping frenzies, and blazing hot sex, on the bed, on the floor, against the walls.

Had I imagined our heavy sexual chemistry? *No way.* It was palpable and hardy enough to push through her hard-set dating rules and the organized chaos that was my life. The constant thoughts of it made me tamper with these wires in this large, and well-secured mechanical room filled with computer components I couldn't name. After all, it was my company, if I wanted to yank this wire or tug at that cable.

Immediately after my deliberate sabotage, half of the tenth-floor lost connectivity to the network. I requested that Travis contact NG for help, and specifically asked that it be Jax that showed up. My behavior was definitely juvenile, but I didn't care. I had a demanding need I was determined to fulfill.

Moments later, when she entered the building, the prospect of seeing her sent a buzz of excitement vibrating through me. After an elevator trip and many questioning side-eye looks from the staff at my unannounced return, I reached the secured door that would lead me to her. I keyed in the six-digit code and stepped into the small entranceway which led to the room housing our network hardware.

I crept into the room, inching closer to the sound of tapping keystrokes. A twinge of guilt sparked at the notion that she was attempting to fix what I had purposely broken.

"Will you save me the trouble of running numerous diagnostics and point out the area you obviously tampered with?"

She hadn't acknowledged me with so much as a backward glance while she spoke. Hadn't even slowed her quick fingers as they danced across the keyboard. I stood at her back a few feet away, stamping down my urge to reach out and touch her. She had drawn me in so fervently, only a determined effort, kept me in place as I relished the feel of absorbing her warm energy.

"I'd—"

"I take my job seriously, Chase." She'd cut me off. "If you wanted to see me again, you should've tried harder. You already knew I wasn't easy the first day we met. Besides, you didn't have a problem showing up at my office, unannounced before."

She glanced back, a smile peeking at the corner of her lip and highlighting her piercing. "I will admit, I did like the potted lavender clematis vine you sent me."

She stood and spun on me; her quick movements surprised me before she glared up at me. The smile vanished abruptly. A serious edge stiffened her body and a hint of frustration sat in her clipped expression. She was in no way afraid or intimidated by me.

"You are fearless, aren't you?"

"Not entirely," she answered. "Everyone has their kryptonite. Even me."

Her admission of having weaknesses, surprised me, as it was in contrast to her aggressive nature. However, it was the haunting glint in her expression when she said it, that caught my attention.

Apparently, *she* was *my* kryptonite. My actions since meeting her was proof that she had weakened my resistance to stay away from her.

"In all honesty, I didn't think that you would have taken my call."

A smile surfaced but disappeared with a blink of those long lashes.

"I would have accepted it, just so I could turn down whatever you proposed, and I would have been nice about it too."

My hand ran up her arm and stilled at her elbow, the touch surprising me as much as it did her. Touching her here, in a way she had not given me permission to, gave her a legitimate reason to report me to human resources, but I was convinced she wanted me as much as I wanted her.

The raw sexual chemistry sizzling between us couldn't be ignored. There was also a tingly spark that caressed me like a glove, a different vibe from what I felt sexually. It was the same spark that had reached across my boardroom and lured my attention her way.

Her gaze was aimed where my hand caressed her silky skin. The connection was so charged, it heightened my senses. The telling notes of goosebumps on her flesh, revealed that the same spark I experienced, had touched her too.

She looked at me. I stared at her. The stare off was awkward until it settled, and I let out the long breath I was holding. She exhaled, her warm breath washing over me.

"I'm attracted to you Chase, I won't lie, but as far as I'm concerned, we're only meant to be business associates. First, I don't do the media, ever, and they follow you around like lost puppies. Second, it would be bad for business. Third, you're not accustomed to not being in control, and I'm not wired to *be* controlled. So, we would never work no matter our attraction. Fourth, I will not be your fetish, the cure for your curiosity, the main topic of discussion among you and your rich friends."

I knew early on to be selective when seeking relationship goals from my family. My mother and father were as different as night and day and barely spoke to each other. They got along well enough, but their relationship, when I was old enough to figure things out for myself, wasn't loving. Blake would tell me often that they were divorcing, but it took years before that happened. Eventually, they stopped pretending, started doing things without each other and even moved into separate bedrooms.

While my father spent his time trying to groom me into a replica of himself as a control freak, it was my mother who would speak words of wisdom so fierce, I was left with no choice but to hear and heed them.

When you meet her; that woman that will open something in you so wide, it will scare you, but you will know it's her. You

will be drawn to her and unable to think of anything but want-
ing to know more about her. Consciously, you may not
understand what's happening or what you may be feeling, but
don't ignore the blessing, Chase. You and Blake are the best
things to ever happen to me, and I know your father and I ha-
ven't been the best examples, but I want you both to experience
the best things this life has to offer. Nothing is better than find-
ing that special someone that can open your heart to true
happiness.

Jax may not have been the woman my mother was talking about, but I wasn't willing to ignore her warning and risk missing out on happiness.

"Your pitiful attempt to convince me that we're wrong for each other isn't working. You can't speak on what you believe you have read in me. You can't make your thoughts a reality of how I might react, or what I may or may not accept. Wouldn't you like to at least see if we can be compatible?"

She stepped to me, closing the little space between us, allowing her warmth to wrap around me. Her fresh honey-citrus scent intoxicated my senses. I breathed her in, closing my eyes as I ran my fingers along her arm.

"I'm not the one for you, Chase, trust me."

Her words hung between us like the resounding sound of a slammed door. If her aim was to intimidate me; it wasn't working. Older men, seasoned business associates, or anyone who assumed a younger man couldn't handle a multibillion-dollar company had been attempting to intimidate me for years. Their efforts had strengthened my resolve to deal with bullies and take an insult with ease. I had never cowered, or backed down when faced with a challenge, so, I wasn't backing down from Jax, even if her warnings were warranted.

"Give me my chance, Jax."

"Why? Am I a challenge you need to master?"

"I'm genuinely interested in you. And I promise to treat your privacy with as much respect as I would my own. And for the record, I hardly know you, but I know that you would never allow anyone to use you as a fetish."

My gaze dropped to her lips, imagining what they would feel like pressed against mine before my tongue slid up the length of hers.

"Okay, maybe not a fetish, but I've piqued your interest, and now you'd like to know what it would be like to fuck me."

My eyes went wide. Her blunt words were like a cold spray of water on my ego. I know she felt my desire for her. What I couldn't understand was why she was fighting so hard to deny it.

"What you're not doing Chase, is listening to the warnings I'm trying to give you. I don't like being told what to do and you are very close to that line. I told you that I prefer being in control when it comes to relationships. I like a partner that doesn't mind being bossed around, and I don't believe you would listen very well. And I'll repeat this in case you ignored it the first time. I don't do the media."

She was right. I didn't give a damn about her warnings. I was just as hardheaded as she was, and the more she pushed, the more I wanted her.

"I believe we may have similar wants, Jax. So, I'm not opposed to negotiating, or learning to ensure your wants and needs are satisfied. Besides, you should know this about me, I give as good as I get."

She took another deliberate step, positioning herself so that her tempting mouth sat inches below mine.

"I'm an *acquired taste*. If we hooked up, there's a probability that you will either stalk me for more, run from the unholy hell I would unleash on you, or put a restraining order out to keep me away from you."

"I want the chance to find out," I replied. My words surprised her based on the way those sexy lips of her had parted in response to her bold statement.

"I'd like the chance to find out what direction your wants might send me. And Jax, I have warnings you should heed as well." I eased a hand behind her neck, making the resistance in her body melt into my touch. "I can be as unholy as you claim to be and as sinful as you need me to be. I have created more stalkers than I care to name, and only the threat of legal action keeps them at bay. So be rest assured that my palate may enjoy your special, *acquired taste.*"

Her pupils dilated before her curiosity turned into a glare, but I saw the challenge clearly.

"I'm not what you're used to. I follow orders in my professional life because it's good for business. In my personal life, I do whatever the hell I want to."

The heat level between us rose with every sentence we added to the fire. She would have liked nothing less than me kneeling in front of her, begging for what I wanted.

However, I stood my ground, staring deeper, acknowledging that her dominating personality was colliding with mine. She was a control freak, but not even she could deny that she wanted me. A thin sheen of moisture was beading on her top lip, and I wanted to lick it away. I would not stop pursuing her until I got a taste of her sin.

"Show me what you tampered with before I forget I'm at work."

Her request put an end to our standoff, but I hadn't missed the impish smile she cast before she took a step back. Reluctantly, I stepped past her to point out the area.

Within minutes the tenth floor was back up and running and I was gifted a tongue lashing for my asinine and juvenile antics.

"The next time you want to get my attention, call me so you can officially know how it feels to be hung up on. I'll even throw in a few vile words to tickle your eardrums."

I fought the stubborn smile teasing my lips. She could care less, that in a sense, I was her boss, or that I was worth billions, and could change lives with my word or my pen. And I loved that! I love that she didn't allow that part of me to influence her behavior around me.

My attempt to ask her out again was cut off when she stepped around me and headed toward the exit, muttering under her breath. I admired the way her jeans hugged her perfectly round ass. The way each step caused a crease to kiss right below the globes, the exact spots I imagined my fingertips would bend into. The way the asymmetrical sleeves of her blouse and collar clung to her alluring figure. I even noticed she wore red and white Chucks—although they didn't match her outfit—which was probably for the ease of walking the busy seven blocks between our buildings.

Her dismissive actions and the wicked words she had thrown at me had me wanting to follow her wherever she was going. Her feistiness was like *foreplay*, a taste of fire roaring below the surface of her seduction.

At Jax's exit, the chill in the room returned, and my gaze remained on the door long after she had gone. The beeping and flashing equipment broke into my thoughts of kissing that sassy mouth of hers.

She made a good show of running, but I wasn't done. My instincts, the ones that led me to make sound business decisions, insinuated that there was much more between us than mere lust. I was becoming desperate to find out once and for all, what was it that drew me to her?

Chapter Seven

Chase

A week had gone by since I saw Jax, who had me strolling into the convention with a single-minded focus. Tonight, I was dressed in a dark gray, Desmond Merrion suit that was tailored to fit, from the legendary Savile Row on my last trip to London. This suit unquestionably highlighted the efforts I put into keeping myself fit, and I had worn it with only one person in mind.

Jax was the only woman that I could recall wanting to impress. Her place in my mind was already established, roped off with a gold-plated reserve sign. I spent the time before this convention on Jax's website reading her bio so many times, it was imprinted on my brain. An impressive start, she had gone to Columbia where she earned her undergraduate degree before working her way through grad school at Cornell.

I found it very peculiar though that she didn't have any social media accounts. None I could find anyway. Did she not like socializing or was there another reason?

The media was the driving force that helped make me a household name. All it took was a few A-list celebrities talking about my company, and how I had made them millions handling their investment portfolios.

When pictures of me and those celebrities started circulating the internet, I became a household name seemingly overnight. Next thing I knew, I was being interviewed by talk shows, in magazines, and on popular internet blogs. Everyone that was anyone was throwing their money at me. People were constantly watching me too, waiting for me to fail, so the pressure to stay on top of my game was the driving force I contributed to my success.

Camera flashes and shuffling feet followed in my wake when I entered with my date, who ate up the attention. She'd stopped me several times to take photos at different angles. My attention though, was in a different zone entirely as I scanned the space for Jax. My hand remained planted in the small of my date's back, but for the life of me, I couldn't remember her name.

"Chase! Chase!" With their bodies bouncing with excitement, two overzealous women shouted my name. "Can we get a selfie with you?"

"Please," they said together like they practiced it.

"Of course," I answered. Although the attention grated on my nerves sometimes, I kept in mind that it cost me nothing to pause for a few seconds to put a smile on someone's face. My date stepped out of the way while the ladies took their place on either side of me snapping away.

When one of the women handed my date her phone to take a photo, she frowned before snapping a few. Their pictures with me were likely already downloaded to social media as they stepped away eyeing their phones.

"I hope that doesn't become a problem tonight," my date muttered under her breath after retaking her place at my side.

Long rows of trade show booths, containing electronics and digital equipment, lined the large open space inside the center. Upbeat tunes buzzed about the space, keeping minds alert and inspiring positive vibes. People mingled, some ogling the latest in tech toys and devices. Owners and investors soaked up the media attention while attempting to hopefully find rich investors that would take their products to the next level.

A bar and serving tables were set up in every spacious corner away from the bustling rows of equipment. Booth owners entertained their guests—some giving presentations and some introducing updates on devices in energetic profit-inspired voices.

A few more fans approached to take more shots. I had never gotten used to the idea that doing my job and being good at it had earned me the status some superstars coveted.

Anxiousness nipped at my bones, biting with a fierceness that added weight to my unrelenting thoughts. "Is there anything I can do to take that bewildering look off your face," my date asked.

"I glanced at her, but images of Jax swayed me from truly seeing her. I finally responded. "I just have a lot on my mind."

The only thing on my mind was Jax. I asked the woman whose name still evaded me if she wanted a drink. A half hour had gone by since my arrival, and I still hadn't seen her.

"You seem distracted." I heard my date say. Just as I thought to respond, a spark of positive energy lit my body. *Finally.* Without seeing her, I knew that Jax had arrived. I turned in the direction of the doorway and caught a glimpse of her entering.

This wasn't the stylish woman I met at the office. With her head held high and her shoulders set in confidence, tonight, Jax was a goddess. Light was in love with her as it caressed the most delicate angles of her facial features. It reflected off her flowing metallic dress, draped perfectly over every curve. She had styled her hair so that three small rows of braids on either side of her head flowed into a stylish mohawk inspired ponytail.

Light makeup made her eyes pop and her glossed lips had me tracing every intricate line and sculptured turn. Her skin tone blended well with the silver dress, which would be dull on anyone else. Her full breasts sat displayed like two tempting treats.

The physical beauty she presented was indisputable, but I knew first-hand that she was much more than what met the eye. My tongue glided across my lips, unaware that my date was observing my every move.

Her throat clearing did little to draw my focus away from Jax's sexy figure. In fact, I did give her a side look before redirecting my attention back to the person I was dying to see since my arrival.

The grin on my face died an unmerciful death, when I noticed something, I had failed to see before now. The person standing beside Jax had taken a hold of her hand. Jax's date—was a woman.

***

Jax

My gaze zoomed across the large space and found Chase as soon as I stepped across the entrance. What was he doing here? It would have been best to ignore him, but I was a glutton for punishment.

Chase's attempt to hide his shock was useless. His jaw ticked when he noticed my date. I sensed his eyes lingering from a distance, as I scanned the newest tech toys in the first few booths we approached.

This was the first time I could recall Chase attending this convention. Had he come for me? Looking over at the woman next to him, she was what I expected. A leggy blonde. One of those prim types whose job was to nab a rich husband and attend social functions.

Why couldn't I stop thinking about punishing Chase in the most delicious ways? It wasn't like we were suited to date each other. The media had leaked that you needed to sign a freaking NDA to even be seen in public with the man, and I'll be *damned* if I signed a contract to go out with anybody. Besides, I did my best to balance staying clear of public attention while networking to strengthen my business.

No less than five minutes after I'd arrived, Chase stepped into my path, stalling my attempt to bring my date her drink. How had he managed to break away from the woman who'd been clinging to his side like her life depended on it?

"Jax."

"Chase."

"You look lovely," he complimented before allowing his eyes to peruse my body. His gaze damned near burned through the material of my dress, making my nipples tighten. His glasses did nothing to tone down the gleaming hunger in his eyes.

Our silent impasse dredged up images of me fucking him cowgirl style, lassoed to a chair until he passed out. My active imagination got the best of me, when I had a worthy muse to fill it with.

"You clean up well yourself." I finally replied, keeping my behavior cool and casual, although, seeing him had kicked up the pounding in my pussy. The man *dripped* sex appeal and the suit he wore tonight highlighted his toned body.

"So, do you date women, exclusively?"

He didn't waste time getting straight to the point. His sharp gaze dared me to reply yes, and if I did, I'm sure he intended to try and change my mind. Chase's date stood stoic, glaring in our direction with her arms folded across her chest.

"Why do you want to know?" If I was reading his body language correctly, he was ready to strip my ass down in the middle of this crowd and fuck the *shit* out of me.

His lips tilted into a mischievous grin before he stepped closer, shrinking the space between us and forcing my lungs to work harder.

"You're well aware that I'm accustomed to being in charge. Apparently, you're in desperate need to find out what you've been missing. I don't believe a woman is equipped to show you all that you're missing out on."

"And I suppose you're the one to show me this, right?"

"You have no idea the things I'd like to do to you." He lowered his voice and leaned closer. "The things you would beg me to do to you."

Unable to stop myself, I leaned in and satisfied my insatiable need to absorb his warmth and breathe him in. He was an invigorating blend, a mélange of black currant, sweet wisteria, and stimulating masculinity.

"I sensed your wild side the moment you touched me with that tight grip you had on my hand. But it was also the moment I knew we would never go beyond mutual attraction. It's been months since I've been with a man, and I haven't decided yet if I want to go back."

"Why not? Afraid you might like it too much?"

My face sat inches away from his when I whispered my crass words, "Just because I haven't been dick-fucked, doesn't mean I haven't fucked in other ways." I turned from him then and found my date in the crowd. "You see that sexy ass beautiful woman over there watching us."

The reality of us being out and in public finally hit him. It hit me as well, reminding that I needed to keep an eye out for the groups that liked to crowd him for pictures.

He took a small, almost deflating step back and glanced in my date's direction.

"I'm going to take her home tonight, and fuck her so good, that afterwards she'll ask me for permission every time she wants to touch herself. Trust me, Chase, once you're mine, you will always be. But it doesn't matter, because we would never work out."

"You're wrong," he stated. The powerful aura of his confidence sucked the air out of the room.

His date strolled up before he could continue, but his eyes remained on me. He didn't bother introducing the woman as she stood staring between us.

"Aren't you going to introduce me to your beautiful date?" My attempt was to offer the woman the attention he didn't.

"Jax, this is…this is…"

A fucking shame was what it was. He didn't even know the woman's name. It took everything in me not to laugh out loud, but I didn't want to embarrass the woman further. Chase Taylorson was something else: a real piece of work.

The lady reached for my hand.

"I'm Amanda Newcastle. Nice to meet you, Jax. You look gorgeous, and I love your dress," she complimented.

I didn't miss the way Amanda's gaze lingered over my body or the hint of sass in her tone when she spoke. Was she flirting? I knew her little churchgoing ass had seen who I strolled in the place with, but it didn't mean I jumped on every cat I found attractive.

"Thank you, Amanda. You look quite tempting yourself," I offered her a flat compliment, flirting to aggravate Chase.

"Maybe we can walk with you guys," Amanda cast a pleading smile in my direction.

The sharp expression Chase blessed her with clearly said, *"Bitch, stay in your place."* For a man who boasted about his commanding nature, he certainly didn't have his woman in check *tonight*. Me? I thrived on my controlling ways. Chase was apparently a lightweight.

After Amanda's suggestion, I glanced at Chase. He wanted to join me and Kara but based on his lifted chest and chin, was too proud to ask. I made his mind up for him. I nodded in his direction before placing my hand across Kara's back, moving us toward the next set of booths.

Chase was in for one hell of a long night. I had warned him about me, but he was determined not to listen.

Chapter Eight

Chase

The ridiculousness of the situation had me nearing my limits. Every time Jax denied my advances, it forced my mind to create defensive strategies that would turn out in my favor. I didn't believe I was a spoiled man by any means, but when you lived in the type of world I was brought up in, where you could afford to have your every need and want met, you became used to people agreeing with you, even when they didn't want to.

Jax wasn't one of those people, and although I struggled to convince myself I didn't like her blasé attitude, I did. Her defiant behavior was a turn on, and I believed she knew it. She posed the kind of challenge I wanted to explore. She was the kind of force that would never be fully conquered, but I would give it my best shot.

She'd been lavishing the ladies with compliments and attention while shooting teasing glances in my direction. "So, what do you ladies think about this wrist-watch phone?" Amanda and Kara would have *oohed* and *aahed* over anything she showed them.

Kara appeared head over heels in love with everything Jax, and Amanda, who a minute ago was glaring daggers at me for my lack of attention, had yet to drop her smile. The longer we followed them around, the more irritated I became. Jax made it clear that she was mocking me, and my irritation was now neck in neck with my yearning to satisfy my craving for a taste of her.

Her warnings were finally starting to sink in. We were the same in many aspects and if we went in the direction I wanted, we would be like two colliding boulders.

It was too bad the realization didn't take away my interest in her.

Every time our eyes met, it made me acknowledge that she wasn't going to be controlled unless she wanted to be. Which was a letdown because I didn't want to control her...just tame her. I contemplated letting her have her way, but only if it meant getting what I wanted.

Her every move drew my focus, so intensely, it alerted me to a new guest. His slight head nod in her direction didn't go unnoticed before he made his way toward our circle. He was a bold one. So bold and self-assured that he elicited female attention from all around the room, including Amanda's. I didn't like it. This night wasn't turning out the way I envisioned.

As the man made his approach, I noticed he didn't stand out to me because of what he wore or how he looked. It was the way he stared at Jax. He wore a dark blue suit, the jacket unbuttoned and giving a clear view of a lighter blue dress shirt underneath. Long brown hair dusted his shoulders and his tanned complexion hinted he either spent a lot of time in a tanning booth or was possibly of mixed ethnicity.

His focused gaze on Jax grated on my nerves. It caused me to be defensive when I didn't have a right to be. His slithering tongue snaked across his lips, and his eyes fucked her before he even said hello.

"Jax *Motherfucking* Saint-Pierre. Fancy seeing you here." He was loud enough that he turned heads. He was a foul-mouthed fool who purposely didn't acknowledge me, Amanda, or Kara. It was more than likely because his eyes were glued on Jax.

She turned slightly with her hand raised in an attempt to introduce the rest of us, but he cut her off. So that's what we're doing, I thought with my head tilted to the side. Amanda was even put off by the blatant show of disrespect, her lips parted in surprise as she cut her eyes in his direction. With a small chuckle, I was preparing to walk away. "I don't have to take this shit from anyone," I muttered under my breath.

I thought Jax was in the midst of a conversation with her friend when she tossed out, "You say something Chase?"

"No," I replied, grasping that she hadn't been ignoring me.

The man made a show of distracting Jax, again, and I was forced to remind myself that I wasn't there with her.

When their conversation reached a stopping point, Jax ushered a hand toward her date.

"TK, this is my lovely lady Kara, and this is Chase and his beautiful date Amanda."

We were only worthy of a smirk and head gesture in our direction. He wanted nothing to do with us because he had a thing for Jax, something I sensed right away. The lust and ravenous hunger in his eyes, when he stared at her, made my jaw clench tight enough to snap.

"Chase! Chase!"

I knew what would follow hearing my name shouted in that manner. Unfortunately, it wasn't just a few fans asking after a picture, but a full-on camera crew. TK placed a protective arm over Jax's shoulder and turned her away from the approaching crew and went as far as taking her completely away from the group. I remembered her warning me that she didn't like the media but seeing TK's arm around her had me frowning instead of smiling for the approaching group.

"Chase, can we get a small exclusive on what you think about the expo tonight?"

"Of course," I answered, plastering a smile on my face like I had trained myself to do. I took one last glimpse of TK with Jax. His hand was at the small of her back, and her date had joined their group as they moved even further away.

Amanda took her spot at my side as she smiled with pride for the camera crew from WNYX, our local news. Thankfully, I remembered Amanda's name when they asked who my date was.

It had taken me fifteen minutes to locate Jax after I was finished with the impromptu interview. Unfortunately, TK was still at her side. Judging by the infuriating expression on Kara's face, she wanted him gone as much as I did.

Jax was the first to notice my approach, and I didn't miss the smirk on her face.

"So, TK, what do you do for a living?"

All eyes were now on me. Was I *not* supposed to participate in conversation?

"I dabble in information technology. What about you?"

"I'm the CEO of Swift Capital. Chase Taylorson," I tossed out my full name in case he recognized it.

"Good for you," he stated dismissively. The son-of-a-bitch turned his back to me and returned his full attention to Jax.

"Let me get out of your hair and see if I can find something at one of these booths," he finally stated.

"So, what does TK stand for? Tech Krazy?" I asked. The hint of irritation in my tone wasn't lost on the group, the way their heads had whipped around at me after my questions. Amanda and Kara's gazes landed on me, but seeing Jax laugh was a plus.

"Actually, it stands for Tech *King*. Don't hate Chase, his skills are impressive," Jax added. Her eyes sparkled with a seriousness I didn't miss, making her history with TK stir my curiosity.

She pointed something out to Kara, not giving me a chance to satisfy my curiosity about TK. Soon after, two fans came storming in my direction yelling my name. Again, I noticed Jax stepping away, not wanting any part in my publicity. Amanda's mean side-eye was leveled on me as well.

After my fans departed, I found Kara and Jax checking out language translator earbuds. Although my interest wasn't in technology, the buds would help out on my next overseas trip.

"Excuse me for a moment," Jax said before walking away.

This was my chance to get her alone again, so I told the ladies I would refresh our drinks and made a detour to follow in the direction Jax had disappeared.

Chapter Nine

Chase

Disturbing thoughts plagued my mind as I paced outside the ladies' room, until Jax exited. Her breath caught when I pulled her by the waist to stop her from moving past me.

"Can I talk to you for a few minutes, please?"

I had never been crazy over a woman, and had no rights to Jax, but she drove me insane, making me borderline stalkerish. Without giving her a chance to answer, I forced her in the opposite direction.

"If you don't take your damn hands off of me, you're going to end up with a size 8 heel print in your face."

The deep scowl on her face made it evident that I was crossing a line. Despite her threat, I kept nudging her back in the direction of the ladies' room.

"What the fuck are you doing?" She questioned me in a harsh whisper, not wanting to make a scene.

Although she demanded an answer, I didn't give her one. She resisted very little when I continued nudging her back. After turning the knob, I kicked the door open with the toe of my shoe. My hand tightened around Jax's wrist, before I spun her and placed the other on her back to give her a gentle shove.

Turning back to the door, I locked us in and checked the three large stalls to confirm we were alone. This was what she had done to me. One touch, a few heated encounters, and I felt like a ravenous beast, finally set free to feed the animalistic hunger coursing through my veins.

"You better have a fucking good explanation for this little scene of yours." Jax shot daggers at me. She stood near the sinks with her arms folded across her heaving chest, her perfect tits bobbing with each breath.

"We need to talk," I told her as I made my approach.

"You're fucking right we need to talk. What the hell are you doing? You've obviously allowed your confidence to over-shadow your good sense. I already told you, I'm not going to be one of your women. Your bed wench, or whatever you rich white men like to label women you have a fleeting interest in. I damn sure don't intend to be the one you can't introduce be-cause you can't remember my name. So, whatever your brain is cooking up, you need to make damn sure it doesn't involve me."

Preventing her from making her escape, I gripped her arm, spun her around to face me and then pinned her against the door. Her breath hitched with how quick I moved before her sharp gaze raced up to meet mine. She was clearly not accus-tomed to being manhandled.

"Jax, you know as well as I do that confidence is the only thing that keeps this world from eating us alive. Besides, my ego is not so big that I need to be in control of everything."

A storm brewed in her narrowed eyes. "This shit you're pulling right now sure as hell appears to be ego driven."

Planting my hands to either side of her head on the door, I caged her in. Her ferocious gaze should have intimidated me, but my need for her was set ablaze by my uncontrolled desires. Unable to stop myself, I explored her body, my hands so anx-ious, they shook.

"What the fuck is wrong with you?"

Her question rushed out on a harsh whisper. She softened her aggressive tone and almost immediately, a persistent need hung heavy in her eyes. Her tongue slid over her lips as her tight grip on the tail of my suit pulled me in closer. Like in the elevator, she was just as turned on as I was.

I leaned into her, one hand sliding aggressively along the contours of her exquisite body while the other circled her waist. "I fucking told you…"

My lips possessed hers before she could fire off another threatening word, and the beast she'd helped to create, broke free. Her lip-piercing was an unexpected delight, the feel of it was foreign until my tongue slid across it. The tap of hardness sneaking into the mix heightened my lust, adding an extra spark of passion to our kiss. The sensation enticed me to devour her mouth as fervently as she devoured mine.

There was no more holding back, I kissed her with the rough passion I'd been dying to unleash. My eagerness was overpowered by hers when she gripped my tie and tugged hard, bending me to her to take control of the kiss I initiated.

***

Jax

I'll be damned if Chase's rough kiss didn't turn me into a searing blaze of lust and provoked an unrelenting need so strong, it thrummed through me, vibrating my insides. I returned his kiss with a force of passion I didn't know I possessed.

At first, my head was a mess of warring thoughts about going too far with Chase. However, he'd gone and gotten me all worked up, and I wasn't sure if I wanted to stop at a searing kiss.

Before I grasped what was happening, Chase had hoisted me atop the bathroom counter. Pinned between my legs, he caressed my tits and eagerly massaged my nipples that boldly tightened for him. He was unaware of my piercing, or that every time his hand moved against my nipple, chilling vibrations soared throughout my body. When he realized that my right nipple was pierced, it drew a groan from deep in his throat that mingled with the erratic gasps I released. His heated words were whispered against my lips. "Hot. You're smoking fucking hot. I want to fuck you so bad."

The heat he was giving off had made me snap, sending my mind back into war. I pushed him, sending him back a few paces as I sat in place, my chest heaving. Fuck, I wanted him, and he knew it too.

Both control freaks, we were warring for power, and I had no idea who would win. I called him back to me with the flick of my finger and he came, eager and ready.

After another searing kiss that made me whimper, Chase lifted me from the counter and spun me so fast, my brain misfired, resetting the process of me figuring out what the fuck we were doing.

His dick nudged my ass as he gripped me around the waist. The hard press of it re-ignited my desire and pushed away a horrific memory from my past that was threatening to take away this moment.

He whispered hot in my ear. "Being bisexual is overrated. I intend to make you forget about women completely."

As hot as he had me, I believed him. Why wasn't I upset about the current string of events? I'd even managed to push away harsh memories from my past that tried to sneak into our scene. Anger should have consumed me the moment he had dragged me back into the bathroom. Instead, the press of his body into mine made me hotter, wetter.

I spun, turning the tables on him before I gripped him by the shirt, and spun *him* into the position he had me in. My swift movement widened his eyes, throwing him off kilter. Although outraged by his overbearing behavior, his determination and confidence had me fully invested.

My breath hitched when he retook control, spun me, and pinned his bulging hardness against my ass. The sensation of him pressed so hard against me made me hot enough to combust. He gripped my waist with one hand and placed the other under my chin before lifting my face to our reflection in the mirror.

Rubbing the side of his face against mine, he whispered, "Damn that's a sexy picture. Look at how good we look together Jax."

Used to being the alpha in my relationships, I kept tensing and releasing, attempting to stifle my unease about being manhandled. Shocked and aroused all at the same time, the confusing mix leveled me, otherwise I'd have hauled off and struck him by now.

His lips caressed the pulsing flesh of my neck, but his exploring stopped at the sight of my tattoo. "Does this vine run all over your body?" His husky voice bounced off me, adding to my aching hunger. It was a question he'd asked the day we met.

Why hadn't I done anything to stop this yet? Chase was taking liberties I had not allowed anyone else. His lips on mine pressed like a waking caress from a wet dream. Warm enough to entice you from sleep.

His hands on me sparked sensual currents that flowed straight down to my pussy. He was clueless as to how drenched my panties had become. My mind screamed, attempting to convince me to take control of the situation, but my body remained deaf to my mental defense.

The slide of my zipper easing down my back, exposing what I knew his lingering curiosity sought, had me as anxious as he must have been. His loud gasp revealed the moment he saw my treasure.

"This is beautiful. *You're* beautiful," he said. "The kind of beauty that has stripped me of my self-control. Wild, uninhibited, and gorgeous." His lips hovered at my ear, his endearing words a whisper.

"I'm completely intoxicated by you, and I fear I have lost my sanity." His words were like secrets I wasn't sure I was supposed to hear. I wasn't entirely convinced he realized he was speaking out loud.

***

Chase

A portion of the vine I had seen on her neck and hand, spanned a large part of her back. The design wasn't thick or messy but elaborate and well defined as it wound around her skin. The beauty and artistry of the tattoo captivated me.

The thin branches were alive with sharp-looking thorns, and a few tiny blossoms that were intricately placed. A tiny flower on her lower back, one behind her right ear, and one on her shoulder. The looping stems grew from a tangle of angry black roots at her lower back.

I believed the tattoo to be a reflection of who she was. Beauty marred by prickly dark pain, toughness with an edge of vulnerability, and a fierce determination coupled with an undeniable likeability.

The expansive detailing of the art suggested the tattoo branched to multiple parts. The sight of the ink made my blood burn in my veins as heat flared and traveled south, causing me to grow unbearably hard.

I couldn't wait any longer; the torture of not being inside her had me gasping to get air into my lungs. I jerked my wallet from my back pocket, thankful I kept a condom in there. I tossed the wallet once I retrieved the condom, not caring where it landed.

Jax watched my every move in the mirror, her eyes stormy clouds of rage one moment, and heavy with need the next. When I reached to take off my glasses, she shook her head.

"Leave the glasses on."

There was no need to tell me twice. I slipped the condom in my front pocket and proceeded to caress the lush roundness of her ass, all the while, waiting for her to stop me.

"Chase," she called back.

"Yes."

"You better make it worth my time."

"I will. I'll make it so good you are going to be calling me every time you want to touch yourself."

My arrogant words, words I had borrowed from her, caused a low chuckle to sound in the swirling hurricane of our desires.

I bent slightly, lifting the hem of her dress and letting my hand slide over her buttery soft skin and ass. Green met brown when our gazes locked in the mirror. I explored her, memorizing the contours as thoroughly as the figures of a multimillion-dollar investment portfolio.

Holding her dress up with my left hand, I swept my right over her ass before palming the firm roundness. My frantic fingers slipped behind her skimpy periwinkle colored thong. Her face creased, and she sucked in a sharp intake of air after I had gotten a good grip and ripped the delicate material from her body.

With the silk wadded in my fist, I watched her face as I sniffed them. Sheer lust fueled me now. I was so amped up on my desire for her that I was verging on crazy.

Based on the heavy accumulation of need in her eyes, I surmised she was as out of control as I was. I inhaled her panties again, the scent closing my eyes and causing me to release a throaty moan.

"They smell good, don't they?" she asked, observing my perverse behavior.

"Yes."

"You better memorize the scent, because this is the only time, you're going to get a whiff."

Her sweet feminine scent intoxicated my senses as well as the air around me, enticing me to seek out the source. "Your mouth is saying one thing, but your body is telling me a whole different story. It's saying you're going to let me have a whiff whenever I want one."

I believe she was enjoying our back-and-forth banter, I certainly was.

"I'm going to make you come so hard, you just may pass out." Her eyes in the mirror dared me to follow through with my cocky statement.

After I shoved her panties into my inner jacket pocket, I removed the condom from my pants and placed it near her mouth, still testing her will to proceed. When her lips parted and she clenched the black and gold wrapper between her teeth, the line she had drawn where it concerned us, had officially been destroyed.

Chapter Ten

Jax

Chase had raised my anticipation so high; I lost all the give-a-fucks about who was in control anymore. This was a first for me. Right now, I was a woman who wanted to be fucked. We had reached a point where stopping was no longer an option—we were either going to fuck or fight.

He kept a tight hold around my waist with one hand, while he worked his belt loose with the other. The sound of his zipper sliding down edged us closer to crossing a line we weren't going to be able to uncross.

Condom clenched between my teeth, I stood in place. Fiery desire remained my motivator, fueling my impulses and setting my body to hum with sexual tension. My need overpowered the fact that my date was out there waiting on me.

With every touch, kiss, and stroke, Chase reminded me that my time with men hadn't been all bad. I hadn't sworn off the opposite sex for good, I'd just decided to take a break from them. I believe he was aiming to make sure my break was a short-lived one.

My conscience screamed for me to stop this uncontrolled affair, but my body continued to beg for attention. My nipples were puckered so tight, they ached. My pussy was leaking so fluidly the juices were already drizzling down my inner thigh. Every hot zone on the surface of my skin tingled in sync with my pounding heartbeat.

Was the heavy bulge Chase had pressed against my ass as big as I was assuming? I could have turned around to find out, but the element of surprise was more exciting.

Once he freed himself, he pulled at one corner of the condom to finish the job of opening it. I clenched my teeth as he ripped the foil away.

"How hard do you want it?"

"Limping hard," I replied to his hungry gaze in the mirror.

We had gone too far, and I was too turned on to stop now. He used one hand to roll the condom up his length while gripping my warm flesh at my waist with the other.

A small part of me wanted to hesitate, however, the part of me that desired a good hard fuck was winning.

Chase explored the front of my body with a possessive hand. He squeezed and massaged my breasts, plucking my hard nipples which sent tingling heat vibrating through me. One of his roving hands slid across the quivering flesh of my stomach while the other inched up until his fingers closed around my neck.

My breath caught, when he used the grip, he had around my neck to lure me into a bent position, sending my ass up as he pressed harder into me from the back. He eyed me in the mirror, observing my reaction to his every move, his eyes, wild and primal.

His free hand skimmed my ass before slipping around my side and lowered. His anxious fingers explored until they found my searing wetness. I was soaked, swollen and pulsing.

When his finger slid across the small piece of metal of my clit piercing, his eyes went wide. He slid his heavy dick up and across my ass creating a lovely friction that my frantic body devoured.

His fingers glided across my wet heat with ease, as our harsh breaths echoed off the tile walls of the bathroom. The heat of our combined hunger burned through the space like an untamed fire.

His wicked fingers teased my pussy, slid across my wet lips and smeared my juices, until he was able to insert two fingers. My eyes slammed shut when he shoved those long fingers, so deep inside me, the action snatched my breath away.

My pussy squeezed his fingers, the constricting muscles unwilling to relax. He didn't remove his fingers until they became bathed in my juices. My eyes snapped open at his voice.

"Tell me that you want me to fuck you," he demanded. He knew I wanted him, could probably feel the need vibrating through me. Patience had disappeared. Common sense had sneaked away, and I couldn't wait any fucking longer. This was a rarity that I didn't want to waste, as I usually had to be in complete control of my sexual partners to get this worked up. Chase had unknowingly accomplished a task I had deemed impossible.

"I want you to fuck me. Right now, you cock-teasing son-of-a-bitch!" I barked my explicit demand at him.

He aligned us before he tightened the grip around my neck from the front and shoved himself into me with a powerful thrust from the back. A harsh breath rushed out of me at the delicious bite of his unapologetic impact. My eyes slammed shut allowing the rush of being filled seep into my body.

His movements were not delicate but not forced either. Right now, he *owned* me. For as much as I controlled the relationships in my past, Chase had me under his spell. He made me eat all my tough words and tuck away my ego.

Our personalities were mirrored reflections of each other, making it difficult for me to remain upset by his actions. If I'd been in his shoes, I would have done the same damn thing. Except, I would have fucked him in one of the three stalls, while women stalked in and out of the bathroom.

I had purposely taunted and teased him most of the night. I expected him to walk away but he endured and was now responding. He didn't care where we were, or how wild he looked. His mind was set on getting what he wanted, and he was determined to prove that he was every bit as dominating as he'd implied.

The first few thrusts took my will and caused me to shiver as my nails scraped along the shiny granite countertop. My pussy was clamped tight, so it took a while for him to stretch my walls enough to accommodate all of him.

Every movement he made shook me. Every bit of resistance raced through me until the juicy flow we created slid over his hard-throbbing head. The tight space of the room reflected our pleasure back to us, adding to our frenzied state of ecstasy.

His whispers were like soft licks echoing inside my ear as the tip of his lips flirted with my lobe.

"You're so fucking tight; it's driving me mad."

Chase had been right about one thing; I didn't need to always be in control. At least, not with him. He'd taken me by storm, and while everything in me wanted to stop him, I couldn't. The sex was just that fucking good.

Chase knew how to scratch every itch, strum every nerve ending, and lick every hot spot. He was giving my pussy an amazing workout, sliding the fat head up and down and against my walls, plunging into me so deep and hard that each stroke ripped the oxygen from my lungs.

"Chase," the rest of my words were stolen, lost on his deep thrust.

"Is this good enough for you? Am I wasting your time Jax?"

"No! Shit no!" I hissed out between clenched teeth. "Fuck!"

Chase was rich and uppity, but his sex was straight hood.

Every thrust drove his length deep enough to snatch my breath from the inside but sparked an emotion that was strengthening my connection to him. The burning hunger he'd built in me had turned into a pleasure so strong, he knew he could rip me apart and make me submit to him even when I didn't want to.

I helped him, shoving back into every long and thick inch of him. The feel of the stretch and the pressure on my walls indicated that he was massive. He stretched me to the point that pain blew kisses at my pleasure, and I overdosed on the intoxication of both. When he went deeper and lingered there, I realized he was waiting for me to open my eyes.

He wasn't tapping into just desire. He licked at something extra, something I didn't have a name for. He was also putting some well-worked miles on my pussy, stamping it with his unique seal.

The quaking in my sex intensified and weakened my legs before it spread to other parts of me. A bundle of tension building in my core was about to snap.

"Chase. Fuck! You're going to make me come!" I heaved loud, struggling for breath.

"Come baby, I can't wait to feel your pussy giving thanks to my dick." Like me, he'd lost all control. Every thrust drove me further into the maddening world we resided in. My heart pumped a mixture of lust and fire, the beat knocking loud enough to vibrate through me. He had my breaths pushing out so hard they gave off sparks of pleasure that was driving me to the brink of insanity.

"Jax!"

Seconds before my heart exploded, my walls tightened around his dick with such force, he erupted along with me. I shivered against him, screaming his name, and showcasing my remarkable use of profanity in both French and English. His teeth sank deep into the flesh of my shoulder, sending peppery currents into my hypersensitive hot zone below.

Our bodies shivered against each other's as we fought to recapture our composure. An orgasm had never rocked me so hard; an amazing realization, since I was convinced that I alone held the key to the ways of stroking my deepest sexual desires.

When we recovered enough to move, he retracted his perfect teeth from my shoulder and kissed the spot where he'd bitten. A reddish imprint was already forming. We glanced in the mirror at the same time, harboring the same pinched expression.

What the fuck just happened?

Like he sensed my thoughts, one of his brows lifted and his eyes remained on me, unblinking. He backed out of my shuddering heat. The wicked expression I offered while he did caused him to avoid my eyes. He staggered to the nearest stall, flushed the condom, and used a wad of tissue to wipe himself clean before zipping his pants.

Stunned, I stood with my dress hanging at my waist on one side and my hip bare on the other. The dress remained gaped open on my back where he'd left it unzipped. He feasted his eyes on my tattoo, fascinated by it and seemingly forgetting the state of our situation for a moment.

My breathing began to level as I processed the depth of the uncontrolled actions that had occurred between us. He visibly swallowed while my eyes bore holes into his through the mirror. Why did it always have to feel so weird afterwards? Now that the dust had settled, my anger had rushed to the surface, more so towards myself for being weak.

Continuing to avoid my eyes, he wet a few of the neatly rolled towels available. Chase had me flowing so good, my juices had dripped down my inner thighs. He proceeded to clean away the mess he had helped create. My chest rose and fell evenly as he wiped me clean. His level of care was unexpected. He was revealing a caring aspect of him that nudged at the irrational knot of anger that had risen up in me.

Once he finished, he started to zip my dress, admiring the view. The material closed around me like a layer of skin.

He slid his hand around my waist and gave a light tug so I would turn to face him. My eyes met his and narrowed. When he moved in for a kiss, I placed two fingers against his lips.

"Don't you dare kiss me, Chase Randall Taylorson."

My voice edged on in a low tone. I had spoken his full name which filled his gaze with curiosity.

He didn't need to know that he had piqued my interest enough to snoop into his life after meeting him. With his resources, if he hadn't already, it wouldn't surprise me if he had sneaked peeks into mine.

"I specifically told you I didn't like being controlled sexually, yet you proceeded to *not* heed my words. But I enjoyed it," I reluctantly admitted. "I enjoyed it a lot."

My teeth sank into my lip, and I shook my head, attempting to process our impulsive actions.

"Damn it was good," I blurted, still having trouble processing what we had just done. "And you better be glad it was." Without another word, I stepped toward the exit and gripped the knob. Before I turned the lock open, I tossed a threatening glance over my shoulder.

"See you later Chase."

An angry-faced woman who was doing the pee-pee dance pushed past me after I opened the door, breaking my visual connection with Chase whose face bore the expression—*What the fuck did I just do?*

Chapter Eleven

Chase

Three long days had gone by since I'd seen Jax. She hadn't made any effort to contact me, and I knew that she wouldn't. One of the first things she told me was that she liked being in control. So, did I. The fact that I had taken that control away from her in that bathroom now resonated.

She would hear the lie in any apology I made because I wasn't sorry. I would do it again. My phone vibrating pulled me out of my thoughts. I was unable to suppress my smile when I noticed it was my mother calling.

I lifted my phone to my ear, and relaxed as I sat in the back of my car, in route to meet my friends for lunch. We'd been planning a get together for a month and had finally carved out the time to meet.

"Mom."

Whether on the phone, or in person, Sadie Montgomery always brought a smile to my face.

"Hi Son. How has life been treating you?" My life had been spiced up the moment I met Jax.

"I'm doing well. About to meet Landon and Ethan for lunch. Working hard and attempting to stay under the radar. Enough about me, how's London treating you?"

"Magnificent. I'm having such a good time; I'm thinking of staying longer. I met a group of American women in my age group who are staying for three months, and they have made my time here unforgettable. We did all of the normal tours, saw Big Ben, the Tower of London, and Buckingham Palace. But things got really interesting when they dragged me into a club."

"You, in a club?"

She chuckled. "My first thought was to flee, but they catered to a forty and up crowd. After a few drinks, I let my hair down, relaxed and just had fun. I even danced to Lil Nas X's, Old Town Road."

My hardy chuckle livened up the interior of my car, happy that she was enjoying herself. After my mother divorced my father over a decade ago, she used her settlement to travel. Each time she returned from her travels, she stayed with me, an arrangement I thoroughly enjoyed. Our roles had reversed in a way as each of my homes had a room for my mom.

"You sound happy. I'm glad to hear that you're having fun. However, the next time you think about clubbing, you need to call me for permission first."

She burst into a fit of laughter.

"How's everyone?" she asked, laughter still in her tone. She had never spoken ill of my father, but his cheating and controlling ways had driven her away.

"Everyone is as good as you'd expect them to be. Dad's still in physical therapy. Blake's still angry at the world."

My family was not a close knit one. My mother's only sister Carol, had died when I was a teenager. The days I got along with my brother Blake were few and far in between.

My father and I were just now starting to build a relationship. He had two brothers, my uncles that I had only met twice. One, Uncle Bruce, sold drugs. The other, Uncle Rich, abused drugs. The hate between the brothers ran deep, pointing at a chaotic history they remained tight-lipped about.

"I hate to say it, but your brother hasn't hit rock bottom yet. *His* rock bottom. When he does, he'll have to make the tough decision to pick himself up. Otherwise, we are going to have to intervene on his behalf."

"I agree, even if we have to force help on him."

We sat with a moment of silence on both ends. Blake was always a tough subject for us.

"I saw your latest photos and interview from the tech expo," my mother said. "You looked good, son. Your date was a pretty girl, but I could clearly see she doesn't make you happy. You two smiled in those photos together, but I could see it on your face, your mind was light years away. I made the offer before, and I'll make it again. All you need to do is accept it."

I grinned.

"Mom, I don't want you picking out women for me. I will have you know that I may have found someone. I really like her, but I think I may have messed up."

"What's her name? And what did you do?"

"Jax Saint-Pierre. She specifically told me what she didn't want. Me pursuing her was one, and I went and impulsively did a second thing that she told me not to."

"You were too aggressive with her, and you're not sorry about it. But you really like this one, so you're reflecting on your behavior with her." Her tone was matter of fact.

The vehicle started to slow, alerting our arrival at the restaurant. The paparazzi that were following us were out of their cars and staging themselves at the entrance to the restaurant, waiting for me. One stood outside my window, the dark tint keeping him from spotting where I sat inside the car.

"Mom, how could you possibly know my current situation so well?"

"Because you're my son, and I know you better than you know yourself. The first thing you told me was that you liked her. I can't tell you the last time I heard you say you liked a woman. You usually say things like; we're going to see where it goes, or we're chilling, whatever that means. But, with Jax, you told me you *really* liked her before you even told me her name."

I hadn't realized what I'd done until my mom had pointed it out.

"I'm interested in getting to know her better, but she is a tough one. She doesn't care about my status, wants no part of the spotlight, and isn't afraid to speak her mind."

Her low chuckle sounded.

"Sounds like my kind of girl. I'm eager to meet her. If you're truly interested in getting to know her son, you have to learn how to humble yourself and show her your intentions are more than physical."

At her words, I realized in this early stage that I wanted my mother to meet Jax. The realization floored me, but it didn't stop my smile from surfacing.

"I know you're meeting up with your friends, so call me later. I want to hear more about Jax. It's not every day my son meets a woman he actually wants to talk about."

This time it was me who chuckled.

"Okay. I'll call you later, about seven or eight your time. Love you mom."

"Love you too son. Take care."

Paul opened my door. I exited the vehicle and presented my practiced smile as the cameras flashed.

Landon and Ethan, my longtime friends would offer me the opposite of the advice my mother had given about Jax. Good thing I wasn't ready to mention Jax to them yet, because I was more concerned about figuring out how to get her back in my good graces.

Chapter Twelve

Jax

The camera was adjusted so that my full body filled the large monitor I saw in the mirror. I stood naked and shivering, but it wasn't the cold that shook me. It was fear. I was terrified of what was coming. Two big standing bright lights on each side of the camera cast me under a spotlight I would have done anything not to be in.

"What are you waiting for, you little dumb bitch. We've done this enough times that you know the routine."

"Aww!" My loud scream echoed through the room when a heavy fist came down on my back for moving too slow. The hard lick caused me to fall into the bed versus climbing in.

"Spread your legs and if you don't smile into this camera, I'll make sure it will be ten times worse."

With tears running down my cheeks, dropping onto the pillow, I forced a smile on my face as I glared at the shiny dark eye of the lens. When the object came into view, the one that would be the primary source of my pain, I lost my ability to breathe. I gasped as I started to shake uncontrollably.

"Please." I begged, crying harder. "Don't make me."

"Don't make you what? You owe me this, you little spoiled cunt, and if you tell your daddy, I'll kill him and make you watch."

My eyes snapped open, and I sat up in bed, clutching my heaving chest and fighting to breathe. My sheets were drenched in sweat again, wetness chilling me now that I had thrown back the covers and allowed the cool air to blanket me.

I've suffered from night sweats for years. It had taken me time and research to find out why I sometimes woke up this way. Sometimes, I remembered the dreams, and other times, they were phantom notes of hate that lingered in my head and affected my body.

The attempts I made to shake away my shivers didn't work, as the memory of my younger self had put me face-to-face with the devil. I could sense the white-hot hate that lingered. A hate so strong, it had the ability to reach through time and space and send shivers through me.

While most people were haunted by things they could see in the here and now, it was my past that ate at the soul of my future.

The bright blue numbers of my digital clock pulled my mind back to the present. Four in the morning. I had gotten a little over three and a half hours of sleep, which was better than usual.

Memories of Chase caused a smile to crack through the fog of darkness that had gripped me. Although I didn't want a relationship with him, I couldn't deny that he had a positive effect on my psyche.

Aside from the relationships I built with the women I worked and associated with, I didn't have but one girlfriend, Lena James. Lena was a flight attendant, so I didn't get to see her often, but took advantage of the times I did. I was one of the loneliest people I knew, filling the void of friendship with work and completing whatever goals I set for myself.

Did I have trust issues? *Yes.*

As far as relationships went, I accepted that I didn't know how to let anyone in. Each time I made a valid attempt, I would do or say something to chase them away. Over time, I became upfront about my desire for casual sex, making it abundantly clear I wasn't looking for longevity.

The idea of letting someone into the inner workings of me and sharing with them my fears and secrets terrified me. They would judge. They would look at me with disgust. They would run screaming for the hills if the wickedness rooted within me was ever spilled onto them.

Swiping my fingers across the screen of my phone, I distracted myself from an issue I knew I needed to face one day. An issue, I fully intended to resolve so that I could eventually have a normal life. I scrolled past twenty work emails, before I found the task guaranteed to keep me busy.

Distracting myself from my past demons was one thing, but not even work was enough to keep Chase from invading my imagination. I'd been avoiding him for a week.

Facts were: Chase had handled me like no one else could, and I could have stopped him, but I didn't. Hell, I couldn't. I craved more of him, but stubbornly refused to give into my unquenched desire for him.

He was an opposing force to my dominating nature. To a woman like me who fed on control, he was my nemesis.

And Chase didn't have a regular dick either, his shit was hypnotic. No other had ever made me not only lose control but give it up. No wonder he had to take himself off the market and bragged about creating stalkers. He could *dick-notize* a woman with one thrust.

Chapter Thirteen

Chase

When my secretary placed a letter from Jax on my desk, I forgot all else existed. The letter was a physical representation that she was thinking about me. Whether those thoughts were positive or negative was a mystery she had folded between thin sheets of paper.

Who sent letters anymore anyway? It was a nice old-fashioned touch I appreciated, the notion brightening my smile.

I resisted my urges to contact her by studying the macroeconomic benefits from increasing infrastructure investments. Studying hadn't worked. I wanted Jax, and now knew it wasn't just sexual chemistry fueling my need for her. Was I on the verge of an unhealthy obsession with a woman I barely knew?

After a moment, I swiped the letter opener through her letter. A smile surfaced as I scanned her neat handwritten words. She possessed the penmanship of a serial killer—neat, clean, and precise. It wasn't a letter but a dinner invite.

The date was set for me to meet her for dinner at seven tomorrow night. I had eaten at the restaurant on several occasions. It was called, The Place, located in Greenwich Village, it sat proudly across the street from the Minetta Tavern, and was known for serving the most exquisite seafood in the area. The smile Jax's invite had put on my face remained for the rest of the day.

***

The drive along MacDougal Street was stop and go. My driver, Paul, reached the restaurant at ten to seven. From the outside, *The Place* appeared deserted and not open for business. Surrounding restaurants and shopping plazas buzzed with the energetic movement of the city as it would any normal Saturday night.

We'd been careful to avoid any tails on the drive over and had used my most inconspicuous vehicle, a dark gray Silverado truck. I scanned the area several times after I exited my truck, hiked the short distance along the pavement, and approached the closed double doors. The heavy wood sprang open at my approach, and I was greeted immediately.

"Good evening, Mr. Taylorson. Allow me to escort you to your table."

"Thank you." I scanned the empty restaurant.

"Where is every…" My words trailed off when she filled my view. The sight of her awaken my senses, coated them with a spice I had never had the pleasure of tasting or smelling.

Jax was beautiful. An encyclopedia of descriptions wasn't enough to define the magnetic depth of her. Her skin shimmered against the light, giving it a reason to exist. The world around her bent to her movement, angling to stay trapped in her glow.

She was dressed in a classic white jumpsuit that showcased the gorgeous body that had invaded my unconscious and waking dreams. She paired the outfit with gold heels that peeked from under the wide flowing legs of her jumpsuit. The chest area dipped low, allowing me to see another piece of the tattoo, which was as much a turn-on as she was.

"You look perfect," the compliment breezed out softly.

"Thank you. You look wonderful yourself," she replied in a smooth, even tone. She stepped closer, leaving only a few inches between us before she placed a light kiss against my cheek.

She pressed her fingers to my lips to stop me from returning a kiss, same as she had done in the bathroom. I nipped at her fingers playfully, causing her to yank them away with a wide smile. My raging curiosity kept me anxious to see how this night would turn out, so I played along, for now.

My eyes only had one setting, her, as she sat in front of me. Our table was the only one dressed in a snow-white tablecloth and set to perfection with serving dishes, glasses, and silverware set for at least three courses.

"Are we the only people here?"

I gave the place another once-over. Jazzy instrumental music mingled with the cool breeze sweeping through the space. A dim glow poured from the recessed lights in the ceiling and a flickering candle set in crystal, sat in the center of our table.

"Yes. We're the only guests tonight. I understand the importance of your privacy, because I value mine as much as you do yours."

She wanted to respect my privacy. The idea enticed an instant smile. The word respect held a lot of power and in my mind, it meant we were officially dating.

"I took the liberty of ordering for you. Figured we'd start with the lobster bisque, followed by a light garden salad, and the final and main dish of crab stuffed flounder. I pared it with a nice crisp Pinot Grigio to drive the flavor of the dishes."

She took a sip of her wine, her sexy lips flirting with the rim of the glass as her eyes flashed heat in my direction above the rim. When she sat the glass down, her eyes sparked with a gleam of passion so heavy I stifled a gasp. The sex appeal pouring through her smoldering eyes had me inhaling deep and hard, in an attempt to calm my frenzied nerves. How could one look, elicit such a strong reaction? Only she was capable of luring such appeal from me.

"Dessert comes later," she said, reading my reaction. Pure seduction dripped off her tone and shot to my dick.

She was seducing me, and I liked it.

"How did you know what I enjoy eating? You've ordered one of my favorite meals," I questioned, aiming to diffuse the sexual tension she had shaken loose.

"I hacked into your phone." Her matter-of-fact tone threw me.

My mouth fell open, surprised at first, but remembering what she did for a living.

"So, Chase…" a long pause followed.

Thankfully, the waiter appeared with our starter dishes as I was reluctant to face what she might have found in my phone. He placed my lobster bisque before me, before placing hers. Known for being the pillar of calm and restraint, I was man enough to admit that I had definitely lost my control with her in that public restroom. However, her resistance wouldn't allow me to hang on to the tiny hints of apprehension that climbed into my head.

"You were going to be mine, there is no doubt about that, but I do apologize for allowing myself to lose control and indulge in what should have been acquired in a more dignified manner."

A lazy smile traced her lips before she nodded in my direction and lifted her wine glass in silent acceptance of my words. There was a trace of challenge gleaming in her eyes, hinting that she wasn't going to make things easy for me.

"As much as I would love to overindulge in the sexual cravings you stir up in me, I want more from you, Jax. I would like to know more about you. I want us to laugh and share our shortfalls and achievements with each other. I'd prefer that we be the kind of couple that communicates rather than let sex solve our problems."

Did I really just let that slip out of my mouth? My forehead crinkled. *What am I saying?*

My conscience answered. *You're saying what you've been thinking for the past few days.*

Based on her reluctant stare, I believed I was admitting too much, too soon, but she hadn't shut me down yet.

"First, I can respect you for wanting more from me, but I don't know when I'll be ready for any kind of relationship. Second, I hardly know you outside of what I read on your phone, or what blogs or headlines tell me. Third, I'm not even sure I want to share my personal business with you."

She spoke with a made-up mind, but I chose to ignore it because I could tell a strong personality like hers would need a lot of persuading. Besides, she seemed to be forgetting that she was the one that had invited me to dinner. Despite my logical mind telling me she may have wanted pay back from the bathroom scene, this was still a date.

With her arms folded across her chest, I couldn't tell what I was reading in her expression—was it amusement or irritation?

The more she tried to resist me, the more I wanted her. Plus, I was starting to enjoy the push and pull happening between us. It excited me, adding a unique flavor to our relationship that I wasn't sure I could get with anyone else.

Around Jax, I wasn't a billionaire businessman, I was a normal guy who could speak freely. I didn't have to be formal or speak in my acting voice. I was simply a man interested in a woman playing hard to get. A woman who didn't cower under the weight of my power, and I respected her more for it.

"Tell me what makes you normal, Chase. I want the real you, not what you show people. What brings you out of the shadow of a billionaire businessman into the light of who you truly are?"

She was at war with herself, resisting me one moment and showing interest the next. However, I was pleased by her show of interest.

"Most people believe I live the perfect life because I have garnered some fame, or because my family has always had money."

Judging by her furrowed forehead, this was her assessment of me as well.

"I'm a prop to some and an ornament to others. A living display. This cold world no longer sees me as a person and could care less about my feelings, how I'm doing, and if I need help. No one cares who I truly am. If I were shot down in the streets right now, I believe a selfie next to my dying body would be taken before I received help."

I imagined my face reflected how certain aspects of my life truly made me feel. A streak of sorrow flashed in Jax's probing gaze before she reached across the table and brushed the lightest strokes of her fingers across the back of my hand. She covered my hand with hers for just a few seconds before she took it away.

She was clueless as to the amount of power she unleashed in that single action, a caring touch that lifted the hairs on my arm. It also revealed a truth about her that I'm sure she wanted to keep hidden. She had just shown me that she cared.

"Having money doesn't equate to happiness, especially when you are raised by a prolific control freak like my father. There wasn't a task or goal set on my behalf he didn't suggest. If I dated a girl who wasn't handpicked by him, he'd do everything in his power to drive her from my life. My dream, when

I was younger, was to become a professional baseball player. My backup plan was to major in engineering, but my father stubbornly suggested business."

A curious smile appeared as she leaned towards me. Her subtle gestures of interest pleased me and induced a spark of happiness that made it easy to share parts of my life with her.

"I'm not saying my life was miserable, but I spent the bulk of it living my father's dream for who he wanted me to become. He was always testing me and my brother. Many of his lessons were carried out by unconventional means."

Her brows pinched tight at the statement, her daring eye zeroing in on mine.

"He has not hesitated to sleep with some of the women we've dated, just to prove that he could. He wanted us as physically strong as we were mentally. To build up those strengths, he enlisted us in several boot-camps that operated with their own set of rules. The kind that flew under the radar, and were allowed to beat, haze, and severely punish their recruits. From one, I was sent home with a concussion, and Blake a broken arm."

Her face bunched in concern. "Damn Chase. I'd have never guessed you would have been put through that kind of hell. Does your father's behavior, or his tough lessons affect the way you treat women? Do they affect the way that you live? It's a horrible way to teach a young man a lesson."

I had never discussed these parts of my life with anyone but found myself eager to share them with Jax. She was the only one who cared enough to ask and sit and listen to what I had gone through.

"Not even my mother knew what those boot camps were. She naturally assumed we were being shipped off to one of the camps she and my father had picked from a brochure. My father's lessons eventually became the examples of what not to do. To answer your question Jax; I don't have all the answers, and there is still a lot I have to figure out for myself, but I do my best to do the right things by women. I do my best to live a productive life."

Her eyes were glued on me, soaking in my words, and I believe better understanding another piece of me. I was eager to know more about her, so I changed the subject.

"So, tell me about the piercing. I like it. I like it a lot, but what made you get it down there?"

My eyes fell to the area blocked by the table. A sly smile crept across her face as she contemplated telling me.

"I got it so that I could learn to control my orgasms. The barbell pings my clit, hitting enough nerve endings to get my attention. For the first month, I had uncontrolled orgasms, until I learned to force myself to think deeper than the immediate pleasure and seek a deeper more satisfying one."

She paused to observe the snicker of satisfaction I was sure was reflected in my eyes.

"Controlling my desire is what helps me enjoy sex even when my sexual partner is garbage."

The statement was unexpected, but I believe we were getting somewhere. Bad sex and underwhelming sexual partners were valid enough reasons to want control, but I believed her need for control ran deeper than she was letting on.

"Why do you enjoy being in control so much?" I blurted the question, unable to keep my nagging curiosity at bay. I wasn't expecting her to give me an answer, but my ears perked when she appeared ready to talk.

"I ended up in a situation that stripped me of all control, all modesty, and all of my dignity. Once I escaped those dark days, I made a vow to never allow myself to be controlled by anyone, and if *I* gave up control of myself it would be a decision *I* made."

A devastating secret she had suffered was hidden within the gloom invading her expression. I reached for her hand, sensing the hurt, seeing it on her face. As lovely as she was, it did nothing to hide the horror seeping from her pores and glancing through her eyes.

"I'm sorry Jax."

She pulled her hand away from mine, not wanting me to comfort her. *What had happened to her?* There was so much more she wasn't telling me. Would she leave if I pushed too hard?

Her set shoulders made me aware that she wasn't going to go any deeper than the surface. Maybe she would someday trust me enough to tell me about it. I kept my hand on the table near hers, letting her know that she could take it if she needed to.

After a silent moment, my mind had gone full circle, reminding me of the threatening promise that lingered in her eyes after our bathroom scene. I glanced around expecting something to happen. However, I sensed this was what she wanted— me being paranoid.

"Are you ready for the second part of our date?"

"We're dating?"

She shrugged but didn't reply. Instead, she asked a second time, "Are you ready?"

"What will the second part of our date consist of?"

Her smile was way too innocent for a woman I believed harbored plans to torture me.

"I thought I would keep things traditional. Dinner, and a movie. I happen to know one of your favorite movies is *Gladiator*. Figured we'd watch it, and I'll fix you a scoop of mint chocolate chip ice cream."

A smile breezed across my lips, despite my anxiousness. I gripped the hand she had reached out to me but was slow to stand. She stepped off, tightening her grip on my hand as I lagged behind with slow uncertainty in my stride.

She was controlling every aspect of this date, and as much as I wanted to resist, my need to see where this would lead was stronger.

Chapter Fourteen

Chase

My reluctance to obediently follow her made Jax drag me along, her firm grip digging into my arm.

"Why are we going this way?"

I glanced back at the exit while she led me toward the kitchen, and what I supposed was the rear of the building. The staff had either left for the night or made themselves scarce.

We exited through the back door which opened to a tight alley. Before I could question why we were lurking in the darkness, she keyed in the code to a side door of the neighboring building. We entered and traveled along an empty and shadowy hall.

My head jetted around in anticipation, waiting for something or someone to jump from a dark corner, and pounce.

"How connected are you to be able to set all of this up?" I whispered my question to the back of her head. I was starting to think that Jax wasn't just a small business owner.

She didn't answer right away as we climbed a set of stairs that led us a level up. After entering another hall, barely discernable music, and distant voices flowed from someplace within the building. I couldn't recall the name of the hotel, but I remembered seeing it in passing.

We shuffled past the lobby bustling with people a level down, but none glanced up, or paid us any attention as we breezed along the deserted outskirts of the action.

I stopped her with a firm grip of her arm. "Where are you taking me Jax? I have had enough of the cloak and dagger mystery."

"You remember dragging me into the bathroom at the expo?" She asked.

"Yes."

"I resisted a little, but I followed you in to see what you wanted, right?"

"Yes."

"Now, you need to give me the same courtesy," she insisted.

This was an entirely different scenario. One I believed was built on revenge for me challenging her need for control, but I decided to play along.

She jerked my arm to get me moving again. I followed, stumping down mounting questions and my irritating anxiousness to see where this was going.

A glimpse of the front desk came into view, a level below us, before we turned into a nook housing a bank of elevators. The word *staff* in big black letters stood out above them. Jax used a key card to open the elevator. As anxious as I was, I did appreciate her going through the trouble to protect my privacy.

I leaned against the back wall of the elevator as she tapped the button for the seventh floor.

"This is reminiscent of the day we met. I was only supposed to walk you to the elevator, but my mind was set on spending as much time alone with you as possible."

Her sneaky smile surfaced, but she didn't respond right away. She was standing in front of me now, in much the same way I had stood in front of her in the elevator the first day.

"What were your intentions if that elevator hadn't stopped?" She asked.

My gaze roamed her leisurely from top to bottom. "I can assure you my intentions were inappropriate for a first meet."

We both laughed and continued to shamelessly stare each other down until the elevator arrived at our floor. Why did it feel like we had known each other for months versus days?

We stepped onto a beautifully decorated hall leading to one of the two suites on the floor. Jax took a firm grip of my hand and hummed while leading me to the door.

The green light flashed on the front door to our suite after she waved the keycard in front of it. Did she have the master key? She gestured for me to enter after springing the door open. She had clearly switched gender roles. I urged myself to cross the threshold, not used to not being in control.

"Why don't you have a seat, and I'll fix your ice cream?" She swung the metal door-catch closed. The finality of the echoing sound sped up my heart rate. She headed for the dining area after dropping the key card on the small wooden table near the door.

The room was impressive and stately with a contemporary décor I appreciated. The open floor plan housed a large wall of windows showcasing a night view of the city through sheer white drapes. At first, it appeared a large television screen was suspended from the adjacent wall, but it was my favorite movie, paused and projected against the wall that faced a large comfortable looking couch.

"It appears you went through a lot of trouble just to have a date with me. Thank you." I wasn't used to anyone doing something this extravagant to spend time with me. It was usually the other way around, so I was flattered, and impressed.

"You're welcome. It was no trouble. I know a few people. You remember that open market you suggested I not fish in anymore? I keep their systems running properly, and they are nice to me in return."

I had offered her that job because I could, showcasing my arrogance. I believe I was also being selfish in wanting to keep her all to myself.

Two shiny marble steps led to a large four-poster bed on a raised marble platform to our left. The headboard showcased intricately crafted hand carvings. Everything on the bed from the pillows to the sheets and lacy shag was snow white and in direct contrast to the darker hues of brown in the living room area.

The rosy scent of fresh cut flowers flowed throughout the space, aided by a light breeze flowing from the area above the couch. The clink of silverware against a dish drew my attention, sending it toward the small kitchen area Jax was in.

She sashayed over and handed me a bowl with a scoop of mint chocolate chip and a mouthwatering chunk of brownie. She had certainly hacked into my phone, and she had gone in deep to find a picture of one of my favorite desserts I had posted on social media over a year ago.

She probably knew more about me than I cared to remember. I wonder if she had discovered that I sometimes used a very exclusive escort service that catered to men of wealth? It was embarrassing and spoke of my laziness where it concerned my lackluster love life.

The most perplexing thing about her knowing my personal business was that I wasn't as upset as I should have been.

"Thank you." I accepted the tasty treat. She observed me cup the bowl and prepared to enjoy my ice cream.

"You'll have to run an extra mile, but what's life without indulgences? And from what I can tell from your phone, you don't indulge in shit but work."

She was right. I shoved a spoon of ice cream into my mouth.

"What are you, my life coach?" I was enjoying her company. I'd never had this with anyone, especially not with a woman.

She pursed her lips, eyeing me with a stern almost possessive glint before joining me on the couch.

"You need one. Shit. Now, I'm starting to understand why you are so aggressive behind closed doors. All the pent-up tension you hold onto for ungodly amounts of time. You're a classic example of money not making a person's life better. You audition women before you date them, most being suggestions from your friends and family. And the escort service."

She paused, shaking her head, but smiling. "Believe it or not, I get it. You don't have the time or energy to invest in the search. And it's convenient if you're not ready for anything long term. You don't have to deal with the messiness of breakups. Trust me. I know. However, you can have anyone you want, so I believe you're selling yourself short."

I want you.

The embarrassment I thought I would feel was minimal as I continued to listen to her quote me a rundown of my life. She knew more than I assumed as she shined light on issues I intended to, but was reluctant to tackle.

"All you do is work. Don't take vacations. You're hunted like a thief in the night by mobs of paparazzi, so your private life is probably crap. When do you get time for yourself? When do you incorporate fun into your life? I'll answer for you. Never. You need me way more than I think you realize."

The fact that she knew my secrets was of no consequence because I didn't get the sense that she was judging me. It appeared her intentions were to help.

"So, Doctor Saint-Pierre, you think I hold onto my tension and aggression too long?" The sarcasm in my voice rang free as I fought a smile.

"Hell yes! Ninety percent of your phone was work related. I was bored as hell, not even a dick pic. You're a damn work-a-holic, and maybe too far gone to be saved."

A hardy chuckle shook my shoulders, enjoying her ribbing, although her statements held truth. I knew I worked too much, had known it for years, and was reminded of it every time I planned a vacation and canceled it to work. "You think I need to be saved?"

"Shit yes. You need saving before you drown under a sea of boredom, profit margins, and bottom lines."

"How do you propose I stay successful, if I don't work hard at improving and maintaining what I have devoted so much time to?"

"It's simple. Find a healthy balance. Be willing to sacrifice something, even if it's for profit. You make tons of money, probably make in a day what I make in a year, yet you don't take the time to enjoy it, all while working a job I bet you don't even like."

She forced me to think and was sounding more like a psychologist over the woman who had spied on me and dared me to challenge her control over this date. However, it was my turn. There were some things I wanted to know about her.

"I need you to tell me about you and TK. What does he mean to you? How would you define your relationship with him?" My swift change in conversation had her eyeballing me with a mean glare. I didn't like the man, but what really bothered me was the chemistry I noticed between them. It was part of the reason I had stalked and dragged her into that bathroom, intending to talk, but taking things much further.

"I have a very few people, by few, I mean two, that I consider friends, TK is one of them. There are no romantic ties, if that's what you're getting at."

"But you're attracted to him, and if not for the friendship, you would sleep with him. I'm sure you already know; he wouldn't be opposed to climbing into your bed if you allowed it."

Her face bunched. I believed she avoided thinking too deeply into her and TK's relationship, just as she was avoiding my attempts at fostering one with her. I sat patiently, awaiting her response as she gathered her thoughts.

"Yes, I can admit I'm attracted to TK, and a time or two, I considered sleeping with him. I'm also aware that he'd like to take our relationship to the next level. However, I've never crossed the line with him and have been honest with him on where I stand with relationships. I've known TK for nearly four years and hadn't given into the flirting temptation between us and believe I never will."

"He's going to push harder for your attention once he realizes you're with me." I enjoyed the expressive looks my budding interest put on her face. If our relationship flourished the way I believed it could, TK was going to be a problem. Plus, he had years of history with her on his side.

"But, I'm not with you," she reminded. I don't know if she believed what she was saying, I didn't.

"You look done." She stood and swiped my bowl from my hand, and the spoon from my fingers before I could get the last of the ice cream into my mouth. All the while a devious smirk rested on her face. I didn't protest as she marched into the kitchen and set the dishes in the sink. I guzzled from the water bottle she had set on the table when she brought my ice cream, attempting—but failing—to calm the anxiousness swirling inside.

When she returned, she stood in front of me and spun, causing me to ease back and glare up at her.

"Will you unzip me?" She glanced over her shoulder, awaiting my response as the flowing warmth from her body enveloped me in raging heat.

Hell yes! Fuck yes! Shit yes! I didn't mind post-phoning getting to know each other for this.

"Yes," I answered with as much calmness as I could muster.

She stood too close, preventing me from getting up to stand behind her. There was no doubt about it, if I stood, I was taking over. My fingers ached to touch her, but I refrained so that I could allow her the chance to be in control. I believed that this was what this night was about. Instead of satisfying my urgent need to take over, I delighted in the task of undoing her zipper.

As the small sliver of metal fell, and the two halves of her jumpsuit fell open, I enjoyed another glimpse of her tattoo. The material slipped down her arms unveiling more of her back. A harsh rush of excitement invaded my senses at the sight of her black lace bra and panties nestled against her luminescent skin. Once the zipper reached the top of her round ass, she wiggled the rest of the way from the jumpsuit until it slid down her body and pooled at her feet.

A blast of intense lust forced me to take in sharp breaths. I placed my hands on my knees and squeezed. How could I maintain a deeper connection with her, if she kept tempting me like this? My tongue glided across my lips, wetting them as my eyes feasted on her lush ass barely covered by sheer lace.

I dug my fingers deeper into my knees, as my eyes traveled the span of her sexy tattooed back. The tattoo met her ass leading to slightly flared hips and shapely long legs.

Having her this close in nothing but black lace, had me tenting in my pants, and conjuring up fantasies of what I wanted to perform on her. My legs were bouncing under my hands, and my brain worked overtime to keep my body and mind on the same plateau. I hoped I'd gain some kind of rewards points for letting her run the show because it wasn't easy.

When Jax stepped out of the jumpsuit, I got the full view of the gold heels she wore. Sexy stilettos complimented her lingerie and made her silky legs a mile long. She turned and her front view had me sliding my hands faster over my now bouncing legs, my action making a knocking noise against the floor.

My mind urged me to be bad, but I held back. *This is her time*, I reminded myself.

My eyes roamed her every slope and curve. The roundness of her tits peeked through the lace, the sight causing me to swallow the raw ache of untamed hunger. My gaze swept the span of her flat stomach, and bellybutton ring and lingered before reaching the lacy black V covering the area capable of making me lose all my senses.

My gaze caught and followed her tattoo, tracking along her left side, before it reached down and zipped across her hip, and finally wrapped around her leg. The sight of the ink flirting with her skin had captured my attention fully.

I worked my way up her body, pausing at the part of the tattoo decorating her exposed side. At first, I thought it was multiple tattoos, but I realized it was one continuous vine with a collection of interesting details growing from it. A flower here, a rose petal there, some thorns in other areas.

"The art on your body is extensive and beautiful. Are you going to tell me the story behind it? I have to know, because this is just too captivating not to have a story to go along with it." My gaze continued to roam. I stopped at her chest, as part of the tattoo inched up to the underside of her perky left tit. By the time my eyes met hers, she wore a twisted smile.

"Maybe," she finally replied. Taking my hand, she pulled me from the couch. Admittedly, I lost all self-control when it came to Jax. My mind went dark, and my dick stood stiff, threatening to rip out of my pants like Bruce Banner from his shirts. I was left unable to stand fully upright because it ached so bad.

"You're not going to chain me down and beat me with hard sharpened objects, are you?"

"Maybe," she replied, but there was no smile this time.

She led me to the bed with a slow stride as I observed the vine sliding down the backside of her leg. She cast the rest of the spell she had started, hypnotizing me.

Her plump, mouth-watering ass was beckoning me. Her tattoo was curling its way around her body, like I wanted my hands to be. I gawked so hard, I tripped.

"Careful now," she stated without turning around. "Two steps are coming up." She knew my eyes were on her and not on the path before me.

Once we reached the foot of the bed, she instructed me to sit, and I complied with quick purpose. I plopped down onto the bed, hard and restless with anticipation.

Jax stepped between my legs and used her knees to shove them apart. When my hands slid up her warm silky legs, she slapped them away. The peppery ache of the strike spiked my anticipation instead of relieving it.

She inched closer, all business and close enough for her legs to rub the inside of mine. Her tits sat right below my mouth and was messing with my concentration. Her legs touching mine sent a fiery need straight to my eager dick. Somehow, I managed to lift my eyes to meet hers, my neck stretching to make the upward journey.

"We're going to fuck, but this time I'll be the one doing the fucking."

My lips parted as I prepared to speak, but she cut me off by placing two fingers against my mouth. "Shh! You don't speak. Day-*one*, I told you I like control, and we have been dancing on a tightrope of push-and-pull ever since. You probably thought you could tame me with your good looks and arrogant charm. Nope. It's *my* turn now."

The seriousness in her gaze was projected like the echo roaring off thunder. My heart wasn't beating, it was using my chest for target practice, hitting so hard I expected to see blood any second. The deeper she dragged me in to this scene, the more excited I became.

Why the hell was I so turned on? She had me shuddering, my insides an inferno of hot need. I had no control. The feeling was foreign, but with her, I didn't feel like my masculinity was being tested. It was more like sparring with a formidable opponent. *Odd.*

"Take off all your clothes, except the tie," she ordered. "Gladly," I replied, with an arrogant smirk. "Just a warning Jax. I'm confident enough in my manhood to step back and allow you to take the reins, but if I see you can't handle it, I will not hesitate to sit you right where you belong." I pointed at the straining swell in my pants. "On my dick."

The level of wickedness in her gaze was her resounding reply. She took a step back to allow me room to stand and undress. I started, but with all my buttons and the cufflinks, it was taking up precious time. However, Jax waited patiently as she scanned every area I unveiled. Each piece I handed her, she sat neatly across the bedside chair.

She stood before me and blazed a trail along my naked body with her eyes. How she managed to ignore my uncontrolled dick nudging her stomach was beyond me. Her fingers traced my tattooed arm, studying the art I had collected. "This is hot. A full sleeve. You keep impressing me Chase, and I'm not easily impressed with anyone," she stated with an intrigued smirk. She took her time admiring my tattoos. When our eyes met, her expression had changed from one of intrigue, to one of domineering control.

Her right palm opened, flashing a set of thorns tattooed there. Dark brown thorny branches decorated the inside of her peachy palm. The level of pain she had to endure for those thorns, was symbolic of what they must have represented. The impressive artistry branched off the vine, snaking around her wrist and extended into her palm like the thin spikes of a rose bush.

"These are indicative of the way I like to fuck."

Those thorns represented, hard, beautiful, pain. Was she telling me that that was what she intended to deliver to me?

My defiant gaze met hers when I lifted it from her palm. I was convinced, there wasn't anything she could physically do to harm me, so if her comment was meant to intimidate, it didn't.

A sassy brow lifted at the doubt I must have failed to keep from my expression. "Have it your way, Chase. You will learn."

Was she addressing the defiant look I had given her? I believe I was receiving more insight on how she felt, when I had taken control of her in that bathroom. I hadn't asked permission then, yet I got the impression that she was standing in front of me now, asking for the same thing I had taken from her.

Chapter Fifteen

Chase

When Jax motioned me farther into the bed with the flick of her hand, I eagerly complied. She reached into the drawer and withdrew a condom before she climbed in.

Standing, she stepped across me with those sexy gold heels straddling my body. The bed springs protested her movement, but she conquered the bobbing springs like she was planning to conquer me.

She stood at my chest, reached down and gripped the widest edge of my tie. I swallowed a yelp when she planted the heel of that golden stiletto in my chest. When she stood upright, the tie tightened around my neck and the heel dipped painfully into my flesh, I believe, scraping the tip of my rib bone as she peered down. Every stance she had taken since we met tonight was one of authority.

Her eyes were an ocean of power, coupled with the authoritative stance that she held, daring me to protest. When she released my tie and removed the heel from my chest, I breathed, realizing I was too awed or excited to breathe properly. A deep pink impression was left in my chest along with a stinging ache that fed my eagerness.

She produced the condom, placing it between her lips as she bent, positioning herself so her sexy ass hovered above my thighs. My dick took on a mind of its own, rising to lick at her heat.

Her fingers raked up my thighs and caused my dick to stiffen, like she had injected it with a straight shot of magic. Her fingers danced along the grooves of my abs and over my taunt nipples, while reaching all around the hardest part of me. The condom remained planted between her lips as she teased me.

"You have a nice body, Chase." She spoke around the condom like it wasn't sitting pinched between her sexy lips.

"Thank you." My choppy words spoke of how worked up she had gotten me.

"Where did you get all this dick?" I swallowed hard, unable to answer when the tip of her finger brushed the leaking head. Her teeth bit into the condom wrapper as she pinched one edge with her fingers and ripped the wrapper apart.

My mouth gaped, and I tensed when she sat the condom in the wide O she formed with her mouth.

She is not *about to put that condom on with her mouth.*

The muscles in my stomach and neck stretched as I fought to get the best view. Of all the drunken, back seat, anywhere we could get it started sex I'd had, I had never had this done to me. When her hot mouth slid the condom over the head, I jerked and gripped a chunk of the bedding to steady my frenzied movement.

In order to unroll the condom, she would have to back her warm mouth up and slide it back down. My tongue licked hungrily across my lips. My ragged breaths escaped, causing my chest to bob in time with my frenzied heartbeats.

My dick stood, strong and stiff, like an armed missile readying itself for takeoff. I was bluntly informed that I had a *"porn star dick,"* so I was anxious to see how far down she would shove the condom with just her mouth.

I craned my neck to capture her every move. The moist heat of her mouth sliding along my dick felt like she was blanketing me with the warmth of a sensual embrace. When she reached a point, it scraped her throat, my eyes slammed shut and my toes curled tight.

A blocked throat didn't stop her sweet mouth from closing around more of me. The wet tightness stunned me, and I moaned harshly as my eyes fought blinding pleasure to sneak peeks.

In order to get the last part of the condom wrapped around my shaft, it had no place to go but down her throat, and down it went. My trembling fingers went for her hair, but debilitating pleasure and blinding intensity, slung my mind into chaos and stopped my journey, leaving me to grip the covers instead.

The growling moan lodged in my throat, ripped free and shook me. Shivers of pleasure coursed through me when my dick squeezed past the tightness of her flinching throat. She didn't stop until every inch of the condom had sheathed me.

Her mouth slid back with ease, leaving a trail of saliva behind. I immediately craved the warm tightness she had surrounded me in. When she sat up and inched her warm pussy closer, my dick throbbed with a different level of eagerness. Recalling the heavenly sensation of being inside her, my mind and body exploded with restless expectation.

When she eased up and hovered her middle at the tip, I froze and lost my ability to breathe. My gaze rotated between her and the sight of my stiff dick, so achingly close to her pussy. In this moment, I was nothing but an addict, preparing for another dose of the drug I was helpless to resist.

Jax hadn't removed her panties, she merely slid them to the side to provide access to the hypnotizing world she owned. Instead of putting me out of my misery, she flashed her palm at me. *Hard. Beautiful. Pain.* Sensing my thoughts, she smirked and closed her hand. When she allowed the first few inches to slide in, I was a hair's breadth from passing out.

"Shit," I hissed with a low groan. What I expected and what I experienced were so far off, I glanced at where we were connected to ensure I'd not fallen into a vivid dream. The exhilarating sensations were better than before, more intense.

Her wet pussy made me want to thrust, to move, to grope the warm lushness of her body. It took everything, and I do mean every drop of my willpower, to lie still and let her control this.

Her movements were way too slow, but I didn't disrupt the way she wanted this to go down. The slow pace commenced until she inched me all the way in. The sensation of my head rubbing against her cervix melted my toes and liquified my bones.

If my deep penetration caused her pain, she enjoyed it as much as I enjoyed being buried inside her. Her face was set in determination, but those eyes—those eyes reflected the way I felt, wickedly good. Each move she made squeezed me with a firm and assured intensity. There was no soft background music, only the groaning springs of the bed and our harmonizing sighs of pleasure.

She increased the pace when the powerful mix of pleasure overtook logic and reason. Leaning into me, she slid her fingers up my arms, digging her nails into my flesh. Winded, my breaths swished past my lips, winding through the parts of her hair that had fallen from her elegant bun.

Her rhythmic movements resumed, her pussy gripping to squeeze pleasure into me and releasing to allow me to glide along her slippery walls, turning me into her puppet. The sensations fascinated me, giving me a taste of the ultimate high.

Jax bent and allowed her lips to hover above my right ear. "Tell me how good it feels," she whispered. "Jax. God. It feels great. So damn good." I heaved. She was fitted so tight around me, I shuttered at her movement. The ache spilling from my fingertips eased when I caressed her thighs which were as smooth and silky as the surface of a rose petal.

Her slight movement when she managed to lean in closer forced me to release a strained groan. "Tell me how much you like me fucking you."

"I like…love you fucking me. Shit!" I yelled at her faster movements. I was cushioned in enough pleasure that she must have induced some sort of mind control over me.

"Don't stop!" I yelled. "Shit!"

The harmonic tones of my moans of pleasure mingled with her chorus of cries, filling the air in the room with a sinful song of our gratitude.

Her hips rotated faster, causing my eyes to roll to the top of my head. I cupped one of her full tits, my thumb brushing the piercing there. "Yes, Chase," she groaned, stirring our desire faster, allowing me to burrow even deeper into her wet heat.

"So good," I forced out, knowing she knew what she was doing. I teetered on the cusp of coming and was unable to hold in the outburst of my words of appreciation as uninhibited pleasure took possession of me.

"Aww! Fuck that feels good!" I shouted between ragged breaths.

She convulsed around me when she came, moaning loudly through the devastating impact with tightly shut eyes and a shivering body.

"Fuck! Fuck! Fuck!" I yelled as she continued to rock her tightness around my dick, enveloping it in delicious heat and friction. She knew that she was riding me to the edge of madness. I couldn't take it anymore. I came so hard I swore stars floated around my head. I kept coming and she kept riding me as cycles of pleasure crashed through me so long and hard, I suffocated on it. I spilled so much come, it had to have saturated the condom and was leaking out.

My orgasm subsided, lessening in its intensity, releasing me from its euphoric trance at its own pace. She eased off me, removed the condom, and cleaned me with a soft wet towel before adding the light strokes of her tempting tongue. She wasn't going to allow me any recovery time. The sight of my dick, still hard for her, surprised me. She adjusted her waving tongue so that the tip massaged the sensitive head.

What started as a bundle of intense sensitivity, was being turned into an aching need that left me in chest-heaving open-mouthed awe. I thought my dick was on the verge of dying, but she had resuscitated it with her special mix of pleasure.

Her amazing tongue action, and throat clenching depth was like nothing I had experienced. The sight of me disappearing into her mouth and the feel of me sliding across her tongue caused one of my legs to shake involuntarily. The extra spark of hardness from her lip piercing added a unique spice that placed this sexual episode some place in the stratosphere.

My muscles twitched and tightened with every mind-blowing stroke. Right before I was set to explode in her mouth, she glanced right at me, and I came watching her swallow my essence with pleasure in her gaze.

After retrieving another condom for the next round, she slid down my dick, her pussy so warm and velvety-tight, the pleasure drove me crazy as I buzzed from erotic rush. I had never been shoved this far down the sexual rabbit hole, where reality and fantasy blended enough to make you think you were truly losing your mind.

This round took longer, and I was more sensitive, but feeling her swirling and wrapping me in all that pleasure, snatched my mind. She was driving me insane, and one of two scenarios were bound to happen: I would pass out or fly off the rails where I would forget how to walk or talk. Every muscle ached, as they were overworked and fatigued, not used to being push this far.

Insanity was calling and I must have answered. Was her tattoo moving? The vine grew around her, the thorns moving along her body as she continued to ride me into a blissful death. Had I been drugged? She rode me hard and fast, and my stiff dick kept charging on like a revved car engine. The urge to come was so strong from the pressing intensity Jax drove into me, it was almost too much.

A series of shutters hit so hard, I felt myself hitting full meltdown mode. The remnants of my cries slid down my throat because my urge to come kept hanging back, torturing me. I was too drunk on pleasure to focus long enough to think, and my vision kept swimming in and out of focus.

"Let me help you get there Chase," I heard her say. I think I shook my head. I was a wrung-out rag, exhausted, and useless. She slowed her pace, interlocking her fingers with mine, and glared into my eyes. She gradually picked up the pace, riding me harder, faster, and gripping my hands tighter while trapping my gaze with hers.

The intensity of this sexual dance and the rhythm of the hot passion burst my senses wide open. I relished every tingling spark and every aching punch of satisfaction until my orgasm raced through me, full bodied. Satisfaction roared through me as her shuttering walls squeezed every morsel of pleasure and strength from me.

When my vision returned, she flashed her palm, a re-minder of how she had planned to fuck me. Acknowledging her ability to not only drive away my control, but make me forget it completely, I puckered up and kissed her palm.

Had she made me her bitch? Didn't matter. She had gotten me to a point where I didn't give a solitary fuck anymore.

Sometimes you needed to be *shown* versus *told*, and Jax had taught me more than I bargained for.

"What does this mean? Are we even now?" My words were low and slow because they had to travel through my exhaustion.

"No. It's not what it means at all. It means you have the ability to allow me to be in control, same as I let you have it. I wasn't aware that I had the ability to let go of it until you. Now, you know you can too."

How had she done it? Her words had me feeling like I had achieved some goal, I wasn't aware I was supposed to overcome. She was the only woman who had taken me this far. When she eased off my dick, an intense tingling sensation had soreness prickling through me. I hissed like a wounded snake who could no longer work his muscles.

The cold air hit my dick and shattered me. She had torn me down past the foundation, had broken me like a gold digger's sabotaged condom. I tensed at every movement she made, my sore muscles aching.

Jax kissed my cheek, her sweet intensity distracting me as she rolled the condom off. She took her time wiping and cleaning me with ease, knowing how sore she had made me.

"I did promise you a movie," she stated. Glancing back, she pressed play on the movie to start it across the room. "I hope you enjoyed this as much as I did." She cast an empathetic gaze at my dick. The betraying bastard had finally quit, sitting limp and curled against my thigh, just as battered as I felt. Jax was the last image I captured before sleep lulled me into her relaxing embrace.

***

The jangling of the door jolted me from sleep. Naked. Alone. Where was Jax?

My heartrate kicked into overdrive, and I prayed it was her on the other side of the door. Wide-eyed, I slung the covers over my naked body at the sight of a dark-haired woman entering the room.

"Can you give me a moment Ma'am?" She turned away quickly at the sound of my voice.

"Yes sir. Take your time." She headed back out the door, leaving me draped in silence. I sat up, listening and hoping to hear sounds coming from the bathroom, but already knew Jax was gone.

Putting my shirt and jacket on was easy. Getting into my boxer briefs and pants came with difficulty. I was sore. I had never had too much sex before. Jax had left me in a mental and physical state of chaos with a raw dick. It was flaming red from too much sex, and my muscles ache like I had aged twenty years.

Once I got into my boxers and pants, I half tucked my shirt, buttoned my suit jacket and prepared to leave.

Thankfully, it was Saturday. I often went into the office most weekends, but today wasn't going to be one of them. I needed to make it home, ice my dick down, and take a bottle of pain relievers.

Where were we going from here? If all we would have was sex and control to sustain us, there was no use pursuing her. We'd each had our turn at the helm with our need for control. I wanted more than that, but did she? All I could think was, *now what?*

Chapter Sixteen

Jax

After the way I sexed and abandoned Chase three nights ago at the hotel, I was sure he would never speak to me again. I didn't want to, but I was starting to like him. We had the ability to park our sexual desire and indulge in productive conversations. Sex aside, I believe we shared a few breakthrough moments at the restaurant, and on the couch in the hotel room before my ego-driven sexcapade started.

The carefully constructed walls I'd built around myself had been coming down for Chase since day one. He was also the only person in my adult life that I had allowed to control me sexually.

My restless mind kept beating back the notion, but there was no other conclusion to make, no other truth to swallow, that something more than sexual attraction was happening between us.

The way he watched me when we were at the restaurant. He looked at me like I was the only thing he wanted to see. Always studying and observing me. It made me feel anxious… beautiful.

When he shared the news about his father's tough lessons, it appeared I wasn't the only one who was dealt a cruel hand in our childhood. And all of those charities, and secret projects he was involved in that I had found on his phone. Providing sports equipment to underprivileged kids, supplying food banks with funding, creating and providing scholarships to low-income schools. He was an undercover humanitarian, but he had chosen to keep the best aspect of himself hidden from the media.

Regret niggled its way into my brain for the way I treated him, but a sinful smile formed when I reminded myself that he deserved it. He needed to be reminded that his status didn't give him a free pass to do whatever he wanted, especially not with me.

The thought of him widened my silly grin. If there was ever a man I wished I could be with long-term, it would be him. He possessed an interesting personality hidden under the fake persona he presented to the rest of the world. I enjoyed the way he could go from being proper and dignified in front of the camera and down to earth and free spirited with me.

Surprisingly, I enjoyed being with him sexually, even when he had control. Letting go and just enjoying myself. Not having to be strong and aggressive. No one but Chase had broken through the wall I thought was impenetrable. How? I couldn't put a finger on what it was about him that drew me in. No one but him had made me come so deliciously hard and blissfully long. Was it the sex? I had enjoyed great sex before, so I didn't think that was it. Even now, my mind worked to process our interactions with each other, a courtesy only extended to him.

After I swiped the face of my vibrating phone, I placed the caller on speaker. The number was unknown, but I had made a habit of answering all incoming calls to make sure I didn't miss any potential new business.

"Hello," I answered, speaking at the phone.

"Hey Babygirl."

My smile grew wide at the sound of my father's voice. No one else in the world could make me happier than Alexander Saint-Pierre.

Except Chase. My inner voice annoyingly teased.

"Dad!" I picked up the phone, swiping it off speaker, before bringing it to my ear.

"How is my Babygirl?" He had a way of making me feel like a kid, all happy-go-lucky and excited.

"Dad, I'm a twenty-eight-year-old woman. I stopped being a girl a long time ago."

"I don't care, you're always going to be my baby girl. How are things going?"

"Things are going well. Just working."

"Overworking you mean? What have you done for yourself? I'm not talking about work related, but something that might bring some joy into your life?"

He was always worried about my happiness. When he wasn't traveling for work, he would set me up on these ridiculous blind dates. How embarrassing. I was such a loser in the romance department, my father had felt the need to play matchmaker. However, I had chewed up and spit out every guy he had set me up with. Some would go crying to him about the 'raving bitch' I was, and he would always take my side, accusing them of doing something that had set me off.

"I went out with someone," I blurted, knowing he'd be happy to hear the news.

"On purpose?" he questioned, laughing into the phone.

"Yes. On purpose Dad. You're not funny. Anyway, I think I might like him," I continued. A lengthy pause followed my admission.

"*Well. Well. Well.* This is a first. You sound happy. What's his name?"

My attempt to shake away the silly smile was useless. "I'm not telling you dad."

"Why not?" He asked before I heard his low chuckle.

"Because you're going to conduct a background check on him."

"And *you* haven't?" He replied with a hint of knowing in his tone.

I stifled a laugh. "Okay, I've done *some* digging, but I may not want you knowing personal things about the man I *might* be interested in. For now, how about I give you his initials. CT."

A funny memory popped into my head. "Remember what you did to that boy Tony for dumping me at that dance when I'd been the one with the attitude?"

"He deserved it. You don't leave your date, *my daughter*, stranded without a ride."

"Dad, you had his car crushed into the size of a packing box and left it sitting in his driveway with a big red ribbon on it."

Our shared laughter livened up the phone lines. My father was the friendliest most caring person I knew, but if you crossed him or me, there was no telling what type of imaginative revenge plot he'd unleash.

"I'll take CT's initials for now, but I would like to hear more about him soon. You sound excited about him."

"I'm not excited. He's just not that bad, and kind of gets my ways."

"Umm-hum," he hummed into the phone teasingly. If my father could tell over the phone I was excited about Chase, did it mean I was unconsciously giving off the vibes?

"Dad, I know you can't tell me where you are, but are you at least safe?"

My father's investigative and undercover skills usually had him working secret missions he was often unable to speak about over the phone lines.

"I'm always safe, but I do have to go. I'll check in with you in a few days."

"Okay. Love you Dad."

"Love you too."

My smile never wavered as I gazed absently at the phone in my hand. Hearing from my father always puts me in a good mood.

✱✱✱

The phone vibrated a second time, disrupting my thoughts. This time the number that flashed, was one I know well. I swiped to answer the call.

"Jax," he greeted.

One syllable of the smooth sound of his voice caused my smile to surface before a foreign sensation lulled me into a relaxed state.

"Chase," I replied, unable to hide the smile in my tone.

"I'm alive if you were concerned about my well-being." His words dripped sarcasm.

"I'm glad you're okay. Are you still sore?" I quaked from the effort of choking down my laugh.

A long pause followed.

"Chase? Are you there?"

"I'm sorry. I thought I heard something. Hang on a second, let me check."

My grip tightened around my phone as my leg started to jump faster with every ticking second. I had read about him being stalked before, to the point that police had made an arrest. The sound of his footsteps eased my tension.

"Okay. I'm back."

"Is everything okay?" I questioned.

"Yes, I'm okay. Thank you. Every time I hear an unfamiliar noise, I check it out. I woke up with a woman standing over me once, watching me sleep, and I woke to another who had snuggled up with me in bed. They'd been clever enough to find a way around security and into this penthouse. Once a man had gotten into my house in the Hamptons and held me at gunpoint for three hours. He had taken gay rumors to heart, had apparently been attempting to date me, but had never been able to reach me by conventional means."

"That's some scary shit. I don't envy your life."

"Sometimes it can be a bit overwhelming, but I've witnessed so much over the years that not much shocks me anymore. Anyway, back to me being left and sore."

"Yes. What about it?" I asked.

"I can wear underwear now but for the most part, I prance around naked inside my home."

The faint sound of his laughter sounded before my own burst free. My pussy had been ripped to shreds by his massive dick, but she'd taken her beating like a champ, and only a twinge of soreness remained.

"So, what's up, Chase?"

"I'm calling to ask, if you'd like to go out to dinner with me Friday?"

He wanted to see me again? Why? We'd both had our turns already.

"If you're planning a revenge situation, save it. I'm not interested in making this an ongoing war."

"I promise; I don't want revenge. I'm asking you out like I should have in the first place. So, Friday at seven, we can decide on the restaurant later. I'll pick you up at your place."

"Okay, Friday at seven," I replied. My forehead crinkled instantly. I intended to reject him, but my brain computed one thing while my mouth downloaded another. Was I making the right decision?

"What about Amanda?" I blurted.

Wait a minute. Why do I care? We weren't exclusive, and we had already fucked the shit out of each other, yet I had just asked him the one question that made it appear that I wanted exclusivity.

"We talked after we left the expo that night." He said. "She understood before our date that I wasn't looking for anything long-term. She made a good attempt at trying to go out again, but we talked it out and came to an understanding. What about Kara?"

"It went about the same as you and Amanda. She knew I wasn't looking for anything permanent. She didn't like it one bit that we weren't going out again, but I always do my best to make my intentions known before I get involved with anyone."

It was poetic how our love lives were a mirrored reflection of each other's.

"You didn't create a stalker, did you? You did imply that you've created a few?" he inquired.

"No. Kara hadn't been around me long enough to get attached. Now, you're a different story. I'm on the twelfth floor and you're probably outside my window right now? Aren't you?"

The sound of his laughter was a pleasant one. I wasn't the person that usually induced genuine laughter in people.

"I hate to go, but I have a business function to attend. As a matter of fact, I just pulled up."

He sounded disappointed.

"Good night, Jax."

"Nite, Chase."

My smile refused to be chased away. Chase's dinner invite was unexpected, but it put a little spark in my heart. It spoke volumes about his willingness to be with me. Though, I did notice he hadn't asked for my address. I expected him to dig into my business, but I didn't understand what was driving him to go that deep?

Why had he taken an interest in me? A young, handsome, billionaire bachelor. Walking out of his door meant being ambushed by paparazzi, and reporters asking questions about his personal life. Not to mention the sea of thirsty women who wanted to suck his money up with the force of a carwash vacuum.

What was it about me that kept him interested? I didn't kiss his ass. I spoke my mind. I assumed he'd satisfied his curiosity with me at the expo. It surprised me when he accepted my invitation to dinner despite suspecting I may have been out for revenge. Now, he had surprised me once more, requesting a date. Where was this going?

Chapter Seventeen

Jax

Strolling through my closet, my fingers ran along the tops of my hangers, making them clank a cozy closet melody. Ideas of restaurants that catered to high society floated through my mind, forming images of Chase enjoying a cozy meal with me. Smart and sexy, he intrigued me. And the cherry on top—his dick.

When Chase had stripped in the hotel room, discipline kept me from gawking when he dropped his pants. I had underestimated his size, which meant he had gotten me so sopping wet in that bathroom, I wasn't thinking straight.

He texted yesterday to ask if I would like to check out this new restaurant called Tantalize, for our *date*. I knew from social media the place was well outside of my tax bracket. If you didn't know someone of means who could extend you a personal invite, or get you added to their exclusive list, you weren't going to lift a spoon inside the place.

Were we dating? *I don't date. Catch and release* was my motto. I was the hard-as-nails chick, who chewed up romance and spit the shit out. So, why the hell was I about to go out with Chase? Why was I standing in my closet with excitement coursing through me as I picked out something nice to wear? Something drew me to him, and I couldn't, for the life of me, put my finger on what it was.

My doorbell chimed as soon as I slipped into my shoes. I peeked to make sure it was him and failed miserably to keep a big grin off my face when I cracked my door open.

"Chase."

The smile I thought I stifled, spread despite my attempt to swipe it off my face.

"Jax."

I stepped aside and allowed him to enter, his presence already causing fiery sparks of energy to flare from deep within. He entered my personal space, stepping so close, his fresh breath kissed my face, before his warm soft lips caressed my cheek and slid down to my neck. His arms were around me instantly and mine had taken a hold of him. It was an unexpected embrace. I lingered in his hold, my insides floating, my mind narrowed to a single thought—Chase.

What the hell am I doing?

I backed away first, attempting to keep my face impassive. I think I missed him. The notion was foreign, jarring in a way that it made me anxious. When he backed away, his smile grew wide, causing me to cast a sidelong look at him. "I missed you, Jax."

My throat went dry and forced me to choke down my hard swallow. His confession had rendered me speechless. Apparently, *he* didn't have a problem expressing what he felt. Other than a pleasant goodbye, I never thought about expressing more.

"Didn't you miss me?" he asked.

My mouth fell open and remained that way.

"Of course, you did, and so badly you can't even find the words to express how much."

I slapped his arm playfully as he stepped past me. He strolled around my apartment like he owned the place, surprising me when he started humming along to Ginuwine's, *"So Anxious"* playing low in the background.

"Your home is impressive, Jax. I don't think New Generations as little as you let on."

His fingers brushed the small, bronzed sculpture on my entryway side table that sat next to a live Dracaena silk tree, with its leaves reaching for the ceiling. "Classy, edgy, tasteful," he offered, glancing around and nodding his approval.

"Thank you." I smiled, appreciating his compliment.

"Is this your father?" He pointed at the picture on the in-table next to the couch.

"Yes, that's me and the old man."

"You look like him. And I can tell that you're definitely a daddy's girl."

I kept the picture visible because I considered my father my hero.

"What's his name? Where is he?" He asked, leaning in to take a closer look.

"Alexander St. Pierre. He works out of DC. He's in law enforcement, so his cases cause him to travel a lot."

I wasn't used to sharing my personal life, but somehow Chase was pulling more out of me than I had ever shared with anyone.

"What about your mother?" he questioned, one of his curious brows stuck in the air.

"Dead." The word fell out of my mouth like hot ash. He must have caught the cutting edge in my tone because he stepped away from the picture and stopped asking questions.

When Chase was satisfied with nosing around my living room, kitchen, and dining area, he met me at the door.

"What's that smile about?" I asked, addressing the cheesy grin on his face.

"I can't be happy to see you?"

"You can, but I see more. Like you know a secret that I don't."

"I'm pretty sure I do." There was a knowing edge to his words that I hadn't missed.

Maybe he did know things that I didn't. I sometimes had trouble understanding the intricacies of my own mind. I certainly didn't understand me and Chase.

"What about the paparazzi?" I had almost forgotten that he always had eyes on him, a testament to how down to earth he could be with me.

"Don't worry. We have it covered."

Although reluctant, I locked my door and followed him.

We didn't exit my building through the front door. Instead, we entered the third level of the garage where his driver, Paul, was waiting at the back door. He was talking into his wrist, communicating with someone. "All clear." Paul made the report to Chase while opening the door for us.

We climbed in and got comfortable. Chase reached out and dropped his hand over mine, testing my responsiveness. Neither of us made eye contact as he swiped my hand, closing it in the warmth of his. The silent connection it spurred was the catalyst for my lack of speech during the drive.

He had shattered my comfort zone, but I didn't have a desire to pull away. Hyperaware of him and of our connection, I squeezed his hand as he brushed light strokes over the back of mine with his thumb.

I was afraid of this but found comfort in the simplistic beauty of the gesture. When a warm tingle started to tickle the hairs on my arms and climbed its way into my heart, I had to say something to distract myself.

"I didn't peg you for a country fan. So, you like country music?" I asked as Kane Brown's "Heaven" spilled softly from some hidden speaker inside the car.

"Yes," he answered. "Country is my favorite, but I often listen to a variety. What about you?"

"I'm into variety also, but my favorite is Classic Rock."

I knew my answer would get his attention. His smile widened, and his brow lifted. "You. Classic Rock. Didn't see that one coming."

"No one ever does, unless they listen to one of my favorite playlist." He stared at and although his smile was wide and bright, he couldn't hide the surprise shining in his eyes.

"I have to admit, I do enjoy learning about you. You are an interesting woman."

"You sound impressed."

"I am."

He still hadn't let go of my hand that had started to ache inside his.

"I'm enjoying dating you." He said out of the blue.

"I haven't decided if I want to date you yet."

"Yet." He repeated. "Call it what you want, but there is a reason you're here with me now Jax."

He was right. "I noticed early on that you weren't a pushover, and I respect that trait in you. I like that you're down to earth and not all proper and high sadiddy with me. I believe I get to see the real you. I think you knew early on that I was bad, that I like to play outside the box, but you don't care. Like me, you'll play with fire, knowing you can get burned. I'm starting to believe you like the burn."

He shrugged and a smug grin sat on his lips.

"What about you? What type of dating life did you have before you were cast into the limelight?"

He stared ahead for a moment before he answered.

"My dating life wasn't any better than it is now. I looked, I liked, I asked, but it was never lasting. The only difference between now, and then, was that I was the one looking for longevity versus now. Unless they have been living under a rock and don't know a thing about me, women can't see past my popularity and net worth."

He wiggled a finger at me, his smile widening. "You're not interested in either. Two of the many reasons I decided I wanted to date you."

Two of many? What were the others? I swallowed my curiosity, choosing not to enrich our connection or endorse a relationship between us. A relationship was a waste of time.

Thankfully, the slowing car pulled his attention away from me. Paul drove us past the bustling front entrance of the restaurant. A line of expensive cars waited there, releasing the social elites who strutted across a rolled out golden carpet to the entrance. Since big-named stars frequented the place, paparazzi and a crowd hung out hoping to snag a money shot, selfies, or an autograph.

Although set to enter through the back door, I left the back of Chase's Silver Bentley, allowing him to escort me into Tantalize like I was a superstar. An enclosed covered area led from the vehicle's open door and into the building, blocking out any lurking paparazzi. The area appeared to have been specifically designed for the wealthy who valued their privacy over fame.

Chase made me feel special, the way he kept smiling and staring with pride. He had managed to sink his claws into me, leaving a mark that pressed deep enough to leave an imprint on my heart. I had returned his embrace back in my apartment. Had agreed to go out to dinner with him. I was starting to believe I wanted this with him when I had never wanted it with anyone else.

Once we entered the back door, a short hall took us into a standing foyer that eventually led into the dining area. We managed minimal contact with the rest of the dining patrons. My face creased in curiosity. *Was that Leonardo DiCaprio?* My intention wasn't to gawk, but I couldn't help myself. I mean come on…It was Leo *DiCaprio*. He lifted his glass in my direction and offered a friendly smile. I waved like the starstruck fan I was.

"Chase, I must say, you make it easy for me to forget you're on the same level as these A-list celebs."

I craned my neck to get a good long look at Lady Gaga, who, like Leo, offered a friendly smile and waved at us. He chuckled, "You make me forget it too. Which is refreshing."

"Let me," Chase insisted once we arrived at our table, and the waiter reached to pull out my seat. He held my chair and waited until I sat down, his smile never wavering.

We were seated in one of the best private rooms in the place although the paparazzi weren't allowed inside the restaurant. Enclosed by dark frosted glass on two sides and bricked in at the head of the table, the small room housed decorative accents that gave it a homey feel. The final wall was a digital screen displaying a live streaming night view from the top of the Empire State Building. The cozy plush leather of the chair slid across my ass like butter. Chase didn't sit across from me, he slid into the chair next to mine, so that he could enjoy the viewing screen, and I believed to stay close to me.

Once seated, we renewed our conversation. "Was that a compliment I heard earlier?"

"Yes, it was. The last time we had dinner. I answered all of your questions except one. You asked me, "What made me normal?""

It was just occurring to me that he hadn't given me a direct answer to that specific question. Now, I was dying to know the answer.

"The answer is you. *You* make me feel normal Jax. You made me remember how to smile, truly smile. And laugh. And listen to the world around me. To soak it in versus glossing over it."

His revelation had me glaring like I was seeing a clear picture of him for the first time. He had placed me on a petal stool so high, I felt lightheaded for a few seconds.

"Wow. Thank you. I…I…"

He chuckled. "I know. I'm so amazing I make you speechless."

I swatted his arm playfully but was grateful he had saved me from fumbling over my words. I wasn't good with sentiment and discussing feelings and emotions.

"Are you this discreet when I'm not around?" I asked, taking in our surroundings.

He leaned closer as if anyone could hear us. "I keep in mind that I have to keep myself out there, so sometimes I serve myself up. However, I've gotten really good at pulling off disguises. I attend live sporting events as just a regular guy who sits in the stands and cheers with the rest of the crowd." I enjoyed the way his face lit up at the mention of sporting events. I recalled him mentioning his dream was to be a professional baseball player.

"Do you enjoy any specific game? Your face is well known, how would you possibly get away with being among us commoners, even in disguise?"

"Beard, prosthetic nose, contacts, mouth-piece. Learned it all on the set of the movie, Shackles of Unrest, when they gave me a cameo. I enjoy attending live football, baseball, and basketball games. Seeing them on television is one thing but nothing compares to the live action, the cheering crowd, the aroma of peanuts, chips, and beer mingling with cigarette smoke and bad breath."

"Sounds like a good time," I said, wrinkling my nose.

"I'll take you to the next game I attend."

I nodded, not refusing him.

Good Girl, my inner voice cheered. Was I finally giving in to this dating thing?

"During baseball season, I'll attend my old high school and college games." A look of longing appeared in his expression before he cast it away.

"May I ask you something?" he questioned before I could inquire more about him and baseball. The strained expression and tone indicated we were diving into deeper waters.

Although reluctant, I nodded.

"Why aren't you on any type of social media? Why does it appear you rarely go out? You have one female friend outside work, and she's rarely around. When we were at the expo, every time anyone came near me with a camera, you wanted no part of it. Also, I couldn't find one photo of you, anywhere, which in this day and age is unusual, especially for someone with a successful business that could benefit from an active social media presence?"

My eyes sat, unblinking. Chase was curious enough to dig into my not so personal business, but he clearly wanted more. I swallowed a heavy load of hesitancy, not wanting to lie, but feeling the need to give him *something* to put a quick end to the subject.

"I was filmed before, without consent, when I was younger. I was exposed to the world when I didn't want to be. I didn't have the means, or even the know-how, to stop it. Because of that, I find it difficult to trust people, so the few people that are in my life, took a long hard road to get there."

He stared, searching his mind for a reply to my surprising yet vague reveal. It would take time and my willingness to open the vault of haunting secrets to tell Chase why I lived the way I did. The reason I had pursued a career in IT had been spurred by my past. They say the past shapes us; I believe my past was still carving out my angles.

"Do you feel like it's something you'd like to share in detail, if not now maybe later? We can talk about anything you want," he added, his voice encouraging.

A memory I tried to force away pushed into my mind before I could give him an answer.

"Keep still. It's just rope you little dumb bitch. It's not going to kill you, but if you keep fighting me, I'm going to put it around your fucking neck."

Sixteen years and I could still feel the rope digging into my wrist, cutting off my circulation and burning like a dry flame. Rubbing my wrist, I shook off the haunting memory.

"I appreciate your interest, but it's not something I would like to discuss."

The empathy expressed on his face spoke to something in me. It made me want to share my secrets with him when all I wanted was to forget them.

"Maybe one day," I offered, because I appreciated him trying, brimming with a genuine interest to know me. However, there were parts of myself I desperately wanted to forget, wishing I could pay someone to wipe the thoughts from my brain.

He changed the subject, recognizing my difficulty in talking about my past.

"What did you do to me in that hotel room?" His keen expression suggested that he truly wanted to know the answer.

"Whatever do you mean?" I asked, playing coy.

He leaned closer, lowering his voice. "My dick wouldn't go down. Usually, I come, it goes down, and re-up after a brief rest. With you, I came three times back-to-back. For a moment, I wondered if you spiked the ice cream you fed me or was it something at dinner?"

I'm sure the smile in my eyes was as big as the one on my face. "I don't know what to say Chase. When it's good, it's good. Once I started, I couldn't stop. I was possessed, ravenous. My body was tired, and I know that yours was too, but I was chasing the highest high until I found it."

"It was incredible." He said, eyeing me like he was about to snatch me out of my chair. I would have let him too.

Chase had one of the most splendidly made dicks I had ever seen. Long, thick, and I believed, masterfully sculpted specifically for my pussy. The first sight of it had caused my ovaries to stand up and do the Nae Nae.

"Where would you like to go on our next date?" His teasing smirk had me fighting back a smile.

He had smoothly ignored the part about this not being a relationship.

"Let's call this what it is, Chase. It's all about our egos. You and I are accustomed to being in a position of authority, taking charge of what's put before us." I glared at him hard, but softened my features, realizing I was being defensive for no reason. I don't think he meant any harm; he was just cocky.

"You have no idea the amount of restraint it took for me to allow you to take me like you did, do you? If it weren't so good, I would have taken control, but I didn't want to. Thinking about what you did in that bathroom makes my nipples hard and my pussy wet."

I enjoyed his reaction. The tension tightening his lust-heavy eyes, the way he swayed in his chair, angling to get closer. His gaze never dropped even as raging hunger took up residence in his eyes.

"What I said our first night about sharing control, authority, whatever you would like to name it. Would you be open for it?"

He was determined, I gave him that. I considered his question. For lack of better words, he was requesting we be a mutually reciprocating couple. I prepared to give my most truthful response.

"If I say yes, I want it understood that I'm *not* agreeing to a relationship of the conventional kind. I'm agreeing to sex and maybe allowing you a pinch of control whenever the hell I feel like it."

Chase tried to stifle his smirk, as amusement and a hint of surprise rode his handsome face. He was going to challenge me every chance he got. I was a handful, but for reasons unknown, I believed he could handle me. His unwavering gaze held mine.

"Okay. Sex, dominance, and you submitting to me whenever the hell I want you to. I think I can deal with that." His cocky grin brightened his features.

This time, I was the one holding in a teasing smile.

"If you think I didn't hear the way you phrased your last sentence, you better think again. I plan on doing whatever the hell I want, and based on your grin, you damn well know it."

His laughter burst free, causing me to join him. The strange effect he had on me was difficult to shake, but I overcame it to concentrate on the menu. The waiter had smiled his way to our table twice and we were so engaged in our conversation we had not even considered our orders.

I ordered the caramelized mud-crab and seafood rice. Chase ordered the stuffed flank steak with prosciutto and mushrooms. He'd hardly glanced at his plate after it had arrived because he was so busy eyeballing and attempting to squeeze more information from me. As much as I hated to admit it, I was eating up the attention he lavished on me. I loved the idea of making a man like him forget about all the power he possessed and concentrate on just me.

The sexual tension between us wouldn't ease up either. It kept building as we pretended we weren't ready to rip each other's clothes off. We had hardly scratched each other's surfaces, so I knew there was more to be desired from him. Despite the sexual tension brimming between us, his keen interest in getting to know me remained.

After we finished our main dishes, we shared a scoop of mint chocolate chip ice cream. When Chase offered his last spoonful to me, I wrapped my lips around it with a smile.

"You're a beautiful woman Jax. You make eating look damned good."

My face warmed and my smile came easier. I think I was blushing. Chase was giving me romance, and he complimented me enough to make me act like a teenager on her first date.

"I think I'm obsessed with touching you. I just can't stop myself. You don't mind, do you?"

I was no longer afraid to admit to myself that I enjoyed his touch.

"No," I finally answered.

His big strong hands delicately caressed my back and shoulders. It almost seemed he wasn't fully aware of how affectionate he was being.

Our conversation resumed. "Since you've been questioning me like a low budget lawyer working a no-win case, why don't you tell me a little more about your past. I'd love to hear about you on your first date."

Chase chuckled, shaking his head at some memory he prepared to share with me.

"She was a twenty-year-old posing as a teen, hired by my father to boost my fourteen-year-old confidence. My father was unaware I'd found out about the ruse, so when I asked the woman, Charlette was her name, if she'd like to have a threesome with me and my father, and I couldn't get it up without him present, she'd turned three shades of red."

My hardy chuckle filled the space of the restaurant. I was starting to think Chase hadn't been as compliant to his father's rules as he'd initially let on. I observed him closely as I prepared to tell him about my first date without him having to ask.

"I'd been so uncompromising with this boy named Tony when he took me to our tenth-grade spring dance. He left my ass on the dance floor and found another girl. He actually left me stranded without a ride home. I ended up taking the city bus home."

Chase attempted to hide it, but his chuckle sneaked out. He thought me getting dumped and left was the funniest thing in the world, and I couldn't help laughing along with him.

We lingered at our table a full hour after we had finished our meals, sharing the ridiculousness of our pasts.

Chapter Eighteen

Chase

My driver circled the block twice, to ensure the coast was clear from any media eager enough to follow me. I wanted to make a quick stop at a little vendor Travis had found that made hand-made jewelry. I'd gotten a bracelet made for my mother's upcoming birthday.

"Why are we stopping here?" Jax turned in the seat, taking in the busy streets surrounding us.

"I need to pick up something. It won't take but a minute."

The hairs on the back of my neck stood as soon as I stepped out of the vehicle. Something was off. I turned and held my hand out, stopping Jax from exiting behind me.

The camera flashes caught my attention before the sound of shuffling feet and shouting found my ears. A small herd of paparazzi came out of nowhere, prepared to swarm us. Paul shoved me back into the vehicle and slammed the door, locking it with the key fob as the herd made attempts to jerk the door open.

Jax sat on the floor on the passenger side in a tight ball with her face buried behind her knees that were tucked to her chest. When I tapped on her shoulder, she jumped before tuck-ing herself tighter.

"It's okay Jax. Were locked in."

She shrugged my hand away from her shoulder. "I don't want them seeing me. I don't want my picture taken."

The heavy pain in her shaky voice wasn't missed.

"You can get up now. They can't take your picture through the mirrored windows."

She had told me from the start that she wanted nothing to do with the media attention, but it wasn't until now that I understood how serious she'd been. She was adamant about protecting her privacy, but I got the impression Jax's paranoia came from a deeper place.

If I weren't mistaken, I would say she was traumatized, triggered in some way by the herd of photographers.

"Are you okay?"

"I'm fine," she answered quickly, not looking up.

"You're not fine Jax. You're shaking." How was I supposed to help her? The information she'd revealed at dinner resurfaced. She was filmed without her consent, and I was starting to think it was some kind of film of a nefarious nature.

"I want to help you, but I don't know how."

She lifted her head, putting on fake bravado. "Just let me sit here a moment I'll be fine."

She didn't sound fine. I slid even closer, being careful not to box her in too much as I placed an arm around her shoulders.

Once Paul managed to climb back into the front seat in one piece and relocked the doors, I told him to take the scenic route to Jax's place. The last thing I wanted was the group following me to her apartment.

"Jax, please. Come sit next to me." My tone was soft, almost a whisper.

It took me ten long minutes to coax her off the floor and back into the seat. She wouldn't let me hold her, but I hung on to her hand, refusing to let it go and hoping she felt some level of comfort.

She didn't make a sound in the seat next to me as we drove out of our way to ensure we weren't being trailed. Paul didn't stop the car until he confirmed we had not been followed.

Instead of allowing him to get my door, I let myself out and quickly walked around to her door to help her out.

"Let me walk you up. Since you're my lady now, I need to ensure that you're safe and cared for. I don't want anyone else getting what belongs to me."

Her dangerous side-eye was worth my bold words. She giggled, not knowing I wasn't *joking*. However, I loved making her laugh, especially after witnessing how upset the rowdy crowd of paparazzi had made her.

This was uncharacteristic behavior for me with her. I believed I was shredding parts of who I was, to find pieces of who I wanted to be. She made me forget about the pressure of being a CEO, and I had allowed myself to have unrestricted fun.

She'd been right. I was a workaholic because I had never found anything else to occupy me, nothing else was of interest or nothing had moved me, not like her.

We'd agreed to an unconventional relationship, but I believed a genuine connection had taken root. It was a bond that breathed a radiating energy and was growing in meaning. After a sample of her so called *"acquired taste,"* it was something I craved with a fierce need because it wasn't one-dimensional.

After escorting Jax to her door, I invited myself in once she keyed the door open. She sat on her couch, kicked off her shoes and reached for the remote control. She began to flip through her channels, as I took a more thorough tour of her apartment. I thumbed through the stack of mail sitting by her door.

"Why two apartments?" I asked.

"I don't want everyone knowing where I live."

"Understandable, but I know where you live. Does that make me a special case?"

"Something like that."

I loved her answer. It enticed a contented smile but didn't stop me from rifling through her things. She didn't even flinch when I picked up her phone and flipped through it. She wasn't this open in life, and the thought that she was this way with only me, pleased me. Like she sensed my thoughts, she stated, "If you were anyone else, I would whip you for being all up in my personal business. You are the noisiest rich man I've ever met."

"You like me being in your business," I mouthed, inching closer to her on the couch. The tingling pull I didn't have a name for yet, had me in its mysterious grips.

Her laptop sat across her lap. I lifted it during warp-speed keystrokes and sat it on the coffee table behind me. Her strong glare met mine when I leaned closer.

"I would love to have a taste of your pussy, if you don't mind?"

Her curious gaze followed my movement when I dropped to my knees in front of her. My fingers slid up her thighs, as I drew closer to her caressing warmth. My eyes were now level with her plush lips. She eased back at my approach, but I continued until my lips touched hers. Her mouth drew tense at first, but her tension eased, and her soft lips melted into mine.

The mysterious tingle had returned with a vengeance and sent my heart into chaos as charged currents prickled up and down my spine. My hands slid around her waist, the tips of my fingers aching. Our tongues met halfway, caressing in a sensual embrace that floored me and opened the doorway for those pent-up emotions to rush through. I had never been impaled so deeply by anyone's kiss. My knees dug into the floor at my desperate need to pull her in tighter.

My intentions were to initiate sex, but something outside my scope of knowledge was pulling the strings.

When her hands journeyed up my arms and met around my neck, I fell deeper into the beautiful rush pulling me under. A low groan sounded in her throat before she tightened her hold on me and slid her tongue from the tip to the back of mine, tasting me, possessing me.

"Jax," I sighed against her lips. She was all I knew. In this moment, she was my every thought, my every desire.

On a sharp intake, she broke the kiss. If she hadn't, I feared we would have passed out from lack of oxygen. We eased back. Her hand slid from my nape to the side of my neck, and mine loosened around her waist.

She sat frozen as surprise tightened the corners of her eyes, no doubt digesting the unmistakable realization of what the kiss had stirred between us. This was more than sex, certainly elevated past lust or desire. I was as stunned as she was, unable to move for a moment since I had never experienced this.

We had a connection strong enough to make me breathless and filled with an intense need to do everything in my power to make Jax happy.

Her hands dropped away from me, and she searched my eyes for the answers to her confusion. There were no answers or quick fixes to us. The truth had revealed itself through an unexpected kiss, and her poker face emerged. It was too late. She had embraced the same rush as I had. She had tasted the unshakable force that had rendered me helpless and frightened me beyond measure.

Her breaths rushed out, the warm flow kissing my skin. The pulse in her neck thumped a hammering beat under my fingertips, in tune with the beat of my heart. The movement of my other hand over her thighs broke us from the gripping trance we were sucked into.

My mind recalled why I had gotten on my knees in the first place, so I allowed the raw need to creep back into my bones, lest I be swallowed by the enormity of our truth. Jax noticed the moment I switched gears and relief washed over her. She would rather deal with desire over the confusing rush of emotions. So, did I. I was afraid of that other thing, the one that shall remain nameless.

My eager fingertips dug deeper into her thighs, loving the way they filled my hands. I dragged her down on the couch as she watched, propping herself up on her elbows. In response to my heated advances, her body recited a story. Her hard nipples poked at her dress, her breaths whispered her desire in its secret language, and her legs fluttered open and close, tapping at my sides.

"I'm about to feast on your pussy." I made the statement with the boldness I often reserved for the boardroom. "Do you have any objections?" I questioned, feeding on the hunger pooling in her eyes.

She shook her head, as I placed my hand on her chest and nudged her back into the cushion.

"Relax, I'm about to make you feel good," I assured, my confidence speaking volumes.

Her tension dissolved, and her eyes volleyed between me and my eager hands, as I reached for her dress zipper.

I enjoyed seeing her in this sexy black dress, but it had dawned on me it could be opened with one long swipe of the golden zipper that ran up the front. "You wore this dress for me, didn't you? With this zip up front, you have been sending me subliminal messages all night, haven't you?"

"Yes. I put it on with you in mind." Her tongue grazed her sexy full lips, wetting them. The subtle movement made her lip piercing sparkle against the light as her eyes blazed with mischief. I unzipped her, dragging the zipper apart with slow ease, loving the sight of her breathless anticipation.

Her elegant brown skin snatched my attention, causing me to take my time admiring each part spilling from the dress. I dragged my eyes over the enticing curves of her full breast covered in thin lace, and the flat plains of her stomach decorated by the small sparkling diamond of her belly button ring. The tantalizing curves that flared out to introduce her hips, filled me with a frantic need.

When I slid the zipper past her underwear, I could no longer take the anticipation. I almost ripped her dress off completely. It fell open at her sides. I looped my fingers into her black sheer panties, dragged them across her thighs, legs, and feet before lifting them to my nose.

Her smooth citrus-vanilla scent was a mouthwatering drug, powerful enough to set my endorphins on fire. I gripped her hips and tugged her closer before I slung one of her legs across my shoulder. With my free hand, I palmed her sexy ass.

My light fingers bit into her tempting brown flesh creating a mixture as exhilarating to watch as she was to touch. I tightened the grip I had on her thigh, dragged her even closer to my waiting mouth, and spread her open.

"You're so wet for me." My tongue introduced itself as I licked her, plying her wet lips and sucking up her juices. I was so turned on; I could feel myself leaking precum. My swollen dick ached with need and throbbed like a swarm of angry wasps trying to break free.

"Mmm," I growled, enjoying the feast that was causing my dick to throb with raging persistence. She was delicious enough to make me savor every drop coating my tongue.

The tiny vertical bar through the hood of her clit slid across my tongue. I eased my tongue past the jewel and found the fleshy hard diamond I was after. Her flavor was sweet and tangy, like a blended mix squeezed from ripe fruit. She was a gift to my taste buds, and I slurped on her.

"Fuck, you can eat some pussy," she stated as her hips swiveled, chasing my exploring tongue. "You make it easy because you taste so good," I replied, before diving back in. She persisted in praising how good I was fucking her with my mouth, chanting her delight between clinched teeth as her fingers massaged my scalp and slipped through my hair.

"Your damn tongue! Fuck!" She shoved my head into her scorching folds, so hard, I could hardly breathe. Each time my tongue would dip low and slide across the star of her ass, I was rewarded with a loud roaring "fuck" from her. If there was one thing I learned, you weren't eating pussy right if you didn't eat everything.

"That's it. I want you to drown in it," she sang.

Her reaction was the kind of motivation that drove me to please her better, harder, faster.

"Holy Fuck! Chase!" She screamed as her nails bit into my neck. Her legs fluttered against my shoulders. Her free hand clawed into the couch. Her shivers alerted that she was at the precipice of sexual bliss.

When I sucked her clit along with the piercing into my mouth, she screamed like an obsessed fan. "Chase. Yes! Yes! So good," she edged out after a series of loud exhausting moans. I kept going after I had licked and sucked every drop of the orgasm from her.

She didn't stop me, even as her body fought to stabilize itself. A minute later she was coming again, and I lapped up every drop of her juices that time too, before I came up for air.

I paid attention to her every move, feeding off her reactions. Jax enjoying my mouth play had my ego floating through her vaulted ceiling.

Through glazed heavy eyes, she cast a sly smile dipped in seduction in my direction as her teeth sank into her bottom lip. Based on the way she stared with dark satisfaction on her face, I had surprised her.

"Damn, Chase. Shit." It sounded like a compliment to me. "Such a deliciously nasty mouth. Such a splendidly wicked tongue." She eyed me with an appreciative gleam, enticing my smile to grow.

I reached up to her shoulder and let my fingers trace the tattoo I was fascinated with. She was insanely beautiful. Something you marveled, and I didn't take my place in her life for granted. I sat back on my haunches and soaked her in, savoring her presence.

I lingered on my knees until the stiffness in my dick deflated. Her eyes were on me the entire time as she used her foot, rubbing it gently, up and down the outside of my thigh. It seemed she understood she needed to calm me.

Once I was satisfied that I had captured her image and saved it to memory, I stood and headed into her kitchen. Her neck twisted in a hurry, following my departure. I had promised myself in the car that I would make this night all about her. The deep well of sorrow she tried to hide when she mentioned her childhood and feeling her shaking on the floor of my car had shown me a vulnerable side she hid behind her tough personality.

Every part of herself that she would let slip, every piece she shared, and every portion that seeped out, I was cataloging. I wanted Jax, top to bottom, inside and out.

It was extremely difficult to refrain from satisfying my own needs, but I was doing better than I assumed I would. Opening her refrigerator, I took a bottle of water and returned to the couch.

She hadn't moved an inch, the low shaven airstrip on her pretty pussy was on display, summoning me for another round. I couldn't not touch her. I sat close and reached for her hand.

"Come here. I thought women like to cuddle after sex?"

We shared a smile at my comment, but I did want her in my arms.

"Not me. I would like to make you too tired to even think about something as lame and punkish as cuddling."

My head dropped in laughter. I had never met such a hard-hitting woman in my life. However, I sensed her hard exterior was her main line of defense against me. I was breaking down her walls, making her deflect my advances. The process required patience, and Jax, assuming who I was, had no idea I had it in abundance. I had decided. She was going to be my woman; she just didn't know it yet.

"Come here. Please. I promise I won't be lame or punkish."

She closed her dress with a huff, zipping it most of the way up before she slid closer. I believe she enjoyed being around me as much as I enjoyed her company, but her ego wouldn't allow her to admit it to herself.

When she drew close enough, I didn't give her a choice, I relaxed into the arm of the couch with her tucked tight against my chest. Thankfully, she didn't fight me on the matter because I had no intention of letting her go.

Jax had lured me into her world and appeared to have no idea how deep. I was falling for her, but it was too quick. I couldn't reveal that feelings had crept into our situation from the first moment I touched her across my boardroom table. She would think I was crazy. Being irrational. Reacting off sexual attraction. I didn't believe I was.

We went on and talked into the early morning hours, about business, my college years and hers. We debated everything from the difference in pay among men and women in the work force, to the economy impacting life and death with respect to affordable medical care.

I enjoyed hearing stories about Lena James, who Jax had been friends with since her freshman year in college. Lena sounded like a character, and I couldn't wait to meet her. When Jax spoke of her I could easily see the caring glint in her eyes. Learning that Lena was born a man that was in the process of saving for her gender reassignment surgery did make me wonder about Jax's friends.

She mentioned that her friends list was small and based on what she revealed, TK and Lena were the only people, other than her father, that she let get close. Getting information out of Jax about her life was difficult, but I was determined and tonight was my biggest breakthrough.

The next thing I knew, and way too soon, the sun's rays were enticing me to open my eyes. We had talked all night, so we had only been asleep for a few hours. Glancing down, I smiled at the sight of my new blanket. For someone who described cuddling as *"lame and punkish,"* she was snug atop me with her face buried in my chest. Reluctant to disrupt her comfort, I didn't want to wake her and became blissfully content watching her sleep.

It had taken her a while to finally get settled as she'd had a couple of bouts of mouthing rapid Spanish and twitching in her sleep. Although they were low murmurs, her unconscious cries were so desperate at one point, I started a soothing stroke up and down her back. She didn't find much peace in her sleep and as badly as I wanted to question her, for now, I believed it was best not to push the issue.

Feeling her body pressed into mine kept a smile on my face. She was so warm and fit perfectly against me, her body folding into my side. My shoulder had become her pillow as the top of her head rested there.

She stirred awake, but didn't bolt like I expected her to, since technically, we were doing something couples would do.

"Good morning." She sat up, shaking the rest of her sleep away.

"I need to get going." I sat up too, preparing to stand. I didn't want to force too much of my "*lame*" behavior on her all at once.

My attempt to kiss her on the lips was derailed. She had turned her head away quick enough for my lips to connect with her cheek. I huffed in frustration. Why did she have to be so damn difficult?

"Not even a little kiss Jax?"

"I tolerated your lameness all night, but I refuse to start my day off with it too." She fought back a smile, but I could tell she was still unsure about where our relationship was headed.

"You don't have to keep your guard up with me all the time. I'm not trying to do anything to hurt you. I just..." She was so much more than a sex partner, but I didn't know what pushing her would do. This was the first time I'd inserted myself into anyone's life this way.

"Just what?" she asked.

"I just wanted a kiss."

Her features softened and a wide grin broke out on her face before she gripped and tugged my arm, pulling me closer. "You better give me what I want, woman." We laughed.

My lips eased into the soft supple bends of hers, and I was drawn into the flowing waves of euphoria our kiss produced. The warm energy she fed into me made my heart flutter and my body jittery. My eagerness to deepen the kiss persisted, and I dragged her into my lap.

We eventually broke the kiss, but I couldn't bear to break our connection, placing my forehead against hers. When I opened my eyes, hers were there waiting on mine. Urgent and demanding, the connection possessed me, and I didn't know how to temper my emotions.

"You're still lame," she tossed at me in a low tone.

I laughed. Her remark was the perfect distraction to stomp down the surge of emotions that had rocked me to my core. She stood off my lap and retook her seat. It pleased me to see her smiling.

Once I had my shoes on, I walked myself out, shaking my head and laughing at her. I called over my shoulder, "I'll call you later, baby."

"Way too lame, Chase," were her last words before I closed the door behind me. If she thought she was getting rid of me, by any means, she could think again.

Chapter Nineteen

Chase

Jax received a call from me every day after my sleepover. She appeared to be getting more comfortable with talking to me. However, today's call would be a bit different from the others.

"Chase," she answered.

"Hey, baby. How's your day going?" Just hearing her voice sent spikes of joy coursing through me.

"My day was good until you rang, calling me by that ridiculous pet name. I'm getting some work done if you don't mind."

"My day is going well also. I'm glad you cared enough to ask." I used sarcasm as my motivator.

"Glad to hear it," she replied. There was an underlying playfulness in her tone making me aware she wasn't pissed like she attempted to pass off.

The sound of her fingers tapping in rapid succession registered. She was behind the screen of a laptop, distracted by her work, but I had news meant to get her attention.

"I'll stop by tomorrow night at five to pick you up for our dinner date," I stated, dying to hear her reaction to my boldness.

Her typing slowed.

"No, you will not be here to pick me up at five for dinner. This is not a relationship, so stop treating it like one."

Like I often did and was smart enough to continue to do, I ignored her protest.

"My father, James, my brother, Blake, and my brother's wife Tonya will be expecting you tomorrow. I already informed them you would be accompanying me."

Dead silence.

"For fuck's sake! You can't do shit like that. You can't go volunteering me for shit, especially not to dinner with your family."

Was that it? I expected more of a fuss.

"My father requested it. He stated, and I quote, *"I want to meet this unicorn who has you walking out of meetings and brushing off conference calls. And, I won't take no for an answer."* End quote."

My father and I weren't close, but we got along. We didn't have the typical father/son relationship. He usually barked orders and delivered tough-love lessons. After having a series of strokes, his attitude had been tempered, but he was still tough as nails.

If I didn't bring Jax to dinner as he had requested, he would call her himself and invite her over. I didn't want him pulling off one of his off the wall lessons. I didn't want him, or anyone doing something that might end up hurting her. I didn't even want to know how my father found out about us. I'd been careful with her privacy.

A long stretch of silence filled the line.

"Jax?"

"I'm here," she mumbled.

"What does your father know about us? You walking me out of a meeting is one thing, but how did that equate to him wanting you to bring me to dinner?"

"He's resourceful." I responded.

"What you're not saying, is that he's used his financial assets to snoop around enough to know that we've been…"

"Dating." I finished for her. "Tomorrow at five. I'll talk to you later, baby." I puckered my lips, made a kissing sound, and hung up before she could protest or curse me any further.

***

When Jax opened her door, her appearance stopped me in my tracks. She was in nothing but a silk, navy-blue bra and panty set.

"Jax?"

"Come in." She stepped aside so I could walk in. "I had work to do today and was dressing when you rang."

"And I respect that about you, but you told me I worked too much and suggested I do something about it, so I took your advice to heart. Now, I'm starting to get the impression that you need to follow your own advice. As a matter of fact, when do you get out for fun, Ms. Saint-Pierre?"

She didn't deny my suggestion, nor had she answered my question as she stepped into a pair of high-waist pants. The legs of the pants were cut in a way that made them look like a skirt. Her jet-black hair was bone straight tonight, silky and long, it hung a few inches past her shoulders. I couldn't wait to get my fingers in it.

I strolled to the couch and took a seat to get a better view as she dressed. Jax was a piece of art, there was no other way to describe her. Sexy and intriguing. Nothing about her was boring. Her body told a story, and I was desperate to read every line.

She paired pale purple slacks with a creamy white lace and silk blouse. The outfit inspired a sexy and elegant vibe.

"Chase, focus." She snapped her fingers to gain my attention. Once I unglued my eyes from her chest, I noticed that her expression held warning.

"You apparently don't know me as well as you think you do, so I'll warn you right here and now. I'm not the girl guys take home to family. I'm usually the one they hide, because I'm not going to pretend to be 'Becky' around your people. I'm agreeing to this because I'm interested in meeting your family, despite my better judgement telling me I shouldn't do this."

A few steps closed the distance between us. "Was *I* who you thought I was?"

She pursed her lips, "No, not at all. You're one of those show-the-world-the-good-side, while you're actually the fuck-me-until-I-pass-out type of man."

The things that spilled from her mouth kept me laughing.

"Jax, I would never suggest you pretend to be someone you're not. I wouldn't recommend you change who you are for *anyone*. But whatever you think of my family, you're probably right. They are spoiled, entitled, and very judgmental."

Was she going to heed my warning? My father requested and I obliged, but if I knew Jax as well as I was beginning to, she wasn't going to bite her untamed tongue for the sake of leaving a good impression. On the other hand, neither would my father, and especially not my opinionated brother.

Chapter Twenty

Chase

Jax's curious gaze scanned our surroundings as my family home came into view. The roar of my Rolls-Royce Cullinan quieted to a low hum as we coasted along the bricked driveway.

"So, Connecticut. The Golden Triangle. The highest of high society. Fitting for your family."

I nodded in her direction. The neighborhood was a little over thirty miles from the city, but with traffic it had taken some time to get there. I exited the vehicle and stepped around to open her door.

I escorted her up the steps, leading her to the front door. Douglas, our butler, opened the door and greeted us. "Mr. Taylorson, so happy you could make it."

His gaze landed on Jax and, although, he covered it, I had caught surprise in his expression, laced with intrigue.

"Douglas, this is my lady, Jax Saint-Pierre."

"Pleased to meet you, ma'am," he stated, his gaze darting from me to her, with a glint of uncertainty resting in his gaze after Jax paid him a pleasant, "Nice to meet you."

He finally aimed his hand toward the dining room. The first steps we took into the room, two additional staff members approached, offering their assistance before I introduced them to Jax.

She leaned into me, her warm words teasing my earlobe. "Surprisingly, I had forgotten how rich you are until I saw this place and all of this *staff,* as you call them. I mean, how many maids, butlers, and drivers does one family need?"

"It was worse before my father retired. He had an assistant for everything."

Before I walked Jax into my family's huge formal dining room, I decided to give her a quick tour of the place, since dinner wouldn't be served for another fifteen minutes.

We marched up the gold and marble staircase where she was shown the apartment-sized bedrooms and the sunroom. Returning to the first floor, we took a quick peek into a few more of the rooms, before exiting the house and strolling through the botanical garden.

Once back inside, Jax stopped in front of the wall of pictures showcasing my transformation from a young unsure kid to a more assured young man. The pictures had stopped when my mother left my father when I was eighteen.

Jax studied my pictures. She pointed at the ten-year-old me. "You were skinny, but a cute kid. You grew into your manhood well."

"Thank you."

She nodded to another picture of me in my baseball uniform.

"Even back then, the glasses didn't make you nerdy or dorky. I think the seriousness in your eyes made you hot."

Her comment sparked a grin.

"I was teased about my glasses, but my mother was the one who made me embrace wearing them."

I pointed out a photo of me and my mom, when I was about twelve. My mother was a beautiful blonde, who always kept her hair short. Her hands sat across me and my brother's shoulders in the picture.

"That's my mom," I confirmed.

"I can tell by the proud smile on your face, you love your mother." She studied the picture with a smile plastered across her face.

"My mother left my father the day I turned eighteen. She handed him the divorce papers and rolled her luggage out the door with her head held high. I was away at college when it happened, but from what Blake described, my father had never been more shocked in his life. My mother knew of his adultery. She had even caught him cheating, not once but twice."

I was proud of my mother; glad she had found the strength to walk away.

"She never voiced a complaint in front of us. My father didn't make it easy for my mother to leave him, but all that time he thought she was being docile, I believed she had just been awaiting the right time. She had pictures of him with other women, some dating back to the early years of their marriage. She had even interviewed two of the women he cheated with. He was left with no choice, but to let her go after she had hit him with the unexpected."

"Smart woman," Jax said under her breath.

"I don't even think she complained to my father, and he was even more controlling over her, than he was over me and my brother. I think she waited until her time came and left with the same grace she entered their marriage with. I believe my father had taken her silence over the years as a sign he owned her no matter what. My mom never mentioned it, but I believed she only stayed with him because of us. With the settlement she received from the divorce, she mostly travels and does volunteer work now."

My smile mirrored Jax's. She enjoyed my mother's story. Her quick tour and the brief history I had given her on my family had taken up the time. We had walked enough that she had relieved herself of the heels I carried for her. I assisted her in slipping them back on before we entered the nearest bathroom to wash our hands.

Jax was likely unaware, but we were more engaging in our interactions with each other. I considered our exchanges the framework needed to build a successful relationship. She was warming up to the idea of us without even realizing it.

As we headed toward the dining room, my family crossed my mind. My brother Blake was living his non-working life in our childhood home. He blamed me, and my father for his shortcomings and didn't mind living free of responsibilities as a result.

Blake believed his older brother status gave him the right to pass judgement on every decision I made. When he had screwed up and flunked out of college, my father hadn't benched him right away, but he started grooming me as backup.

The hard work and training I poured into becoming a professional baseball player, had earned me the honor of having scouts show up to watch me play during my junior and senior years in college. My dreams were shattered when I suffered an unfortunate knee injury.

Wild parties, drinking, and women consumed most of Blake's life during and after college. After my knee injury, my father informed me that he wanted me working as his apprentice instead of Blake.

Blake had been bitter since, labelling me, the favorite son. My father and I tolerated him because he was blood.

Upon seeing Jax when we stepped into the dining room, Blake's mouth fell open and remained so. My father's lips twitched, and his eyebrows inched up on his forehead, but he appeared more amused than surprised.

At least my father remembered his manners and stood, although he had failed to hide his surprise as he gawked at Jax. Blake stood after his wife, Tonya, tapped his arm.

My father remained standing at the head of the table, aided by the cane he started using after his second stroke three years ago. His health issues were one of the reasons I had taken control of the company so early in my life. "Dad, Blake, Tonya, this is my lady, Jax Saint-Pierre."

In true Jax fashion she greeted, "Dad, Blake, Tonya, nice to meet you all."

After Jax's greeting, I detected a hint of surprise in my father's crooked posture, but he swallowed it quickly before a smile surfaced on his lips. The stroke had taken away his ability to control the muscle memory in parts of the right side of his body. As a result, when he smiled only one side of his mouth would turn up. However, the sight of the smile surprised me. Tonya stared, her expression as telling as Blake's, who had finally managed to close his mouth.

After an awkward silent moment, Tonya fixed her face with a smile. Blake smiled, but it was one of those smiles you had to work at maintaining to conceal the underlying frown.

"Jax, it's nice to meet you, young lady," my father stated. His smile deepened before he reached out and shook her hand. My father was the most formal of us all, so I expected him to reply to Jax with a comment of discipline about her greeting, but he simply greeted with a pleasant smile and handshake instead.

"Nice to meet you, Jax," came Tonya's late greeting. Blake sat in place eyeing us both, the contempt in his expression hard to miss.

I assisted Jax into her chair before taking my own. She sat across from Blake, and to my father's left at the head of the table. I planted myself across from Tonya.

Blake stared a hole in Jax across the table as my father prepared to interrogate her.

"So, you own an IT company?"

"Yes, sir, I do."

Before Jax could continue, my father had moved on to the next question.

"...and *we* are one of your clients? How did you pull it off? Your track record in the IT arena must be unmatched?"

"It started when my company replaced the network at Jefferson Reed's, brother's company," Jax said.

Jefferson was one of Swift Capital's portfolio managers.

"He was impressed with the work I did for his brother. He was so impressed that he informed me that Swift Capital was considering upgrading *their* network. He talked me up to the rest of the company, and I received the callback to set up the new network." James had lifted a brow at Jax words but remained silent. "From there, my background was checked, they found that we had worked with a number of other big named companies, and we negotiated a contract for my company to manage the network."

"Where did you attend school?"

I leaned into Jax. "I'm sorry you have to go through this but as soon as he gets it all out of his system, he'll settle down."

She squeezed my leg under the table as her reply. "I went to Columbia for my undergrad and then Cornell for my masters."

At those highlights, Blake and Tonya's eyebrows rose. Any minute now, I expected Blake to start with his questions. The last woman I had brought home at my father's request, he and my brother had ripped to shreds.

Glancing at Jax, I was confident she could handle whatever my family threw at her.

"So, how did you become associated with my son outside of work?"

A teasing smile eased onto her lips. "I was dragged, mentally kicking and screaming, into one of his meetings. Once inside the dreary place, I was ambushed with technical support issues that could have been handled by the in-house team. Chase ordered his assistant to introduce me to him and here we are."

"So, you'd worked for the company for eight months and you two had never met before?" Intrigued filled my father's tone.

"Correct. We hadn't officially met until a month ago. I believe Chase was away on business during the time we'd set up the network," Jax confirmed.

"So, what are your intentions toward my son? Have you signed an NDA?"

With each new question, Jax's hand rose, sliding up my thigh. I fought to keep myself from jumping when her hand rested on my dick at his last question.

"Sir, I haven't signed an NDA to date your son, and I don't *intend* to sign one. An NDA is for girls who seek the temporary afterglow of someone else's fame and fortune. I'm a woman who chooses to shine in my own light. And, honestly, I can't say at this table what my intentions for your son are. I can assure you; they're not decent."

At those words, I choked on the water I had just sipped. Tonya stared at Jax, stunned. She was likely wondering if she imagined what she had heard. Blake glanced between Jax and my father, his mouth agape.

Me? I sat with my elbow on the table, my hands cupping my mouth, struggling to keep my composure as my dick throbbed in Jax's firm grasp.

"Are you going to let this woman talk to you this way?" Blake asked, glaring at my father, but not getting an answer. "Oh, I see. It's your favorite son. He could get away with this ridiculous relationship. If it were me, I'd have not gotten to within a foot of a woman like that."

"What the hell do you mean, a woman like that?" Jax shot her words across the table at Blake, as I fought to keep her calm and in the chair.

How my father maintained a straight face was beyond me. When he took too long to reply, Blake cleared his throat and prepared to continue, but he had no idea who he was preparing to tangle with. Jax's mean glare was still set on Blake, who appeared anxious to start an argument with her.

"My brother is one of the wealthiest men in this country, and you're a glorified tech support clerk. Since your status is nonexistent, you're no doubt with him for one of two things, money or your fifteen minutes of fame. I hope you don't think this is going anywhere, you're nothing more than another one of his impulsive decisions."

Jax sipped her drink and took her time before she prepared to offer Blake a response. A low groan escaped when her fingers tightened around my dick. Her hard stare was leveled at Blake. She was going to rip him to shreds, and I wasn't going to stop her because he deserved it. I kept my mouth shut because Blake would taunt until I became angry enough to hit him. Besides, Jax was doing a good job of keeping me distracted.

"I prefer to work and pay my own way. Unlike you, I don't live off the backs of my family. I don't make millions, but I work hard to make enough to be proud of. Every time I swipe my credit card to make a purchase or to pay my bills, the funds come from money I worked for. I don't need Chase's money. I have never asked him for money or gifts, nor do I ever intend to. With that being said, if he offered me gifts of his own free will, I'd be a damned fool to say no to him. But, make no mistake, dear brother Blake, I won't ask, nor will I drop my drawers in exchange for anything. And has it ever occurred to *you* that *I* might be the one making the impulsive dating decision?"

Blake sat frozen. Jax may as well have slapped him because he wasn't used to anyone confronting him, especially not a woman. Tonya couldn't hide the smirk shining on her lips as she sat in awe of Jax.

Blake scratched his head and grumbled before he took a sip of water. My father sat unusually still, one of his bushy eyebrows stuck in the air as his glare volleyed between Blake, Jax, and me.

After the verbal whiplash Jax had given Blake, the table remained at a loss for words. I hadn't realized it until she mentioned it, but she was right. Money had never come up in any of our conversations. She had never asked for anything, and I believed she never would. Besides, she was doing just fine on her own.

"So, Dad, did you know Jax started her business in the same manner as you, right out of college, no favors?"

The smile on Jax's face when her eyes met mine was priceless.

"Is that right?" My father asked. "Independent and willing to work hard to create your own path. Very respectable."

Thankfully, my father was interested in anything business related. It defused the tension at the table. The expression on Jax's face showed she wasn't aware of me knowing about her accomplishments. Blake decided to cling to his frustration, refusing to release his tight expression, perched lips, and hiked shoulders.

Jax could care less about Blake and wouldn't dwell on it. She focused her attention on my father who had already fired off three back-to-back questions.

Surprisingly, the rest of our dinner went well. Except for Blake, we enjoyed pleasant conversation about wine, followed by a healthy debate about politics and the state of our nation.

My father appeared comfortable with Jax. His smiling gaze and engaging words with her was another in a line of surprises, because James Taylorson never accepted anyone if it didn't benefit him. He was tough and firm and often unbending in his ways. He questioned Jax about the direction she planned to take her business.

When she engaged him in a discussion of her business plan, my father was in heaven. As well, I was impressed with her level of knowledge on the savage business world she was blazing a trail through. She had managed to pull my father's attention from her tattoos and piercings, and he was now in tune with her intellect.

Personally, I enjoyed both. While Jax and my father talked, Blake sulked.

"Why don't you two spend the night," my father proposed. "It will keep you guys from battling the evening traffic."

My father's suggestion nearly gave me whiplash.

What the hell is going on here?

No one I dated had received an invitation to stay overnight. Besides, there was no way in hell I was letting Jax stay anywhere near my father. Although I knew Jax wouldn't stand for it, I didn't know if I fully trusted that my father wouldn't try and teach me one of his lessons by coming on to her.

"This is ridiculous," Blake muttered under his breath, but loud enough for us to hear. He stood abruptly, causing his chair to grunt, before he stalked away without excusing himself. His fuming words made their way back to us.

"Next thing you know, they'll be getting *married* with no pre-nup."

Tonya stayed in place, unwilling to follow her grumpy husband. Blake had a chip on his shoulder the size of the White-face Mountains. Drugs, alcohol, and gambling had cost our family millions, and he still hadn't taken responsibility for any of his actions.

After losing the deed to our family's Palm Beach home in a card game, he had caused a near devastating car crash that caused Tonya to lose their baby. He later started treating her like damaged goods when she was unable to conceive again.

"I would love to spend the night, if for nothing more than to irk Blake's nerves. Unfortunately, I'm working on a project I need to finish," Jax finally answered my father and sneaked a wink in my direction.

"I can respect hard work." My father grinned. A laughing sound actually came from his mouth. Jax was clueless as to the miracle Tonya and I gawked at. Maybe she *was* a unicorn like my father described because it appeared he had fallen under her spell.

Chapter Twenty-One

Jax

After dinner we sat around the table and chatted a while longer. Blake returned and requested to speak to Chase as we prepared to leave. I could imagine what he was about to tell his brother.

The family assumed we were a couple, and I followed Chase's lead, allowing the lie to settle. Tonya pointed me toward one of the ten bathrooms in the house as Blake dragged Chase into the study near the dining room. He shot an evil eye in my direction before he eased the door closed. In return, I gifted him with the hardest swiveling eyeroll I could manage.

Before I sauntered off to the bathroom, I eyed Tonya. Her easy smile indicated she knew exactly what I was about to ask.

"I'll give credit where it's due. The Taylorson men are blessed with good genes, but why do you stay with Blake?" I spat his name, making Tonya giggle.

"If I had a dollar for every time someone's asked me that question," she chuckled. "Can I be frank with you Jax?"

"Please."

"I consider myself lucky to have gotten into this family at all. I was trailer trash. The only thing I had in my future was bartending and drunken one-night stands. I met James through an exclusive escort service I worked for. First night, he pulled me out of there. He kept me as his mistress for a full year.

"He told me that he'd never marry me, but I could continue on in our relationship as is. I really didn't want that. We'd had some good times, and he showed me things I would never otherwise see, but I wanted more and told him so. That's when he decided that I would be better off with his son, so he introduced me to Blake."

My bottom lip hit the floor at Tonya's revelations, and I lost my ability to blink. She didn't appear bothered by my expression.

"Blake knows about you and his father?" She had my curiosity on lockdown, and although it wasn't polite to be nosey, I couldn't help myself.

"He knows everything. It's part of the reason he acts the way he does. He hates his father and hates Chase because he thinks the two are in cahoots to wreck his life."

I wanted to feel sorry for Blake, but he was still the king of assholes in my book.

"What about you and your happiness?" I scratched my head, staring a hole in Tonya and wondered if she was still sleeping with James.

"Trust me, I live well, and I get to play, discreetly. I would take this life any day over going back to the trailer park."

To each his own. I would have been in trailer park heaven, saving up for my monthly trip to the flea market.

Her hand brushed my arm. "I have to go, but I'm pretty sure I'll see you again. James is certainly interested in you."

"Okay. Hope you have a good evening." I watched Tonya walk away.

Finally able to uproot myself from the spot I stood in, I went to use the bathroom. On my way back, I couldn't help being drawn to Chase, and Blake's raised voices as the noise seeped through the cracked door.

"Why do you even care who I date? You're desperate for me to fail. If you think she's so bad for me, why say anything at all? Why not let me make the mistake?" Chase questioned his judgmental brother.

"Because you're a billionaire, and she's a piece of trash who is after your money. Frankly, I don't understand why you can't see it for yourself."

Son of a bitch!

I bit deep into my bottom lip, and my fist clenched so tight, my nails dug into my palms. It took every muscle to keep from busting through the door to slap the judgement from Blake's brain for calling me trash.

"Watch your damn mouth!" Chase shouted at Blake. The volume of his tone shook my insides. "She's not trash. She's one of the smartest and most hardworking women I know, and since she's headstrong and brave enough to confront you, you can't stand it."

My hand covered my heart, which had flooded with pride for the way Chase defended me against his ass-mouthed brother. All Blake was good for was shitting judgmental words from his mouth.

"No matter what kind of show she puts on in front of everyone else, you must realize she's beneath us. I mean, for God's sake's Chase, the woman has her damn nose, lip, and lord knows what else, pierced and tattoos all over her neck and arms."

Blake lowered his voice, causing me to shove my ear closer to the crack in the door. "And she's… Black." The word hung in the air like toxic fumes coming from his mouth. He'd spit out Black like I was a walking disease.

The rumbling of furniture scraping across the floor had me ready to bust the door down. From the wider crack I opened, I saw that Blake had landed against the large oak desk. The shock on his face at his brother's reaction was priceless. Chase had pushed him and had his hand around his neck.

Breaths heaving, wide mouth, and eyes aimed like two missiles, Blake knocked Chase's hand away from his neck.

"Take your goddamn hands off of me!" Spittle flew from his mouth.

Chase pointed an angry finger in his face. "So? What if she was purple? What damn difference does it make? There are only a few reasons you wouldn't want me with her. You sense that she's good for me, or she is exactly what you have always wanted, and you can't stand seeing her with me." Chase's irritation roared with each word. I loved this more aggressive side of him that had come out in my defense.

"Don't be ridiculous. I didn't think you were into Black women. Mark...my...words, that one is trouble," he said, pointing a finger toward the door I was nearly kissing so that I could be nosey. "Based on what you've always chosen and considering I have never seen any of the men in our family dating one, it makes me question your decision."

"I don't know if you're drunk or crazy, but you better watch your fucking mouth where it concerns Jax before I put my fist in it!"

"But she..."

"Are you finished?" Chase cut him off. He aimed a stiff finger in Blake's face, as ready for the conversation to end as I was.

"Hell no, I'm not finished," Blake said. The man didn't know when to shut the hell up.

"Open your damn eyes. She's nothing but trouble. She's a distraction you need to get over, quickly. Have fun with her and move on. Dad hasn't intervened because he's in shock, and too sick to realize what's going on. You know he isn't going to go for this. I'm trying to warn you. She has no status. She can't contribute to the Taylorson legacy. She's too much of a risk; too damn mouthy."

Chase heaved a sigh. "This is classic, Blake. You love advising and telling everyone else what they should do, but you never follow your own advice. I find it difficult to believe you graduated from NYU with a mind as narrow as yours. Frankly, Blake, I don't give a fuck what you think about me or Jax. I'm leaving now before I do something I can't take back."

No one except my father had defended me the way Chase had. It touched me in a place I'd been guarding since we met. Chase was wiggling his way into my heart, and I didn't know how to stop it.

I rushed away from the door before he caught me eavesdropping. I would have loved to smack Blake upside the head with a hardy dose of reality, but he wasn't worth it. The man could be the anomaly who could freeze the hottest pits in hell. Thankfully, he and Chase were nothing alike.

Chase walked out with a tight angry frown on his handsome face. The moment his eyes met mine, his expression melted away into a charming smile.

"Did you hear us?"

"No. Just walked up." I lied.

When he placed his hand in the small of my back so we could leave, I glanced back at Blake and winked. A frown grew so deep in the asshole's face, it could rip a hole in the shit-pile he called a brain.

Chapter Twenty-Two

Jax

My lips refused to remain closed as Chase walked me toward the floating, five-star hotel that was his yacht. Until we'd approached it, I was once again reminded about Chase's wealth.

"Be willing to sacrifice something, even if it's profit to give back to yourself. You don't take the time to enjoy it."

He had spat my words back at me, reminding me he was taking the advice I had given him. We'd been driven to New Jersey to gain access to New York Bay. The bay would empty us into the Atlantic Ocean and set us free to roam. I could imagine the large amount of behind-the-scenes planning, fees, and paperwork filed to give us a weekend of peace.

Since we had linked up, I didn't get the impression Chase's aim was to impress me with money. We talked about the intricacies of running a business, but he had never turned to subjects about his material possessions or his bank accounts.

He didn't allow his status, or popularity to affect our time together. I appreciated that aspect of him. His ability to be real, to not power trip, or make demands of me that he expected to be followed. He had the ability to fascinate me and keep my interest.

He could step into his everyday life, get what he wanted with the snap of his finger, but with me, he was just Chase. During the week he would find any excuse to call and I obliged him, enjoying our silly talks and serious ones.

He wasn't like anyone I'd dated. He was observant and paid attention to issues and concerns I didn't think he had noticed. He noticed that I avoided conversations about parts of my childhood, and although he didn't push, he asked me to share stories with him.

In talking to him, I found Chase to be funny, and more down to earth than I had given him credit for. He harbored the incredible ability to make me laugh and could keep a conversation going for hours. Throw in the best sex of my life, and it had become difficult to distance myself from him.

I had never had this type of lasting back and forth with anyone. I believed we were becoming friends in the midst of him attempting to convince me into a relationship. Despite the questionable decisions I was making where Chase was concerned, serious second thoughts plagued me as we closed in on the yacht.

The same evening, we left after having dinner with his family a week ago, I'd allowed him to talk me into abandoning work to spend this weekend with him. He had also walked boldly into my apartment, ripped my clothes off, and fucked me senseless against my front door. Like before, he laid with me on my couch, and held me afterwards, daring me to protest.

Despite all the warnings and doubt I presented to him; Chase kept pressing onward. A mountain of reluctance kept badgering me to end it with him, but he hadn't given me a reason to. *Your past is going to seep out and destroy him. Name one successful relationship you've ever had. You're not built to carry on a long-term relationship. Your number one rule; avoid emotional attachments. Keep it short and sweet to avoid hurt and pain.*

I shook away my irritating thoughts and concentrated on the little slice of happiness I had finally agreed to after Chase had spent hours convincing me that I should have fun.

Last week it was his family home that made the most extravagant five-star resort resemble a shack, and this week it was his yacht. I squinted, adjusting my focus at the name, *Acquired Taste,* in big fancy letters printed on the boat's stern.

"You did not!" I shouted before cupping my mouth with both hands as a pleasurable chill of elation ran through me.

At the sight of the words, my feet shuffled against the thick wood of the dock before I stopped in my tracks. I stood there stunned, my breaths rushing out to keep pace with the hammering beats of my heart.

"Yes, I did," Chase replied, laughing at my reaction. "I was determined to find a way to get you to toss away doubts about spending time with me," he stated, reading me and my reluctance like a pro.

There was no description for the feelings that had so suddenly flooded me. Pride, happiness, and the unshakable notion that I was falling for Chase. No one had ever done anything for me so awe-inspiring or romantic.

Raw emotion surfaced as I studied the words that were painted in purple, my favorite color, on the white surface of the boat. The beauty of his gesture touched me so deeply I was forced to shake away the sting of tears that formed at the back of my eyes.

We walked side by side, his warm hand cupping my lower back. My head dropped against the side of his shoulder, the weight of his surprise leveling me in the best possible way. I grinned the rest of the way, as the name disappeared from the stern view and grew larger as it was also painted on the starboard and port sides.

Unable to wipe the silly smile from my face, an overwhelming sensation of joy overtook me and caused me to hold tighter to Chase's hand, after he had taken mine. The gesture pleased him, so much so, he lifted my hand to his lips and pressed a warm kiss to the back.

The footfalls behind us, reminded me that one of his staff members was following with our luggage. After Chase had picked me up, he'd informed me on the drive that six staff members would be joining us on the boat. All of his staff signed NDA's, which made me feel comfortable about our privacy being protected.

There was Timothy, the yacht's Captain, a portly middle-aged man with shaggy hair and a ready smile. Cathy, a middle-aged graying blonde who was the skinniest cook I had ever seen. There was Frank, a beefy younger man from the security team who followed with our bags. Those were the ones I had seen so far. There were already three aboard the boat, preparing it for our weekend getaway.

I tilted my head, eyeing him with a squinted eye. "Chase, are you sure six staff members are enough?"

He paused his steps, chewing on my question.

I placed my hand atop his when he retrieved and lifted his phone preparing to make a call. "I was joking," I teased, chuckling.

Chase had an army of people at his fingertips, ready and waiting to fulfill his every request. Once aboard, we took a moment and enjoyed the view from the deck before he escorted me further.

When we walked into the saloon, I took in the opulent décor. Everything in my line of sight was varnished hardwood finishes with gold trimmed edges. An authentic Persian rug adorned the hardwood floor that was as shiny as glass.

Every piece of furniture appeared handpicked by a top designer and flown in from wherever it was purchased. There were beige leather couches and chairs, crystal tables, and silver trimmed plant stands. A glass and wood staircase resembling a beautifully rounded suspension bridge sat in the far corner of the room. There was a hall on the other side of the stairs that provided access to the quarters.

Chase's face was lit with excitement that I could practically feel bouncing off his body. "What would you like to do first?"

Without answering him, I bolted to our sleeping quarters, with him hot on my trail. We laughed and shouted down the walls, racing to an unmarked finish line. It took me a hot second to throw on my bikini and find my way back to the deck. The staff had made themselves scarce, and although I knew Chase and I weren't alone, it felt like we were.

By the time he made it to the deck, I was lounging in one of the comfortable chairs enjoying the view of the shore as it became smaller. Beach towels, cold glasses of fruit-infused water, and a fresh tropical fruit tray sat waiting on our lounge side table when I arrived. A small remote sat on the table as well. Upon closer inspection, I noticed the service-call button on the device, which further proved Chase could have what he wanted, whenever he wanted it, at the push of a button.

The endless living portrait of the pale sky kissing the dark ocean waves stole my attention. The July heat on water wasn't the same on land. Out here, the heat caressed you like you'd been dropped into a thick cloud of warm hugs. The water danced as the waves created a song. The sun caressed the clouds, making them blush hues of orange and red.

After a quiet moment of the warm flowing breeze, Chase approached and stood above me.

"I could get used to this," I stated, expressing a bit of the joy that had started to settle into me.

"Good. We can do this whenever you want." His statement sounded like a promise.

His eyes roved, checking me out with meticulous intensity. The two-pieces of white material I wore covered the parts society decided needed to be covered, but not much else.

Almost frozen in place with my hand tucked behind my head, I fought the urge to react to his probing gaze. It was difficult to keep my eyes on the dwindling shore, while sensing his eyes teasing every inch of me.

"Jax," he called.

The sound of his voice turned me on, making my pussy ache with thirst and hunger. I glanced up, unable to keep a smile from surfacing.

"Yes."

"You are the sexiest woman in the world." The truth in his words shined through his eyes.

"Thank you," I giggled. His compliment made me feel special, silly, and anxious.

When I stood, Chase pulled me into his arms, his heat soaking into me enough to reach down to my bones. The blue and white swim shorts he wore hung low on his waist, giving me a show of his tight abs. Seeing and touching his body again was wreaking havoc on my libido.

Tall, fit, and with bulging muscles in all the right spots to highlight his strength. My hand ran up the length of his arm while I basked in the softness of his skin covering the pressing strength of his muscles beneath.

Appreciating our height difference, my gaze trailed the slide of my hand. Without shoes, I was eye-level with the top of his chest where it ran into his broad shoulders. I raked the tip of my nail across one dark pink nipple, making it pucker, before my gaze found his.

"And you're the sexiest man I've ever laid eyes on," I finally replied, hoping he found truth in my words. The astute bad-boy vibe had drawn me in from the start and hadn't let go.

The blogs and magazines were right on some accounts. Chase was funny, handsome, and charming. What they didn't know was that he could fuck like a mythical creature created specifically for the task.

His hands slid around my waist and rested on my ass. I didn't believe he'd intended the action as a sexual one, but I would be damned if a rush of wet heat hadn't leaked from me. He must have sensed my mood because he lowered his mouth to mine and feasted on my lips. It didn't take but the tip of his seeking tongue on mine before he lifted me, and I wrapped my legs around his waist.

I had locked lips with many before Chase, but it had never felt so relaxing, freeing, a gateway drug to more potent emotions. This was a level of intimacy I wasn't used to. I hadn't allowed myself to go this far with anyone but him.

The staff was forgotten along with us being visible to the shore, and the fact that it was broad daylight. I don't know what kind of spell he was casting on me, but I was hooked.

What the fuck am I thinking?

I wasn't one to get hooked as I usually cut the shit short before emotions were even a factor. However, Chase had the keys to unlocking a set of emotions I didn't know needed satisfying.

My legs slid down his body until my feet touched the hardwood deck. With one last kiss, my lips fell away from his. His forehead creased.

"What's wrong?"

"We're like two horny teenagers?" When I glanced around him, the shoreline had transformed to a bouncing line riding the waves. How long had we been stuck together?

"You're America's favorite billionaire," I reminded him. "People watch you, stalk you, and I don't want my picture splattered all over the tabloids and Internet."

His hand remained at my waist. "You're right. I should know better. It's why I instructed the driver to take us hundreds of miles out."

My mind reeled. "Does that mean we'll be sailing towards international waters?"

"Yes. The distance will also be a deterrent to any vultures, angling for a picture, or to get a story. I want us to get as much privacy as we can. I would like this to be *our* time and not *their* story. If I knew how to operate this boat, I would have left the staff, but they have instructions to remain invisible unless we need something."

He took my hand and walked me to the side rail before placing me in front of him, hugging me from behind. My head fell back against his chest as the breeze licked my exposed skin.

Chase leaned in and kissed the top of my head before he tightened his grip around me. From the corner of my eye, I noticed the smile on his face had deepened. I rejoiced in the fact that I could make him happy.

During one of our many phone chats leading up to this trip, I had promised him I would do my best not to be so *hard* as he suggested I was.

Minutes later, he insisted on giving me a massage. I didn't mind returning the favor, and he was thrilled to have my hands on him. He always started shit when I tried my hardest to be a good girl.

His ripped muscles pushed against my gliding fingers, taut and rolling and helping the process of setting my lust levels on high. For as much as Chase worked, I didn't know when he found time for the gym, but his body spoke of the time he dedicated.

His skin was buttery soft over muscles that tightened and flexed underneath, making it the perfect combination to highlight his maleness and entice me to explore every part of him. His back when he flexed it just right, made me wet.

There wasn't a part of him I hadn't checked out. The sight of him enticed me to be generous with my affection, groping and caressing all six-foot-four inches of him.

After my detailed exploration, I surveyed his handsome face with the ability to go from innocent to charming to demanding in a heartbeat. However, the emotion I saw reflected in his heavy gaze stopped me. There was enough passion pouring from him that I felt the energy of what he was putting out. Did it mean he saw the same thing from me?

In an attempt to stamp down the unnerving bundle of emotions fluttering in my belly, I kissed him. The heat of our passion tightened its grip on me when I straddled his lap to get closer without breaking our kiss.

When the body contact didn't turn me into a raging inferno of sexual tension, I sensed that something different was happening with us. Sex couldn't rescue me from the torrent of this fantastic storm, and from the looks of it, Chase was caught in the surge.

The intercom buzzed, startling us. We were so lost in each other that the cook, summoning us to dinner, was the only thing to break us apart. He pulled on a T-shirt as I donned my swim cover-up.

We entered the beautiful interior of the yacht and took our seats at the dining table elegantly set for our meal. The full-sized kitchen and dining room, the boat's galley, I had caught a glimpse of earlier, sat off the stairs and opposite the hall leading to the sleeping quarters.

Chase must have informed his staff of my love of seafood, because our dinner consisted of delicious shrimp etouffee over a bed of fluffy white rice, a pot of steamed split lobster tails and scallops, and fluffy seafood biscuits. I didn't know which of us had started the conversation, but we had latched on to the topic of marriage, of all things.

"I don't think a couple needs to be married to be happy. It's just a piece of paper that provides no real purpose that I can see. Think of all the marriages based on everything except love, like financial gain or citizenship. Marriage is no longer looked at like it used to be, nor is it respected like it once was."

He nodded at my argument and prepared to start his own.

"I agree somewhat, but what makes the connection more meaningful is the act of having the ceremony, of sharing your happiness with friends and family, of a couple having their union blessed. It adds more significance to it simply being a piece of paper."

My brows pinched in thought, as I chewed on a piece of the tasty lobster.

"So, you're saying two individuals that are together and not married, their relationship is less meaningful than the ones that have been legally married."

He shook his head at me.

"That's not what I'm saying and you know it. Let's say we've been together a year. We don't have any plans to get married because we're happy just the way we are. However, six months later we decided to get married anyway. Marriage would legalize us, making our union more binding in the public's eye. It says to the world, this is my wife or my husband by law. I'm worth a lot of money and knowing my brother the way that I do, he would sink his claws into every dime I have. With you and I married, all I own would be left to you."

I lifted a brow. The notion that he would leave me everything, although we were speaking in example, had me feeling warm and wanted.

"Okay, you make a good point looking at it from a legal standpoint, but a will is a piece of paper that can do the same thing."

Our healthy debate about whether or not marriage was a necessity in this day and age went on for about thirty minutes. I enjoyed this bantering with him. Most of our phone conversations were the same way, our way of learning about each other's views.

I devoured my meal, savoring the lemon, garlic, and buttery flavors of the lobster sauce dripping over my fingers. I forced myself to consume only half the food because I didn't want to carry around the fullness later. I had resisted Chase sexually, for as long as I could, and there was no telling what would get unleashed when we closed the door to our sleeping quarters.

Judging by the way he watched me, it was safe to say he felt the same.

"I'm going to skip dessert and go and take a shower," I announced, as I marched my fingers across his shoulders on my way. His wide grin and the spark of mischief in his gaze spoke volumes, letting me know he knew what I was thinking about.

Chapter Twenty-Three

Jax

The view from the balcony, the breeze, and the therapeutic sound of the ocean had swept me into a deep state of relaxation. My eyes had fallen closed and the sensation that I was floating and being carried away by the rolling waves had taken over. When I heard Chase entering the room, I eased my eyes open and an automatic smile surfaced. A glance across my shoulder, showed him slipping into the bathroom.

A few burning rays of the sun peeked above the darkening horizon and stole my attention until a set of strong hands slid around my waist and stole it back.

Chase spun me so that my ass kissed the railing. I loved his mountainous size and powerful build. The idea of climbing him, of mounting so much power, of taming all his hard masculinity, and of being able to endure the potency of him, made me breathless.

I didn't intend to stop whatever was about to go down. I'd been waiting for it. He scooped me up with ease and carried me across the threshold of the door like we were a pair of newlyweds.

After he laid me across the oversized bed, he leaned in, not merely staring, but his gaze *bore* into mine, so firm, it froze me in place. A mix of care and concern rested in the depths of his eyes.

"I want to make love to you, Jax." The serious gleam in his eyes stalled any protest I aimed to form. Right now, I didn't want the serious vibe he was giving off. Instead, I wanted to be seriously getting fucked.

"Chase, what are you talking about now? Can we start fucking already?" It had taken me all these years, to figure out that I could even allow someone to fuck me, now he was sounding like Boyz II Men, talking about making love to me. Agitation had started to sneak into my head, causing my lust level to heighten versus lowering.

When he joined me, laying flush against my side, he lavished me with tender kisses to my cheeks and forehead.

"Please, Jax. I want to make love to you."

A deep sigh was released as I rolled my eyes and kept them aimed at the ceiling. I think he enjoyed us being more intimate, like a couple. Maybe, I did too, but this thing between us had me confused and indecisive, two words I fought hard to keep out of my vocabulary.

He slipped his hand under the cover up I had thrown on over my underwear and squeezed my tits with just enough pressure to make me moan. If he fucked me like the first two times, he could name it whatever the hell he wanted.

His lips never stopped caressing various parts of my neck and shoulder, the delicate strokes causing light shivers to radiate through me.

"If you let me make love to you, next time, you get whatever you want," he offered.

This was his way of getting what he wanted. He was willing to face my wrath again just to make love to me. He sucked a small pocket of skin under my ear before he sank delicate teeth into me. My fingers flirted with the soft hairs on his chest despite my hesitation.

"Please," his husky timbre melted on my skin, sending the warm flow across my neck and chest. My breaths quickened, enjoying his play.

He was speaking my language with his bites and sucks, but I wasn't going to make this shit easy. Especially when he was asking me to do what I didn't want to. I rose high on my elbows as his lips chased my neck on the way up.

"If you insist, you're going to have to beg for it. I've always wanted a puppy." My eyes leveled on his. "On the floor and get on your hands and knees and beg." My attempt to look and sound serious was messed up by the smile I couldn't keep off my lips. I enjoyed roleplaying. Before Chase, I almost always had to have it to get my juices flowing. Chase, however, made me want to skip playing so we could get to the good stuff.

His eyes followed the area I pointed to. His tongue slid across his lips as his dick jumped against my thigh. Instead of being offended, or even hurt by my request, his lips turned up into a grin.

He kissed my stomach on the way, sliding off the bottom of the bed to the floor. I rose and scooted to the edge to get a better view of him on all fours. With his glasses discarded; his big green eyes sparkled with anticipation.

I stood, glaring down on him. My intentions were expressed when I slipped my cover up, off and tossed it. I was left in my thin red bra and panties. Like a good little doggy, his warm wet tongue slid up the side of my leg, tracing a portion of the vine tatted there.

"You are the only one I ever wanted to make love to. The only woman I want to cherish. To worship."

His eyes flashed heat, his soft words were dissolving my resistance, and his scorching tongue blazed a trail up the side of my calf that elicited a fiery need. I may have initiated the begging, but, like I was learning, Chase was never going to fully submit to anyone. He was working me slow. If making love would be this hot, maybe it wasn't such a bad idea.

I ruffled the top of his hair before reaching under and rubbing his belly for effect. At my action, he stifled a grin. I retook my stance, turned on by my elevated position over him.

"Since you're such a good little beggar. This is a one-time only treat. Do you hear me?" I fought not to laugh, shaking a stiff finger at him for effect. "I'm going to need you to be a good boy and not beg for this anymore after today."

"*Ruff, Ruff,*" he barked, causing me to laugh out loud. This moment had started out as me attempting to flex my ego, but it had turned into a precious silly one that I could look back on and smile about.

My breath caught when his eager tongue slid the rest of the way up my leg and stopped at my inner thigh, under the flowing heat of my pussy. His hand followed and didn't stop until it had slid across the swell of my ass and had gotten a good grip on the top of my underwear.

He tugged them down until his face was back at my throbbing heat. The caressing warmth from his mouth rained across my pulsing center before his tongue reached out, slid across my piercing, and brushed my clit.

"Fuck," escaped on an exhausted breath and a full body shiver. The man knew what my pussy needed.

A few more flicks and a push and Chase had me spread across his bed panting and staring at him in helpless anticipation. When he dipped his face back between my legs, he feasted on me, sucking my lips, as his twirling tongue massaged my inner walls.

His mouth and my pussy had a special connection. Only he could get me off with his superb, tongue action without my intervening words or selfish pelvic maneuvering. My body and his mind meshed well, either knowing what the other wanted.

My head fell against the cushiony mattress and my entire body sighed with breath-heaving relief at the feel of his tongue, so heavenly and sinful sliding into me. *God.* He knew how to get me blazing hot.

My shortened breaths kept getting caught in my throat as my chest heaved. The fingers of my right hand sank into his silky hair and got a good grip while the nails of my left stabbed at the covers. *His tongue.* Tight twirls, sensual slides, long and deep strokes, and languid licks. It took mere minutes and he had me about to…

"Oh fuck!" My heart galloped in my chest, mimicking the pounding hoofbeats of a prized stallion in full stride. On the cusp of exploding, I started shoving my pussy in his face, desperate to seek out the pleasure he unleashed.

"Chase. Shit. Don't you dare fucking stop!"

He eased my legs wider as he tunneled deeper into me. I desperately wanted a peek at the image of him getting me off with his tongue and how he moved it to get my juices flowing so freely. However, I was wedged so deep in desire, I was unable to lift my head.

The orgasm struck so hard, I feared I would fall apart from the jolts of pleasure quaking through me. "You're fucking me so good with your tongue! Magic!" My compliments spilled out a mile a minute before my mind numbed, and I sizzled with explicit pleasure.

Chase didn't give me time to come down. He slid his shorts off and fitted his strong body above mine. His hand slid between the tight space of my back and the mattress, his fingers raking my skin before he located the clamp and undid my bra. His actions were delivered all while his mouth made love to mine.

His hard thickness nudged the inside of my thigh before his shaft teased my greedy core.

Once he got my bra off, he dropped it over the side of the bed and proceeded with manipulating my body. Every part of him was used to stimulate me. His legs massaged mine. His tongue played a slippery game with mine. It was like he had four hands as they massaged my ass one moment, my tits the next, and even managed to get a hold of and grip my hair, setting it free of the ponytail it had been in.

When he lifted himself and his thick dick licked across my piercing and sat at my entrance, my eyes flew wide open.

"Chase, what are you doing?" Breathless, my hand found a way to his chest.

"I'm about to make love to you."

I cleared my throat. "Aren't you forgetting something?" One of my eyebrows rose high on my forehead. "Like a condom?"

He shook his head. "No."

What the fuck does he mean, no? My inner voice sounded like she had an attitude over this shit.

The heat he had built up within me, was dissolving into a simmering boil as he slid his hardness against my dripping wet lips and brushed over the source of my heat. I was getting lost in the sensation again, but my senses snapped back in a flash and I tensed.

"Chase, what the fuck do you mean, no?"

"Please, Jax. I want to make love to you without anything between us. I know you're on the pill, I've seen you taking them?"

The man knew *all* of my damn business, probably knew which doctor had prescribed my pills. And I'd allowed him the freedom to peek freely into my life.

"Yeah, but…" I couldn't believe he was asking me this. "I've never…"

"Been with someone unprotected," he finished my sentence. "Allow me to be the first. Please."

The sorrowful glint in his eyes complimented the sincerity in his tone, the combination dredging up an endearing spark in me, and stirring a part of me I thought unreachable. He kissed me again and rubbed his tempting dick all over my pussy, spreading my wetness with the head, making more wetness seep out with each swipe.

"Please. I'll stop with the lame stuff afterward. I want to know what it's like to be with you this way." His hot whispers in my ear fueled the need he was building in me, making my body respond with desperate waves against his.

Why was Chase putting me under this type of pressure, while his hard length stroked my pussy? To add more weight to his persuasive actions, he flashed me the full force of his hypnotizing eyes.

He gripped my jaw so that I couldn't turn away from the deep impact of his gaze. "Jax, I've never wanted this with anyone else. I've never wanted anyone the way I want you."

God, he was making me weak. His lips covered mine, caressing my mouth deep and sensually.

"Yes," I murmured against his kiss, causing him to draw back to make sure he'd heard me right.

With our eyes locked, his hand slid along the side of my body before reaching between us. He raised up enough to take a hold of his dick and positioned it against my sopping wet heat. The swollen head shoved at my opening as his powerful gaze imprisoned mine.

"You want this dick? Tell me you want it."

Fuck, he was driving me nuts as the tip teased my slick lips, calling my flowing juices to the surface.

"I want it. I want your dick." I breathed my words out over a rushed whisper.

At my admission, he added enough pressure that the tip entered, and I could feel the head breaking apart my raging heat. The moment had arrived, he was entering me, and I was letting him do it without a condom. A prayer echoed some place in the back of my mind, one of hope that I wasn't making the biggest mistake of my life.

He kept pushing but didn't force it. Instead, he glided in with a long thrust that took a blessed lifetime to end. It was so damn good my mouth fell open and my head dipped to the side. I swear, a tear slipped past my clenched eyelids. I had never experienced anything so all-consuming in my life.

"Jax," he whispered my name like it was a fresh breath to his starved lungs.

Once he was planted deep, he paused, relishing the heightened state of us being joined with no restrictions.

"Is this okay?"

What kind of question was that? He knew damn well it was okay.

"Yes," I finally answered.

He drew half out and instead of another long thrust, he shoved into me with such slow and meaningful intent, I synced with his movements, latching on to the slow hypnotic rhythm. I was being taken by pure sensation. Feelings. Emotions.

I had never experienced this type of sensational tension that was driving me mad one moment and filling me with pleasure the next.

"I think I'm obsessed with you, Jax," he whispered. He kept going, kept on feeding me pleasure like he hadn't said what he had just said.

"What? What are you s-s-saying?" His words were as alarming as the emotions he was pouring into me. The rest of the story I was too afraid to hear was reflected in the intensity of his gaze. There was a song playing in his eyes, a beautiful silent melody that sang to my heart, unique and only for me. He was scaring me, but at the same time making me acknowledge feelings I never knew I was capable of experiencing.

He kissed me with the same slow intensity he worked my body with, and I loved every minute of it. His hands roamed as he bathed my skin with his tongue, my neck, my shoulders, and my chest.

He cupped my full breast with light squeezes, tugged my nipples between his teeth, and toyed with my nipple-piercing with his tongue. Every touch ignited and sent raging heat to the rest of my erogenous zones. How did he know? How could he know my body like this?

Everywhere he stroked sparked emotions that tightened our connection, melding us together in a way that we may never be pulled apart. He did an exceptional job of capturing me so completely I was aware of every kiss, touch, and thrust.

We had connected sexually. We had connected with explicit lust. But this? This was something capable of making us go against every principle we had set for ourselves. This could steal away our control for good. This was the kind of connection that had you busting windshields out of cars and peeking into windows in the middle of the night.

Control had been relinquished because we had given into a bond stronger than us. I was convinced that Chase was expressing through his body how he felt about me. The deep hard thrusts reflected how intensely he was falling for me. The shallow ones reflected the tender caresses of a friend, willing to lend me a shoulder or ear when I needed it. The deep lingering thrusts sparked a dash of pain, revealing he was in tune with the darker side of sex. When he backed all the way out, sat the head at my opening, and pounded into me with maximum force, he was proving he was very much in control of his actions. He was letting me know he could be everything I needed, but I needed to be willing to let him.

"You feel incredible. So wet. So hot. Perfect." The sensual heat of his words wound into my ear and added to our sexual energy that saturated the room.

He settled on the deep lingering thrusts for a moment, his powerful leg muscles flexing against my quivering inner thighs. The long pounding thrusts got me sopping wet as I fought to keep from clawing the skin off his back.

He knew what I craved and would enjoy most. The man could sling dick like nobody's business, but I didn't think he realized the extent of the emotional effect he had on me. I was linked into something much deeper than our amazing sex and found myself embracing the notion for the first time. My grip around Chase was so tight, I could feel myself shaking against his body, yet it still didn't feel tight enough.

His every rolling thrust created spine-tingling aches as fiery sparks of emotion consumed me, turning my mind into a realm of lit fireworks. I teetered on the edge of orgasm; the sharp currents were strong enough I feared they would stop my heart.

Filled up with mental and physical pleasure, I was reduced to a weeping mess as my lazy moans filled the room. The few understandable words I managed to squeeze between gasps were, "Chase. Chase. Shit, Chase. Fuck."

Covered by his full body, he used every part of himself to stimulate me. He sent me soaring straight into the stars, my body shooting off like a probe sent to explore space. I embraced my perfect death, clinging to Chase as he followed me into the sensational crossover that shattered reality.

We remained stuck together for what seemed like hours, breathing, meditating, committing our lovemaking to memory.

When he eased out, I was too satiated to move, not even a flutter from my eyes seemed possible.

He positioned himself at my back and spooned me. Once he draped his arms around me, he squeezed, securing me in his hold, unwilling to allow me to run away from the connection I could no longer deny. This was a new revelation for me. I breathed in the undeniable magic I had never shared with another, the intoxication of it lulling away my apprehension.

His lips brushed the back of my neck, and his warm breath caressed me as much as his embrace. A deep breath filled me with fresh air and allowed me to relax into Chase's warmth.

"Would you like to talk now? You're good and relaxed, and I meant what I said about wanting us to be the kind of couple who communicated with each other. Sometimes it feels like we are living our relationship in reverse. We touched the hot uncontrolled passion first, then the spine-breaking sex, and now something more meaningful. However, it doesn't matter how we got here, as long as we're here. You can tell me anything."

A strained pause followed the tension creeping back in, but he squeezed me to him, chasing away my anxiety, until I relaxed again.

"Why are you so afraid to talk to me?" He breathed against my hair. "By now you should know I would never do anything to hurt you."

His words were meant to calm me, but my determined mind dredged up wicked sins from the past, causing me to coil like a viper ready to strike.

"Please, Chase, can we go to sleep?"

"Okay but let me say this first: You are not your past. It impacted your life, but it doesn't make you the you that you are now. I know it's easier said than done, but don't allow who you were, to interfere with who you're becoming. You're amazing, a breath of fresh air to me at a time when I found myself suffocating and waiting for the day that my heart turned cold. You may not think so, may not have even noticed, but you have a lot to offer in a relationship. You've offered me friendship, compassion, laughter, support, and advice. You make me happy."

His warm lips brushed my cheek before he settled into a relaxed position, pulling me into his chest.

"I'm not going to hurt you." He squeezed me securely against him, the tight caress provided a relaxing warmth I enjoyed.

"Says your mouth," I replied.

"Says my heart," came his simple response.

Dammit Chase!

His words clasped around my heart so tight, I choked down a sob. Although my mind fought it, I believed he deserved to know more about my history.

I swallowed hard. I was scared, and I wasn't afraid to admit it to myself. I was shouldering some massive shit. Something capable of keeping me from embracing my emotions fully. I believe Chase sensed that.

He placed his lips to my ears. "Whenever you're ready. I'm not going anywhere."

Chapter Twenty-Four

Chase

Jax turned and placed a sweet kiss on my lips before she sat up, reached over, and turned on the lamp. I lifted and placed her pillow so that it would cushion her back before cushioning my back to the headboard. An awkward silence stretched between us as we sat, staring straight ahead. I didn't have to ask to know that her inner turmoil was stirring.

"You were right, Chase. You should know more about my history, and why I'm afraid to talk about it. I trust you, Chase."

She went quiet again, but the emphasis she had placed on the word *trust* wasn't missed.

"The first time I overheard my mother say she never wanted kids I was five." Her voice trembled with a vulnerability she rarely showed.

"The first time I overheard her tell one of her girlfriends she wanted the abortion, my father talked her out of getting it, I was seven. The first time she wished I were never born, I was eight. It became pretty clear, even in my young mind, my mother didn't want me. She was a party girl, born to a wealthy family, the Ramos' who disowned her when she became pregnant with me at eighteen.

Her words soaked into me as I sat tensed with anticipation, and a touch of fear for where the story might go.

"The plan was for her to finish college, and then marry one of the wealthy suitors her family would pick out for her.

Instead, my mother had chosen my father. At the time, I think she may have loved him, but he was poor, a part-time college student who had decided to go into the police academy."

Based on the blank stare set adrift in her eyes and the tension that crinkled the corners, she was struggling to sort through the tough memories.

"I think her pregnancy became the turning point. My father had always wanted me and made every effort to show me he loved me. He worked hard because that was the type of man he was. Most of my young life he worked two jobs, one as a cop, the other as a security guard, to make sure we had everything we needed. But my mother, having been raised spoiled and entitled, wanted what her friends had. Designer clothes, fancy cars, and social status. Looking back at it, I believed she was pathologically obsessed with having money and status.

"She used me several times, attempting to wiggle her way back into her family's life. Dressing me up and flaunting me in front of them, like a prized show pony. But, like her, they didn't want anything to do with me. She often left me and my father, sometimes weeks at a time. He had to hire a nanny to take care of me whenever she did because he had no immediate family. My mother would eventually return, and my father would take her back every time."

Jax absently scratched her head, her stare cast against the wall as she sorted through what was likely a mountain of emotions and recollections. I watched her like a hawk, studying her every move and gesture as her face transformed from stressed to impassive.

"My mother had grown into this wicked woman, filled with hate and resentment. She yearned for the life she believed me and my father had stripped away from her. She didn't have a maternal bone in her body. There was no help with homework, hugs at night, or bedtime stories. All the love and care I ever received came from my father. Unfortunately, his law enforcement career meant long and demanding hours that kept him away and was also our only source of income."

"In addition to the hate and resentment my mother aimed at me and my father, she was also a cheat. I suspected my father knew about it for a while, and finally grew tired of it, so they decided to divorce. My mother had never wanted me, so I believed her threat to take my father to court for custody was out of spite. She knew that separating me from him would hurt us both."

Her head fell back, her concentrated gaze aimed at the ceiling. I was reluctant to disturb her, but the deeper she dug into the memories, the more her body started to knot with tension.

"I was the happiest on the days, or weekends I spent with my father. The only time I felt loved was when I was with him. He would sit and talk with me like I was a little adult, asking about my week and all that I had done while we were apart. He would take me out to the movies, the park, game rooms, everything a kid looked forward to that my mother never bothered with.

"When my mother wasn't leaving me alone in the house to sneak off with her friends, she was belittling me about everything from my darker complexion, to my quiet nature, to my being ugly because I looked like my father. She hated everything about me. She didn't want me, but she didn't want my father to have me more. She drilled it in my head that love didn't exist, and promised it was as made up as the tooth fairy."

When her breaths started to quicken and the weight of her past appeared to push down on her, I ensured she knew I was there by pressing the right side of my body to the left of hers.

"My mother never gave up the quest to live the life she believed she deserved. Instead of working a normal job, she opted for one that would provide her fast money. She hooked up with a seedy producer that helped her launch her own porn site. The money made her happy for a while, as she could afford the material possessions she sought, and showed off to her entitled friends."

Her mother's type was a constant in my circle. Unfortunately for some, they were raised to only seek out and associate with the social elite.

"It wasn't drugs or alcohol, but my mother's greed, and her need to fit into a certain social status that became her obsession. She was willing to do anything and hurt anybody to get what she wanted. When she figured out, she could make more money by introducing a featured guest on her show, she looked to *me*."

"No." I choked out; the word barely audible. I prayed her mother wasn't crazy enough to carry out what I think Jax was clearly implying. Jax never wrung her hands, so when she started, I sat my hand atop hers, feeling the light tremble in them.

"Here. Take my hand." My tight grip didn't ease the anxiety that had a tight hold on her.

"She did a weekly mother-daughter show, where she made me…p-p-perform…"

Her trembling top lip was pinched into the bottom, as she struggled with how to release the memory. I eased closer, unwilling to let her relive the horror of her past without knowing that I was there for her.

She'd been molested by her mother on film and forced to perform sexual acts, all while knowing she was being watched by a sick audience. People who didn't see abuse. Ones who used a child's torture for sexual gratification. Only a monster from the deepest pits of hell was capable of forcing a child to endure such horror.

"She would beat me if I didn't do what she wanted. She didn't care if the acts hurt, didn't care if I screamed, yelled, or begged. My pain and torture was a part of the show."

She choked down a series of sniffles before swiping at her flowing tears. The story had my nerves so torn apart, it had my stomach queasy and clenching. I started to suffocate on the grief I felt for her, pulling in deep inhales and blowing out harsh exhales

"Each time I disobeyed, didn't perform to her standards, or protested the things she did to me, she made the one threat I was most afraid of. She promised she would pack me up and take me back to Venezuela where I would never see my father again. He'd always been all I ever loved because he'd been the one in my life to make me feel important and wanted. The one who had shown me I was worthy of being loved. My relationship with my father meant more to me than anything, and she knew it. I was too naïve to know that she was using my relationship with him to keep me in line. I didn't tell anyone about my abuse, especially not my father."

In the moment, I was her listening ear and shoulder, but Jax needed more.

"She hurt me badly, Chase. So, so bad." She spoke through her cries. "The first time I had sex at seventeen, I didn't even have my virginity to give, because my mother took it. It was captured on film as entertainment."

Dear God in Heaven.

Jax's eyes were deep pools of sorrow, the depth being filled with the blood spilling from my ripped apart heart. She stared at me, but at a glance, I sensed that she was blinded by the memory of her mother's horrific abuse. The grief heavy in her eyes told me it was ten times worse than what she could describe. The pain of it emanated from her trembling body. She had survived an unimaginable darkness, one that pulled apart a person's soul.

I moved to kneel in front of her and glanced through the haze of sorrow clouding my eyes. The pain etched in her face, the hurt that seeped through every syllable of her words, put a death grip on my heart.

"Why did she hate me so much?" Her watery gaze was on mine, her chin trembled as she fought to contain her crushing emotions. I couldn't answer her question. No one could.

"I don't know, baby. I don't know. She was a rotten horrible person. Come here."

She recoiled from my proximity. Her retelling of her horrific past likely had her questioning me wanting her.

"Nothing about your past will ever chase me away Jax. I need you to believe me."

She nodded, biting her lips, and avoiding my eyes, her body rocking back and forth. Her sorrow had imprisoned her, locking her behind impenetrable bars of sadness. I would find a way to break her out because seeing her this way had taken my will to be free without her.

I lifted her into my arms before adjusting us on the bed. Pulling her into a tight hold, I planted her head against my chest. She released some of the pent-up emotions she carried, through body racking cries. She shook so hard; I was afraid she might break. The heartbreaking tone of her cries raised goosebumps on my arms. Hot tears stung the backs of my eyes, and I allowed them to spill freely as I clung to her.

"I should have found a way to make her stop. Why didn't I make her stop?"

She wept, deep and hard, her body jerking within my arms, as her tears wet my chest. God, I wish I knew how to take her pain away. The ache of her deepest sorrow had made a home in her heart. The pain of her past remained, and I sensed she felt it as deeply as she had when it happened to her. Now, I understood her need for control, and her unwillingness to forge relationships.

You never knew the true depths of someone else's pain, the closest you could get was through loving them. Jax carried around a hell I wouldn't wish on anyone, but her strength had endured and allowed her to carry the heavy burden that could have destroyed her.

The story also brought to light why she was never inclined to speak about her mother, or her childhood. It explained why she couldn't find peace in sleep. Having her picture taken or being filmed was a trigger, a reminder of the physical, and mental torture she had suffered at the hands of her own mother.

After a moment, her cries dwindled, leaving our mingling breaths and her chest racking sniffs. We clung to each other until her sniffles died down and the rhythm of our breaths made the only sound.

She backed out of my hold, regaining the strength she'd let slip. Unwilling to let her go fully, I used my thumb to wipe away her tears. I didn't care if she saw my puffy, tear-filled eyes or heard my weeping sniffs. She needed to know I cared. That I felt a touch of the hurt she had suffered, and the pain that still punished her.

"Jax, baby, you were a child. You didn't do anything wrong. There was no way you could fight what was happening to you. It wasn't your responsibility to make it stop. It should never have happened." My quick breaths rushed out in fits and starts. My ability to control my emotions was ripped away, but I fought to remain strong for her.

"She messed me up. I can't hardly connect with people. Have difficulty forming friendships. Having a camera of any kind aimed at me makes me nervous. What she did to me, chases me in my sleep, and sometimes while I'm awake. Some days, I can't even stand to look at my own body."

She fingered the part of the tattoo starting on her hand.

"I started off cutting myself. I didn't understand why I was doing it, but the pain was a tolerable one that I endured, because I was in control of it. I didn't stop the cutting, until I started getting tattooed. I begged my father to let me get my first tattoo at fifteen. He said no, but I sneaked off and got it anyway, just to see if it would take the edge off my anxieties."

Her hands brushed caringly over the tattoos on her arm. I think the tattoos and her piercings were some type of healing balm in some way.

"Tattoos are the scars we choose. They hurt, but they scab over and heal, leaving only the beauty behind. These tattoos are a reflection of what I wanted to see in myself. Something beautiful and meaningful."

She unconsciously fingered the start of the tattoo on her wrist. "Looking in the mirror, and seeing my naked body was an unpleasant experience for me. The sight made me feel dirty and nasty. Sleazy. My tattoos have become more than just pretty body art, it's like my protective cover."

Pain thundered through her like a freight train, the telling signs radiating from the heavy glint in her eyes and tense set of her body. All I had to offer as relief were soothing words and a caring embrace. I shook my head, but nothing could shake away the horrific images of a younger Jax being tortured by her mother.

"After this had gone on for quite some time, my father became suspicious. Since my mother didn't work, her new car, clothes, and jewelry were a red flag. She would tell him they were gifts from her rich boyfriends. From the age of nine to twelve, she used me in her films. A few months after my twelfth birthday, is when the shit hit the fan. My father figured out what she was doing to me. When I visited him, he started noticing that I was withdrawn, sad, and not my usual self around him. I would lie to him about how I got certain bruises when he found them. I guess he started watching me closer than I realized.

"My mother was a part of a group of porn stars, working under the umbrella of a shady internet producer that knew how to keep the films underground. He had set it up so that only exclusive members knew how to gain access to the type of illegal porn they sold.

"This is another reason why the media attention terrifies me. Not knowing when or if someone that saw me then, would recognize me now. Not knowing how many of those recordings were saved by that sick audience. Are they still watching that sad and broken girl as a way to heighten their dark, sexual desires?"

I searched her eyes for some respite but found none.

"Since my father was in law enforcement, he had access to the type of resources needed to investigate my mother. He had done enough digging to track down members of the underground pornography ring. With the evidence he found, he sent a lot of people to jail. The night he confronted my mother about me, she denied any wrongdoing. She told my father:

"What I'm doing is payback for you, and that brat, messing up my life. I told you I didn't want her. I wanted to have an abortion, but you, you wanted her, begged me to keep her. This is your fucking fault."

"After her rant about me being my father's fault, I watched as he started strangling her. I believe until this day that he truly didn't know the woman he had married and had a child with. I harbored so much hate for her, I didn't feel an ounce of sorrow, nor did I help when she reached in my direction. I backed away from her flapping arms. By the time my father blinked away his rage and loosened his grip on her neck, her tongue was hanging

214 · KETA KENDRIC

out of her mouth and her body had gone limp. He placed his body between me and hers when I asked if she was dead."

My teeth sank deep into my bottom lip, fighting to keep my composure and hoping Jax couldn't read the satisfaction I felt at the knowledge of her mother's suffering. For the first time in my life, I hoped for another human's death.

"My father took me to my neighbors, telling me he and my mom had to talk when she woke up. I was twelve, I knew she was dead, and I think my father knew it too. He picked me up from the neighbors the next morning and told me that I would be staying with him. He and I rarely talk about my mother. She is still a tough subject for us after all this time. Although I asked after my mother a few times, we never spoke of the last moments I saw her or what happened to her afterwards. My father made sure I talked to several child psychiatrists back then, about what my mother had done to me. I don't believe it helped.

"My father said my mother was the wickedest seed he had ever encountered. He beat himself up for being blind to the evil within her and for leaving me with her. Even now, I can tell he's still haunted by what happened to me. He can be a bit over-protective at times, conducting background checks on anyone he suspects me dating. He is convinced that I'm living proof the most wicked people have the ability to produce roots that grow into beauty and perfection. His words have always stuck, but not in the positive way he intended them to."

My face creased, attempting to understand.

"I was planted in pure evil, so when I took root, I grew from the wicked source, fed from it, lived and thrived within it. Since, I'm the root of the wicked, I must be evil too. It's what I have always believed. My mother was a beautiful woman on the outside, so no one, not even my father suspected how truly evil she was on the inside. I vowed to do everything in my power to keep the evil she planted within me from destroying others. The fear of someone finding out my secret. Having to explain why I'd rather lurk in the background than be in the spotlight. The anxiety issues. It's too much baggage. So, it has always been easy not to have long-term relationships.

"It wasn't until I was old enough to understand it and after more therapy sessions, my father forced me into, that I realized I also avoided friendships, mainly with women. Until you, I believed control was *the* way to keep people from getting too close. You have been the only person I have been with long-term, and although I sense a change in me, I'm still afraid for you Chase. What if I snap and become like her?"

"Baby, you're not evil. You're not going to snap. Your self-sacrificing behavior is all the proof you need. A truly evil person wouldn't care about protecting others. Only someone with a caring heart, would sacrifice the possibility of happiness to protect someone."

She sat in silence, thinking on my words before she continued.

"Although my father has repeatedly sent me to therapy, it never sticks. I never want to talk about it or face how my mother's actions have impacted me. How being exposed to the world on film at such an impressionable age has affected me. Some nights I wake up drenched in sweat, reliving every sick detail. No one wants to deal with someone that broken up inside. Do you even want me now that you know the disgusting things that was done to me by my own mother?"

I palmed her face, turning her to me.

"There is nothing that has happened or that you can say that will chase me away. I'm here for you, whatever you need, whatever you want to talk about. I'm never going to stop wanting you. No matter what. Do you hear me Jax?"

She nodded.

I squeezed her to me, hoping she believed me and felt the strength of my words through my caress. When she returned my embrace with strength and nuzzled her face in my neck, I believed it was her way of reassuring me that she had accepted my words. We sat in the embrace for minutes before she let go.

She had bared secrets that had held her captive. Her warm tears spilled over my fingertips as I swiped them from below her puffy eyes. She swallowed, attempting to hold back the sadness that continued to grip her.

Through the tears, a smile tinged with relief eased onto her face, the sight warming my insides. I placed my lips against her ear.

"I'll always have your best interest at heart. I'll always do my best to protect you. I would do anything to take away the pain I know you feel."

My words squeezed past the tightness in my throat, and escaped the thick sorrow pressing down on me. I kissed the top of her hair and squeezed her even tighter.

"Thank you for sharing this with me. I'm sorry you had to suffer through such a traumatic time with the one person who should have encouraged and loved you. Your father was right. You're nothing like that despicable woman, and no matter what kind of seed you came from, you took root and grew into someone smart, beautiful, and loving."

I brushed a soothing stroke along her arms and back attempting to but knowing that nothing I did would ease away the deep well of sorrow she had to pull from. She needed to come to terms with what had happened in her past.

The notion that she was sparing others from the kind of evil her mother had tortured her with, she was willing to sacrifice her own happiness. But, that was only a part of it. She feared having to share with anyone what had happened to her. She feared what would show up in films from the past. Being with me was a hazard to someone with a phobia of being filmed. And Yet, there were still more layers to her story.

Did she not want to love anyone else because she feared it would be used against her, like her mother had used her father, to keep her locked into a horrific situation?

Did she blame herself for how her mother had turned out? What about her mother's family, since their decision to disown her put Jax in the she-devil's wicked path? There was also the tattoos and piercings I believe she used as therapy and cover, something to shield her from a past she hadn't gotten over, or truly confronted. What took her father so long to figure out what was going on with his daughter? Jax had shouldered a lot of the blame for her past when she was the only blameless person in the entire situation.

"If you would like to go to therapy again, I'll help you. It may help you deal with the hurt and confront the mental pain that you're suffering through. I'll go with you if you want me to."

She nodded. "To be honest, I've given it a lot of thought in the past few years. I know what demons are Chase, and I also know that I am far from being healed. For the sake of my future, I have to confront my past. I've been planning to find someone to talk to. As you said, I need help. I need to focus on getting myself together enough to be normal."

My fingertips brushed her cheek. "Look at me Jax." When she did, the endless depth of sorrow in her eyes put my emotions in a chokehold. "You are normal. There is nothing wrong with you. Talking to someone that may be able to help you sort through your feelings doesn't equate to wrong, or abnormal."

The crease of her smile deepened before she leaned in and placed a sweet kiss on my neck.

Patience had gotten me this far with her, and I believed it was the key ingredient to help me help her heal. I pressed my lips against her forehead before I tightened the hold I had on her.

"I'm here for you. To talk. To listen. To support you. Whatever you need."

She lifted her head enough to capture my gaze. The warmth that surfaced in her expression this time stopped my spiel. I would be everything this woman ever wanted because she had always been everything I ever needed.

Chapter Twenty-Five

Chase

I stood at the side of the bed, studying Jax while she slept. She hadn't called out or twitched once in her sleep last night. Was it a sign that her healing had begun? Her trusting me enough to share her horrific past meant more than she could ever know. She needed help, and I wasn't naïve enough to think that I was enough.

As far as our relationship, there was no denying our connection, but I don't believe she was aware of, how deeply she had embedded herself into my blood. She had tattooed an indelible imprint on my heart that would never be removed.

An annoying and uncomfortable idea crept into my head. I had revealed in the heat of uncontrolled passion that I was obsessed with her. A part of me knew I had spoken the truth, knew that I was willing to do anything for her, but letting it slip had been a mistake. Hearing her story had only amplified that feeling.

She stirred and I jumped back, pretending to walk in. "Hey, sleepy head." I handed her the glass of orange juice I was holding.

"Chase," she uttered what had become her greeting for me. Her gaze met mine, and left my words hanging in my throat. After making love to her last night, my feelings had grown into something I was sure I couldn't hide anymore. I also knew her well enough that she wasn't going to tolerate me feeling sorry for her, but her story had gutted me.

"Breakfast is ready if you're hungry."

"I'm starving."

She sat up and sipped from the juice. Unable to stop my probing gaze, it dropped to her perky tits.

"Let me take a quick shower first," she said, smiling at where I had aimed my eyes. I had already showered, but it didn't stop me from wanting to join her. However, I resisted the urge because I had asked enough of her.

Last night had meant more than I could explain to Jax. It meant more than being CEO of Swift Capital, more than the prestigious titles and accolades given to me, more than all the money in the world.

Jax had taken possession of me when she walked into my meeting. She had taken my mind the night in the hotel. Last night, she had taken all of me, and I don't believe she realized it.

After breakfast we relaxed in what I learned was her favorite part of the yacht, the atrium. I tugged off my T-shirt and took the lounge chair next to her in my swim shorts. I gawked as she stripped off her swim cover-up, revealing a tiny royal blue bikini that highlighted a body with the power to drive me insane. I was left unable to pull my eyes away and she knew it.

The entire time she stripped, she kept her eyes on me. Walking past her chair, she approached and stood above mine.

"Let me help you with that sunscreen," she offered.

I swiped the bottle and handed it up to her.

"Help me with anything you want." My restless gaze followed the tattoo up her leg, across her thigh, up her side, and to the underside of her tit, until my gaze returned to hers. She didn't move an inch until my greedy eyes were fed.

She sprayed until the sunscreen wet her palms and rubbed me down so good, I swore I was approaching the rush of a climax.

My offer to help her apply her sunscreen was ignored when she straddled my chair before sitting and positioning herself across my lap. Immediately, my dick tented in my shorts and pressed into the warm inside of her thigh. Hot spikes of need coursed through my hard length and caused the leaking head to ache despite her weight pressing down on it.

Grinding into me, I moaned under the movement of her warm sensuality. She gripped my chin and turned my face to hers. Her commanding ways didn't allow her to see what was right in front of her face.

I was under her spell, had fallen for her so deep I couldn't see straight. She could easily find the telltale signs in my eyes. She only needed to listen to my erratic breathing every time she came near me, or the way my heart pounded when she touched me. The chaotic beat had set to a unique rhythm that only occurred for her.

For now, she could think whatever she wanted. I think she was operating under the guise that we were still warring for control, but that line had been destroyed.

"It's my turn, Chase, and you know I like to push things way too far." She flashed a wicked smirk. The determined glint in her eyes reinforced her words. She was about to fuck my head up worse than it already was. However, after last night, I believed she was capable of more than she projected through her tough words and aggressive actions. It had taken a tremendous amount of strength for her to tell me about her childhood, and although she was determined not to show it, I knew that she was mentally drained.

Her kiss started with a tender caress until the sharp pinch of her teeth sank into my bottom lip and hit me like a punch.

The ache slid down my throat. As quickly as she shot blissful agony into me, her hot pussy turned on my dick and promised it more pleasure. It was so hard, it throbbed with the heavy need she evoked and only she could drive away.

Her soft lips sat against my ear. "We are going to play a little roleplaying game. It's a simple one since we don't have any props to play with."

She glanced instinctively behind us before continuing. I'm going to fuck you right here, right now and all you have to do is keep your shit together."

An involuntary shiver churned in my stomach, and my breath quickened to keep up with my screaming pulse. Her hand slid from my chin, down my chest, and between our bodies. She ripped apart the opening of my swim shorts and stuck her warm hand inside. When her hand wrapped around my length, my mouth fell open, but I didn't dare spit out a word.

Her hulking gaze remained on me, stalking me like prey, waiting for me to call attention to our play. I hadn't a clue as to what she'd do if I failed, however, she'd instilled in me an urgent need to find out what was coming next.

The waving, dark waters of the Atlantic, the breeze, and the eighty-degree temperature cast the perfect setting. While her hand worked my hard shaft, her eyes drifted away from mine for a look around the main body of the yacht.

She slipped her bikini bottom to the side and raised up, hovering her pussy above my dick. I didn't know if I could sit there and take it, not from Jax. There was a vast mental and physical difference in being inside her with no condom, and I rejoiced in the fact that she wasn't about to use one.

The tip dipped into her warm tight grip, causing me to rest my head on her shoulder, and I released a deep groan. I did my best to swallow my gasps as my fingers pressed into her arm with a bruising force. It didn't go down smoothly as a choking grunt escaped.

Her fingers retook my chin as she hovered in place with the tip of my dick inside her. "Look at me, Chase. I want to see your every reaction, while I'm fucking you."

She wasn't going to make this game of hers easy. I was already on the verge of losing it, and she wasn't going to stop until I lost it.

When she sat down on my length with slow ease, a sensational tingle took a hold, capturing me in its maddening grip. Her inner walls pulsed around me, and her slippery heat coated me. I moaned as the resistance pressed against my dick the deeper it went.

My head fell back against the chair as my breaths hitched in fits and starts.

"Look at me Chase. I want those eyes on me."

She rolled her hips with such slow pressure her name fell like a slow drip from my mouth. "Jax."

She leaned in and kissed me, sending her tongue deep into my mouth as she worked me even harder below. My grip fell from her arm before I tightened my hand around her waist.

Her wicked actions had my emotions all over the place. One moment I was into the sex, my mind latching on to how good it felt to be deep inside her, the next, my emotions would rise to the surface and deepen our connection. The urge to tell her how I was feeling surfaced, but the fear of scaring her away stalled it.

When she spread her legs wider, it allowed me to go deeper, and I didn't know how much more I could take. A loud gasp escaped as I fought to keep from shouting the army of curse words resting on my tongue.

The commanding power she held over me was an unrelenting force that I respected and hated. I wanted us to find a balance in our relationship. One where she wouldn't have to prove her ability to control me.

The pleasure was a monster who ate my control piece by piece. The agony of keeping it together when all I wanted was to fall apart left me in the best kind of distress, jittery and aching all over with pleasure.

"Do you feel how wet my pussy is? Do you feel how deep inside me you are? I want your hot cum inside me right fucking now."

Her sinful words had undone me, the fiery spark of our passion had melted my mind. I came so hard, I lost mental focus, as I gripped her ass and tugged her hard against me.

Harsh and ragged, my words rushed out. "Jax, fuck. You're driving me insane."

A series of shivers I failed to overcome ripped through my body. I made a feeble attempt to shake off the lightheadedness I felt, and for a second feared I might pass out.

Jax had fucked me into oblivion, and I was helpless to do anything but enjoy every second of it. When she moved to climb off me, I kept her in place, unable to bear the thought of letting her go.

"Stay here for a minute. Please."

She indulged my request, allowing me more time to stay linked into our connection.

"Jax."

She stopped me, sensing my emotional intentions.

After last night, I seriously doubted she didn't believe in us and our relationship. However, she was still trying to put up a wall that I was determined to keep knocking down.

Jax

The last thing I wanted was to back away from Chase, but I couldn't let him know he had a hold on me. One, so tight I couldn't shake it loose no matter how hard I tried. He made me lose my shit as much as he lost his.

He made me forget the rest of the world so that I'd only concentrate on him. After last night, I needed to know if he had destroyed my ability to be me. He had made love to me so damn good; I would let him do it again. Hell, anytime he wanted to. He knew how to manipulate my body and make me his in a way that I could abide.

I had also shared with him my darkest secret, one I was prepared to take to the grave. One that still played devious little tricks with my mind. I thought I would be sorry that I told him, but all I felt was relief. If he was being truthful about going with me to therapy, I think I wanted him with me.

After using the towel to clean up, I adjusted my bikini bottom and walked to the boat's rail. I had to take a break from Chase. He made me drunk, and I thought about things that may never be. Did he know that my little sexual stunt was a test to see if he still wanted me? He said he did, but my tangled mind had to know with all certainty.

The shimmering water trapped under the beaming sun rays caught my attention. It was in the same predicament as me, helpless under the incredible presence of the magnificent sun.

When Chase's strong hands wrapped around me and his soft warm lips caressed my neck, I didn't protest. The goosebumps that pricked my skin spoke of how magnificent he made me feel. The man gave me chills in the middle of the summer, standing under the sun. He turned me so that I faced him.

"I'm going to finish what I was telling you a moment ago."

He spoke matter of fact and, although I wouldn't tell him so, I loved the authoritative tone he often took with me. I enjoyed the challenge he presented and found our butting natures more appealing than off-putting. How was I supposed to know I would like it? No one had ever really challenged me until him.

He lowered his lips to mine and stole a sensual kiss. The soft peck had me wanting him again, and not just the sex. His forehead pressed into mine before his words brushed my lips.

"We're not just fucking, Jax."

I wanted to argue, but I was out of reasons to give in my defense. We had blossomed into something out of my sphere of knowledge, and it would be foolish of me not to at least acknowledge it.

His hand slid across my ass and the rest of me automatically wrapped around him. Arms around his neck, legs around his waist, and pussy resting against his dick, which was as hard as it was moments ago.

"You're determined to make me fall for you, aren't you?"

"Is it working?" He asked with a teasing grin.

"I would rather not answer that question."

He chuckled before kissing the tip of my nose. He eased back enough to capture my gaze.

"In my family, money and prestige are substitutes for happiness. Until you, I've never known what true happiness felt like. I want a chance to make you happy too. I know more about you in this short time than I know about friends that I have known for years."

My face bunched with skepticism at his remark. His expression was laced with knowing, and I was willing to bet that he was about to wipe that doubt right off my face.

"Your favorite color is purple. I believe you can eat seafood every day for the rest of your life, you love it so much. You laugh the loudest at the corniest jokes. The tattoo on your back is laid out in a way that it doesn't cover your birthmark, two small interlocking hearts. Your nose crinkles when you first wake up, like the idea of waking stinks. The picture of you and your father, sitting on your living room coffee table is your favorite. Clematis, the "queen of vines" is your favorite. I can go on for hours."

Lips parted and eyes stuck on his face, his words left me stunned because he was reciting intricate details he couldn't find through a background investigation on me.

"I want you, Jax. While you've been thinking up ways to reject the idea of us, I've been paying attention. You're a pretty extraordinary woman. You were keeping your guard up because of your past. You don't have to do that anymore."

Reaching over his left shoulder, I rubbed my hand along the back of it, until I found the large scar there. I did the same to his lower back, tracing my hand along the ridges of the long gash he had there. Finally, I touched the one on his bicep covered by his tattoo.

"I learned some of your personal business from your phone, but I'm pretty sure you got all of these scars from the unorthodox bootcamps your father put you in." The surprise in his expression held a boyish charm that put a sparkle in his eyes. "You missed one," he said. "You mean here," I added, easing my fingers over his inner right thigh. "They almost got the family jewels, but I'm grateful they didn't." We both laughed before he eased me back into his caress.

We were so close, my rushed breaths bounced off his face. My heart knocked against my chest so hard, I know he heard it. He accomplished his goal and captured my full attention, so I could no longer hide the feelings I had for him. They were pouring off me and wrapping around him, mending us closer and strengthening our connection.

"This is not just attraction between us. We're more than a single emotion. Jax, I…"

His words stopped so abruptly, my breath caught and my gaze shot up to follow his.

"What were you about to say?"

"Jax, baby. Don't look back. Lay your head on my shoulder, and I'll take you inside."

"What? Why?"

His voice was laced with panic. So, of course I peeked. The mini replica of a black helicopter hovered in the sky above us, the sound of its buzzing engine broke into my focus.

"What the fuck? Is that a fucking—"

"Drone." Chase finished. "Just one time I would like to be left alone," he growled, anger lacing his voice. He backed away from the rail with me snug against him, my legs still around his waist. I did as I was told for once in my life and placed my head on his shoulder.

Under the protection of signed NDAs by his staff, who'd assured us privacy, I had foolishly allowed myself the freedom to live, only to have it crumpled into a tight life shattering wad.

My mind whirled. How much of us had that thing seen? The gravity of our situation hit like a wrecking ball. I had just fucked Chase with a fucking drone lurking around us.

Chapter Twenty-Six

Jax

Once Chase got us into the interior of the yacht, I hopped off him. He sat on the couch and I paced a hole in the beautiful glass-wood floor.

A fucking drone spied on me and Chase as we were having a private moment?

I stopped pacing long enough to glare at him. "I fucked you in the wide open, on the deck of your yacht with a fucking drone lurking in the sky. I thought we were safe from that shit." I stated the obvious, too dumbstruck to think.

"I know, baby," he answered.

I dropped onto the couch next to him.

"I don't want to be a tabloid whore. If you know how to fix this, please enlighten me." He had experienced this type of situation before and employed fixers who took care of things like this for him.

"I have a few ideas, but we need to head back home."

"Yes. Back home," I agreed, talking more to myself than him. My mind worked at warp speed, but not forming a single logical thought. At home, I had computers and equipment I could use to find out who did this to us.

Amped up on adrenaline and anger, my leg bounced non-stop. Chase took my hand and kissed the back. The level of stress in his eyes mirrored my own.

"A fucking drone, Chase. They were probably recording us the entire time we have been here. If so, it means we could have at least two sex tapes out by now."

His eyes grew wide as he stood up from the couch. I followed him to the captain's wheel.

"We need to return to shore as quickly as possible!" He said in an elevated tone. I had never heard Chase yell in anger, so his sudden outburst had scared the poor man half the death. "Doesn't this thing have a tracking system? Sonar? Let me see it." He was never like this. He wanted answers and he wanted them like he was used to getting them in the office.

The captain didn't appear to know what task to start first. Get us the heck back to shore or show Chase the tracking system. I hated to throw a monkey wrench in his idea, but with the kind of tracking the boat had, it wasn't equipped to locate the drone.

Chase gathered the group of employees and proceeded to question them like a lead detective.

"So, you're telling me no one noticed a damn drone flying around the boat?"

They all shook their heads.

"No, boss."

"No, Mr. Taylorson."

"No, sir."

Chase continued to question the crew relentlessly as I paced one second and sat the next, stood and paced again. I personally didn't believe his staff was involved with the drone.

Whoever operated the drone was probably returning it to its home base and based on the type of technology they used, whatever they recorded had likely been downloaded already.

Another slew of curse words spilled from me.

"Fucking, mother fuck, I should've brought my fucking devices." I didn't even have my cell phone. Chase had requested I leave it all, and I had foolishly obliged. He had planned for us a quiet retreat from technology and his media stalkers. All we had were a few satellite phones aboard.

Chase and I had managed to avoid the media before now, but his high-tech stalkers were on some next-level shit with that drone. The captain set the boat on a course to return to shore and explained to Chase the tracking on the boat wasn't designed to hunt a drone.

Chase turned to me. He didn't have to tell me he was sorry; it was written on his face.

"I apologize, Jax. I promise I will do everything I can to rectify this situation. I'll sue whoever's behind this as soon as I find out who the hell it is."

He drew me into his arms. My body easily melted into his. Unfortunately, my mind remained in a state of upheaval, preferring to troubleshoot ideas to clear the hailstorm threatening my life. My fingers tingled, eager to strike at the keys of a keyboard.

My hold around Chase's neck grew more constricted. My fist tightened, my nails digging into my palms. "Someone is going to pay. If I find a clue, a picture, a film, or anything that could lead me to them, they are going down."

Chase eased me back, holding my bare shoulders in each of his strong hands. "Jax, your version of paying someone back is never painless. Would you let me handle this, and if my method doesn't work, we'll unleash you?"

I intended to smile, but my lips refused to bend, sticking to the true nature of my mood.

"You can't keep me on a leash, Chase. The best you can do is pet me and make me sit for a few minutes."

His expression drew tighter, the concern in his eyes shining through. He appeared more stressed about what I was planning over what was going to happen if a sex tape about us was released. Did he not care about what a sex tape would do to me? My career? My mental health?

"What are you going to do? I don't want anything to happen to you because of me, because the media won't allow me to have a private life. This is all on me."

We were going public, with a sex tape no less. The notion left my nerves so charged I was forced to slam my eyes shut against the pulsing currents.

"I know this isn't your fault. I know you didn't want this, but I won't sit around while someone is out there making what was supposed to be a private moment into a nationwide—" I gasped when a ton of ideas flooded my brain. "—fuck you're a billionaire! A successful, popular, sexy, and intriguing billionaire. They are going to make this shit an international spectacle. I knew this shit could happen, but I didn't listen to my own damn warnings."

I palmed my throbbing forehead and squeezed my temples before I slammed my eyes back shut. Bent at the waist, I choked down a surge of nausea by swallowing the large gasp of air I sucked in.

"Holy! Fucking! Shit!" My shouts were aimed at the floor, each word releasing a tight knot of tension, before I lifted. "This is bad. There is no way I can't do something. This can ruin me. My business. My life."

Chase made a valid attempt, but there was no talking me down once my mind was set to do everything in my power to find the drone stalker and make their lives a living hell.

***

When we reached shore, a media storm was waiting there for us. Paul stood at the edge of the dock, attempting to hold the crowd back.

"What are they doing here? Where the fuck is security!?" Chase shouted.

I stood with my back to the crowd, pinned against Chase, and gripping him around the waist. It appeared they'd been clever enough to stay out of sight while we were sailing closer and sprang out as if saying, *"Surprise!"* as soon as we stepped off the boat.

From the boat, the walk along the dock, and to the car hadn't appeared too far away. As soon as the crowd of about fifty or more paparazzi came into view, riled up at our arrival, Chase's car may as well have been ten miles away.

"Sir, you can use this to cover her." Cathy, the cook said. She handed Chase a black cashmere throw she had gone back and pulled from the interior of the boat. Chase used the throw as my shield. After tossing it over my head, he drew me tightly into his strong chest.

How did they know where we would dock? Someone had to have leaked our location and arrival time. Chase had assured that no one knew our docking, or embarking location.

Once we cleared the dock, a horde of shuffling feet and waving arms fought each other to have their voices heard. The throw covering me didn't stop me from spotting the camera flashes, nor did it stop me from catching snatches of their dancing shadows cast on the ground. A million questions were being shouted at us from every direction.

"Frank, clear us a path." I heard Chase shout to his boat security guy.

The flashes, the shouts, the idea of them filming me, snapping pictures of me, fighting to get my face on the news and Internet had set my nerves so far on edge, the tremble in body intensified. The buzzing in my ears competed with the shouts growing more anxious and louder the longer Chase avoided answering them. My breaths started to stall, I couldn't breathe properly, and I didn't think it had anything to do with the soft material covering me. It was a panic attack.

"I've got you. You're going to be okay." Chase reassured, squeezing me tighter against him.

It wasn't until someone shouted, "Young lady!" did I realize they were aiming their questions at me. "Miss, what's your name?" I gripped the throw in my fist, squeezing so tight my hands shook as I fought to keep my face hidden.

"Mr. Taylorson, tell us her name."

"Who's your new lady?"

"Show us her face."

"What happened to Amanda?"

Eager fingers poked and prodded, each touch a shock to my system, each causing me to yell out uselessly. I needed a decent flow of oxygen. My head swam and my body became heavy, but Chase kept me afloat, supporting the bulk of my weight.

"Timothy, watch her back. Don't let them touch her," he yelled out, calling back to the boat captain.

Everyone wanted a piece of me and Chase. While they yelled and pushed at us, I could hear Chase whispering that he wasn't going to let anything happen to me. I concentrated on his voice, the only sound keeping me from falling apart.

Soon after, my forearm was gripped and I was yanked sideways before I was snatched into an abrupt stop. The harsh actions made me lose the little sense of direction I was clinging to.

"Take your fucking hands off her, or I will sue the shit out of you. You know better!" Chase barked at one of the prowlers, his booming voice sending relief rushing through me at the notion that I was still in his grasp.

They kept shouting, stalking, pushing, and attempting to get me to uncover myself. They pleaded for Chase to unveil me and tell the world who I was. This was shear torture to someone like me who usually didn't hesitate to speak my mind. However, in this case, fear kept me quiet. Fear of being filmed, of having my photo taken, and of being made a public spectacle.

"Let us see your face!"

"Let us see her Chase!"

It was funny. I could stare a grown man in the face and be ready to punch him in the teeth if he crossed the line, but having my picture taken or facing the threat of being on film had the ability to turn me into a frightened child. This was one of the only triggers capable of crushing me, mentally and physically.

"What's your name?"

"Give us your name!"

Another harsh shove almost disconnected me from Chase's tight grip.

"Stay back! Paul, secure the car. They are trying to climb into the damn car!" Chase shouted.

It wasn't until I was lumbering through this bed of disturbed fire ants, that I comprehended what Chase had been living with. I had seen the way parts of his life was splashed out all over the television. It was because he valued some privacy that a part of his life, mainly his work, and some of his private life was kept from the spotlight. How could I have been stupid enough to think that being careful would work?

It was why he'd been interviewing women just to have female companionship and taking extra precautions to see me. He had done his best to protect me from this nightmare the entire time, one I had taken care to avoid myself.

The sound of the car door being snatched open, caused a gust of oxygen to break through and flood my lungs. I sucked in deep breaths as Chase kept me pinned to him. Once I stumbled into the back seat, I kept the throw over my head, despite my desperate need for fresh air.

Chase tugged me into his side, cradling my trembling body. "You're okay. I've got you. I'm not going to let anything happen to you." He kept repeating those words and kissing the top of my head as I clung to him like a lifeline.

Although Chase informed me it was okay to uncover myself, I kept the throw around my head and peeked through a small opening. Once my eyes adjusted to the dim interior, I made out the tinted windows as his driver fought the crowd to get into the driver's seat.

When Paul opened the door, the hounds reached in and snapped shots around him. Chase drew me in and covered the small, exposed portion of my face with his hand. I'd never seen anything like this. This incident was more proof that Chase was being his true self with me. I had become the late breaking news in his life. While most women in my situation would've been glad for the exposure, it was one of my greatest fears.

"I'm sorry," he breathed against my hair as my head rested against his strong chest and fast beating heart. "I didn't call ahead for security because I didn't think we'd need it. I tried to be careful with you, I promise."

My tension lessened and the shakes had calmed, but my fingers clawed into Chase like those of a cornered cat.

"I'm sorry boss." Paul called from the front seat. "I called for security, but they got held up. The company wouldn't even release your helicopter to me. I honestly don't know what's going on. I also tried to call you on the satellite phone to warn you about this but couldn't get an answer."

"Thanks Paul. Take us to my house in Westport. It will be difficult for them to get onto the property there."

I didn't care where Chase wanted to go, I just wanted to get away from this crowd. I was willing to bet a year's pay that whoever managed that drone also found a way to hold up Chase's security team and his helicopter. As badly as I wanted to go home, I knew we couldn't risk leading the mob to my place.

Chapter Twenty-Seven

Chase

Jax had been skittish about forging a relationship with me, and the media attacking us today would send her packing for sure. She made it clear from the start she valued her privacy, and although it was difficult, she had chosen to share with me the reasons why. Even without knowing about her past, I had tried to be as careful with her privacy as my own.

We'd returned a day early from what should've been a peaceful trip. She was certain we had a sex tape either out, or one on the verge of being released. Was it possible since we had no idea how long the drone had been spying?

There was a handful of people who knew where I was taking the yacht, and they had all signed nondisclosure agreements. One way or the other, I would find out which of them leaked my location with Jax to the media.

Hearing the helpless sound of her gasping for breaths, and the way her body had trembled against mine, had killed me. How was I supposed to help her when it was my fault she was suffering? The crowd had triggered the traumatic event she had suffered when she was younger. I couldn't imagine what she felt, or what was going through her mind.

There were clear signs shown today that she was suffering from post-traumatic stress disorder. Jax needed help, and I was going to make sure she received it. She had fallen asleep clutching me. Carefully, I shook her awake when we pulled into the driveway.

"Where are we?" She looked up groggily, peering through my window. Her head swiveled to my colonial style gated villa. The place offered privacy and a tranquil form of peace that was hard to come by in the city.

"We're at my house in Westport, a little over fifty miles from the city. Here, the media may lurk, but they can't get in. You'll be safe here, I promise." I brushed my lips along her hairline.

After exiting the car and walking around, I reached for her hand to help her out.

I held her tighter than I ever had before the paparazzi intervened in our lives. My firm grip was glued around her small hand as I escorted her up the steps. Morgan, the house manager, waited for us with the front door open.

"Good afternoon, Mr. Taylorson. After receiving word of your impending arrival, we started preparing your rooms and meals."

"Thanks. This is Jax St. Pierre." I gave a quick introduction. Although Jax wasn't feeling her best, she graciously shook Morgan's hand.

I led her to the living room couch, where I tucked her into my lap, folding my arms around her anxious body. I couldn't lose her already. Not like this. When Jax drew away, my heart sank to the bottom of my chest.

"I need a computer. And a phone," she flashed me an expectant glance.

I nodded and stood, flooded with enough anxious energy to send me in the wrong direction in my own house.

A short while later, I returned with my extra phone and laptop. She fired up the computer as soon as it hit her restless hands. "Don't worry, I'll make it so no one will know I'm using or have used your computer."

Was that even possible? Was she about to do something illegal?

"What are you going to do?" Concerned, I got in her face to ensure she answered me.

"I'm going to figure out where that damn drone came from or at least where it's at. If we don't have a sex tape out already, I'll do my best to stop it from getting out."

"You can do that?"

The mischievous glint in her eyes and the cunning twist of her lips revealed she was about to put action to what she had expressed. With calls of my own to make, I eased up to the window with my cell Paul had retrieved from the car. I alerted my team, praying at least one knew how to put an end to what was brewing.

My next call was to my father. He had dealt with several situations of this magnitude; therefore, his advice and guidance would be invaluable.

"I will call Mark Romero, see if he could help you fix this," my father said after I had given him a quick rundown of our situation. Mark was our family lawyer and fixer. There wasn't much he wasn't able to find a solution to.

While my father spoke of who could fix what problem, I couldn't help tuning into the side of Jax's conversation that I could hear.

"TK, I need you." Jax sounded desperate. And of all people, she had called TK. He had appeared crazy enough for her attention to be willing to kill us all?

Nonstop, they chatted. Her speaking their secret, virtually indecipherable language.

"Chase, are you listening?" My father yelled, his voice loud enough through the phone to make Jax glance up.

"Yes, Dad, I have jotted down Karl Vicente's name and his number. He has the inside track on the most popular media outlets and is the man to go to when you don't want something getting out."

Jax's eager fingers worked the keyboard so fast, it didn't appear she was typing anything that made sense. With the phone I gave her on speaker, she typed like a mad woman.

"I can't tell you why I need this done. I'll owe you. Can we leave it at that?"

TK took a long while to give her an answer.

"Okay. You'll owe me, and you know I'll collect," he replied.

"Stop fucking thinking about me owing you, and fucking do what I asked you to do. I don't have a lot of time." She yelled toward the phone with such fierce intensity, the vein in her neck appeared to vibrate. The way she cursed at TK, I was sure he would hang up, but he seemed more cheerful after her harsh words.

"Sure, J. I'm already on it. I can narrow down the places the drone could've passed and may have been spotted on camera flying back into this city. Finding it could lead us right to the operator. Finding the media outlets, they may have submitted something to is even better and will likely be easier to track down. Let me know if you need anything else."

Jax thanked him before she swiped the phone off.

This wasn't the time to be trivial, but it bothered me knowing TK wanted her. She refused to acknowledge it, but they had a special bond. She owed him now, and I wasn't okay with what he may want to collect.

"Thanks, Dad. I'll call you back later." I hung up before his reply.

A stack of questions sat on the tip of my lips, as I sat on the couch next to Jax. My eyes landed on her working fingers.

"Are you sure you should be asking someone like TK for help. He wants you, and I don't like it."

"Unfortunately, he's the only one I know who can give me what I need right now."

The statement hurt, burning my heart to ash before the flakes were carried away by the wind.

She paused her typing, considering what she'd just said. "Need, as in technical help."

And just like that, she had replenished my devastated heart.

I lifted my phone to my ear after dialing Karl Vicente like my father suggested. I hadn't realized I'd been on the phone with Karl for fifteen minutes, but he was sure he could identify what news outlet or outlets that may have received updates on us. Before I updated Jax with the positive news, and apologized again, she raised a hand to stop my words.

"I know, Chase, but I can't sit idly by and not make attempts to protect my privacy. I'm starting to build my life. I don't want it derailed before it's had a chance to start. If my name gets blasted in the media, I want it to be about my mind, not about who I'm dating. Plus, I can't possibly take being exposed to the world again. It's a shot I'm not willing to take. This is one of the reasons I specifically told you I didn't want to get involved with you or anyone else."

She was lashing out, but I understood her anger.

"I didn't want any of this to happen, and I've done my best to protect our privacy." She turned away, still mumbling her frustration.

A mixture of anger and irritation was written in her tight expression. She'd never stopped typing. Her expression changed from anger, to confusion, to worry, her face frowning one moment and relaxing the next.

She didn't acknowledge me after I leaned in and kissed her on the cheek. She kept going, building her own brand of damage control. The phone I loaned her started to chime as I prepared to make more calls.

"It's for you." She pointed to the phone. "One person knows to call me on that phone, and I promised you I wouldn't compromise it or your computer, so the call is for you."

Unsure, I eased the phone up to my ear. "Hello."

The frantic voice on the line, stalled me. "Chase, what the hell are you doing? It's about time you answered your phone. Turn on the television."

Blake's irritating voice grated on my nerves, but my gaze was already dancing around the room for the remote.

"Did you call Dad's fixer? He's kept dad's many affairs out of the news many times."

Running around the room, I hunted for the remote. There was no need to search for a channel, the first thing I noticed flashing on screen was Jax's beautifully tattooed back and her rear end barely covered by her tiny blue bikini. Her sexy legs encircled my waist, her head rested on my shoulder, the backdrop of our photo was my yacht. My face was a surreal mixture of shock and awe, staring up into the lens of that fucking drone.

"Chase, I hate to say I told you so, but I told you so. I told you this would happen. Told you she was trouble. You need to let her go before things get worse." Blake badgered on.

The television highlight stopped Jax's incessant typing. She stared, as slack jawed as I was. I flipped through the channels, and to my horror found us on every station. They all wanted to know who Jax was, where she had come from, and how long we'd been dating.

"If her back view is that beautiful, we can't wait to meet Chase Taylorson's new girlfriend," commented one of the reporters. A slew of more comments followed, scrolling across the news ticker at the bottom of the television screen in big red and white letters.

"The secretive billionaire bachelor Chase Taylorson's hot new girlfriend."

"The sex kitten the billionaire Chase Taylorson's been hiding."

"Billionaire Chase Taylorson, secretly married."

What happened to the days when reporters had standards? The highlights flashed across the screen as Blake's grating voice pounded into my ear.

"I told you to have your fun with her and dump her, but you didn't listen. I tried to help you and you threw my help back in my face."

A quick swipe across the face of my phone put an end to the frustrating sound of his voice before I tossed the phone onto the coffee table.

My personal life, one I had fought to keep that way, had become serious news. I had hired a few extra men to increase my security team that I was likely going to fire for failing to show up earlier today.

Aside from Paul, I employed an extra driver, Ian, whose job was to scout my routes to avoid the paparazzi. He and Paul also used decoy tactics, sometimes driving two look-a-like vehicles to throw the paparazzi off my trail. There was also Marvin Lomax, my look-a-like I had started using as a decoy when necessary. Jax had no idea the measures I was taking to protect our privacy.

A few of the news outlets had enlarged Jax's tattoo. They couldn't legally ask the public to identify Jax but blasting her photo would lead everyone to try and figure out her identity. When my main phone buzzed, I knew it was social media notifications about the latest breaking news of my life.

The more I flipped through channels, the more questions surfaced about the sexy, or beautiful, or gorgeous woman I was dating. Thankfully, and to my surprise, they weren't concentrating on race, and turning our relationship into an excuse to bring up a sore subject in our country.

Several news sources had posted the photo of her glancing back at the drone, but the sun had shadowed the profile of her face, and thankfully, it wasn't clear enough for them to identify her.

"I got you, you motherfucker," Jax muttered under her breath behind me.

I glanced in time to see her all but growling at the monitor.

"What did you get?" I inched closer, my curiosity getting the best of me.

"TK was able to get me into the network that purchased our pictures. He took it a step further and reverse tracked where the link came from. Right now, I'm making my way up their asses, about to get linked into their shit and they don't even know it."

"Are you saying you already have a digital footprint of where those pictures came from?"

"Yes." Was all I could get from her as her fingers beat the letters off the keyboard.

My desperate need to keep her safe had me in a tight coil of biting helplessness that wouldn't release. I had managed to do something I rarely did. I had failed.

Chapter Twenty-Eight

Jax

"The bastard has skills. He's not a run-of-the-mill crook, I'll give him that. Either he's working with someone, or he has created a convincing shadow. Asshole," I spat, aiming my words in no particular direction as my eyes remained glued to the screen. "He has a multi-layer firewall set up, but I'll worm my way through his shit one way or the other." The bad news was, I didn't know if I was hacking him or his shadow. Either way, I would take out my target by aiming my anger at both.

Chase stared like he didn't know me anymore. If he knew how many laws I had broken to preserve my privacy, he'd be terrified. I refused to be labeled a billionaire's interest of the week and lose my livelihood because of a fucking breaking news story.

News with a shelf-life of a week wasn't going to ruin my life forever. What was worse, I was exposed, half naked and vulnerable for the world to see. It was my body, along with my life being uncovered. I couldn't let it happen.

"One down, two more to go," I muttered, smirking at the screen.

Chase scowled. "You broke through their firewall?"

"Fucking right, and I'm about to get through the other two and fuck up his world."

Chase caressed my hand and squeezed to draw my attention. "Jax, I have people working on this too. Don't do something you're going to regret or something you'll get into trouble for."

"I shouldn't get into trouble, but if I do, it will be worth it, if it means helping to preserve my life. I can't let them release more than they already have. If a sex tape gets out, I'm over. I'm not some celebrity who can expose a sex tape and become famous for it. This can't happen, Chase. I can't let it." My emotional outburst caused an even deeper crease of concern to pour over his face.

I paused my typing long enough to point a finger into my chest. "My life will be fucked up, blown apart, and you, all you'll get is a *hoorah* for fucking me."

Chase didn't argue, because he knew I was right. I had lost count at how many times his face was plastered on the news with different women, and it did nothing to hurt his business. On the other hand, a female in the same position would lose respect, business, and associates for doing the exact same thing.

"You're right," he said. "The last thing I want is for this to hurt you."

His face was a deep crease of questions and concern. "Remember, I know that this goes much deeper than your career. Talk to me, baby."

"One more to go, and the motherfucker is going to crumble," I muttered, my eyes glued to the laptop, projecting a hint of madness. I heard Chase talking, but I didn't want to talk right now. Besides, I was in my zone. Either I was about to save myself or make the situation worse.

"I'm in!"

Chase's eyes went wide at my shout before our gazes locked. He understood me better than anyone, but I don't think he could ever fully understand all that stood against me. He had never had to claw his way through a business world that viewed a female more as a nuisance, or as something they had to tolerate in a world they believed meant for men. He'd had his fair share of run-ins with duplicitous females, but he had never been exposed in such a savage manner it caused him to obsessively guard his identity. It was why I preferred to have the world think I was a man, and only showed my face when I had to. He had never been used and abused and riddled with such raw hate that death became a better option.

"Does you being *in,* mean you're inside the computer of the person you suspect sent our photos to the media? How? It's only been a few hours."

"Yes, and I'm a few clicks from sending him a virus, so vicious, it will fry his computer and seek and destroy everything he's sent. Hopefully destroying those damn photos of us."

I expected Chase would be upset about my update because of his earlier concerns about what I was doing. Instead, he smiled.

My gaze settled on the television as flashing red notes about me and Chase scrolled across the bottom of the screen. The notes were what helped to finalize my decision to hit the send button.

"Jax, if your actions today come back to you, you could be in serious trouble. That being said, I need you to know that I'll have your back."

Only Chase could make me smile at a depressing time like this, his support easing my distressed mind.

"I appreciate your help in this Chase. I know that you'll do everything in your power." I leaned over and placed a quick kiss on his lips before my attention was pulled back to my task of destroying the stalker's world.

"If he's sent the pictures or even a sex tape to anyone, the virus would seek out his *sent* items and destroy them."

I attempted to ease Chase's mind because I cared about him. However, he didn't appear convinced of what I was saying. "Me and TK are certain we've found the right person, but if we haven't, your efforts will come in handy. However, if there is one thing I'm certain of, this level of exposure will send me into permanent hiding. This will kill any future I have. All of the work I've done to get this far will go down the drain, and I will never be taken seriously again. With the mention of my name, the world will change my title to Chase Taylorson's latest conquest."

Chase prepared to reply but the phone sounded.

"Hey, you know the deal. I need you to make my footprint disappear. Nothing on this side of the bridge survives, I'm talking full blown digital burn."

TK's voice boomed into the phone. "This is digital black ops level shit. You are going to owe me big."

"Got it, now get the shit done already and stop flapping your lips."

TK's chuckle was the last sound I heard before he hung up. The crazy fucker was enjoying this shit because it connected us on the level he lived on.

All I wanted was to stop this stalker and clear my head. I didn't want to divulge too much in front of Chase because it was best he not know. Plausible deniability. My father began teaching me information technology at twelve, and I dove headfirst into the field, soaking up every lesson, every trick, every clever bit of knowledge.

Even with all the knowledge I had gathered, TK was on another level. He was able to get into and do things I had never figured out. He claimed he didn't want to share some of his secrets with me because he didn't want me triggering a trap capable of getting me locked up. So, whenever I ran into tech issues of a questionable nature, I looked to TK to help me.

The computer virus I unleashed had the ability to wipe out an entire news station for receiving the photos on their network from the laptop of the drone stalker. This was a part of my plan I hadn't shared with Chase. He didn't need to know how desperate I was to keep myself from the public eye. I was more afraid of being exposed than of losing my business.

He knew I was making questionable maneuvers but hadn't made a strong attempt to stop me. In his own way, I think he understood why I fought so hard to hang on to my life and career. Maybe he felt responsible for my exposure.

"Can I go home? Is there an alternate route?"

He shook his head. "No. Please, stay here tonight, and maybe the coast will be clear tomorrow."

A deep sigh did nothing to ward off the stress of the day or keep it from siphoning the last of my energy.

"Maybe tomorrow? Are we stuck here?" My shoulders ached; they were drawn so tight with stress.

"I spoke with the guys at the entry gate, if you go out there now, the media will pounce. They've caught the scent of blood, and they're going to stick around and stake out every place I've been spotted."

Chase's strained expression encouraged me to go to him. He sat me across his lap. The warmth of his solid body eased some of the tension from mine.

"I apologize for being an asshole. I know none of this is your fault." I cupped his cheek, loving the way he leaned into my hand before closing his eyes.

He turned his face so that his lips brushed my palm before he folded me into a tight embrace.

"There's no need to apologize, I understand better than you think."

Neither of us spoke again until his house manager entered announcing that our dinner had been prepared.

"Thanks, we'll be right in," he answered, his breath warming the top of my hair.

My appetite was nonexistent, but I wasn't going to be rude either, no matter how foul my mood.

After we made our way to the beautifully set table, I absently picked at my scallop piccata with sautéed spinach, while Chase spent his time staring at his plate and shouting instructions at people on his phone.

"Goddammit, you find out who it is. If you can't, I'll find someone who can!" Chase slammed his phone on the table making my dinnerware jump and clink together. I expected to see the face of his phone shattered but it had survived the violent blow.

This situation affected him as much as it was affecting me. I reached out and gripped his hand. The moment his wrapped around mine, his features softened, and his caring expression surfaced.

Chapter Twenty-Nine

Chase

After dinner, we strolled down the hall leading to my bedroom.

"I asked Morgan to prepare you a room, but I prefer having you right next to me."

Her face squinted in confusion.

"If you wanted me with you, why in the world would you let Morgan waste her time preparing me a room?"

"I was being respectful of your feelings by requesting to have you a room prepared, but your clothes are already in my room. The offer was made as a courtesy, but you're coming with me."

She smirked before flashing me a daring glint. "Is that so?"

After gripping her arm, she glanced down at the area I had taken a tight grip of but didn't offer a protest. I dragged her down the hall like a disobedient child and slung my door open before placing my hand in the center of her back and shoving her inside.

The heat burning in her eyes spoke for her. It was telling me that my aggressive behavior was turning her on. She stood at the foot of my bed with a small portion of her bottom lip tucked between her teeth. The piercing at the corner of her lip sparkled against the candlelight I'd had Morgan set up.

"Before you do whatever you're going to do, I need to take a shower first." We were still in our clothes from the boat.

"You're welcome to join me," she offered, the hungry seduction in her tone apparent.

"I intended to," I replied before aiming a demanding finger in the direction of the bathroom.

We peeled off our clothes on the way in and were naked by the time we stepped inside. Morgan had drawn me a fragrant bubble bath, the steam flowing from the huge garden tub filled with hot water and fluffy lavender-scented bubbles. The jets hummed, as the water swirled in a rhythmic pattern.

Jax dipped her toe in first before climbing in. I followed. After seating myself behind her, I plucked one of the fluffy white washcloths from the edge of the tub, squeezed some soothing citrus soap into the cloth and proceeded to wash her.

An extended amount of time was spent between her legs. Once my hand dipped below the warm bubbly water, it got lost down there. There wasn't much verbal dialog passed between us. Instead, it was her body communicating, accepting my tender wet massages and soapy caresses. When she rose and turned with her own cloth raised, I knew it was my turn to get washed. She did such a good job of scrubbing me clean, she left me panting.

She straddled my legs, shoving her body against mine, so close, her hard wet nipples grazed my chest. At her sensual touch, my eyes slid closed, and I embraced the urge to wrap myself around her. I leaned in for a kiss, but she wouldn't allow it. Instead, she gripped my hair and yanked my head up, while she slipped down my wet-hard length. My scalp ached where she pulled, but the pain fed into the red-hot pleasure she lavished me with.

"Yes! Shit! Oh!" I cried out. "Holy fuck!" She was the only one capable of turning me into a blubbering mess of curse words and loud outbursts of gibberish.

"Chase." Her breaths flowed against my cheek. Her slow rotation had stalled my ability to speak. She called out once more, "Chase."

"Yes." My word escaped on a quick exhale. The slow grind she started created sparks of burning pleasure that left my lips parted and my breaths short.

"Am I feeding your obsession?"

"Yes." Maybe she *had* been listening when I mentioned being obsessed.

"You're feeding mine too," she admitted, low and throaty in my ear.

My eyes widened. She admitted that...out loud? The clouds of desire overtaking my brain were parting. When I glanced into her eyes to grasp her meaning, she yanked my head back with an even tighter grip on my hair. She quickened her movement, forcing me to think of nothing but our explicitly delicious sex.

Once I got a grip on her luscious ass, I helped her along, although she didn't need my assistance. The sound of water splashing onto the floor added to the symphony of our heavy breaths and moans of pleasure.

My release was an invaluable gift, a pleasurable feast fit for a king. My dick strummed against her walls, seated deep in her smoldering heat. I came hard and long, my body seizing, skin stretching tight, and muscles clenching tighter. A hard shutter wrecked my body at the feel of my hot cum coating her insides.

The one function I succeeded in performing, was to slam my eyes shut and pray my heart didn't stop in the process. My labored breaths rushed out, and I gripped her, so tight, I was sure I was hurting something.

When we were conscious enough to think, she relaxed against me and sluggishly draped her arms across my shoulders and looped them around my neck. I drew her in, keeping her in my tight caress until our breathing leveled out.

I was still planted deep inside her and ready to give more if she wanted it. After all, she had given me the ultimate lesson in keeping my stamina. I had never been this ravenous with any woman, nor had I ever had a desire to give one all of me.

Chest to chest, my heart pounded against hers, each beat translating my feelings into sound. She indulged me in a tender hug before she backed away, taking her magic with her. A shudder danced through me as I slid from her cozy warmth.

She stepped from the tub and walked into the shower, leaving me to sink low in the water and relax my head against the back. She could have finished bathing in the tub, but she was putting on a show for me in the see-through shower. I didn't move a muscle until she had finished, stepped out, and wrapped herself in a large white towel.

"Where did Morgan put my clothes?" The tips of her fingers traced a feathery stroke across my arm, sending a chill through me. After pointing her to the bathroom closet, she picked out a few items and headed into my bedroom.

I finished my bath in the cooling water. By the time I stepped into my bedroom, she was under the covers and fast asleep. After such a long crazy day, I threw on a pair of shorts and joined her. When I drew her into me and wrapped her in my arms she didn't protest.

A refreshing feeling of contentment washed over me at the feel of her sleeping form draped over my body. I whispered against her hair. "You are what has been missing in my life. Before you came along, all I had was work and a one-sided empty world I couldn't fill, no matter how much I accomplished. No matter what happens, I would never leave you. Neither would I stop fighting for you."

"You too," she whispered. She lifted and allowed her soft lips to brush my cheek before nestling her head back into the nook of my shoulder. She hadn't been asleep. Her two-word reply had called back that feeling of contentment I enjoyed.

Chapter Thirty

Jax

The day after the paparazzi attack, the coast had cleared enough for Chase to sneak me home without confronting a media mob. He walked me to my door and gifted me a kiss that left my body sizzling and my mind fried.

The deep smile on my face was set, spurred by the excitement of being home. I walked through my door, kicked off my shoes, and was stopped in my tracks by a male's presence.

"Dad?"

Although he was the only person I had ever given a key to my apartment, it always surprised me to see him. At a towering six-three, solidly built, and hair faded so low it verged on bald, my father's appearance was just as imposing as his reputation in law enforcement. Where I was a smoky caramel, my father was the true definition of cocoa, dark and smooth.

He stood from my couch when he saw me, a big smile across his face. I didn't walk, I ran to him, tackling him as he lifted me into a big bear hug. He released a playful growl as he squeezed and twirled me around playfully.

"What are you doing here?" My question was spoken into his neck, muffled but understandable.

He set me on my feet as we stood grinning and eyeing each other from head to toe. I hadn't seen him in four months.

"I thought you were on one of your top-secret assignments?"

"Do you think I would stay away after seeing my Babygirl splashed all over the television?"

My eyes fell closed for a moment. The idea of my father seeing me, draped around a man and thrown in the midst of what could turn into a more scandalous situation, left me feeling defeated.

He placed his hand atop both my shoulders when I dropped my head in embarrassment. "I know this is not easy for you, but you're strong. Start at the beginning and don't leave anything out."

I shook my head. "No Dad. I refuse to let you swoop in and fix this for me."

"I'm your father. I'm supposed to swoop in, dive in, jump in, and do what is necessary to make sure you're okay."

He ushered his hand towards the couch. He wasn't going to drop this, and I knew better than to argue.

"I have a friend who is helping me. We did some things, not all of them legal, to track down where those pictures were sent from. We started at the station that aired the photos and worked backwards."

He nodded. With some of the tools at his disposal, I wouldn't be surprised if he knew more about TK than I did. When my curiosity had gotten the best of me a few years ago, I'd asked him if he would check into someone's background for me. After a thorough interrogation on why I was asking, he had smoothly told me no. He did add that I had nothing to fear or question. I never asked again.

I eased into the couch, tucked my legs and got comfortable. Alexander St. Pierre was going to want every detail, and he would hang on to each one like it held the key to the answers we sought.

Two hours of questions and recapping had left me mentally drained, but my smile remained at having my father present. He was a walking, talking, damage control device if there ever was one. I felt sorry for the person responsible for spying on me and Chase. My determination to find the culprit, coupled with my father's would eventually put a face on the person.

"I don't believe Chase is involved in this," he started. I didn't think he was involved either, but my father's opinion on the matter added to my confidence in Chase.

"If one was made, the only reason they would keep the recording is for leverage or to later use it as a stronger incentive to break you two up."

"You think this is motivated by someone trying to break us up? Why? We've been careful."

"Not only is this person trying to break you two up, it's someone you both know. If you were as careful as you say, then only someone inside your inner circle could do this type of damage. It could also be a determined ex, or a super fan of his."

The one guy on the planet, I actually enjoyed being around, could inadvertently be the cause of casting me and all my demons into the spotlight.

"You like Chase." It wasn't a question, so I didn't give an answer. "In light of what's happened, you haven't separated yourself from him." It was a revelation my father pointed out that I was well aware of.

"He's nothing like he's portrayed in the media, a billion-aire playboy and financial genius who lives a glamorous lifestyle. He admitted to being lonely, his childhood wasn't a cakewalk, and he is strangely in tune with me. Where most men are intimidated by my strong personality, he isn't afraid to challenge me. He has also made a valid effort to respect my privacy, especially having faced his own issues with the media."

"Does he know? Everything?"

I nodded. "Yes. I trust him."

My father's thoughtful smile was aligned with his eagle-eyed stare. "If you trust him, then so do I."

It touched me how readily he'd accepted my judgement when I didn't always have confidence in myself. However, I still sensed that there was a, *but* coming.

"I will do everything I can to help track down this person or persons. But, there may come a time, depending on how swiftly we can resolve this, when you may have to step away from Chase. If that time comes, please be assured, I'll do everything in my power to make things right."

My face tightened at the thought, but I understood where my father was coming from. Staying away from Chase could be the key to us finding the suspect. I didn't like the idea, and Chase would hate it, but we weren't left with many options.

"I have to depart early in the morning," my father said, looking as disappointed as I felt.

"Nooo," I whined. "New assignment?"

His smile grew wide. "Current assignment, but I decided to take a break to check on something more important."

"Dad. Aren't you going to get into some kind of trouble?"

"Maybe, but the way I see it, they need *me* to solve *their* problem. So—" He shrugged like impeding a federal investigation wasn't punishable with jail time.

That he was willing to risk his freedom and job to check on me was the main reason my father was my hero.

The following morning, we ate together at one of our favorite breakfast spots, Buddy's. A short while later, I took him to the airport, where he left me with a sad smile and watery eyes.

Chapter Thirty-One

Jax

Five days had gone by since I had last seen Chase. We were calling each other non-stop. Phone sexing, and texting in the midst of the serious conversations we were having about us. He was getting good at pushing me to talk about us more.

Despite not being able to get him off my brain, my fascination with him didn't stop me from putting in the necessary work to keep my name out of the public's eye.

I had invited TK to my apartment; the spare one I used for company and mingling. It was the one-bedroom studio I had rented before NG's profit margins increased. This was where I took dates I didn't want to know about my main residence. Only Chase, and a select few were special enough to know where my home was.

TK, in my opinion, was one of those people who was so smart, he blurred the line between intelligent and insane. His life was sort of a mystery. I kept things from him, because I sensed he kept them from me as well.

Everyone had a digital profile of sorts. TK had nothing. My curiosity had gotten the better of me once, but just as I had a past I wanted to keep buried, I had to respect that maybe TK did also.

All I knew about him was what he volunteered, and I accepted that it was enough. I believed the less I knew about him, the more unlikely I was to get any closer to him. After knowing him for nearly four years, I remained clueless as to how he made his living. I believed the bulk of his work was based on illegal operations, but I didn't judge and never called him on it.

There were times when he would disappear for weeks at a time and return unexpectedly. I stopped asking, when I gathered he wasn't going to tell me his secrets until he was ready. He often got this look like he wanted to tell me something, but so far, he hadn't.

Why would I choose to keep associating with a man like TK? Chase had asked so often; I was sick of hearing the question. The best answer I could come up with, was he was one of the smartest men I knew in my field and, in all the time I had known him, he had never given me a reason to distance myself from him.

I had met TK at a tech convention. He had introduced himself, and I quickly became engrossed in his vast knowledge in the field. When he swerved across the line and admitted his attraction, I let him know I wasn't interested. It wasn't that I wasn't attracted, but I valued his mind, more than I was interested in taking him to bed. If there was such a thing as minds having the ability to marry, me and TK's would have been hitched.

The music of our fingers striking keys made the only sound until the doorbell sounded. *Who the hell is at my door?* My eyebrows pinched into a tight V in my forehead when I stood and prepared to answer the door.

A quick peek revealed Chase standing outside my door. My heart skipped a beat before it reclaimed its pounding rhythm. I glanced back at TK sitting at my small dining room table.

This wasn't going to be pretty. After having only met him once at the tech expo, Chase didn't hide the fact that he didn't like TK. Every time his name was brought up in conversation,

Chase's face would tense with a mix of irritation and disapproval.

Chase knew I kept two apartments. He had discovered this one while rifling through my mail when he visited my main residence.

We were supposed to lay low because of the hornet's nest our leaked pictures had stirred up. But, telling Chase to stay away was useless. Crazy thing was, I didn't know if I could have stayed away from him for long either.

The door creaked, sending an elongated whine into the space when I opened it and stepped to the side. Chase was poised to speak, but his words halted at the sight of TK. A firestorm brewed in his gaze, so strong, it reached across my living room and collided into TK's sharp glare.

Before I could utter a word, Chase pulled me in and crushed me against his hard body. His hand slid across the swell of my ass, squeezing me through my jeans. He was putting on a performance for TK, but his possessive actions had me cracking a sly smile.

Why was I getting turned on? I believe I enjoyed being marked and claimed by him, a revelation that I would never have admitted a month ago.

As always, Chase smelled like sugary sin; his fresh fragrance washed over me as quickly as the strength brimming from him. His long strong body pressed against mine, was all it took to get my juices flowing.

"Chase."

His lips sat against my neck as his fingers remained spread wide across my ass.

"Um hum," he answered huskily.

"I've got company."

"So," was what I think he had muttered.

I backed out of his hold. "Chase, you remember my friend TK from the expo?"

He glanced in TK's direction before his lip turned up like a snarling dog's. Who said rich people weren't petty? His dismissing gesture was so slight, I'd have missed it if I weren't standing so close to him.

The men's gazes were welded so tight to each other's, my head swiveled between the two. Did either intend to blink again?

When I closed my door and walked away to return to my laptop, Chase was right on my heels. The tension in the room was thick enough to choke on by the time we reached the table. Chase took the chair giving him a view of us both since the table was a perfect square.

"We're attempting to track down the drone-driving spy who leaked those photos."

Chase's glare finally left TK's to acknowledge my words. "Didn't you send a virus to find and murder his computer?"

"We won't know who it is until the asshole powers it up and the virus starts doing its job. I'm hoping he doesn't know how to keep us from identifying him, or that he hasn't trashed the computer to avoid detection."

Right when Chase was about to speak, TK pointed at the laptop's monitor. He spun it around so I could study his findings.

When my eyes lifted from the monitor, I caught the mean squint Chase had leveled on him. This was going to be a long day if I didn't find a way to separate the two.

***

Chase

If he licked his lips at Jax one more time, he was going to find out I was more than a suit. I glanced at Jax who appeared oblivious to the longing in TK's eyes, and his obvious interest. She tolerated him because he spoke her language.

The team my father had working on the situation hadn't turned up any suspects either, but like Jax and TK, they managed to keep eyes on all the major networks in an effort to prevent anything else from being leaked.

"So, baby, dinner tomorrow? I'll make you whatever you want," I said to Jax as I spied *him* in my peripheral.

The way his jaw flexed, I could tell I was getting on his nerves. *Good.*

Jax covered my hand with hers, and I could feel my smile deepening. Her pretty purple-nailed fingers wrapped around mine before she squeezed.

"I would like that, but we should be careful around these media hounds from hell. God forbid they find out who I am and latch on to me too."

My lips parted, ready to continue talking with *my woman*, but TK interrupted again.

"J, look at this. He did a digital sweep to hide his trail, but his broom is broken because I see right through the shit."

"*J? Who the hell was J?*" No, he hasn't given my woman a nickname.

"Didn't know your nickname was J, Jax. It doesn't suit you," I told her while my eyes were locked on TK's.

She let my hand go and walked around to his side of the table. Concentrating on something on his screen, she stared above his shoulder. He had stolen her attention again, and it had my damn blood boiling in my veins. When he glanced at me with a smirk, it took everything in me not to punch his lights out.

"I was talking before you rudely interrupted me," I said, spitting the words at him. I was coiled with so much tension, I was ready to rip out the jerk's spine. Jax and I had enough outside influences threatening our relationship, we didn't need want-to-be boyfriends adding to the confusion.

"And I'm here attempting to find the asshole who intends to mess up Jax's life, which is more than you're obviously doing. Is there a specific reason for you being here?"

I shoved an angry finger in his face. "You have some fucking nerve asking me what I'm doing here. I'm here to check on my girlfriend, and it's a good thing I did. The way you're eyeballing her, she appears to be in the midst of being bitten by a rabid stray."

"It's not *me* she has to worry about," TK responded. "You're so fucking thirsty, I wouldn't be surprised if you planned this whole thing just to keep your claws in her. I'm sick of you rich assholes thinking you can do anything you want and get away with it."

We both leaned across the table, like two snarling wolves, ready to rip each other's throat's out.

"I wouldn't be surprised if *you* set this up to get her attention. You're probably here now as a way of covering your own trail," I added before pointing an accusing finger at the laptop sitting in front of him.

Jax walked around TK and stood between the two of us.

"Guys, cool it. I don't need the two of you bickering. It's my fucking life on the verge of falling apart." She huffed out, folding her arms over her chest. Five days had passed, and although nothing else had gotten leaked, tracking down the suspect was proving more difficult than we expected.

Jax focused her attention on me. "Chase, TK's help in finding this drone spying bastard is invaluable."

At those words, TK's smirk grew deeper as one of his eyebrows twitched. I wanted to knock that brow clean off is face.

Jax turned and focused her attention on TK. "Chase is my boyfriend, TK, so he has a right to be around me."

"Thank you baby." My smirk couldn't be contained. Hearing her refer to me as her boyfriend was a dramatic step up in our relationship, and I loved the sound of those words coming from her mouth.

After fifteen minutes of listening to them peck the hell out of their keyboards, I prepared to leave my woman with a man who clearly wanted her.

When I glanced at her and was met with a sincere smile, I knew she wouldn't cross the line with the flea-infested stray sitting across from her. However, it wasn't her that I was worried about.

I was distracting Jax, but a part of me didn't want her alone with TK. He was just the type to poison her mind and have her thinking I was involved in the drone situation. If he could do half of what she claimed he could on a computer, he could certainly make it appear that I was involved.

She walked me to the door with her arm around my waist. I'm sure TK hated the passion-laced kiss I gave her. I made no attempt to acknowledge him when I walked out, relishing that the last thing he saw was me kissing Jax.

Chapter Thirty-Two

Jax

A few hours later, TK and I were still hard at work. The asshole who sent those pictures was a slippery bastard who had taken every precaution to prevent being caught. If there was one thing I was sure of, if I couldn't figure this out, my father or TK would.

"Hello," I answered the phone when I saw it was Chase.

"Jax, something bizarre is happening to my laptop," he shouted into the phone, his voice troubled and laced with uncertainty.

"Tell me what you see," I told him, turning my gaze to meet TK's.

"It's blinking and flashing like a strobe light, and there's a big black blinking Pac-Man eating up my file folders."

"What the hell!? I set up extra protections so your laptop wouldn't be affected." There was no way I had left a trail to his VPN. I was too seasoned to be that sloppy.

"It's not the laptop you used at my house acting up. I'm in my office at Swift Capital."

"Fuck!" I yelled. "How could I have fucked up your work laptop?" I questioned myself while a hundred different scenarios popped off like camera flashes in my head.

TK's probing gaze landed on me. He didn't speak a word, but I had an idea of what he was thinking. The realization socked me in the center of my forehead, but I chose to ignore it.

The responsibility of Swift Capital's Network fell on me. The virus had my signature, my coding, therefore the chances of it finding its way into the network I had help set up was possible. If Chase's work laptop was being affected by the virus I had sent out, it meant he was directly connected to the person who had stalked and leaked our personal business to the world.

Chase's shouting echoed though the phone. "Jax. What's happening? You're going to have to explain this to me."

TK's voice was pinging my ear at the same time as Chase was asking for an explanation.

"Jax, don't be an idiot. The rich asshole is the one who those files came from. His laptop's probably been off. He hired his people to record you. The people he claims are working to help you are probably the ones running interference to keep us from discovering their cover-up. He wants to destroy your name and livelihood, so you can be dependent on him for help."

Chase's voice came through so loud; my phone may as well have been a bullhorn in my hand.

"Jax, what the hell is going on? Are you listening to me?"

To shut TK the hell up, I flashed him my palm. In the calmest voice I could muster, I spoke to Chase. "Power off your laptop, and I'll be there in about fifteen minutes."

"Let me come with you," TK offered.

"Thanks, but no. I don't need you two biting each other's heads off, while I sort out what's going on."

He attempted to utter more, but I held my hand up and shook my head at him.

"Please, let me handle this," I stated, my tone firm enough to quiet the words scratching to spill out of him.

He gritted his teeth and coiled with irritation, but thankfully, remained silent.

"If you leave before I return, lock the door from the inside and pull it close," I called over my shoulder before I snatched my purse and slipped on my shoes.

"Okay, I got you." His smile widened at the idea of me leaving him alone in my apartment.

By the time I arrived at Chase's office he was pacing the floor with his fists clenched tight at his sides. When his gaze found mine, relief swept away some of the stress he carried.

"Thank God," he stated. Not even his stress had stopped him from placing a sweet kiss on my lips. I glanced around to make sure none of his staff had witnessed the intimate gesture.

A virus, set off by me, may have destroyed his work and business dealings, but he had acknowledged me with a kiss. The sentiment made me smile despite the serious situation. Once I sat at his desk, I powered up his laptop and as he'd described, the black Pac-Man continued to devour his files.

The visual evidence on Chase's computer was telling a story I didn't want to believe. Chase couldn't have set up the drone. He wouldn't have done something like that to me on purpose, would he? I had given him my trust and had opened doors for him that I hadn't for any other man.

The diagnostics I was running would tell me if his computer had been tampered with, or remotely accessed. Disappointment started to rush through me when my findings didn't net the results I prayed for.

I sat staring at the screen, shaking my head and attempting to ward off my anger, not wanting to believe that Chase was behind the drone scandal and photo leak, the whole time.

Why else would this virus be destroying his computer?

Unwilling to give up on him too easily, I ran the test again. My eyes fell closed before I lifted my fingers and let them hover above the keypad. My eyes felt like two weights in my skull, but I managed to lift them and stare daggers at Chase. His mouth dropped open after his questioning gaze met my deadly glare.

"What? What's wrong?"

I stood too fast and wobbled.

"You...you. Fucking fucker," I huffed out, pointing an accusatory finger at him. "How could you? You of all people should understand the hard work, and effort that goes into building a business and name in this industry. You know what this type of exposure could do to me, but you don't care do you?"

"Jax, what are you saying?"

Tears slid down my cheeks, and I quaked with racking emotions. The hurt of who betrayed me opened deep wounds; some I knew would never heal. Chase had broken me.

He stood, pretending he didn't know what I was talking about, shaking his head, and lifting his palms up in question.

"The virus was built to destroy the source of where those files came from. Now that you've triggered it, it will destroy everything. Like a heat-seeking-missile, it will also seek out and destroy every picture and file *sent* from this computer."

"Jax, you can't *possibly* think I did this to you. I was not the originator of those pictures, and I damn sure didn't leak them to the tabloids. Why would I do that, especially after what you shared with me? I'm not that heartless. The last time I was on this computer was the day we traveled together. It's been here in my office on my desk. This is the first time I've fired it up since."

"You set this up before I let my guard down and told you everything."

My forehead fell into my palm before I closed my eyes and just breathed. I had told him the one thing that hurt me the most, and he had still allowed this to happen.

"You're a billionaire. At the snap of your fingers, people will do whatever you tell them to. You didn't have to be here physically for your orders to be carried out. All the proof I need is staring me in the face. You're going to lose every file on this computer, and I hope the accounts are worth millions."

"Jax, please. Stop this. I didn't leak those files. Someone is setting me up."

A smile formed on my face despite his imploring words. "I figured you'd say that," I barked, shaking with a blinding rage I couldn't keep contained.

"I was so fucking stupid. I can't believe I trusted you. I let my guard down for you, and it's come back to bite me in the ass."

When I stepped from behind his desk to head toward the door, he attempted to stop me by planting his firm hand on my shoulder. My glance traveled to the area where his hand rested on my shoulder before the deadly intent I projected in my glare met his apprehensive one.

A tense mixture of fear and panic etched his face. The sight of him set my nerves to a jittery beat. I was upset enough to hit him.

"Please, Jax. I didn't do this. I wouldn't."

I shrugged his hands off my shoulders. "Don't touch me. You said you were obsessed, and I actually took it as a compliment. You wanted more than I was willing to give. But destroying me to get what you want; it's low and unforgivable."

"Please. What would I get from destroying your business? Your life. Your name."

My stiff finger was aimed at his face, dangerously close to poking his left eye out. "You'd get me with no restrictions, no distractions, nothing to get in the way of you getting what you want. And if the media knows about us, it won't leave them much room to hound you about me."

He caught my wrist, but when I went still and glared at his hand, he lifted both hands in surrender. "Jax, you don't believe this. The times I convinced you to skip out on work to spend time with me were for the same reasons you convinced me to do the same. We work too much and simply needed a break."

"Why didn't I see this before? You could do whatever the hell you want to whoever you want to do it to. You blinded me to that side of you so I wouldn't see it coming when you ate me alive."

"Jax! Jax!" He kept yelling my name. He ran after me until he was able to block my path with his body.

"Jax, please. You can't believe any of this. You mean more to me than this company, and especially more than fame and popularity. For God sakes, I love you!"

Time froze and all the air was sucked from my lungs before it solidified and turned to stone. As much as I wanted to one day hear a man tell me those words, and mean them, this was not that time. I believed Chase meant them, but the words didn't have the effect they were meant to have because they were being used in desperation.

I stood immobile; my legs fixed in place like two slabs of concrete.

"That's why you weren't worried about the aftereffects of the photo leak or stopping them from being leaked at all."

Tears had gathered in his crazed eyes. He was a fucking stalker. I had called him one before, and he never denied it.

"Jax, you have to believe me. Think about this logically. I would never hurt you like this."

I stopped listening. I was done.

Tears clouded my eyes because of how much I had begun to care about Chase. A toxic mix of rage and hurt, threatened to blow my head off. I had allowed myself to fall for him. My dumb ass had stopped listening to my mind and had allowed my heart to open up.

I marched past him brushing his arm as he persisted in pleading his case. "Jax wait. Let's talk this out. You're upset, not thinking straight."

"Now, you're a fucking shrink." I released a hollow laugh at his remark even as my heart was exploding from the hurt he'd put there.

Once I stepped out of the office, I slammed Chase's office door so hard, it vibrated the thick glass surrounding the frame. Every head on the floor stopped and peaked from desks and cubicles like I was the devil.

Richard, one of the research analysts I occasionally spoke too, approached with a question, but I scooted him out of my way, same as I had done to Chase. I kept stepping until I reached the elevator and attacked the down button.

Without glancing back, I sensed him behind me. If people didn't know it from the photos displayed on the news, they would figure it out that I was the woman in the picture with him now. However, I no longer cared. All my give-a-fucks on the matter was set on fire.

Chase stood behind me. "Jax please. Just listen to what I'm telling you."

With an angry sweep of my hand, I knocked his hand away from me and kept my gaze aimed at the elevator. The shiny stainless steel elevator door gave me a warped reflection of him standing behind me.

My words seeped out through gritted teeth. "You've been watching me work my ass off attempting to figure out who did this. You even sat at my dining room table watching me and TK work to solve this, and it was you the whole time."

He backed against the wall, putting some space between us in an attempt to see my face.

"Someone is setting me up. I don't know how to prove it, but I can promise you, I won't stop until I do," he choked out his desperate words, his face drawn tight in anguish as tears stood in his eyes. The sad sight of him gave me pause, but the evidence flashed though my brain and reminded me not to fall for his charm.

When the ding indicated the elevator had arrived, I stepped inside, not allowing the doors to fully open. I beat the hell out of the lobby button the same as I had the down button. Chase was smart enough not to climb in with me.

Chapter Thirty-Three

Chase

Pain gripped me in a chokehold. Its bone chilling fingers tightened and shook me with enough force to rattle my teeth. I had lost Jax. I had the world at my fingertips, but she was all I wanted.

In order to get her back, I needed to find a way to prove my innocence. First, I had to find a way to stop this virus. The members of our IT team took turns working vigorously to restore my computer, as I stood hovering over their shoulders. However, they were at a loss as to how to stop something they or I didn't fully understand.

My gaze fell to my ringing phone as Pac-Man continued to eat my files. It was Landon calling. I was in no condition to talk to anyone, but I picked up anyway.

"I can't talk right now. I have shit happening that I need to fix."

"I know. Travis called and said I needed to check on you. He said you had a big fight with a woman that yelled at you loud enough to melt the paint off the walls." When I didn't answer, he continued, "Are you okay? I'm driving over right now. Is this about the new lady you've been seeing? The one you hinted about at lunch when you asked me and Ethan about interracial dating. I saw the pictures, Chase. She looks good on you."

I didn't need or want his opinion on the matter. I needed to call our security team to pull surveillance footage. If someone had gotten into my office, it would be a major security breach.

"You didn't go through with one of those plans we talked about on how to trap a woman, did you?" His tone lowered to an audible murmur. "Did you try out one and it backfired? Is this what the fight and these pictures circulating the news and Internet are about? Chase, man tell me something."

"I'll talk to you when you get here. I need to make some calls."

I hung up before he could start up again. He wasn't going to stop until he bled me for every bit of information on Jax. My mind was on one track, implementing damage control measures to fix this situation so I could get Jax back. My obsession with her had forced me to make questionable decisions I wasn't proud of, and I needed to fix it.

Me without her wasn't an option. Even if I had to lie, plan cover-ups, and bribe, I was willing to do anything to get her back.

***

My words started spilling out before my phone reached my ear. The members of our IT team were still at it, working, but failing to stop the virus. At this point I had lost business, deals were going to fall through, and a ton of money was being lost, and I didn't care.

I snatched my phone up, making the tech currently working on my laptop jump.

"I need you to find me the best IT expert in this city. Search this country if you have too. I don't care what you pay them. I need them in my office right fucking now!"

Travis was the lucky recipient to catch the brunt of my frustration. I yelled enough about work that he was used to my outbursts.

"I hear you, sir, but one of the best tech people I know just left your office."

The veins in my forehead and neck nearly burst, I yelled into my phone so loud.

"Did I ask for your opinion? Find another one or two if you have to. Get someone who knows what the hell they are doing into my office ASAP!"

The hard slap of my desk phone on the receiver sounded like a cannon blast. It surprised me I hadn't cracked it in half. On the business aspect of the situation, I could find ways to savage my contacts by using my managers and analysts. Even my assistants, whose computer should have almost mirrored mine. However, I was losing the only woman I ever loved, and it was my own damn fault.

Knowing I was the reason for Jax's distress, sent me into a restless mixture of fear and anger. I glanced at my phone, but determined it wasn't wise to call her while she was so upset.

Jax was smart. She would clear her head and figure out I'd not done this.

Would I do about anything to keep Jax? *Yes.* However, I would never do anything to hurt her.

The people, or person setting me up was doing a hell of a job. *Why?* Minutes before Jax had shown up at my office, I had gotten a call from our R&D department confirming a Swift Capital Drone had flown across international waters on the date and time we were spied on.

The kicker, the drone had been signed out by me. The moment I had cast a glance across Jax's shoulder, and spotted the drone, I suspected it was one of ours, but how had someone made it appear that I had requested to use it? If only I had informed her of my suspicions before things had gone this far.

At this point, the only way I was clearing my name, or getting Jax back was by figuring out who had set me up. If people hadn't figured out who was in the leaked picture before now, I'm sure they would soon have an idea.

Two hours after Jax stormed from my office, the help Travis had enlisted arrived. At first glance, he looked thirteen. His thick glasses sat on the bridge of his nose, and his clothes hung loosely on his lanky frame.

He reached out his long, boney hand. "Nice to meet you, Mr. Taylorson. My name is Max MacKenzie."

It must have been my pinched expression Max noticed because he answered the question on my mind.

"If you're wondering about my name and my father, the answer is yes. I'm Mack MacKenzie's son. Unfortunately, I didn't inherit his looks or his popularity with women."

His father was a millionaire playboy I had met at a few social functions. He was a prick who treated women like trash, and rumor had it, his son was the key to his success of their telecommunications empire. They provided cable and internet services to over a quarter of the industry.

I was grateful that Travis was able to get Max at all.

"It's nice to meet you, Max. I have quite a situation I hope you can assist me with." I pointed at my laptop sitting atop my desk.

The young man had the laptop powered and was typing code into it within minutes.

"Shoot," he uttered.

The pinch in his forehead and tightened lips revealed my dilemma.

Max's speedy fingers hadn't stopped working, and he glared at my laptop like it had come alive. He tapped his forehead, his eyes never leaving the screen. Was he contemplating his next move or was there not a move to make?

He started talking as he typed. "Sir, I can't stop this. The only one who can, is the person who initiated it. It's like attempting to disarm a bomb, made by a bomb maker I don't have a profile on. The best I can do for you at this point is attempt to save the data you have left."

"Please, save what you can," I instructed, hopeful that all wouldn't be lost.

He bit deep into his bottom lip, his eyes squinting at the screen. "Who did you piss off? I've never seen anything like this, and I've been a techie since before I hit double digits. Despite what they say about data still being out there, there are ways to make it disappear."

"Disappear, as in vaporized with no backdoor way of making it reappear?"

He nodded as his fingers worked.

"I can't retrieve what's gone after it's been taken. It's being sent to a place I can write my way into but can't exit. If I execute a command without proper syntax, it can cause the program to fail. Whoever did this created a digital black hole, and if I go chasing after your info in there, I could risk losing everything, faster."

His updates left me speechless, and I stood there gawking at him before I uttered, "How much is gone?"

"Thankfully, it's slow-moving. So far, about forty percent of your data is gone. It took out everything that was backed up first," he revealed.

Half my data, gone. Data that I was never getting back. My only hope of saving some of my pending business deals rested on my team.

At this point, I took a seat. Hearing what Jax had already confirmed, made my knees weak. Losing everything on my computer was depressing but losing her had wounded me so deeply, it shredded my heart.

I dialed my father, needing to find out who had set me up. Disclosing to anyone how I had gotten the horrible virus was out of the question because it would implicate Jax. Whoever sent those pictures to the media, had sent them from my computer or had found a way to make it appear that way.

Max stopped his rapid finger strokes when I approached and stood over him.

"This is happening because someone leaked files from my computer to the tabloids. Is there any way to locate those files and trace them back to who used my computer to send them? I scanned the past week of surveillance, and my computer hasn't been touched, until today. By me."

"I will have to stop saving data to hunt for what might already be gone."

"Shit!"

I was being forced to choose between saving what was left of my data or figuring out who had set me up.

"Do it. It's more important to find out who used my computer to leak that information."

Max's brows lifted at my comment before his typing commenced.

Glancing back at the past week may not have been a long enough timeframe, so I instructed the security team to review the camera feeds for the past month. Who else had been in my office?

If my laptop was used remotely, I prayed the teenager who sat behind my desk, was clever enough to track down and identify the user. Otherwise, Jax was never going to speak to me again, especially when she found out where the drone came from.

Chapter Thirty-Four

Jax

Lying flat on my back, I stared into the wide-open nothingness above me, my mind, a mine field of exploding thoughts. "Fuck!" I shouted into the darkness of my bedroom.

Chase's pleas kept echoing inside my head. What if someone *had* set him up? The virus would destroy all evidence of it.

We'd been through so much together in such a short time that he had managed to earn my trust, and I had bared my deepest sorrows to him.

I sprang up, snapping on my lamp.

"The drone," I whispered to myself.

A few days ago, TK had sent me snapshots of the drone, captured from a CCTV camera, when it was being flown back into the city. We attempted to identify the drone, but the images were so blurred, it had taken a while for them to be sanitized.

Less than thirty minutes after I had thought to give Chase the benefit of the doubt, my heart was broken all over again. The letters flashed across my screen in big fancy red letters, the diamond shaped logo with the letters revealing the name of the owner. Those letters formed words I had seen a number of times—Swift Impressions.

The drone belonged to Chase's company. Swift Capital had several imprint companies that produced products sold on the market. Swift Impressions was one of those companies that happened to be in the same building as Swift Capital.

The doubt I had about Chase being set up was doused in gas, and instead of a match, I imagined myself using a flamethrower to obliterate it.

The only time my father didn't answer my calls was when he was out of the country. He would also record his voice mail message in French for me when he would be unreachable. I regret that I couldn't tell him how badly I had fucked up by choosing to trust Chase.

When I turned on the television, things just kept getting better. Every channel I flipped to had my face plastered on the screen. They had identified me as the woman draped around Chase's waist. My efforts to stop this shit hadn't worked. I had officially become a billionaire's play toy, and every eye wanting to have a look, could now see me.

I made no attempt to stop the flow of my tears after a surge of raw emotions had set them free. Being filmed during a private moment, with the possibility of being exposed without my consent, stirred painful childhood memories that gave me a headache.

My nerves had gone up in flames, and I was unable to contain the toxic level of anxiety flowing through my jittery body. Snapping back the covers, I ran to my small living room bar, searching for the liquid courage I needed to get me through the night.

The doorbell sounded while I was finishing off my third drink. I was such a mess, I staggered to the door, ready to use the liquor bottle in my hand to beat Chase upside his head. However, my blurred vision made out TK standing on the other side of the door.

When I let him in, he took one look at me, and pulled me in for a strong hug that I desperately needed. He took the bottle of vodka from my hand and sat it on the table before closing and locking my door.

Although I had never officially given him the address to my main residence, it didn't surprise me that he knew where I lived. He didn't taunt me with, I-told-you-so's. Instead, he walked me to my couch, and sat holding me as I cried into his shoulder.

"You're going to be okay. This will blow over in no time." His reassurances went on until I drifted off to sleep.

***

A day later.
"I'm downstairs. Get your ass up!"
It was a text from Lena. She called nonstop after I stopped answering my phone a few days ago. I'd shared with her that I was dating someone, but I hadn't given any details about who it was. She knew my dating situation well, so she hadn't asked after how things were going, assuming it wouldn't last past a week.

After I buzzed her up, I left my door cracked so she could step inside. Otherwise, she would beat the door down and disturb my neighbors. I sat waiting on the couch with my feet tucked under me, my energy depleted. It appeared something in nature knew that I needed the few people in my life I counted on. Lena showing up a day after TK had spent the night was the closest they had come to meeting each other.

She was going to let me have it for not answering my phone and making her worry if the seething voicemails and text messages she left me were a sign. She would also lend me her ear and a sturdy shoulder to lean on.

A burst of positive energy coursed through me at the sound of her approach. Using the tip of her finger, she pushed my door the rest of the way open and looked the door up and down like it had offended her. I felt like shit, but the sight of her made me crack a smile. She stood in place, hand on her hip, eyes zeroed in on me.

It was eight in the morning and her hair was styled in a perfect shoulder-length bob with thick bangs. Her make-up was painted flawlessly over her creamy mocha skin. She wore a blue silk robe-dress that was stylishly draped over her body with black ankle kissing boots.

She did a once-over the interior of my apartment before she strutted in, hand fixed on her small hip, and eyes on me. She stopped in front of my crumpled body on the couch. Glaring down on me, she wiggled only her manicured nails in a gesture for me to give up whatever drama I was holding back.

"Spill it and don't leave anything out," she said before dropping onto the couch next to me.

She took my hand, interlocking her fingers with mine as I struggled to gather my words.

"Tongue can't do this to a person. That man must have put some super dick on you. You don't answer your phone. You got my damn blood pressure up worrying about you. Look at your hair, and this ratty ass robe. Jesus Jax. You're my fucking inspiration, my prime example for what I want to end up resembling when my transition is complete."

I didn't need the mirror to tell me I looked like shit, I felt it. Her calling me out for it only made me feel more of the impact Chase's betrayal had left.

It took an hour of me stumbling through my words and being pulled into the tight hugs Lena lavished me with for her to hear the parts I wanted her to hear.

"I know your secrets-keeping-ass isn't telling me everything. How the fuck are you going to go out with one of the sexiest men in this world, and not tell me who it was?"

I shrugged. "It doesn't matter now. He wasn't who I thought he was."

"What if he is?"

Her question drenched the room in silence.

"What?" I asked, peering intently at her.

"What if he really was set up and you didn't stick around long enough to figure it out? The way I see it, you were waiting for an excuse to get away from the man."

"What?" It was the only word I had the ability to squeeze out. I thought she would take my side on this and go on a male bashing rant against Chase for what he'd done.

"Whose side are you on?" I finally asked her. "You really think I wouldn't at least check to see if the evidence I saw was legit? His actions could cost me my company, my livelihood. How am I supposed to show my face, and be respected if all the world remembers is seeing me draped around a man looking like a slut? What happens if a sex tape pops up? I get screwed out of my life, and he gets a pat on the back."

She twisted her lips at me, one eyebrow stuck in the air.

"What?" I asked her again.

"None of what you're saying has happened, and it may not happen. You are more upset about what *can* be, instead of concentrating on what has *actually* occurred. I know how this world works. If more pictures or a sex tape comes out, things will more than likely unfold just as your predicting. And, I will be the first one to show up to kick ass and take names for you. But. What if he really was set up?"

She held an exaggerated stare until I squirmed.

"I don't understand all that computer stuff you do, but from what I do know; you computer geeks can make anything look legit. I think you jumped the gun on him too fast. You don't let a man like that go that easily."

She knocked on my head, as one would a door. "Hello, is the Jax I know in there? The strong-willed one that will latch onto something like a fucking pit-bull until *she* decides to let go. The one that doesn't run away from shit, no matter how bad it stinks," she said talking to the top of my head. She shifted her eyes, dropping her gaze on mine. "I think you're afraid that what you had, just might have been real, and you don't know how to handle it."

Lena had never bitten her tongue with me. It was one of the reasons we'd been friends for so long. I didn't argue with her logic because she brought up a point that I considered myself. Even after finding out about the drone, I still didn't want to believe that Chase had betrayed my trust.

"I don't think you should cast him aside so quickly. And, I'm not saying it because he's a billionaire, or sexy as hell-flaming sin. I'm saying it because you paused with him. There are times I've seen you go out with and drop three dates in a week. I've been telling you all these years, the moment one makes you pause, he more than likely is, *the one*."

The irritating mix of regret and indecision hovered like a swarm of annoying insects. Her words had me rethinking my decisions.

"This is just my take on it, but if it were me, and Chase was guilty of setting up the drone, I still wouldn't leave him. Do you have any idea what I would give to have a man like that, pull a stunt like that, to keep me? All I'm saying is think deep and hard before you make any final decisions."

I nodded, biting my lip. Lena knew that I had gone through a rough patch in my childhood, but she didn't know the specific details or that it was at the hands of my mother. She didn't know the depth of the pain, or the wounds those leaked photos had opened.

Chase knew. *Shit!* I had told Chase my deepest secret after knowing him for a month, and I hadn't even told Lena. The revelation floored me.

Lena released a deep sigh like she knew what I was thinking. She rubbed a tender hand up and down my shoulder before pulling me into a strong embrace. "Can you get yourself together now? I can't stand seeing you look like somebody's old, dried up side chick."

I lifted my heavy head from her shoulder and glared at her. "Damn Lena. You're really cheering me up right now."

"You know how I am. I'm not about to let you sit in this house looking tore up. Now, go straighten your crown, and let's go have breakfast in the overpriced restaurant down stairs."

Drained, I eased up off the couch. I'd been drinking and hadn't eaten much in the last few days, and my stomach was punishing me for it.

"And you're paying," Lena called after me as I headed towards my bedroom for a much-needed shower.

***

At the start of the third day, and after Lena had pep talked me into dropping my pity-party campaign, I eased out of bed with a little less sorrow in my heart. She'd been excited about her upcoming trip to Dubai. Her secret dream was to meet an Arabian Prince that would make her his number one wife, while allowing her to live a work free life of leisure.

After a quick shower, I prepared to check back into my life. The first thing I did was to log into my laptop and set up a conference call with my small staff.

Did I still have a business left to salvage? If it were only me, I would become a recluse and stay hidden in my home, but I was responsible for employees who needed their jobs.

When I sneaked a peek out my window, a crowd similar to the mob that met us at Chase's yacht, waited in front of my building. They glared up at my moving drapes, but I remained in the shadows. Thankfully, I was twelve stories up and you had to have a keycard to enter the building and elevators as well as a six-digit pin to gain access to my floor.

The first sight of the inside of my office space lightened my mood. The group sat around the table of our small board room with their laptops in front of them. I saw them, but they would only see a black screen as my voice would represent me. Helena had her cordless desk phone tucked between her ear and shoulder while she typed on her laptop.

She waved at me before she bent and stared into the camera. Her tone was low, but clear enough for me to understand her words. "After your identity as Chase Taylorson's secret girlfriend was leaked, everyone in the world wants to hire us."

"*What?*" I paused, not fully understanding her update. The few times I had called to check in, my staff had confirmed that things were going well, but I was convinced that they were telling me what I wanted to hear just to keep me calm. I had convinced myself that it was only a matter of time before the downfall of NG began.

Jeff walked in lifting the mic of his wireless headphones from his mouth before leaning way too close to the camera. "I don't know if you meant for your business to get out, but we're going to become millionaires because of it."

Again, all I managed to squeeze out was, "*What?*"

I didn't understand. I hadn't slept a wink in two days. I had ignored most of my phone calls, wallowed in the stench of my own self-pity, and wondered if I would still have a business when all was said and done.

Helena and Jeff talked at the same time, and I didn't understand a word from either. My concentration was shot. All I picked up was something about new contracts and business pouring in.

Lulu also had a phone pressed to her ear while she scribbled on a notepad, but it didn't stop her from smiling and waving.

Bits of Quentin's phone conversation revealed him sweet-talking his way into a deal he would later sweet-talk me into taking.

Helena and Jeff took turns explaining that my being outed as Chase's new girlfriend was apparently good for business.

When I Googled myself, pictures of my employees popped up with mention of me having a successful tech company, along with the few photos they had captured, and leaked of me and Chase.

There was no way Chase could have known leaking my pictures would have a positive impact on my business life. Could he?

There were hundreds of comments, most of them positive, highlighting my success in business. Them mentioning that Chase was dating a fellow business mogul, was a great step up to the airhead model types he'd been dating. I wasn't a business mogul by my standards, but the update was a blessing compared to what I expected to be called.

I swiped at beads of sweat that had gathered on my forehead, still battling the anxiety that plagued me at the notion of being exposed. This could have been worse. Clients could have canceled scheduled work requests, and open contracts could have been pulled since most were at-will. Relief swept through me, easing a little of the stress I had allowed to make me sick over the past few days.

Chapter Thirty-Five

Chase

It took Max ten days to track down a semblance of a lead on the person who had set me up. Each time he had made any headway on clearing my name, he would hit a roadblock that would take him two steps back.

The media had done just as Jax predicted they would. My popularity shot through the roof, and everyone that was anyone, wanted an exclusive interview for Jax's official reveal.

Max was convinced that someone had the inside track on his every move. He explained how thorough the suspect was at using untraceable efforts to cover his tracks.

"Each time I come close to closing in on answers, I believe my efforts are being sabotaged," he informed.

I believed Max. I believed whoever we faced, would do whatever it took not to get caught. My mind dredged up TK.

Some of Max's updates were in computer jargon I had to ask for clarification on. "So, you're confirming that someone remotely accessed my laptop, but you can't figure out who it was?"

Working around his own busy schedule to help me find answers, young Max seemed as obsessed with finding my hacker as I was.

"Whoever it was, used a public Internet café."

My pacing ceased at his words.

"When I checked to see who used the computer at the café, I found a user was a person with the screen name, *Surcum Sized*. And he knew where to sit to avoid the cameras."

I hung desperately on every word.

"I was unable to pick up his reflection off a cup, glass, or window," Max continued.

"Who the hell is this guy?" I mumbled under my breath. Max had recovered a portion of my workload, and thanks to my assistant, I had enough to immerse myself in work. I had lost millions, had lost some clients, but the fallout hadn't been as substantial as I had anticipated.

Work kept me from thinking about Jax. Somewhat. It saddened me that she had to hide now. I hadn't seen her in the news which said she had found a way to stay unseen.

What I wouldn't do to have one of our debates or phone chats. Our dinner dates would lead to some interesting revelation about her that I was always grateful to receive. I could even go for one of her snappy comebacks to some smart comment I would make.

"He hid well, like the digital invisible man. This virus however wasn't fooled. The computer he used to remotely access yours, is being destroyed with the same virus that nearly destroyed your laptop. It's like it's on a search and destroy mission and knows something is up with that computer. Your laptop was targeted as the source, and I believe I may be able to figure out how he did it."

I paused, digesting what Max was telling me.

"So, you can't identify this guy, but you have enough to prove that someone did, in fact, remotely access my laptop to send those files to the media?"

Max nodded. "Yes, I've discovered enough to prove you were set up. But, finding out who was behind it, will be difficult."

The corners of my mouth turning up into a smile felt foreign. "Thank you. I'm grateful for your time and dedication to proving I was set up. Please, do whatever you need to do to find out who it was. Whatever you need, don't hesitate to notify me."

"You're welcome, Mr. Taylorson." I had never heard his words expressed with the deep level of excitement his tone currently held.

"Max, can I ask you something?"

"Sure."

"Why did you agree to take on this job? You don't need the money, or the headache for that matter."

"Me and Travis are frat brothers. When he called, he gave me a few details about what he had seen on your computer. I love a challenge and what he had described intrigued me. And your right, I don't need the money, which is why I won't be charging you."

I pinned him with a hard stare. "I can't let you do that. Why would you do that?"

"I respect what you have accomplished in such a short time in business. You're a good example to follow. And, I respect you as a person. I have never seen you act like a douche to people, and the people I know who have met you, all say that you are a genuinely good person."

"I appreciate that, Max."

The first thing I needed to do was call Jax and update her on the new discovery. I would also write a check in Max's name to a charity of his choosing, since he didn't need or want the money.

***

Jax

What was wrong with me? My running app was telling me I had gone just under two miles. Why was I so sluggish? My attempt to shake off the fatigue didn't work. Turning my music up and slowing my pace didn't work either.

Foot traffic in the park today was minimal, just the way I liked it. Running had always been one of my outlets, a form of therapy. It was my saving grace, when I had no other options. It even kept me company when I was the loneliest. I would run until I was so exhausted, I would collapse into a dreamless sleep.

I slowed my choppy pace and stood on the outskirts of the path I ran on. No other runners lingered on the spiraling and beautiful wooded trail, so I stood in place and took in deep heaving breaths.

The insects serenaded with a lullaby as a light wind left feathery kisses against my cheeks. The earthy scent of pine and a flowery blossom teased my nostrils. Why wasn't this perfect scenery setting the tone for my therapy run?

During my short affair with Chase, my exercise routine was sliced in half, but with all the sex we'd been having, it must have evened things out because I hadn't gained an ounce.

Not being around him was proving that Chase had left a profound impression on me. Despite what he had done and my feelings on the matter, I still missed him. So much so, I made myself sick thinking about him. Every time, those three words, *"I love you,"* crept into my head, nausea followed because a part of me believed he meant them.

He'd wiggled his way into my heart, but I was never letting him know how much he had gotten under my skin, and how much he made me care for him.

What if he *is* innocent? Lena's probing question kept echoing in my head, making me second guess my actions.

A surge of pain climbed from the bottom of my stomach and inched to the top before it crawled up my esophagus. The bowl of cereal from last night's dinner was threatening to make a second appearance. The retching sting of the bile burned my throat, forcing me to bend at the waist as I spit and gagged.

Here I was, surrounded by nature's beauty, hugging a tree. Sick about a man I was only supposed to be having a good time with. I heaved deep and hard, my throat clutching nothing but the air I was sucking in.

Sex was all there should've been between me and Chase, yet I'd sat at his table and ate dinner with his family. I'd been on his yacht. I even shared my controlling ways with him.

Everything inside me was projected out, until I was left dry heaving. The painful quakes were slow to cease as they battered my body.

My tight grip on the tree loosened so I could lean against it for support. It took great effort on my part to breathe the nausea away, but I managed. I removed my baseball cap and used it to fan my hot face.

After minutes of praying, the ugly feeling started to subside, but I was forced to take a seat at a random bench before I made my slow trek back to my apartment. Although the media hype had died down, I adopted the habit of dressing in oversized clothing as an extra precaution. Thankfully, September in New York welcomed the arrival of some fall attire, allowing me a better shield to protect my identity.

My mental health was questionable before I met Chase, but now my physical health was starting to suffer as well. What the hell was wrong with me? Was Chase so addictive that I was having withdrawal?

Once back home, I scanned my living room, no doubt resembling a crazed lunatic. I didn't know what I was searching for, but I'd stepped inside and stood in place. I was hoping that something in the space would give me an answer to all the questions tearing me apart.

After locking my door, I shuffled to my couch and fell into the soft cushions. My attempts to ease into a relaxed state of mind failed, allowing my thoughts to sprang up and remind me that I had let a man do this to me.

My body was fighting itself. It craved Chase with an insatiable hunger. His never-ending caresses, the sound of his voice, and the quick little kisses he had a habit of placing all over my face and neck.

Screw him! I wanted him one minute, wanted to kill him the next, and to fuck him after that. Closing my eyes, I sucked in a deep breath and released it slowly. How the hell does one get over someone they had fallen for?

The ping of my phone drew my attention. I swiped the face to find a message with a video attached. After reading the threatening message, urging me to stay away from Chase, it took me a moment to soak in what I was watching on the video.

Nausea and lightheadedness struck at the same time, causing me to sway as I struggled to stay upright. My phone tumbled to the floor from my shaking hands, and I slumped into the couch, leaning into the cushions for support.

My father had warned me there may come a time, when I may be forced to stay away from Chase. Just when I had talked myself into one of the many requests Chase had left on my voicemail for us to meet up and talk, this call had given life to my father's prediction.

I sat immobile; my watery gaze stuck on my dropped phone as my ten-year-old terrified eyes stared back at me. My worst nightmare was playing out before my eyes, one-click away from being aired to the world.

Chapter Thirty-Six

Chase

It had been six weeks since I'd seen Jax, and I didn't know how much longer I could forgo feeling her snuggled into me, hearing her voice, or inhaling her precious scent.

Numerous calls and texts from me went unanswered. I ended up sending members of my security team to spy on her just to see if she was okay. Paul would drive me past her building just so I could feel close to her. I missed her so much, I was reaching out for her in my sleep, and waking up with her name on my tongue.

Max was successful at tracking down the drone that had snapped photos and recorded us. However, the task of discovering who deployed the drone on that fateful day was a well-kept secret with all the evidence leading back to me.

Someone had gone through a lot of trouble to pin this on me. It had to have been someone who knew both me and Jax. If the stunt was to break us up, it worked.

The media hype had died down, but it didn't mean they wouldn't still try to get a story.

Sitting behind my desk, I dropped my face into my shaking hands. Jax had become a part of me and no matter how much time had passed, I couldn't shake the notion that a part of my life was incomplete.

The vibration of my cell phone drew my attention. I swiped the screen when I noticed it was Landon. His animated voice came through the speaker. "How are you, Chase? Got your girl back yet?"

"I'm not doing well. I feel like shit and, no, I haven't gotten my girl back."

Landon yelled over the line. "Learn how to drive son-of-a-bitch!" He was projecting his road rage at some unsuspecting driver when he was more than likely the one in the wrong.

"I thought you told her you'd found evidence that proved you were set up?" He must have concluded his road-rage episode.

"You're talking about the evidence I was forced to share with you to convince you that I was set up? You're supposed to be my friend, yet you believed the media and Internet over me."

"I believed you in the beginning. I was just angling to get the exclusive because I have known you long enough to know when you're not telling me everything," he laughed.

"I tried to set up a meet, so I could show Jax the evidence, but she wouldn't meet with me. She said being around me would keep her in the spotlight, and she doesn't want to live like that. For some reason, I got the impression that she wasn't telling me everything. She just didn't sound right."

"What's your plan for getting her back? I know you have one, right?"

I shook my head even though he couldn't see me.

"Nothing yet."

"Chase, I know you. For you to be this troubled, it highlights how serious you are about Jax. From what you told me, and from what I've read about her business success, I understand why. She's not a gold-digging schemer after your money, or a spotlight chaser. She's very much in command of fulfilling her own dreams."

His low chuckle sounded on the other end. "From the few other photos that were leaked, I could understand why you're so into her. The woman adds spice to the word sexy. Smart, hot, and hardworking. What more could a man want in a woman?"

"Exactly. She had me, the moment I saw her."

It was Jax's looks that had gotten my attention in the first place, but I was drawn in further, when I found out how hardworking she was and how funny and outgoing she could be.

"I told you, man. All of this could have been avoided if you had done a *Greg*." The comment caused me to laugh in spite of the absurdity of the subject matter. Greg, one of our friends, who'd been obsessed with the woman he wanted to marry, had gone through great, and very questionable lengths to keep her.

"The shit Greg did to keep Kathy was downright devious, and I believe illegal," I spoke into the phone, shaking my head.

Based on the hint of laughter in his tone, I knew Landon was joking. As desperate as I was to get Jax back, I wasn't *that* desperate; or was I?

"Landon, I can't do something so deceitful. I care about Jax way too much to trick her into staying."

"It's a solid plan, if you're left with no other options," he reminded me, a teasing glint in his tone. "But all jokes aside, I do hope you get her back. I haven't met her yet, but I know she means a lot to you. Seriously, let me know if I can do anything."

I thanked him before we ended our call. He'd been calling me more often since he found out about me and Jax's break up. He, along with my father, appeared to understand how much I cared about Jax.

"Dad," I answered when I noticed it was him calling.

"Hello son. How are you?"

I stepped away from my desk, keeping my cell pinned to my ear.

"I'm still on the quest to find a suspect," I replied.

Approaching the bank of windows, I peered out absently. The view called, but I didn't really see it as my mind was stuck on Jax.

"Did the outside security team I hired help at all?" My father asked. "They were an eager bunch, very motivated."

"Yes. They were the ones that discovered that my signature used to sign for the drone was a clever forgery. However, they weren't successful in figuring out who was behind it. They also couldn't link the person who signed for the drone, with the one that leaked the photos."

We haven't yet confirmed why, or if it were one or a group of people behind the attacks launched at me and Jax.

"I wish I could do more for you. I noticed from our brief meet at dinner that the young lady meant a lot to you. I know I wasn't always the best example for you and your brother, but I hope you can understand that I pushed you because I have always wanted what was best for you."

"I know dad. I appreciate all the help you are giving me. I'll see you later tonight for dinner."

Family dinner nights were a regular occurrence now. Although our family was a long way from being close knit, we all managed to show up and break bread together. Blake was still being Blake-the-Fake, feigning concern and urging that it was for the best that me and Jax weren't together anymore.

"See you later son."

My father's support wasn't something I was used to, but it meant more than he could have known. His efforts proved that even the most controlling person I knew, had the ability to change.

Chapter Thirty-Seven

Jax

The night sweats came more frequently, releasing demons from my past to wreak havoc on my mind while I slept. The exposure, and extra attention I had gone out of my way to avoid, had taken my already paranoid state to an all-time high. It was only a matter of time before the tape holding me together ripped apart, and I was clueless as to what would seep out of me.

I'd been ducking and dodging Chase's calls, but I had finally given in and agreed to meet with him. Despite the newest threat lingering over my head, I believe it was time we talked. We'd agreed to meet at his house in Westport, since it was the most secure in keeping out the media.

Morgan, the house manager, escorted me into the house and my eyes found Chase immediately. He waited just inside the door. He was so handsome and put together, my damn breath caught at the first sight of him. He was dressed conservatively in black slacks, and a light green button up that intensified the radiant sparkle in his eyes.

"Hi, Jax. You look lovely as always." His words sounded as sincere as the expression he presented.

"Thank you."

Although he didn't say it, I didn't miss the way his eyes lit up at my presence. The sight caused my heart to flood with unexpected emotions, the kind that had me wanting to wrap myself around him. I didn't notice the tremble in my body, until he stood close enough for me to feel his warmth. Had he noticed my breathing had hiked up a notch?

His smile didn't help things either. Seeing him smile, made my lips turn up on their own accord. After he scanned me, his eyes locked with mine, and didn't drop.

His sinful scent caressed me next, the spicy and relaxing mix invading my senses. Although I was sure I was failing, I pretended his presence didn't affect me.

"I missed you Jax. I have honestly been pretty miserable without you."

I missed you too.

My damn mind needed to shut the hell up, or had I said that out loud? Based on the way Chase kept smiling at me, I had.

"Come. Have a seat please." He ushered his hand towards the dining area, and waited until I was aligned with him, before he placed a delicate hand on the small of my back. The initial touch caused me to stifle a gasp, as I fought not to react.

"What did you want to speak to me about?" I asked.

"I wanted to talk to you because we've discovered more evidence proving I was set up."

Intrigued, I sat up in my chair. He had already told me he was innocent, but I was left with no choice but to refuse to meet with him when he called me the first time. The threat of exposing a video of my worst nightmare was hanging over my head, still was.

"What kind of evidence?" I asked.

He handed over a tablet and talked as I scrolled. "Someone went through a lot of trouble to set me up. The signatures on the documents required to use my company's drone were from digitally enhanced copies of my signature. Someone at the Alien Gang Internet Café, took remote possession of my laptop and sent those photos of us to the media. This person knew the café well enough that we were unable to pull a full facial shot from the security cameras."

I scanned the tablet's screen, scrolling through the pictures as I attempted to pick up on anything that stood out. Nothing registered.

"Whoever set me up, I believe their aim was to break us up."

My gaze lifted and connected with his. "Maybe they did us a favor," I offered, feigning nonchalance.

"You and I both put forth a lot of effort to spend time with one another. You survived my family. Whether you admit it to yourself or not, we *were* good together."

Although I returned my attention to the picture I was studying, his words remained with me and I sensed the hurt in his tone from my casual behavior.

He sat motionless, as I examined the evidence he presented. After a long while of studying the data, I glanced up. I had accused him of something he didn't do and soon after, I stopped digging into the case where it concerned his innocence. I'd promised him, the night after I revealed to him my secret that I would never stop fighting for him and ended up doing the opposite. If I had kept digging, maybe I would have found he was innocent.

"Chase, I am so sorry. Please forgive me. I apologize for not believing you when you told me you didn't do this. And I apologize for damaging your laptop and destroying your data. I had no idea any of my fallout would affect you. I never believed you were involved in this, until I saw what I believed was solid evidence."

"Thank you, and as hard as it might be for you to believe, I understand why you did what you did. You think I don't understand your position because I have always had money. I clawed my way out from under my father's shadow, because I wanted to make a name for myself. The task wasn't easy having access to millions, so I understand how difficult it was for you to accomplish it without money."

He reached across the table for my hand, but I didn't give it right away. He kept his hand there, not caring about my stubbornness. The deep affection he continued to aim at me was my undoing.

When I placed my hand inside his, I immediately relaxed. My mind eased and my tension disappeared. I could breathe. Damn, I didn't know how much this man affected me until he'd put his hands on me.

Chase had helped me weave a path through a minefield of horrific memories. He unknowingly kept me from falling into the abyss of darkness that constantly clawed at me. I believed *he* was the path to healing I'd needed all along.

He squeezed my hand. "Jax, I apologize for what has happened. It was never my intention for you to get hurt or caught up in my drama. I need to know that you're okay."

I nodded. "After a week, the hype died down. Caps, shades, baggy clothes, and taking scenic routes have been working to keep me discreet so far."

He blew out a breath, pleased that my life was once again manageable. His hand clung to mine tighter. "What about us? You think we still have a chance?"

I swallowed, unsure now that I was so close to him, touching him. His hopeful gaze was making me weak.

"Please, Jax. I can't lose you because some jealous person doesn't want us together. I promise you, I haven't, and I won't, stop searching, until I find out who did this. I understand how badly being exposed hurts you. Is there anything I can do to make things better? Is there anything you need me to do?"

My hand tightened around his because I knew he was sincere.

"Thank you. I believe you *will* do what it takes to find out who did this, and I'll help you. However, we can't get back together or fall back into a relationship. Being with you puts me at serious risk for more exposure."

He didn't reply but gave a defiant glare, letting me know my words had gone in one ear and out the other.

Was this the right time to tell him the latest threat that was wreaking havoc in my life since we'd been apart? Besides, seeing him at all was a risk.

"Chase, I'm—" I was too fucking nervous. "I didn't stay away from you because I didn't want to be with you. I was afraid. I—" I glanced at my phone sitting on the table before me and stopped talking. It was too soon to put the weight of another situation on top of what we were already dealing with.

"What is it? You can tell me anything Jax."

I shook my head. No, I was keeping my issues to myself. Telling him could spark a firestorm of a different kind. I had to stay away from Chase. It was for the best that I did.

We enjoyed a nice dinner, but I didn't miss the questions in his eyes. Chase knew something was up. The way his gaze kept probing me. The way he kept studying my every move.

His behavior was reminiscent of the first day we met. He had studied me across that table like he knew something I didn't. He wasn't going to leave me alone until he knew what I was keeping from him.

He followed me to the door. When I reached for the doorknob, he placed his hand over mine, stopping me while boxing me in. If I turned and looked at him, it was over. He was too close. He smelled too good. He felt like my own personal heaven.

"Jax," he called, his voice vibrating off my flesh and touching a few of my hot zones.

"Yes." I still hadn't turned around.

"I need you to turn around and look me in the eyes. I want you to see the truth of my words."

Reluctantly, I turned. His serious gaze locked with mine as I fought to get myself under control.

His fingers slid up my forearm, leaving a trail of goose-bumps that prickled like hot whispers against my skin. He knew exactly what he was doing to me, what he had the ability to do to me. Nipples, hard. Pussy, wet. Neck pulse, every pulse, pounding.

"You're not telling me everything. I'm not going to rush you but call me when you're ready to talk."

He paused.

"And, Jax—"

I think I said yes. My eyes had dropped to his lips as I stood fighting a shiver of anticipation.

"Let me give you something to remember me by."

He didn't give me time to reply because his sexy lips were on mine and his heat seeking tongue was stroking the inside of my mouth. His strong hands roamed, causing my body to react to each stroke, swaying and bending to savor every squeeze and caress.

By the time he turned me loose and opened the door, I could hardly walk, and he had thrown my vision off by a degree or two.

Chase

Jax hadn't allowed me to escort her back to her house, but nothing was going to stop me from inserting myself back into her life. I was convinced she needed me, whether she admitted it to herself or not. It also appeared she wanted to tell me something, but was continuing to be her hardheaded self.

She looked gorgeous, and her skin was alive with a natural glow, making her more beautiful than I remembered. However, the stress behind her eyes told me she hadn't been sleeping.

Our short dinner date, the caring glint in her eyes when she had taken my hand, even her apology, it all drew me right back into her world. I was more determined than ever to find out what was wrong.

Her words resonated, the ones about us not returning to our relationship, but I had chosen to ignore them. I wasn't letting her go again. I had waited long enough. If she hadn't shown up tonight, my next move was to waltz into her apartment like I paid the rent there. There wasn't a doubt about what I wanted, and I was willing to risk anything to get it.

I'm sure she received my response to her demand that we not return to our relationship, loud and clear, while I was kissing her.

***

Jax

A few days later, a glance at my watch showed me and Chase had been talking for nearly two hours. A knock at my door startled me, and I prayed it wasn't TK. I didn't feel like entertaining, talking, or putting in investigative work. All I wanted was to keep talking to Chase, since an active threat and fear was keeping me away from him.

"Chase, hold on, there's someone at my door."

"It's too late for someone to be at your door. If it's not Lena, tell them to go away."

I laughed at him as I ambled to the door. A quick peek had me grinning from ear to ear as I sprang the door open and clicked off my phone.

"Chase? What are you doing here?"

Instinctively, I peeked around his sturdy shoulder.

He didn't say a word. Instead, he stepped in, closed and locked my door and turned to face me. His lips were on mine so fast, I had no choice but to give in. We were in so much trouble.

Less than five minutes later I was spread out across my coffee table with Chase kneeling before me, making me call on the lord with the reverence of an over-zealous choir member.

Chapter Thirty-Eight

Jax

I managed to keep Chase away for two weeks after he'd shown up at my door and commenced stroking me every which way but loose. We had gone at it like animals, fucking until daybreak.

Keeping Chase at a distance was the best thing I could do if I was ever going to figure out who was threatening me. However, keeping him away was easier said than done.

Based on Chase's interpretation, James Taylorson was a womanizing cheat with questionable parenting skills. Lately, he was making positive efforts to redeem himself. For reasons I had not figured out, James liked me, and had extended another invite to family dinner.

"Why all the family dinners? Based on the last one, I would think your father wouldn't want me back, or anywhere near Blake?"

"I don't know. This is a first. I think he likes you because you're strong, independent, and you can speak his language where it concerns business. Also, he and Blake have such a strong love-hate relationship, that he would invite you just to spite him."

An hour later, I was staring across the table at Blake whose nasty gaze was slapped away by the sharp sting of mine. After the media drama, and being officially labeled Chase's new woman, I figured I owed the family another face-to-face.

To my surprise, and the rest of the family's obvious surprise, James hobbled up and placed a delicate kiss on my cheek. Although the older man stood relying on a cane, he towered above me, reminding me of where Chase had inherited his height.

His free hand brushed my shoulder as he took a step back and flashed a crooked smile. "You look lovely, simply lovely."

I shot a quick look at Chase before I returned to James. "Thank you, I appreciate the nice compliment. You're looking pretty dapper yourself." I hope James didn't think he had another Tonya on his hands, just because I gave him a compliment. There was no way, ever in the history of this life, past, present, or future that he'd ever have a shot.

James couldn't contain his grin. I'm sure he wasn't used to someone like me, who wasn't going to tell him what I think he wanted to hear. He turned and glanced at Chase. It appeared he intended to say something, but before he could, Chase sent his arms around his father.

The hug was awkward and fumbled at first, until James softened and returned his son's hug. This was a new action for the men. Chase had breezed over the topic about hugs and kisses being passed out by his mother, while his father worked non-stop and dished out tasks, orders, and discipline.

Staring at the men embrace each other, I presumed James was attempting to change, and give his family the care he had neglected to give in their younger years. Tonya sat in silence, gawking at the exchange. Blake appeared stunned, jealous even, as he cut his eyes at his brother and father's display.

When James released Chase, a smile lifted one side of his face before he patted his son's shoulder and hobbled to the head of the table. Once James was seated, Olivia entered, on cue, with a serving tray filled with a variety of drinks.

When Blake aimed his predatory gaze in my direction, I sensed an insult on the horizon.

"So, Ms. Saint-Pierre, I see you've managed to become quite the celebrity. How far down your checklist is the baby, and the joint bank account? Or, is the plan to get married first?"

Why was that demon so invested in me and Chase's business? It wouldn't surprise me one bit if he had hired spies to watch us. However, I believe he would have dropped a bombshell to the media the moment he found one.

"Blake," both Chase, and James called to him in warning. He ignored them by taking a hard sip of his drink and eyeing me over the glass.

"Your kind makes it hard for *decent* women. You, with your so-called black-girl-magic. How you get unsuspecting white men to buy into that shit, is beyond me."

Chase jumped out of his seat, and I gripped his arm, his strength nearly lifting me out of my chair. His body heaved; every muscle pulled tight with anger. If that table hadn't been between him and his brother, I'm sure he would have hurt Blake. James and Tonya sat deadly still, afraid for Blake who was smart enough to stay quiet.

So, this was how Blake was planning to start the dinner. My intentions were to remain nice to him tonight, but his words had caused my motivation to dissolve into a cloud of black vapor.

I tugged hard at Chase's arm and was finally able to get him to sit. James and Tonya visibly breathed after he had taken the seat.

My mind wouldn't be still. It wouldn't allow me to ignore the things Blake had said. I wasn't going to play nice.

Tonya kept her head downcast, eyeing me under her lashes. She appeared to be anticipating my response to her husband.

James sat at the head of the table with a poker face, sipping the tea the maid had placed in front of him. If the frown Chase aimed at his brother grew any deeper, it would put a crack in his flawless skin.

He leaned in with the intent of letting his brother have it, but I placed my hand on his forearm to stop him. When my gaze met Blake's, the fires of hell had risen, and I fully intended to light the bastard up. His daring glint met my vicious one.

He was at the top of my suspect list for who had spied on me and Chase, which added to my serious dislike for him.

"When I discovered you had one nut, from a car accident you caused no less, it gave me a better understanding of why you have so much bitchiness in your attitude." Tonya spit her drink on the table, a series of loud coughs had overtaken James, and Chase tugged at *my* arm this time. "Jax," he called to me in a hushed tone. He knew I was about to be a petty bitch, and he was right.

I had someone threatening me with a nightmarish film from my childhood that I was too afraid to tell Chase about. I couldn't sleep. My emotions were all over the place, and we still hadn't found out who had spied on us and set Chase up to take the fall. So, yes, Blake was about to get lit on fire.

"The lack of testosterone has not only affected you physically, but it has also weakened your mind, which has never been fed anything but bullshit. My words are probably echoing in the void you call a brain right now. It's glaringly obvious you want your brother's life, but you don't have enough *balls* to take it. Since you don't have the *cojones* to take his thunder or to even replicate yourself a copy, all you have left is your misguided opinions and your imprudent judgement."

Chase shook my shoulder, attempting to stop me as Blake sat frozen, too stunned to spit out a word in response. "Jax. He's not worth it."

The sound of everyone's breathing became amplified like microphones sat at their mouths and noses. Every eye was locked on Blake, including mine. Olivia had frozen in place behind Tonya with the serving tray in her gloved hands, her eyes aimed at Blake.

Blake sat taller in his chair; his jaw clenched so tight he was a second from chipping a tooth. Chase sat as stunned as the rest of his family, his hand gripping my arm in a tight hold like he was afraid I was going to get up and attack.

Blake reared back in his chair with a stiff neck and astonished eyes. His voice roared across the table. "How dare you talk to me that way? You are beneath me."

He glared in his father's direction; his chest puffed out like a prize winning rooster. "Dad, aren't you going to say anything? I'm doing what you would normally do in a situation like this." All eyes pivoted to James. "You know damn well if she was associated with me, you would have found a way to get rid of her."

"Stop talking Blake." James' rigid tone had us all glancing in his direction. "You still don't know when to close your mouth. We're here to enjoy dinner. Let us." James sipped his tea like the matter was handled, but Blake blatantly cut his eyes at his father and returned his attention to me.

What was his problem with me that he would defend Chase? Based on what I gathered of their relationship, Blake spent a lot of his time plotting against Chase to gain control of the company. He hated me more than his quest to sabotage his brother. Why?

Olivia raced toward the door, either to get out of the line of fire, or she was in a hurry to get whatever she intended so she could return and witness more drama.

James appeared to be amused by the sparring contest Blake wanted, and I fully intended to give. Tonya's facial expression surprised me. A smirk rested on her face, as she stared between me and her husband. She had even leaned forward, like she didn't want to miss a word.

Blake's ugly scowl called to my anger. He wasn't done. His father was right, he didn't know when to shut up. He had an unrelenting will to get me upset. Was he in some way getting a thrill out of the harsh words I lobbed at him?

"You're the kind of low-class trash that thrive on men like us to increase your social status. I come from a family of wealth. I have a name, so I'll always be more than you. You are nothing other than a no class charlatan who has poisoned my brother and maybe even my father, but you don't fool me. I don't intend to sit idly by and say nothing while you manipulate your way into this family."

"Jax. He's not even worth the energy," the voice in my head said. Head-voice be dammed because I wasn't listening. I couldn't stop the words gathering on my tongue like poison, as I prepared to reply to the insults Blake had spit out.

"All you'll ever have is a name, Blake. Instead of worrying about your brother's life and my actions, you should be working on a plan to build yourself one. One that doesn't involve jealousy and self-hate. As soon as Chase and I leave this house, you will slink back into the cesspool of darkness you crawled from and fade away. No one will see you; no one will hear you; no one will miss you, and no one will even care that you're not there. Your opinion means about as much as an old dog's waning bark. You mean nothing."

My words sailed toward Blake, the harshness of them leaving his face red and tight with biting anger. I was leaning so far across the table Chase had both his arms around my shoulders.

Blake had touched a nerve, a live wire I had juiced with maximum wattage. I didn't realize I was in tears, until they were sliding down my cheeks. Hot angry tears. Why was I allowing this man to wreck my nerves? How could I let his meaningless opinion reduce me to tears?

Blake's severe gaze landed on everyone at the table, I believe wondering why no one raised a voice or jumped in to defend him. When he was done eye-slapping his family, he looked back to me. Chase had released me from his hold, but his strong hand kept a grip on my arm.

The hate between me and Blake was real, strong enough to bend chromium. The man didn't want me with his brother, or anywhere near his family. What was it about me that vexed him?

Chase reached out and covered the hand I had fisted on the table. His caring caress lingered there, until my hand was cupped inside his. Blake glared exceedingly long at our interlocked hands.

When I spotted the searing jealousy in his eyes, I had found my answer. Blake wanted Chase's life. I made his brother happy and, worse, his brother reciprocated my feelings.

Chapter Thirty-Nine

Jax

It had taken us an exceedingly long time to reach my apartment, due to us having to lose a car chasing paparazzi. He'd been hanging out outside the gates of Chase's family home. He showed off his boldness of driving while snapping photos of Chase's car, not caring that he endangered other motorists.

The rush of the car chase appeared to have done something to us. Once Paul released us safely into the garage, we moved with swift purpose to gain access into my apartment.

I was in such a mad rush to get the door open; I nearly snapped my key off in the lock. Chase's hands were filled with my tits as we shuffled over the door's threshold, not even bothering to flip the lights on.

The glow from the lights outside, shining in through the drapes, gave the scene the only romantic touch it would get. All we cared about, in this moment, was fucking each other; raw and hard.

Chase released my tits long enough to slam and lock the door. I dropped the keys on the floor and was lifted and whipped around so fast, I lost my breath. The next thing I knew, my silk blouse was gripped and torn open as I was hiking my skirt up.

We were so crazy for each other; buttons were popping as clothes continued to be ripped. The harmonic sound of our anxious heaves livened up my dim living room, sounding like some new communications technique we were forming.

On prior occasions, Chase had fucked me against my door and on my coffee table. This time, when he lifted me, he appeared to be searching for a place to park us. I pointed at the wall behind him. I didn't care where he fucked me, I just needed him inside me as soon as possible.

My underwear, like the pairs before, were ripped away. My legs were spread wide, and my hips gripped tight in his strong hands. With my back pinned against the wall, my breaths heave so hard in anticipation, it emitted a low whistling sound. Chase drove his thick length into me with such force, I believed he'd knocked my soul backwards in my body, putting it in time out.

We devoured each other with hungry kisses, exploring hands, and tempting squeezes while he fucked me with a wild need that mirrored mine. He was going home with some scratches tonight because my nails dug deep and my fist clenched hard as a way of dealing with his powerful thrust.

"Chase, you're too deep!" I yelled. "It's too much. Oh, God, it's too much."

"You can take it. Let me see your face. I want to see you taking it." Was his reply. He started pushing into me harder and deeper, making me gasp as he threatened to knock some internal organ loose.

"Oh God, you're pounding me so hard. And it's so fucking good," I panted and yelled between sharp breaths.

My ass and back were going to be bruised, but I didn't give a damn. Chase knew exactly how to make me lose my shit and forget about all the drama surrounding our lives.

"I want you to miss this dick while I'm not around." If that were his mission, he was accomplishing it.

"Aww! Oh shit! You're about to make me come!"

We both came, loud, hard, and sinfully delicious, my pussy pulsing and raining over his throbbing dick.

***

After Chase's departure, the best I could do was stagger to my couch. He had done such a good job of pleasing me, I found myself slipping in and out of sleep. My heavy eyes attempted to drag themselves back open each time they slid close.

My ripped shirt still managed to cling to my body by a thread and my bra only covered one tit. My skirt had survived the action, and although it was twisted, it had managed to fall back over my legs.

Chase was the sleeping pills I had prescribed myself. His sex was a cure for all that was wrong with me. Night sweats be damned, once Chase got a hold of me I slept like a fat baby in a dry diaper.

My face pinched when my eyes picked up on movement in the mirrored portion of my small bar area. Was that someone attempting to tip toe across my dark living room? Had I fallen asleep? I blinked hard to make sure I wasn't seeing things.

My skin tightened on my bones and an instant chill erupted over me. *Someone's in my apartment.* My heart rate skyrocketed, but I was so stunned, I froze in place.

The intruder must have waited until I had fallen asleep to make an escape. How long had they been inside my apartment?

When I snapped out of my trance, I reached under my couch. My hand went fishing around for the gun my father had taught me how to use. Fortunately, I had never had to draw it on anything but targets when my father would take me to the gun range.

Just as my hand tapped the hard grip of my gun to unsnap it from the leather pouch it was sheathed in, the dark figure ran

324 · KETA KENDRIC

towards me. His shouting registered, but I didn't understand a word because my mind was focused on freeing my gun.

His heavy fist came down at me and although my quick sideways movement dodged his hand, it knocked me off balance. Taking advantage of my dilemma, he shoved my shoulder and sent me off the couch to the floor.

He didn't appear to have a gun, and I couldn't afford to let him get a hold of mine, so I kicked at his legs with all I had. My attempt worked as he yelped in pain and limped away from me, realizing I was going to fight.

I scrambled forward, legs kicking and arms flailing, sliding on my stomach to get back to my couch. Once I had my gun secure and in my hand, I lifted and pointed it at the man. Scrambling across the floor on my ass, I pushed my back against my couch to get myself to a standing position. He had made it as far as my door.

The metallic *click* of my Glock froze him in place, just as he was reaching for the front door lock.

"Take one more step and I will be painting my walls with your fucking brains."

His hands reached for the sky, one holding what appeared to be a dark camera or recording device. I maintained a steady aim at the man, as I reached blindly onto my coffee table for the remote to turn on my lights.

The man was clearly scared shitless, holding what I noticed was a high-powered camera in one of his shaking hands.

"Drop the camera asshole!" I yelled the order once the room was fully illuminated. The sound of the camera hitting the floor pleased me as the trembling asshole appeared ready to piss himself the way his knees were knocking. He was young, at least early twenties, slender with a buzzed low haircut.

"Who the fuck are you? How did you get into my apartment? Who hired you to spy on me?"

"I'm sorry. I needed the money." His muffled voice sounded as he was still facing the door.

"Turn your ass around and tell me who hired you!" I shouted, my anger taking over. "Are you the asshole who has been spying on me all this time?"

I hadn't realized I was inching closer to the man, until I was about four feet away. My closer positioning frightened him as I noticed his body, visibly shaking. He couldn't have been behind something as sophisticated as the drone spying. He was more than likely a pawn, a disposable entity as the mastermind maintained his cover.

"Unless you have a superpower that will allow you to eat nineteen hollow point slugs, you better start talking. And please know, I'm crazy enough to empty this clip into your ass, stand over your bleeding body, reload, and empty another clip into you."

He raised his hands higher in response to my threatening words.

"I was hired over the phone. They sent me a key card to this building in the mail, along with a key to the door, and two different six-digit pins to get on to this floor. I never met them. They wired me five-thousand to break in and promised to wire the rest, when I got any information on you."

Six residents lived on this floor. If someone wanted to break in, they would have six chances of getting a pin, and could easily steal a key and key card, or get one copied. This was classic proof that no place was truly secure.

"So let me get this shit straight. You broke into my house. Hung out. Watched and recorded me having sex, and tried to sneak out when you thought I was asleep? How long have you been in my apartment?"

"I-I-I came in right after you guys left. I'm sorry. I didn't mean any harm."

"Of course, you meant harm, you asshole. Did you not just hear me list out all of the crimes you've committed? I should pull this fucking trigger."

"Ma'am. I'm so, so sorry."

He tried to wave me off, shaking his head as tears started to spill when my hand tightened around the pistol grip.

"It's too late to be sorry. You weren't sorry when you attacked me. If I killed you right now, I won't spend a day in jail."

I took a few steps back and picked up my cell phone.

"Yes. I would like to report a break in. I'm holding the intruder at gunpoint. If he tries anything, I'm shooting to kill, so send someone quick."

The dispatcher continued to talk on the other end of the line. I placed the phone on speaker and continued my conversation with the dispatcher while I texted Chase.

"Intruder in my house. Have him at gunpoint. Come back quick. Cops on the way. 911 online w/me."

Chase text back immediately.

"On the way. Ian will be there in a few minutes. Shoot the intruder if you have to."

Ian was Chase's extra driver. Had Chase been leaving the man to watch me this entire time? Why else would he be two minutes away?

Ian arrived along with the two officers. I buzzed them all up on the same elevator trip. My want-to-be criminal intruder had become a sniffling mess of tears as snot bubbles blew from his red nose.

I had slung every question I could think of at the man before the cops arrived, discovering that there must have been some truth to his story. He didn't know shit. As scared as he was, I was sure he had revealed to me all that he knew.

Chase came in just as the cops were questioning me. Ian stood at my window like my secret guardian. After Ian and the officers left with the crying intruder, I threw myself into Chase's arms.

He kept checking me over and suggesting I see a doctor just because I had a small scrape on my arm. "Come home with me Jax. I'm afraid for you staying here tonight. At least stay with me until you get your locks and security information updated."

I nodded before glancing up at Chase. "I took that asshole's Camera." I marched over to my couch, reached underneath it, and dragged out the intruder's camera. "He admitted to planting some listening devices too, I took those as well, to see if I can track them back to a location. I threatened to kill his ass, if he told the cops I took his equipment. The asshole recorded us. He was in here while we were…" I couldn't finish. The impact of the situation had finally taken its toll on me as my tears started to spill.

Chapter Forty

Chase

The next evening, Jax sat across from me devouring the dinner of prawns in plum sauce, and fried rice I had cooked for her. She had found it entertaining to learn that I knew how to cook and was convinced I would burn the house down until she tasted my food.

The plan was to cheer her up, since the camera, and listening devices she had taken from the intruder, hadn't produced any viable clues as to who was behind the attacks being lobbed at us. The man had also been released on bond, and the authorities were being tightlipped about the release.

"Jax, I want you to be *my* woman. I want to be *your* man. I want to take care of you in every way you might need it. I most certainly want to be the only man you're touching, kissing, and caressing." I blurted.

If she thought I didn't know about all the time she and TK was spending together since our separation, she had seriously underestimated me. The way he looked at her and reacted to her indicated that he wasn't going to abandon his quest to cross their bond of friendship.

She sighed in mid-chew but didn't appear as upset about my demanding request as I had expected she might. I hid my smile as she sat considering my request.

"Chase, there is something I need to tell you first. The real reason I stayed away from you after you told me you were innocent of the drone and picture leak."

I sat my fork down, giving her my undivided attention.

"When I was a child, my nightmares were recorded for anyone willing to pay to see them. Over the years, I along with the help of my father, have poured a lot of time into tracking down a lot of those people who were members of that porn site. Our efforts have led to the arrest of others who own sites just like that one."

She handed me her phone. "I stopped seeing you even after you proved your innocence because being with you would mean that this would get leaked."

After only a few seconds of seeing the video, I stabbed at the button trying to turn it off.

"Jax, I'm so sorry this is happening to you." I reached for her hand, as my brain processed what her being with me truly meant. "You being anywhere near me means your risking them leaking that video."

This was what she was keeping from me. This was why her and TK had been together so much. This was much more serious than leaked pictures or even a stalker. This situation was several horrific crimes caught on film. Rape, incest, and child pornography just to name a few.

"Jax," I called her name. A low whisper was all I could manage because my heart was breaking for her. "Someone is dead set on keeping us apart. We need to report this to the authorities as soon as possible."

Someone wants us apart so bad, that they were willing to go to these disgusting lengths to try and destroy her reputation.

"Why would you see me, knowing what your risking?"

She shrugged. "Being exposed like that is one of the worst things that can happen to me. But, there is something much more important than my exposure at risk, and it took me way too long to realize it."

Being forced to participate in child porn and having evidence of her torture resurface as a threat to keep her away from me, was not something to take lightly. They were using an illegal piece of evidence to threaten her.

"I don't understand. What could possibly be more important than protecting yourself from the kind of nightmare I know you suffered?"

Her phone sounded, and I prayed she didn't answer. What we were discussing was much more important at the moment.

She answered.

At first a slither of worry moved across her face, before angry creases lined her forehead. She listened to the caller, not speaking a word. Dislike for what she was hearing, played out in her facial expressions. They were probably telling her that they were about to release the video for being with me.

She slammed her phone on the table, startling me and sending the plates and silverware rattling.

"I'm about to play a recording I received from an unknown caller. I need you to explain this shit to me, Chase," she barked through clenched teeth.

What now?

She swiped the face of her phone with hard angry flicks. The sound of my voice spilling from her phone froze me in place, taking everything except my ability to hear.

"She's the first woman who has introduced me to the word 'no,' in a long time, and it drives me crazy. I want her to be mine. I'm willing to do anything to make it happen."

"If you want her that bad man, do what Greg did to Kathy. Trap her. Women do that type of shit to men all the time."

The conversation was one I'd had months ago with Landon. We had a similar conversation recently when he'd called to check on me.

"Hey, that's not such a bad idea. It will be easy to sabotage her birth control."

I closed my eyes and prayed.

Ho-ly Fuck!

If this was another attempt by someone to split us up; it was going to work. If Jax's eyes were weapons, my family would have been planning my funeral. The words confirming that I was joking on the recording during the conversation were conveniently left out.

Jax leaned across the table, in the same manner she had leaned towards my brother at dinner yesterday. The sight of tears gathering in her eyes, tore at my heart. I reached for her, only to have my hand slapped away.

"How could you do something so despicable? I was ready to agree with you, until this shit. I'm risking one of my worst nightmares getting let loose just to be with you."

The words I attempted to spit out weren't making an impact, until I put some base in my voice.

"Jax, the conversation was of me and my friend talking shit. Whoever did this, didn't play the whole conversation. We were kidding, and—"

She stood in a rush, cutting me off. "I can't believe you did this. I can't believe you trapped me. What the hell is wrong with you?"

What the hell was she talking about? I hadn't trapped her. Her tears started to flow as she swiped angrily at them. I had never seen her this upset before. Not even when she believed I had leaked those pictures.

"I respected you, Chase. I would have never intentionally done anything to hurt you. I never missed a single pill when we were together."

"I know. I used to see you taking them."

She snatched her hand back when I reached for it again.

"No, you don't understand. You don't understand a damned thing. That call explains everything. It was you. You and your clever plot to trap me."

She wasn't making any sense. "Me. What? What are you talking about?"

"Like you don't know, Chase. Imagine my surprise, when I go in for my checkup, and laugh at my doctor when she tells me I'm pregnant."

My world stopped spinning. I stopped breathing. All movement had stalled. Jax picked up her knife and pointed it at me, the plum sauce glistening on its shiny edge like fresh blood. My eyes went wide and shock consumed me as I fought for words or at least to make sounds. I couldn't think about anything but what she had just revealed.

"You're p-p-pregnant?" My voice came out low, and shaky as uncertainty raced through my veins and sent my pulse slamming against my jugular.

Jax aimed her knife closer to my face, but her words had me so flustered, I wasn't in the right mindset to back away.

"Why are you acting surprised? Isn't this what you wanted?"

"You're pregnant?" My voice grew louder and more demanding now that her revelation had wrapped a fist around my brain.

My gaze landed on her flat stomach, the news short-circuiting my brain and stalling my ability to speak. *I'm going to be a father.*

My heart flooded with instant happiness, as a smile danced across my lips. Jax's loud fussing had faded into the background, and I didn't care that she waved a butter knife in front of my face.

My ears and mouth may as well have been stuffed full of cotton. I was flooded with deafening thoughts of Jax being pregnant with *my* baby. I had always wanted kids, wondering if I would get lucky enough to find the right woman to share the privilege of raising them with.

When I noticed Jax's flowing tears, and her body shaking in distress, I jumped from my chair and ran to her. She backed away, shaking the knife at me.

"I'll never forgive you for this. You have not only crossed the line this time, you've destroyed it. How could you mess with my pills, and do this to me?"

Jax's words ricocheted through my brain. She believed I had done this. I had, but not in the way she was assuming. I was unable to concentrate on her accusing words because I kept focusing on her confirmation that she was pregnant.

The harsh words she slung hadn't yet put an end to the happiness that had so suddenly flooded me. I had to straighten my stance when my legs threatened to crumble under the overwhelming weight of the news. Jax proceeded to rip me a new asshole, but I couldn't care less. She was pregnant. *Pregnant!*

I stepped into her striking distance, hoping she didn't rear back and hit me, or worse, stab me. I removed the knife from her hand before placing it on the table and steadying her shaking hands.

"I hope the devil drags your trap-a-woman-planning-ass to the deepest, fiery pits of hell for what you did."

My words cut through the hail of curse words she was raining down on me.

"Jax, baby. Please take a moment to think about this," I suggested, my tone calm.

She blinked and glared into my eyes, appearing to finally notice my closeness.

"Why would you receive a random voice mail, of a private conversation I had with my friend months ago? Someone, likely the same person who pulled off the drone incident, has been invading my privacy, screening my calls, and probably has my house bugged."

She remained silent, allowing my words to seep in.

"I didn't tamper with your pills. I wouldn't. I want a lasting meaningful relationship with you. Why would I mess up my chances by doing something that deceitful?"

Her beautiful eyes darted left and right before returning to mine.

"Baby, someone is determined to break us up. When you decided to see me despite the latest threat they lobbed at you, they added this to the mix. They want to split us up by any means necessary," I urged, attempting to get her to hear reason.

In an attempt to help her lose the tension, I rubbed her shoulders, light and gentle.

"You're pregnant. Are you sure?" I glanced at her stomach again.

She pinched her lips tight and nodded as a tear slid down her cheek and joined the others that had gathered above her lip.

Smiling at this moment was going to upset her, but I couldn't help myself. "Don't cry. We'll be fine. I want this baby as much as I want you, but I didn't mess with your pills, just like I didn't send those pictures to the media."

She studied my face.

"You want the baby?"

"Of course, I want our baby. This news makes me happy. Excited. I want to announce to the world that I'm going to be a father." My excitement was hammered away by my plaguing thoughts. We had to address the recurring problem we had.

"We have a serious problem to confront. The pills could have just not worked, but if someone tampered with them, you could be in danger. They are also threatening you with an illegal video which is more proof of their ruthlessness. And the intruder was the most dangerous awakening yet. I can't let anything happen to you and our baby. We still don't know who set me up. I believe it's the same person who sent you the recording."

My grip on her hand tightened. I now had two people to protect. The realization of the news remained, nailing its way into my brain and bringing to light our child could already be in jeopardy by the person attempting to rip, his or her, parents apart.

"Do you have the last package of pills you started so we can have them checked for tampering?"

She bit her bottom lip, the action lifting her lip piercing. "About that. . ."

Her eyes didn't dare meet mine, as she sucked in a deep breath and released it with a noticeable uneasiness.

"Jax? How long have you been pregnant?"

She mumbled her words, causing me to cup my ear in my hand.

"You're going to have to repeat the statement a bit louder, because it sounded like you said two and a half months."

She nodded like a child on the receiving end of a serious scolding. It meant she had likely gotten pregnant on the yacht.

"Jax! How could you keep something this important from me, for so long? What if something had happened to you? What if something had happened to me? I would have never known about one of the best gifts I could ever receive."

Her eyes widened, surprised by my words. "It's not like I've known the whole time. We were at odds because I thought you were the drone stalker. Then, I was threatened with the one thing I thought would keep me away from you. Also, I was afraid to say anything because I thought you would be upset, and..."

With a *shush,* and a finger to her lips, I cut her off. I don't believe I had ever shushed anyone this way before. I could feel a deep crease, denting my forehead as I shook my head.

"Why on earth would I be upset?" I caressed her shoulders and rubbed her back, attempting to relax away the tension she clung to.

Uncertainty glimmered in her tight expression. Now, I understood the visible changes I had noticed in her. Her skin that I had always found beautiful was even more luminescent as it glowed under the lights. Although her posture was a little hunched and unsure, she kept her hands to either side of her midsection, unconsciously protecting what was there. I glanced at her flat stomach, covered by her blue fitted top.

"I know one of the reasons you had women sign NDAs was because they had made attempts to trap you. This pregnancy didn't happen that way. I'm not one of those women. I don't want to be labeled as one of them. I was upset with Blake at dinner yesterday because I was sitting there with your baby in my belly, and his words hit closer to home than I liked."

My head rocked side-to-side, disappointed she still didn't get it.

"I'm disappointed in you." She stared speechless. "After all this time, you don't get it. Making you sign an NDA has never crossed my mind. You're carrying our child. He or she is more important than anything. Now, I understand why you would risk your worst nightmare being released to see me. We have to stick together, now more than ever, to figure out who this person is and why they so badly want to keep us apart."

"The last thing I want to see is one of my worst nightmares being released for the world to see, but..."

Unconsciously, she touched her stomach.

"I can't let you put your life, and our baby's life in danger by going back to your apartment. I will have Morgan collect everything you need. I'll have whatever else you would like moved."

"Okay Chase," she said with a smirk.

My arms flew around her, ensuring I placed her mouth against my shoulder. I was not about to give her a chance to change her mind.

When she embraced me in return, I lifted and turned with her locked in my tight embrace. My muffled laughter bounced off her neck and breezed through her ponytail as her giggle mixed with the jubilation of mine.

"You have no idea how happy you make me," I voiced while setting her back on her feet. "You too," she said in a low apprehensive tone. She wasn't comfortable expressing her feelings to me, but I sensed her trying. At once, I exploded with concern over the way I had just handled her.

"I didn't hurt you, did I, tossing you about. What about all the reunion sex we have been having?"

She giggled. "I doubt he's the size of a plum, but as far as I've read, and from what my doctors say, my condition doesn't make me breakable. I can do everything I did before with a little more caution."

My lips twitched and my cheeks rose high. "He? You called him he? You know the gender already?"

"No, but I believe he's a he, because I can't possibly live with the idea of a mini version of me roaming the planet," she admitted, causing an outburst of laughter to rush from me.

My cheeks started to ache, I grinned so hard. I was going to be a father. *Me.* Although he was the size of a plum according to Jax, I couldn't resist reaching out to stroke her belly. She placed her hand over mine and smiled up at me.

There was no movement of any kind, but I didn't care because my son, or daughter was in there, and although Jax smiled now, she would hate me later. If she believed I was an obsessed stalker before, I hated to think about what she would label me now that I knew she was carrying our baby.

Chapter Forty-One

Jax

Chase was establishing himself as the rock in my life; the kind of support I had never allowed myself to have. He was the only man besides my father that I had let fully into my life. For the first time, I felt positive about the prospect of improving my life, not only for myself but especially for our baby.

However, Chase's overprotective attitude where it concerned my pregnancy was a whole different matter. It was nice to know he cared enough to want to protect us, but I was starting to suffocate.

Two weeks was the amount of time it had taken for my smile to drop. If he asked me how I was feeling one more time, I was going to scream.

I'd grown attached to the little peanut in my belly, but Chase was taking things too far too fast. He was treating me like the Queen of the Seven Kingdoms. Daenerys watch out.

I couldn't walk to the bathroom without him or his house staff offering to guide my way. Did all men get this excited over their first child?

Thankfully, the little fellow in my belly was being kind. Although occasional nausea would hit, I managed to keep my food down and the morning sickness phase according to my doctor was nearly over.

If the father was as kind as his son was being, I may survive this thing with my whole mind intact. However, I needed alone time. Fresh air. I needed to stretch my legs. Maybe return to work. There was only so much I could do teleworking from home. Goodness, Chase was killing me softly.

There was no doubt Lulu could handle the workload at the office while I was hiding in my baby daddy's mansion. However, I wanted to work, not hide from a madman I was beginning to think wasn't real.

If I had to guess, I would venture to say it was one of Chase's exes or one of the hundreds of women stalking him on social media. Blake had always been at the top of my suspect list. Hell, it could have been one of my one-night flings. I didn't know who, but they didn't want us together.

Chase requested that my apartment be rescanned for bugs along with his house. I volunteered to conduct the preliminary scans on his equipment, since I knew what to look for.

Did I have a stalker? Did Chase have a stalker? I didn't know, but with all the money he had access to, and my ability to hack and cyber spy, you would think we would have found the answer to the questions by now.

Approaching footsteps brought me back to the here and now.

Oh God. Here comes my baby daddy.

As I forced my lips into a smile, not even I believed what was planted on my face as Chase made his approach. He carried two large bags, stuffed with clothes and toys for the baby. For the past few weeks, he worked half-days and always returned home with shopping bags in tow.

He hired a contractor to turn one of the bedrooms into a nursery, so the sound of construction buzzed, and thumped most of the day as I switched back and forth between teleworking and watching the soaps on television.

As Chase sat next to me showing off the outfits that wouldn't fit the baby until he was two or three, thoughts of how

I had gotten pregnant filled my head. Nothing made sense anymore. My life had gone from a full-time businesswoman who had the perfect formula for keeping people at arm's length, to a woman thrust into a whirlpool of swirling passion and drama. Add to that a baby, and my life was as dramatic as the soaps I was becoming addicted to watching.

Chase was still talking about something. I looked him up and down, lifted a brow like I was listening and continued with my thoughts.

At first, the idea of being pregnant had me thinking crazy things like postponing it until I was ready. Now that the reality had set in and this little fellow had taken root, I found myself embracing the idea of becoming a mother, and of wanting to be a better mother than *my* mother. I believed I was already better than her. There was never any doubt that I wanted my baby from the moment I found out I was pregnant.

Chase and I expressed our happiness in different ways, his in voice and expensive baby purchases and mine with silence. It all became overwhelming at times, but I considered how he had grown up, and realized that spending five-thousand dollars on a baby rattle was his norm.

"So, what do you think?"

What had he asked? He wasn't flashing clothes anymore, so I couldn't get away with a *"that's nice,"* answer.

"What do I think about what?"

"Us getting a bigger house. Something *we* want," he stated, awaiting an answer.

I squeezed my eyes shut, meditating to stamp down my hormonal irritation.

"Chase, you live in a mansion, how much more room do we need?" I questioned him, thinking of the eight bedrooms, seven bathrooms, game room, study, four-car garage, pool,

pool house, movie room, and something I was probably forgetting, that I'd seen since my stay.

Oh! Fuck!

I had messed up and let the word, *we,* fall out of my mouth. The grin on his face revealed as much.

"Chase, slow down. You can't go out buying houses. Eventually, I'm going back home," I reminded him.

His defiant expression suggested otherwise, as one side of his lip tilted up and his glare shot to my belly. He'd made it known without uttering a word, that I wasn't going anywhere as long as his baby was inside me.

Chapter Forty-Two

Jax

Instead of James calling for another dinner night, Chase had volunteered us this time, telling his father that we would be there this evening. The last thing I wanted was to have dinner with his family, but we were having a baby together, so it appeared I was going to have to learn how to deal with them.

An air of elegance zipped through me in my high-collared, light blue body-hugging dress. It highlighted my best assets, kissing parts that would soon swell and stretch and become hard and sore within the coming months.

When I reached to strap into my sand colored, strappy stiletto, Chase appeared, taking the shoe, and strapping me into it with ease.

Walking into Chase's family home an hour later wasn't an easy task, as my stomach started fluttering. I usually didn't care what people thought of me, but when the numbers would be millions, it counted no matter how much I wished it didn't. However, I still didn't give a damn what Blake thought of me.

James greeted us at the front door, the maid, butler, and assistant maid at his back. His wide lopsided smile was the first thing I saw. Did he already know about his grandbaby?

Chase stood so close; his father had to squeeze past him to place a soft kiss on my cheek. "Nice to see you again, young lady," he stated, giving me a once-over.

Thankfully, James's greeting felt sincere. I would have hated to toss some of the hate I had stored up for Blake, at him, if he attempted to make a pass at me. Besides, the way Chase was staring at him with me, I didn't think I had anything to worry about.

His father had displayed a similar behavior toward me at the last dinner, and it was obvious that Chase wasn't used to seeing this more accommodating version of his father. The men shared a quick embrace, which went smoother than their last awkward hug.

James turned to me when they were done, allowing his hand to caress my elbow before he led me to our destination.

Chase maintained his close stance, hovering at my back. His overprotective posturing had me reaching behind me to shove him a few paces back.

"I was informed that seafood gumbo is one of your favorite meals. I hope the team has prepared it to your liking." James's cane thumped and echoed through the house, reflecting his chaotic movement.

"I'm sure it will be delicious." I glanced back at Chase whose protective behavior would spill our secrets before our words did.

When we entered the dining room, Blake and Tonya were already at the table. The sight of Blake standing and greeting me with a barely there head nod paused my steps for a moment.

"Nice to see you again, Jax," Tonya said, smiling.

Chase assisted me into the high-backed leather chair. An awkward silence fell over the room, and no one took their seats until after I'd taken mine.

As if things couldn't get any stranger, James's and Tonya's smiling gazes had never dropped from me. If my third appearance in their home was shocking, wait until they heard about the little nugget rolling around in my belly.

"Jax, I noticed you handled your encounters with the media and the leaked photos well," James stated as the maid placed dishes of soup in front of us. Why the hell would he start dinner with that shit? I'd had my mouth fixed for some gumbo, now my taste buds were all messed up thinking about that mess. It was his table, so I guess I was going to play along.

I noticed the question in his tightly pinched brows when Chase faced my direction. How was I planning to address his father's statement?

"Sir, I didn't exactly handle it well. I used every trick I could come up with to find out who leaked those photos. When I found out it was one of your company's drones, I gave your son hell, until he proved he'd had nothing to do with it. The crook is still out there. He thinks he's safe, but he's not." My stiff-eyed gaze was aimed in Blake's direction. "I've latched on to his scent, and I won't stop until I sink teeth in his a... in him," I corrected, proud of myself for not cursing.

Ever since I found out about the little fellow I was carrying; I had cut back on a number of my bad habits.

"I have no doubt that you'll figure out who did this. We're also investigating to get answers," James stated.

The chatter continued about the drone, and my and Chase's leaked photos until Blake, like nails scratching a chalkboard, interjected his voice into the conversation.

"Comes with the territory. If you enter a relationship with a billionaire, you should be smart enough to expect you'll not find any level of peace or privacy." Disdain dripped from him like wet paint.

My teeth sank into the inside of my lip as my eyes adjusted and used the lighting to blur Blake from my vision.

"So, Dad, how have you been? How's the physical therapy going?" I questioned James, knowing Blake would hate me addressing his father as Dad. Making matters worse, James answered my question with a wide smile.

"I'm much better. Things are going better than expected. Thanks for asking." A gracious head nod complimented his reply. His scanning gaze paused at each of us as he prepared to speak again.

"Chase tells me you guys have some important news you'd like the share?" His bushy brows lifted in anticipation, looking like two sleeping caterpillars sitting on his forehead.

I glanced at Chase. Was I going to let him put the bombshell out there? I was sure I'd be hearing about it on the news later when Blake leaked it to the media. Chase cleared his throat. I expected him to be nervous, but a big shit-eating grin was plastered across his face.

"I'm going to be a father! Jax is pregnant!" His body bounced in giddy satisfaction, unable to contain his excitement.

James's mouth dropped open, before a slow smile lingered in his eyes, getting used to the idea of a grandchild, I supposed.

Tonya made her way around the table. She stood above me and Chase, and embraced us over our shoulders, before she placed unexpected kisses on each of our cheeks. Her gesture pulled at my heartstrings, reminding me that she couldn't have children.

"Congratulations, guys. I'm happy for you. I'm excited to become an aunt." I believed her sincerity was genuine.

"Congratulations!" James stated. "I was hoping I'd get the chance one day to hear the shrieking cries of a baby again. Little feet scampering over the floors. Tiny hands pulling and breaking expensive pieces. Vomit and drool drenched shirts. I missed most of it with my sons, but I don't intend to miss it with my grandson," he voiced, surprising me and Chase, who sat frozen in his seat and gawking at his father.

My eyebrows lifted. They were taking the news well, so well in fact, I was waiting for the other shoe to drop.

"Congrats."

The word didn't surprise me; it was whose mouth the word had come from. Blake had labeled me a gold digger, and had blatantly suggested I was nothing but trash, and a low budget tech support clerk. He suspected I had planned my pregnancy and wedding to Chase from the start. I expected more of a fight from him, but he remained at peace, and I was grateful he had.

Chase and I thanked everyone, between conversations about baby names. We shared our decision to claim the baby as a boy, although we had no idea of the sex. Blake didn't participate in much of the conversation. He put on a decent performance, but he didn't like it one bit that I was stealing the spotlight. Occasionally, I would catch his pinched eyebrows and irritated gaze aimed at me.

By the time we had dessert, the little lemon in my belly had a college fund, life insurance, a top-of-the-line medical care plan, a nanny until he was eighteen, stock in Swift Capital, and a house that hadn't been built yet.

Tonya appeared happy about becoming an aunt, and likely took the opportunity as her chance to experience a touch of motherhood. Chase couldn't stop his infectious grin, and Grandpa James hadn't stopped going on and on since Chase broke the news.

Blake was the evil lurking entity at the jovial event. He'd never relaxed his face or unclenched his jaw. The more I was in his presence, the more I was becoming convinced he had somehow pulled off the drone scandal and sent me Chase's recorded conversation.

By the time we left his family mansion I was sure of one thing. I wasn't returning to my own apartment anytime soon, and my unborn child was ten times richer than I had ever been.

At the notion that his family had accepted the baby, Chase's grip on me and his son had tightened more than when we'd arrived, and the gleam in his eyes shined brighter. I welcomed his happiness because it reflected my own.

Chapter Forty-Three

Jax

All I wanted when we returned to Chase's mansion, was for him to pin me down and fuck me until I passed out. Instead, what I received was a belly rub and food shoved in my face, like I was his favorite four-legged pet.

It had been weeks, and Chase hadn't fucked me yet, even after I had begged him to. He'd gone back to believing sex would hurt the baby because of our tendency to get carried away sometimes. My hormones were so stirred and mixed, I was on the verge of unleashing my pent-up vixen if Chase didn't give up the goods willingly.

"Chase, will you stop rubbing my feet and look at me?" I fought to keep frustration from my tone.

Glancing up, he kept my foot planted in his lap; his hand still wrapped around flesh that was months away from the swollen stage.

"Chase, I'm only asking once more: Are you going to fuck me or not?"

"Maybe later. When we're ready for bed."

Was I in a fucking nightmare? I could feel my face and lips pinching at his unbelievable words.

Fuck this shit! A woman has gotta do what the hell she's gotta do when she's horny and the man who could give her what she wants was letting a baby the size of a damned lime stop him.

I jerked my foot from Chase's grip, causing him to cast a set of wide eyes at me.

"I'll be right back," I tossed over my shoulder as I stormed away. Chase had denied me one time too many. Hell, I wasn't even fat yet.

When I reentered the room ten minutes later, Chase's mouth dropped at what I had changed into. It was an Angel of Death costume; black leather covered the essential parts. Five-inch black leather hooker-heels and large black wings attached to my back accentuated the costume.

Chase hadn't gotten but a touch of my roleplaying persona because he usually took control and made me forget all about it. This was his reminder that if he wasn't going to control things, I had no problem doing so.

His wide eyes roved over me before he fell back and into the couch, his throat bobbing sporadically. His lips opened and closed several times, but he couldn't manage words. His gaze locked on the black whip gripped in one of my hands and the shiny black grim reaper scythe in the other.

Since confined to the house, I'd ordered all types of items he hadn't seen yet.

"If you tell me no one more time, you're going to lose some blood tonight one way or the other."

I raised the whip and followed it up with a dramatic display of the scythe, making sure he got a look at each.

Pretending I needed to fix my shoe, I propped my leg up on the couch next to him, fully aware my pierced pussy was on display from the crotchless portion of my outfit.

"Take off your clothes, Chase." My low and calm tone edged out as I kept my eyes aimed at my shoe the entire time. He reached for the buttons of his shirt, fiddling with them with frantic hands.

"Umm. Jax," he called.

"You're moving too damn slow!"

He jumped at my roaring voice. When I raised up and cracked the whip across the couch near his ear, he hopped up like the couch was on fire.

The familiar sound of his buttons hitting the floor pinged my ears when I got a good grip of his shirt and ripped it off with his help. I'd made a habit of popping his shirt buttons; therefore, he should've been investing in more of his shirts instead of baby clothes.

One of his shoes went sliding across the floor as the other skittered a few feet away from him. He jumped around, yanking one of his legs from his pants as the other clung to his muscular thigh for dear life. Once he'd finished the struggle with his pants, he snatched his boxer briefs down and his dick sprang up like he'd set free a big pink jack-in-the-box.

He stood before me ready, the sight of him sending my blood pressure through the roof.

"Kneel right here before me." I pointed at the area where I repositioned my leg, propping it up higher on the couch. He complied, but his gaze traveled to the whip hanging in my hand. When he got a close view of the scythe and noticed it was a real blade his eyes snapped up.

"Yes, it's real and if you don't start licking my pussy like a good death-fearing soul, I'm going to gut you and send your soul to hell." Embracing the role as the Angel of Death, I projected my menacing, sexually frustrated growl.

His warm hand caressed my inner thigh as his tongue slid across his parted lips, wetting them before his eyes landed on my exposed pussy.

"And Chase," I sang. My voice stopped his approach, his mouth inches from my pulsing heat when he looked up at me. I wanted him to feel the pressure for making me wait.

"If I don't come within five minutes, you better have a prayer ready. Your Angel of Death is an impatient bitch, who would love nothing more than to snatch your soul."

No further words were needed. Chase stood and turned me with ease, assisting me onto the couch. He didn't let me keep the scythe, placing it on the table behind him. The whip, I had refused to let him take. He didn't waste a second sinking his wicked tongue into my sizzling heat after he had spread my legs.

Oh my God. His tongue. Fuck five minutes, he was about to do it in two. My pussy wept with joy as the wetness he didn't catch, leaked down my inner thigh. Chase had his tongue buried so deep in my drenched heat, he made me drop the whip and my eager fingers gripped his hair to stir his head.

The fire roaring in the pit of my stomach reached out and burned the rest of my body so fast, all I had the ability to do was yell his name, loud and urgent. "Chase! Fuck, Chase!"

He didn't give a damn about the whip and scythe anymore and neither did I. He didn't allow me time to recover either. My thighs were gripped in the midst of my spasms, and he dragged my ass to the edge of the couch. Every breath was a difficult task, but lust kept me bold and determined.

"You better fuck me like you've been daydreaming about my pussy for months."

A smile slid across his lips before his eyes darkened. "I never stop daydreaming about *my* pussy. You're about to get fucked so good, it's going to take you a month to remember your own name."

After his possessively arrogant words, he plunged into me with one heaving thrust, bowing my spine and sending my head falling back and grinding into the couch. I don't know if it was that we'd not done it in the past weeks, or if it was my hormones, but dammit if this wasn't the best hard fuck Chase had blessed me with. I was one scratch from clawing a hole in his back, one scream from losing my voice, one twitch from falling apart.

The poor house staff must have overheard his name shrieking out like a screaming eagle and let loose in the living room. The word "fuck" was used in so many different ways, they had likely assumed a 10-16, a domestic disturbance, was in progress.

Every powerful, pelvic pounding thrust set loose a spark of magic, dissolving my bones until it left me hanging over the edge, and screaming for madness to take me.

"Lord-Jesus. Chase. You're so fucking deep!"

The sound of our bodies slapping was as loud as our moans. Sex with Chase had always been the best I had ever had, but this, this was downright unimaginable. The series of sharp, body searing currents made me lose control of myself. My heart was on the verge of exploding. Everything hit me all at once and I shattered, full body, mind, and even my soul screamed, *have mercy.*

Chase erupted a second after me, his roaring appreciation mingling with mine. We lay there long after we'd climbed back into our bodies, our runaway breaths bringing normal sounds back into the room. I couldn't move if I wanted to, and neither could he.

His lips brushed my cheek before he placed a sugary sweet kiss against my lips. "I love you, Jax."

The feeling of elation had taken such a hold on me, I responded on impulse.

"I love you too."

We froze as the endearing words hung in the air between us.

Chase jerked his head away, eyeing me with such adoration my heart melted in my chest and leaked into my fluttering

356 · KETA KENDRIC

stomach. Pretending I hadn't said what I'd said, I leaned in to reignite our kiss.

Chase placed a firm hand on my shoulder and eased me back so he could glance into my eyes. He wasn't going to let me downplay this monumental moment.

"You just said..." He couldn't finish his statement.

"I did and I do. I love you," I stated with confidence, realizing it was time I revealed my feelings for him.

"I love you too Jax. More than you could ever know."

He drew me in, tightening his hold on me enough to make me squeal in delight. His relieved laughter warmed my heart, causing it to kick faster in my chest.

After a moment of us savoring each other's closeness, Chase eased his way out of me, shuddering and hissing before he slid to the floor. His smile never dropped. He crawled to a sitting position and laid his head back on the couch, next to my open thigh.

A silly smile rested on my face, as I shoved my fingertips into his damp hair from the back to the top of his head, leaving the shorter strands sticking up. I attempted to sit up, but my body and mind hadn't aligned, so I laid there, pussy on display, air drying.

After a relaxing minute, Chase found the strength to join me on the couch. My eyes remained closed to the soft stroke of him, brushing a few wet strands of hair out of my face. "Why didn't you tell me?"

It took great effort to lift my hooded gaze to his handsome face. He'd given me a big shot of the something I was craving, and it left my body and mind calm and relaxed.

"Why didn't I tell you what?" I frowned, curious about what I'd forgotten to tell him.

"I heard rumors of pregnancy sex being good, but I had no idea it was like that," he muttered while glancing at my pussy.

I shrugged, as I let a smirk light my face. "I've never been pregnant, so how was I supposed to know?"

Our poor baby. His parents were freaks, and he wasn't going to get any rest during this pregnancy, if we had anything to do with it.

Chapter Forty-Four

Jax

A month and a half had gone by, and I had managed to keep my sanity together, staying caged up in Chase's mansion. I'd been teleworking, but it wasn't enough to keep my busy mind occupied.

Not having any social media accounts shielded me from a lot of the negativity that came with being thrust into the spotlight, but there were so many outlets and methods of dispensing drama, comments still made their way to me.

They had labeled me every name in the book, but I was surprised to find the positive feedback on me and Chase's relationship, far outweighed the negative. The positive vibes lightened my anxiety about the situation tremendously. I was a long way from being ready to stop and smile for the cameras, but Chase was the perfect remedy in helping me face my childhood horrors.

In a week, he was set to accompany me to the therapist I had agreed to see. We had spent weeks searching for the perfect doctor. I wanted my son to have what I didn't, a mother. One with a stable mind.

The little meatball in my belly had started to flutter, the sensation, although, scaring me at first, now had me smiling like Chester Cheetah.

Chase had returned to a regular workday, but he phoned, or texted every hour on the hour to check on us. Since our drone stalker who remained nameless was still some place lurking, Chase didn't believe it was safe for me to return to my office.

He took overprotectiveness to a new level. I'd never had anyone care for me in that way, therefore I found that I was more flattered by his behavior than upset. He'd even kicked things up a few notches and had hired around the clock security.

He had also put a set of rules in place, banning me from going anywhere unless he was with me, and suggested I stayed clear of strangers to avoid diseases and viruses. To keep me from losing it, he often pointed out all the unresolved dangers we still had lingering over our heads like a dark cloud.

The only other places we visited were his family home and my doctor's appointments. Since his father knew about the baby, he'd requested we visit weekly. We kept to a Saturday evening dinner plan I had gotten used to. Grandpa James had gotten so relaxed in his interactions with me that he touched my stomach. Even Blake had started to speak complete sentences in my presence.

***

At nearly five months pregnant, the swell in my belly was noticeable. My baby bump was official. At first, I believed I would be disappointed at the growing roundness but seeing the effects of my baby growing gave me a great degree of pride for the little fellow.

I rubbed my stomach and often sang to him, but I wasn't crooning lullabies.

"Don't worry, little fellow, we're going to make our great escape from our captor, your father. He means well, but he's a bit stalkerish."

My new situation involved a lot of pampering that I enjoyed, but it was the being watched and under guard and key part that drove me crazy. For the first few weeks I didn't mind it, fearing facing the crowds because of the media attention. Or inadvertently running into the drone stalker who still didn't have a face.

I missed freedom, independence, and my ability to come and go as I pleased. Being cooped up was too much. I'd been studying the security team's every move, either by eye, or by tapping into the security system.

I'd made plans to get out and breathe, like I'd done twice before. Chase had given me keys to the house, as well as the alarm and gate codes. With a fully charged phone, all that was left was to duck out on the security team. A few hours of freedom, and I would be back and in the house by the time security even knew I was gone.

Two hours was enough time to stretch my legs and clear the clutter from my brain. I'd come to terms with the fact of becoming a mother, but I remained on the fence about becoming a full-on instant family. Every time I convinced myself that we would be okay, the demons from my past would pop up and crush my positivity.

My phone was programmed with everything I needed to trick the security system, and to open and close the gate without setting off any alarms. An Uber was set to meet me at the front gates.

Drone stalker or not, I was taking back my independence, in two-hour increments.

Chapter Forty-Five

Chase

Tony, my security lead's desperate tone came through the phone, commanding my immediate attention.

"We can't find Ms. Saint-Pierre. The surveillance footage showed her on her laptop in the living room before noon, but hasn't provided us any clues as to when, or how she got off the property. We canvassed the neighborhood to see if she'd gone for a walk, but so far nothing. We've made several attempts, but she won't answer her phone."

To calm my sparking nerves, I rocked back in my chair.

Don't overreact, I told myself. Jax wanted alone time. Numerous times, she complained about being cooped up in the house. She was a walking computer, so she probably manipulated the surveillance so she wouldn't be seen leaving.

"Tony, hold on. I'll call her."

After dialing Jax's number and hearing it go straight to voice mail, three times in a row, the fire lighting my nerves blazed uncontrolled. She always answered me, no matter how much my overprotectiveness pissed her off.

My anxious steps filled the space of my office. I paced, attempting to settle my nerves that had gone haywire. I aimed my desperate words toward the sky.

"Please God, let me be overreacting."

The idea that Jax could've been taken had me plagued with horrific ideas of all the things someone could do to her and my son simply because she was with me. I called her job, but no one had seen her. Her friend Lena, who I hadn't met yet, was back in Dubai, based on their last chat. I had also heard her speaking to her father on the phone, but I was clueless as to how to contact him.

Think Chase.

I pulled up the *Find My Friends app* that we had installed on our phone the same day I found out she was pregnant.

A glance at my watch showed twenty minutes past one in the afternoon. I redialed Tony.

"Check the house thoroughly, and send someone to check the main gate entrance. Her phone is nearby, so I'm hoping she just went for a walk."

***

An hour later, me, Tony, and the security team had searched every corner of the house and grounds. The overcast sky hid the sun, projecting a gloominess that spoke to mine.

Tony's pitying gaze met mine. "I'm sorry, sir. I called as soon as we discovered she was gone."

My gaze lifted past Tony's shoulder to another member of the security team, Chris. He was approaching with the over-sized black purse Jax usually carried. The sight of him with her bag caused my heart to turn to dust in my chest.

"The guards at the main gate said she climbed into a blue sedan that they believe was an Uber. I did a walking search of the area and found her purse just outside the view of the main gates. It appeared to have been tossed from the car," Chris informed us. "The security team pulled up surveillance, but it only shows her climbing into the car of her own accord. The view of the driver was unclear."

The information being given, wasn't translating to her being taken. There had to be an explanation. My arm jerked from the weight of the purse when it was handed to me. Somehow, I found the strength to rifle through it.

The sight of her phone in the small inside pocket, siphoned the last of my strength. My legs threatened to buckle as they wobbled under my weight. The air around me grew thick and my lungs fought hard to keep up with my harsh breath.

I had never loved someone so deeply, that the idea of losing them could bring about my own demise. The threat of *them* being taken from me, of something happening to them, was too much. My heart was beating too fast. I couldn't breathe. I think I was having a panic attack. I clutched my chest with my free hand, my gaze still aimed inside the purse.

"What is it?" Tony questioned.

My throat clenched so tightly with fear; I couldn't speak. Tony took a careful step closer and followed my stuck gaze. He did what I was too afraid to. He reached into the purse and retrieved Jax's phone. With no purse or phone, she had no way to call for help, a clear sign—someone had taken her.

My vision blurred as fear seized me and kicked my anxious energy up to full-blown panic. She'd managed to find a way off my property with security on the premises and was driven away from our guarded, and gated community without setting off any red flags.

This led me to believe the danger we'd been flirting with, went far beyond someone leaking pictures and paying off spies. Tony placed the call to the police, as I probed my mind attempting to figure out where else she could have gone besides work.

"Yes. I'd like to report a missing person: Jadzia Saint-Pierre. A twenty-eight-year-old African American female. She's about five-foot-six, one-hundred and forty pounds; she was wearing a green T-shirt dress, and green and white tennis shoes. She's five months pregnant. She was taken from the area near *1252 Jennings Court, Westport*. She's nowhere on the grounds. We found her purse outside the main gates with her phone inside. Will you dispatch someone immediately?"

I kept my eyes on Tony as he spoke with the dispatcher. His lips moved, but I didn't compute all the words because my brain was overrun with negative thoughts. He shook his head at whatever the dispatcher was saying. When he hung up, his gaze locked with mine.

"They are sending two detectives. When I mentioned Jax's name, they knew who she was because of the recent news. They usually require more time before they render someone a missing person but based on the media attention you two have recently gotten, that didn't seem to matter."

On one hand, if Jax wasn't missing, she was going to kill us all because Tony had confirmed to the dispatcher, she was pregnant, which meant the media would blow up the story.

I could picture the headline:

Billionaire's Pregnant Girlfriend Kidnapped.

On the other hand, if Jax *was* missing, the media could work in our favor in helping to find her.

Chapter Forty-Six

Chase

The detectives weren't motivated enough for me in their quest to find Jax. With no confidence in them, I was prepared to call a man I disliked. If anyone could find Jax, I believed he would do it swiftly and without question.

"J?" TK answered with his nickname for Jax since I was using her phone.

"It's Chase," I told him. "Jax is missing. She skirted security, left the house, and I believe someone has taken her from this community with security and cameras watching. Her purse and phone were discarded right out of the view of the community guard station. The detectives, the local authorities assigned to work the case, are not motivated enough to find her. Will you help me?" I hated begging, but for Jax, I would bend both knees.

TK didn't reply. A paused moment followed, but I could hear him typing, so I waited.

"I've already tapped into your cameras," TK answered.

"How? You don't even know my address." *Should I trust this guy?* Jax trusted him, so maybe I should as well, I thought. My instincts had led me to calling him, so I decided to stick with my gut.

"I tracked where her phone was pinging. You should really consider updating your home security system," he suggested.

He amazed me with how quickly he was able to find that much so fast. *Is it really that easy to find people these days?*

"Thank you," came my late response. As far as the security system, Jax had given me the same advice.

"TK, she's pregnant," I blurted. Dead silence had me checking the phone to ensure he hadn't hung up. The seconds on the phone continued to count down, alerting me that he remained on the line. Although he wasn't talking, I heard his fingers striking the keyboard.

"She climbed into the back of a Blue BMW. I'm using CCTV to track the vehicle's location," TK relayed to me.

Maybe he *was* as smart as Jax insisted. It had hardly been ten minutes and he was providing updates that two trained detectives hadn't discovered yet. As far as I knew the detectives were at the guard station scanning surveillance my security team had already checked.

"I have an address," came TK's voice.

No fucking way!

"You do? How? I'm on her phone, so there isn't anything on her person for you to track her. How could you possibly have a location?"

"Closed-circuit television and even traffic cams are powerful tools if you know how to use them. I tracked the license plate of the Blue BMW that picked her up, tapped into various other devices and followed the plate."

"This all seems too simple and fast. Is there a possibility we're being led into a trap?" I was concerned TK was tricked, and possibly left breadcrumbs leading him to the wrong location.

"I don't know, but I'll meet you there to be on the safe side," TK added.

"Okay," I agreed. I wasn't going to sit around and wait on two detectives who appeared unbothered by Jax's disappearance. I would rather chase a false lead with a man I didn't like.

"200 Circle Hill Road," was the address TK recited. "Can you repeat that address for me?" He repeated it, and I prayed I had heard it wrong the first time.

"I'll meet you there. Don't approach, let me go ahead of you and check it out first," TK suggested. He hung up before I had a chance to reply. My words had stalled because the address he had quoted had left me in such a state of shock, I was unable to untie my vocal cords to speak.

***

TK was on my heels like a stalker. The bumper of his silver Tahoe, flirted with the bumper of my black Bentley Continental GT. Although he had vehemently protested, I insisted on leading him to the address since I had no choice but to disclose to him that I'd been there before.

His glaring eyes met mine in my rearview mirror, as I entered the neighborhood with ease. My body was fixed, coiled so tight, I was one stiff mass of exposed nerves.

TK glared at me through his windshield like he wanted to punch me in the face, especially when I entered the code for the security gate. He followed me onto the property and parked behind the blue BMW I had never seen before today.

Why would Jax be here?

"Where the fuck are we, Chase? How the fuck did you know the security code to the gate, not to mention the guards who opened the front gates to this well-protected community and let us in like they knew you." Deep aggravation tightened his brows, as a storm brewed in his eyes.

I didn't answer him. All I wanted was confirmation that his clue had led us to Jax.

"Jax!" I called out, scanning the front of the house. The front door was rarely locked due to staff being on duty around the clock, and the community was gated, and guarded by security twenty-four-seven.

I slung the front door open and rushed in with TK on my heels. Running from room to room, I yelled Jax's name.

"Jax baby! Where are you? Are you okay?"

TK followed, lobbing questions and curse words at my back. The sight of him with a big shiny gun in his hands slowed my stride.

"What are you doing with that?"

The shiny piece wasn't aimed at me, but the menacing gleam in TK's eyes was just as threatening.

"You are going to tell me where the fuck we are, right fucking now!" He shouted his demand, his voice roaring like thunder through the room. His gun remained aimed at the floor, but he appeared ready to use it if I didn't give him an answer.

"This is my house. My family home. I grew up here," I stated, causing his puzzled expression to glaze over his anger. I didn't have time to rationalize an explanation. I needed to find Jax.

Where the hell was my father and the staff? What was going on? I hadn't seen Blake's car either. I took off toward the kitchen and dining area, my hard steps echoing against the shiny floor.

"Jax! Jax! Are you here?"

"Chase," her muffled tone floated low and hollow into my ear. The desperate plea in her voice sent me flying in the direction of the sound. TK raised his gun and gripped my arm to stop me from going blindly into a situation of uncertainty.

"Let me lead." It wasn't a suggestion. He shoved me out of the way and took the lead. He was acting like the arrogant asshole I had met at the expo. However, his gun was displayed in confidence, revealing his familiarity with one. Who was this guy? As a matter of fact, there wasn't much I knew about TK, other than him being Jax's friend who wanted more than friendship.

We crept down the basement stairs toward Jax's call. Once we cleared the stairs, we froze at the sight displayed before us. Behind Jax was someone I knew.

"Amanda?"

Amanda stood behind Jax with a gun pressed into her side under her right arm. The sight of Jax being held at gunpoint sent fear ripping into my tendons and vital organs. What the hell was going on? How had Amanda gotten a hold of Jax and gained access into my family home? Why would she be here? Was Blake behind this?

Amanda shoved the gun deeper into Jax's side each time my gaze landed on her. I think Amanda saw my concern for Jax as a sign of disrespect towards her.

"You don't have to do this. We can work something out. Where is everyone? How did you get into this house?"

TK had his weapon aimed at Amanda, which caused her to tighten her hold on Jax and clench the gun tighter. My eyes met Jax's watery gaze. "You're going to be okay baby." I unclenched my hands and reached for her as I cast a pleading gaze at Amanda.

"I'm the one with the fucking gun!" Amanda yelled. "She's not going to be okay. You think it was okay for you to treat me like your throw away? Take me out and you can't even remember my fucking name. Then, you leave me waiting, looking like a desperate idiot, while you're fucking this bitch in the bathroom?"

I held my hands up in surrender. "I'm sorry Amanda. It was our first date, and I shouldn't have treated you that way."

"It wasn't our first date, you arrogant, inconsiderate, entitled, son-of-a-bitch!" she snapped, her hands trembling, causing the gun to shake against Jax's side. Jax had wedged her hand between the gun and her stomach.

Amanda must have been mistaken. I would remember if I had gone out with her before.

"We can work this all out. It was all just a big misunderstanding," TK added, keeping his aim steady.

"Shut the fuck up!" Amanda yelled at TK. Her shout had caused the gun to jerk in her hand, and her finger to stiffen on the trigger.

Amanda aimed her deadly stare at TK. "You're just as rude and arrogant as Chase." She seemed unphased by the fact that TK kept his gun aimed at her.

"How can we fix this?" My eyes were back on Jax, who stood stiff and still, anticipating the gun blast.

"There are no fixes. I want the both of you to suffer, starting with me blowing this bitch's brains out."

She lifted the gun to the back of Jax's head, and TK immediately took up a more aggressive stance.

"Please, let her go. I'm the one you want. Take me," I pleaded with my hands stretched out in front of me. The mercy I sought with my heart and mind for Jax, and our unborn child was squeezed out, and I'm sure was projected on the anguish set in my tight expression. Seeing her in this situation was my worst living nightmare.

"You don't want to do this Amanda."

TK's pistol remained aimed in Jax and Amanda's direction, his stance firm and strong. Tears slid from Jax's bloodshot eyes as she cradled her small baby bump.

My hands, shaking in fear, were lifted into the prayer position. "Please," I begged with my glazed eyes locked on Amanda. I took a step closer, unconcerned about my own safety. TK was aligned with me, moving closer as well.

"Stay back!" Amanda yelled, pressing the pistol harder into the back of Jax's head. When she lowered the gun and pointed it at her stomach with a teasing sneer, my heart dropped, hit the floor and shattered.

"You think I didn't know about your love child?" Amanda smirked in my direction.

"Please, don't. I'll give you whatever you want, don't hurt her," I sobbed, my voice ragged, tethered, brittle. I was fighting to hold myself together, unable to control my erratic body movements. I had to find a way to get Jax away from Amanda by any means necessary.

"Get the fuck out of my way Chase!" TK shouted behind me now. "You're going to get yourself and Jax killed. You're blocking my fucking shot."

"Amanda, we can work this out. You don't have to do this. I didn't mean to hurt you. I apologize for any hurt and pain I caused you."

"You can't remember my fucking name, so I know you don't remember the first two times we were together either. Let me remind you," she said. "Most recently, in January of this year. I dyed my fucking hair black to get your attention, and you ended up leaving me in a fucking hotel room. Your assistant was nicer to me than you."

"I'm sorry. The paperwork you signed says…"

"Shut the fuck up about paperwork!" She yelled, shaking the gun at me. The tension in her face was pulled so tight, it appeared she was wearing a mask. "Three years, two months, two weeks, and four days ago was the first time we went out. I wore my natural brown hair then. Our pictures were plastered all over the television and internet. They said we were the *it* couple. They predicted marriage and babies in our future. We hit it off so well, I thought the same. After a month, you just got up and walked away, no calls, no text, nothing."

"Hea...ther?" Her name edged over my tongue, each syllable flying breathlessly across my lips.

"Bingo," she replied quickly, with a sneering laugh.

Back then, I had engaged in a couple of relationships, but none lasted more than six weeks. One of the women had been named Heather, but I couldn't remember the last name. Had she had a facelift? She looked nothing like the woman I remembered dating as she was now a blonde.

"Please accept my sincerest apology for the hurt I caused you. I was upfront about my relationship goals. The media sensationalized our relationship, turned it into something it wasn't."

I took another step closer with my hands raised. TK inched up as well, his feet shuffling .

"You better stay the fuck back!" She barked with a tone so menacing it stopped me in my tracks. Her eyes bounced back and forth between me and TK.

"You tossed me away like I was a sack of shit, when all I ever wanted was to love you?"

"I'm sorry if I made you feel that way."

"You sat there, staring me in the face months ago and interviewed me. I figured the third time was a charm. But you looked me right in my fucking face, and not only did you not know who I was, you remembered nothing about me. Do you know how much that hurt? Our time together, it meant nothing to you but, it was everything to me. We were good together. You told me I was good for you, then you threw me away and went out with the next woman on your to-do list."

Three years ago, Heather had convinced me to take her to Vegas. We had gone out on four dates in a months' time. One of the dates included a weekend in Vegas. A lot of drunken sex was involved, but there were never plans for a future together.

She had managed to get me shitfaced and attempted to convince me into a quickie drunken marriage. It was one of the reasons I had decided to let her go. She was coming on too strong, talking about marriage and children.

TK and I both took another cautious step that stopped us both when Amanda aimed the pistol at him, then quickly back on Jax.

"Come any closer, and I'm squeezing this fucking trigger!" she shouted.

"There must be a way we can work this out. What can you gain from hurting Jax? She didn't do this. I aggressively pursued her."

"Satisfaction," she said. The disturbing scowl she cast resembled the snarl of a lioness aiming to rip her prey's throat out. "The satisfaction of knowing I finally got your attention. That I made you hurt. And to think, I got new tits for you." She hit herself hard in the chest with her free hand. "A new ass, nose job, and changed my hair color twice to get your attention, and it still wasn't enough."

Her crazed eyes filled with tears, the left twitching at the corner.

"Put that damn gun down!" A roaring voice from above sounded like it had fallen from the sky.

Thumping footsteps sounded on the stairs, drawing our attention. TK kept his gun aimed at Amanda, but like the rest of us, his attention had landed on the man making his way down the stairs.

"Dad?"

My father approached, his cane knocking loud against the floor with each step. I was concentrating on Amanda with Jax so hard that I hadn't heard him until he'd spoken and was midway down the steps.

He stood behind our group during our standoff, leaning on his cane and glaring at Amanda with fire in his eyes. My attention shifted back and forth between the two. Did he know her? I couldn't worry about their connection right now. I had to find a way to get Jax away from Amanda.

An overpowering force took a hold of me at the sight of her threatening to hurt Jax and our unborn child. Tunnel vision had started to set in, making me mindless and not caring about danger or getting hurt. I only cared about getting Jax away from Amanda.

"Chase get out of the fucking way!" TK yelled, wanting to reclaim his aim at Amanda.

"Stop pointing that gun at my son!" My father had lifted his cane, pointing it at TK.

"Chase, move Goddammit!" TK shouted.

"Chase," Jax's low tone sounded. It was the only voice I cared about hearing.

I continued to step forward, ignoring the voices of the men shouting behind me, with my gaze locked with Amanda's. She lifted the gun, aiming it at my chest. My desperate moves had pulled her attention away from Jax, and her concentrated gaze remained pinned on me.

My mind overflowed with enough rage to make me fight for the control I needed to keep from doing bodily harm. My veins pop under my skin. Fire had replaced the blood coursing through me. Although I suspected that Amanda was hurt enough to shoot me, it didn't stop me from advancing on her until the gun touched my chest.

"Chase. No." Jax cried in a low tone.

"Chase!" I heard my father yell behind me.

With Amanda's teary eyes on mine and the gun jammed into my chest, I reached blindly, shoving Jax out of the danger zone.

Reaching up with caution, I brushed a delicate hand along Amanda's cheek and fought a grimace when she leaned her face into my palm. The gun shook in her hand, knocking against my chest and giving more depth to her fractured mental state.

"It didn't have to come to this Heather. Do you really want to hurt me? Whatever I did to you, I can assure you, it wasn't intentional."

TK had lured Jax into safety behind me which urged the storm in my blood to churn harder. The notion of being outside myself took a hold of my mind. The gun sitting pressed against my chest could have gone off but knowing that Jax and our child were safe was enough in the moment.

"Chase!" Jax's shout had managed to break through the black cloud of rage surrounding me. I smiled at Amanda, but I ached to strangle her. I slid my hand along her cheek, lowering it with a delicate touch until it brushed the top of the pistol shaking in her hand.

"I love you, Chase. I always have, from the moment I met you," Amanda confessed, meaning every word. The true definition of crazy had manifested itself and was staring me in the face. Once I had a good grip on her gun, I snatched it from her hand and shoved her until her back struck the wall behind us.

"How dare you threaten the woman I love and our unborn child? Are you crazy?"

"Chase. Please. We were so good together. I can make you happy," she choked out. She saw nothing wrong with what she had done, nor did she harbor empathy for the lives she had placed in jeopardy. TK or Jax had taken the gun from me, but my focus was concentrated on Amanda.

"Chase please stop! She's not worth it. This is not you. *We* need you!"

I hadn't realized how tight a grip I had around Amanda's neck until I felt Jax tugging at my arm. The steady flow of her voice had broken apart the rage that had engulfed me.

TK stood on the opposite side of me, unphased by my behavior. I believe he would have stood there and let me kill her. I hadn't heard my father yelling for me to stop, until my mind had realigned itself.

I backed away from Amanda with my hands frozen in the position they had been in around her throat, until I was a safe distance away from her. TK gripped Amanda's arm before turning her roughly to face the wall and proceeded to frisk her for more weapons.

Jax kept her tight grip on my forearm, whispering to me in hushed tones. "I'm okay, Chase. We're okay." The sight of her, and the sound of her soothing voice was what had dragged me back to the present. A smile broke through my haze before my gaze fell to her stomach.

"Are you sure you're okay? You're both okay?" I scanned her thoroughly.

"We're fine." Her tender stroke brushed my jaw. Fresh tears leaked from her eyes and slid down her cheeks before she cast a glance at Amanda, then back at my father who stood observing us.

Chapter Forty-Seven

Jax

Chase kept me close and tucked into his side with a protective arm around me. My kidnapper's anguished groans lured my face from Chase's strong shoulder to TK's rough handling as he continued to search Amanda.

"Let me go, you fucking lunatic. I told you I don't have any more weapons!"

I suppose Amanda hadn't been expecting Chase to find me, especially at the one place he would not think to look. The knowledge of him reaching out to TK for help proved how desperate he was to find me. When he ran up on Amanda pointing a gun into his chest to save me, to save us, it was crazy, but proved he loved us more than his own life.

Seeing TK with a gun and how well he handled it was a surprise. I believe the illegal life I suspected he lived was being revealed.

The fact I was taken to Chase's family home and had witnessed Amanda gain access, led me to believe that Blake was working with her. However, it was the older Taylorson standing in front of us that my gaze landed on.

"Dad? What the hell is going on? What is Amanda doing in this house?" Chase's face was squinted tightly into a heavy mask of confusion. TK stood staring at James with one hand keeping Amanda pinned to the wall, as she squirmed and fussed under his hold.

"Chase, tell him to let me go," Amanda called back, but received no reply.

James hadn't answered Chase's question, instead he hobbled a few steps closer, thumping along as his cane knocked against the floor.

He continued to ignore Chase's question as he aimed his attention at TK and Amanda. "You." He pointed at TK. "Would you remove your hand from that young lady's neck?"

TK didn't acknowledge that James had given him an order. Instead, he shot the older man a pointed look and continued to hold the back of Amanda's neck, pinning her face to the wall. The position looked painful. *Good.*

Chase stood deadly silent, staring at his father like he had never seen him before. I attempted to take a step, but it did nothing to break Chase's hold on me. With a finger aimed at Amanda, my attention was focused on James.

"Do you know this woman? Did you hire her to kidnap me and hold me at gun point?" I attempted another step, but all that moved were my feet, as I was pinned to a brick wall. Amanda continued to call out for Chase. *And I thought I was crazy.*

"Yes, I know her, but I would have never advised her to hold you at gunpoint. I simply told her to bring you back here so we could all talk," he answered without an ounce of remorse. Me, Chase, and TK gawked.

"You dirty ass dog!" I yelled at James. He'd been playing me and Chase, pretending to be on our side when he'd been plotting against us the whole time. Since Chase was holding me in place, I leaned forward so I could glare into James's eyes.

"You did all of this, didn't you? The drone, sending the paparazzi to attack us, hiring someone to break into my apartment, intercepting my Uber by sending that mental patient to pick me up, spying on me and Chase, the video…"

At this point my tears restarted, but not from sadness or fear. My tears now fell from pure unadulterated anger. I lunged at James, but a set of strong arms stopped me.

"You goddamn bastard! How could you do this to someone and stand there, smug, and arrogant like your actions didn't rip apart two lives. You selfish son of a bitch!" I screamed at the top of my lungs as Chase held me around my shoulders, and TK kept a raging Amanda in place.

"I will find a way to send you to prison for the rest of your life," Chase growled at his father. "It will become my mission to see you suffer. Why would you do this? Why?" Chase questioned; his words choppy from the deep well of hurt his father had caused. His body trembled, and I didn't know if it was from rage or hurt.

James smiled. The old rotten Billy goat stood his ass there and cracked a smile, making my anger flare higher as I attempted to get away from Chase.

"You dug up an illegal video of me being tortured to use in your plot to keep us apart. When that wasn't enough, you hired someone to break into my apartment." TK glared at me; his eyes squinted with curiosity. He had no idea about my childhood horrors. The fact that James had dug up my past proved how sick and devilish he was.

"Just a few times, Chase. Please. Let me bust him upside his fucking head a few times with TK's gun, and I promise I'll be okay."

James, with his wide eyes, for the first time appeared afraid. I knew I resembled a mad woman, hair all over my head, wild yelling, and attempting to break away from a man who towered above me and was a mass of muscle and unbreakable strength.

"Jax, please calm down. You're going to hurt yourself and the baby," Chase said, but his calming words had no effect. I wanted to lay hands on James Taylorson. It was clear he had manipulated Amanda, but it didn't stop me from wanting to put a foot in her ass too.

"Why would you do this?" I barked in his direction. "Why would you play with our lives like this? Risk the life of an unborn child…" I was so upset, I was unable to finish my sentence, as my tears continued to fall.

James pointed at us. "You two are too upset right now to understand my reasons. My grandchild was never in danger. It was my gun she took, and it was empty."

"But mine isn't," TK pointed out. "I could've killed her. Chase *would* have killed her. What's wrong with you?" TK spit his words at the older man, sneering at him.

"Have you lost your fucking mind?" Chase snapped. His words had knocked the wind from the room and his father's chest. James had jumped at the sound of his son's booming voice, his steps faltering as he moved back.

For the first time, Chase moved his hand from my waist. He roared in anger, a deep resounding growl that called for complete silence. He took a step closer to his father, every muscle in his body pulled tight enough to snap.

His gaze had gone blank like he'd hidden his soul away from his evil intentions. He was going to kill the old fart; I could sense it. I gripped his arm, his powerful muscles flexed so tight they felt like iron under my fingers. There was enough rage flowing through him to scare me, but I couldn't let him go to jail for murder.

James was smart enough to take a few more careful steps back. Amanda's yells continued in the background as Chase's murderous gaze held his father in place. James lifted a hand in surrender.

"Chase, I couldn't allow you to expose a five-billion-dollar empire to just anyone? When I noticed how serious you two were about each other, I had to intervene." He cast his gaze in my direction. "No offense Jax, I like you because you're smart and you're not afraid to work hard, but you don't have enough clout to be a good match for my son."

"What the hell are you talking about with your crazy ass?"

James ignored me and my question and concentrated on Chase. My fist tightened, ready to punch Amanda in her mouth, if she didn't shut the fuck up with her useless yelling that no one cared about.

"There is only one place Amanda could have gotten your gun, and that's from your bedroom. You're a despicable son-of-a-bitch. Let me guess. You allowed this woman to get a hold of your gun, then send her to pick up Jax." Chase took another step closer, dragging me along now, as his father took two more steps back.

"Heather Amanda Newcastle. Does her surname ring any bells to you?" James asked Chase, like this was the time to be playing twenty-one questions.

"I don't have time for riddles. You better tell us what the hell is going on before I do something I can't take back."

"Heather's the daughter of Lieutenant Governor, Herbert Newcastle."

"So what?" I blurted. "I don't have a single fuck to give about whose daughter she is. The bitch kidnapped me at gunpoint and belongs in a mental facility."

Chase's mind must have latched on to something because he shook a stiff finger at his father.

"You're at it again. You're the reason Amanda kept getting to the top of my dating list. She didn't have the privilege of being raised by you, so she had no idea that you were using her. Blake married who you chose for him. Now, you want me to marry Lt. Governor Newcastle's daughter, so you can somehow claw your way into more power."

My teeth bit into my lip, still aching to rip the man apart. This was all about power. James was attempting to pimp his son out to a possible soon to be Governor's daughter. Was this a sample of the kind of lessons, and overbearing guidance Chase was exposed to growing up? He'd mentioned on several occasions how tough a son-of-a-bitch his father had been.

How had Chase turned out so normal if this was who had raised him? Without his mother's influence there was a good chance that he would have probably turned out just like Blake.

"Nothing about what you've done is right, yet you stand your balled-up ass there like you're the god of all decisions. You're a delusional, power-hungry dick-faced asshole!" I shouted my angry words at James, somehow hoping they had the power to punch his ass in the face.

James cut his eyes at me. Chase was good at holding his piece, but I wasn't. James made me look normal when I'd believed myself broken beyond repair.

"Let me guess. Your plan was to break me and Jax up so that I could marry Heather? The only reason you would have for wanting to talk to Jax alone would be to get her on board with whatever sick plan you've hatched. Has it ever occurred to you that the Lt. Governor is using you for your money? His daughter marries me, and he gains exposure to an endless supply of campaign money."

"Son, this would be an excellent opportunity on your part as well. This endeavor can groom you for a possible seat in the government. Your celebrity status would make it an easy transition."

"Are you serious right now?" I asked James, not wanting to believe it, but knew he wasn't joking. It appeared he wanted to live Chase's life for him, or better yet, live his own life through Chase. I glanced at Chase and started talking while James was in the middle of his sentence.

"Is this the twisted kind of bullshit you've had to deal with all your life?"

Chase nodded while staring daggers at his father.

"Hey asshole!" I called out to James whose gaze was reminiscent of Blake's. I pointed at my stomach. "I'm pregnant with Chase's child. How did you think a marriage with another woman was going to factor into your fucked up equation?"

Off a deep sigh he shook his head. "The pregnancy was never supposed to happen, but what's politics without some scandals? Besides, you're carrying a Taylorson now, you would have more privilege in his life than some wife. With Chase as his son-in-law, Herbert would be a shoo-in for governor. In return, he would groom Chase."

James said all this with a straight face. Like this type of twisted shit was normal. Amanda's angry scowl revealed that she was getting a true depiction of what she'd been buying into.

"James, you're a fucking lunatic. You're the kind of crazy that runs too deep to be reasoned with. I'll climb through the fires of hell before I let you anywhere near this baby, and that's a fucking promise," I spit the words so intensely at him, I forced Chase to recapture me.

Chase aimed a stiff finger at James as he struggled to contain his blazing anger.

"So let me get this straight. You and Herbert, your golfing buddy if I'm remembering correctly, planned this. Use me and your money to help him become Governor. In return, you get to run the state for him, playing him like the puppet you would turn him into. Then, groom me for politics to keep the power train rolling."

James didn't look bothered by Chase's breakdown of his plans.

"You think you're helping me? How far does this go? The drone, my signature, sabotaging our efforts to find you out, exposing my private phone calls, digging up an illegal video to threaten Jax, and sending someone to break into her apartment."

Chase shook his head in disbelief when James didn't answer. Instead, he stood there blinking at his son. The man we assumed was helping us, was who'd been manipulating the hell out of us the whole time.

Angry tears streamed down my cheeks, as I prayed for Chase to let me go, so I could beat the shit out of this old man and pray for forgiveness later. I thought Blake was a snake, but he was at least man enough to tell me to my face what he thought.

"Yes, to the drone, but I recently discovered that Amanda had kept a key she made to your penthouse years ago and must have found a way to record your phone conversations. I didn't hire anyone to break into Jax's apartment either."

All eyes landed on Amanda.

Chapter Forty-Eight

Jax

Amanda glared back at us and didn't appear to be sorry that she'd been invading Chase's privacy for years.

"I took the key from her." James informed Chase, like it mattered. Chase didn't acknowledge his father but continued to cast an infuriating gaze in Amanda's direction.

"You," Chase pointed at her. "You've been in and out of my penthouse for years, spying on me. All those times, I sensed that I was being watched, hearing things, it was you, wasn't it?"

Knowing who her father was, Amanda was able to get away with things that a normal person wouldn't. Then, linking up with James, gave her a wealth of infinite knowledge on how to be wicked.

"I'm sorry Chase. I waited for you. When I saw you sleeping with all those other women, I could have reacted, but I swallowed the hurt and sat by and waited for you. I tried to figure out what you saw in them, so I could give it to you." She had the nerve to look embarrassed.

Chase had very little privacy, but she was confirming that he'd hardly had any. His life was being stomped on by a bunch of lunatics who wanted to shape it the way they saw fit, despite his feelings.

"It took a team of ten to stop your cyber-attack and to keep you and *him*," James stated, aiming a finger at me before pointing at TK again, "From launching a full-on cyber war and destroying a major broadcast network. You two were always a step from finding out the truth, despite the team I employed. Max MacKenzie gave the team a run for their money also. Your determined efforts would have forced me to reveal the truth sooner or later."

James paused, and I could imagine all that crazy inside his head fighting to come out.

"Amanda's erratic behavior is what drew us all here today and forced me to reveal too much at once." He pointed a crooked finger at Amanda, still pinned to the wall breathing like she was running on a treadmill. "Honestly, there's not much the team can do anymore to keep you from uncovering the truth anyway." James finished.

Chase pointed an angry finger at his father with hurtful tears standing in his eyes. "Tell me this, and I want an honest answer from you."

James nodded.

"The knee injury I suffered in college that ended my base-ball career, you did that to me too, didn't you?"

Another nod came from James. "You were concentrating too hard on your hobby instead of a career that could last you a lifetime."

The hurt in Chase's face stirred something in me, making my anger toward James flame to an all-time high. Through the years, Chase believed his father's tough love was for his bene-fit. He glanced down, placing his hand against my stomach while glaring into my eyes.

"We're the roots of the wicked, but we're better than what we were born from. The truth of your father's words were re-flected on me too. The roots of wicked seeds are capable of growing into something decent and producing something spe-cial."

A sheen of raging anger covered Chase's face when he glanced back at his father.

"James Arthur Taylorson, you are the wickedest man I know. I pushed myself to impress you. I swallowed my dreams to pursue yours. I shelved my happiness to bring you yours. I see you. I see the deceit and evil that has always resided in you."

He tensed harder, attempting to contain the rage, tightening his muscles and coursing through his veins. My firm grip on his arm tightened as it seemed he might snap and deck the old rabid possum standing in front of us.

"Somewhere along the line, you lost your mind, I'm sure of it. You could have crippled me for good. You could have killed Jax and our unborn child with these stunts of yours. I didn't need my life turned into a living hell to know how much I love this woman. No matter what you did, I would have never left her," he expressed with a level of emotion I felt.

"Despite what you may think of me, my instincts have never failed me when it comes to choosing what's best for myself. Especially, when it came to ignoring the fucked-up lessons you attempted to teach me and Blake. You're the reason Blake is so screwed up."

James had the nerve to look hurt. He was truly a hot, delusional mess of a man.

"Why don't you tell the group why I truly took over the company, *father!*" He spit the word father out like it had burned his tongue. "Tell them how the board members ganged up on you and voted you out. How they threatened to buy the company out from under you. If I hadn't taken over, there wouldn't even be a company."

Chase had sacrificed the life he wanted to save their family business, and James didn't appear to be the least bit grateful.

All he was interested in was power. Since it had been taken from him one way, he sought it in other ways.

"The main reason Swift Capital exploded into a billion-dollar company was because I followed my own instincts. I never wanted to be CEO, still don't. I stay because the company needed someone better than you or Blake, and I had enough confidence in myself to know it was me."

I lifted a brow; proud he was venting his frustrations.

"James, over the years, I have allowed you to believe your ideas and input actually mattered. Your ego driven power plays wouldn't allow you to see I was not the puppet you assumed I was. It took me a while to master the skill, but I figured out how to feed your ego enough to let you think you had the control you so desperately desired, when I was in control the entire time."

James was too stunned to comment. I side-eyed Chase. Is that what he had done to me? Had he fed my ego to ultimately get what he wanted from me?

"Why?" The heated tone of Chase's question reverberated throughout the room and yanked me out of my thoughts. "Why send Amanda to pick up Jax, knowing she is unstable? Why not sit us down and tell us how you felt? I started to believe you had changed, but even with parts of your brain damaged by strokes, your mind is still as warped, and twisted as it has ever been. Shame on me for believing that a man wicked enough to hand his teen sons over to two sexually deviant oil baronesses, in exchange for a board seat, would ever have anything other than sewage pumping through his rotten heart."

"Chase," I whispered, appalled by the impact of what he had just revealed. I was flooded with the same depth of hatred for James as I had felt for my mother. The tears standing in Chase's eyes crushed my heart, but I realize they weren't tears of sadness, they represented the blinding hatred he fought to keep under control.

"I'm so sorry that happened to you," I whispered to Chase. "And that you grew up with this colossal asshole." My grip on him had grown so tight my hand shook from the force of the squeeze.

"It's okay," he whispered. "They both died horribly when they got a hold of the wrong teen boy."

All eyes landed on James who showed no remorse for how he had hurt everyone, especially Chase. Amanda had even quieted and relaxed enough that TK allowed her enough room to twist her neck to get a look at James.

"Son, I thought you understood that every decision I made on your behalf was to make you stronger. As far as you and Jax, I thought breaking you two up early on would do the trick in keeping you apart. I was keeping you both from making a mistake."

This mother fucker was talking like his son hadn't just called him out for pimping him out as a sex slave when he was a teen. What kind of fucking devil was James? He just kept right on with his explanations, like his words alone were all it took to smooth things over.

"Son, love is nothing but a fallacy that people foolishly convince themselves is real. I give the two of you six to eight months, max. Why go through the stress of maintaining a relationship that is doomed to fail anyway?"

Chase's laugh was a deep rumble that shook his chest and vibrated against me. Blessedly, Amanda remained quiet behind us. I had broken several of my nails attempting to jump out of her car until the crazy bitch had pulled that gun on me. I aimed my broken nails at James when he twisted his mouth, preparing to feed Chase more bullshit. I was sick of listening to him.

"I'm calling my father. See how smug you'll be when Alexander Saint-Pierre gets a hold of your raggedy broke down ass. Your money can't save you from everything."

"Jax," TK called, but the raw fury coursing through me stopped me from answering him. "Jax!" TK yelled, yanking my attention from the asshole I wanted to kill.

"Please don't get your father involved in this." The stress in his pinched gaze, and the desperation in his tone wasn't missed.

"What the hell do you know about my father?" My gaze was stuck on his face. TK, for the first time, appeared to struggle with what he had to say.

"TK!" My loud shout caused my nails to sink deeper into Chase's arm.

"He's never revealed the reason why to any of us, but an order from Alexander Saint-Pierre is always followed. And it's not money we want to be paid with. We're paid with training. There are people that would kill to work under your father, taking on the side job of keeping an eye on his daughter is a very small price to pay for what we receive in return."

"What the fuck are you talking about TK?" The secrets and lies were flowing like the rapids of Terminator, one of the most technically challenging river rapids in the world.

"From twelve to fifteen you had Sabrina. She was much more than your nanny. From sixteen to eighteen, the new nanny, Kim, was put in place. Your college years, Chad, the friendly jock who lived next door to you the entire time, wasn't a college student. The friendly neighbor, Mr. Harrison, in the first apartment you rented after college. And finally, it was me." TK finished, leaving my mind blown.

All eyes were aimed at him, as I attempted to pick my jaw up from the floor. My father blamed himself for what my mother had done to me. He'd often told me how much he wished he could've prevented it or noticed the signs earlier. And now, years later I recalled his words as he held me the night he killed her.

"The most precious gift to ever enter my life, will never be left unprotected. I'll never allow anyone to hurt you again. From this moment forward, I'll do everything in my power to keep you safe."

On one hand, I was grateful he kept his vow to protect me, but on the other hand, his methods of doing so were as far-fetched as James's attempt to run Chase's life.

With murder on my mind, my gaze remained on TK, who dropped his gaze away from mine. Amanda struggled to pull herself from his grip but failed. I would apologize to my son later for the cursing I had done and was about to continue to do.

"The fucking plot keeps getting thicker. My life's a fucking maze of secrets. Anyone else feels the need to spill more secrets while we're airing all this dirty ass laundry?" My infuriated gaze was pointed at each person and finally stopped on Chase.

"Can we get the fuck out of here, before I find a way to beat the shit out of two grown ass men?"

TK was on my shit list as much as James, and my father. He'd been lying to me for years. I considered him a friend, and this whole time he'd been one of my father's watch dogs.

"I'll deal with you when the idea of murdering you no longer brings me pleasure." I spat my infuriating words at TK. Despite my anger, thoughts of how often TK had been there for me when my father couldn't, kept me from blowing a fuse.

"We're not going anywhere." Chase stopped me from moving.

"We need to reveal another secret, starting with who the hell your father is?" His hard glare cut into TK before it rested on me.

James glared at me expectantly, wanting to know as well.

Chase housed a hint of anger in his eyes, but when his gaze dropped to my protruding belly, it disappeared.

"We have a long talk ahead of us," he said, and it wasn't a request.

I nodded, knowing I should've disclosed to Chase that my father had stopped being a regular cop a long time ago, especially with us bringing a child into the world. It pleased me that James's money hadn't been able to buy my father's cover.

No one was supposed to know my father was CIA, not even me. I glanced at TK. Was he CIA too? I was too upset with him to find out, and I wasn't sure if I wanted to forgive him for deceiving me. If my father hadn't been on assignment, I would phone him and unleash the hundreds of choice words I was saving for him.

James called out to Chase when we started towards the steps. "Son, please try to understand my side, why I did this for you. Please say you'll forgive me, and we can talk about this later."

Chase stopped a few paces in front of his father, his gaze deadly, his body coiled so tightly, the anger was spilling from him in heated waves. I would remind him later to change his locks and update his security at each of his residences. His father claimed to have taken Amanda's key, but there was no telling how many copies she had made. Also, there was no guarantee that James wouldn't start using the key himself.

The deadly glare Chase cast on his father made me flinch.

"You better be glad my mercy prevails over my wrath or you would be dead for all that you've done. Don't call me. Don't come near me. Don't even consider me your son anymore. If I see you again, I'll punch you in the face until it's unrecognizable. I'll never forgive you. I never want to see you again." James had enough sense not to keep pushing Chase. Whatever he was about to say next, he kept to himself.

Chase released a devious laugh, one I had never heard from him before. "You know what? You should marry Amanda. That way you both get what you want. You get access to more power, and she'll get a Taylorson. I'm pressing charges on the both of you for reckless endangerment, kidnapping, breaking and entering, and whatever else applies."

Chase's stiff finger sat an inch from his father's face. "You evil, black-hearted bastard. You're the reason I know how it feels to hate."

Proof of how wicked James was sat on his self-righteous face. He wasn't sorry he had attempted to pimp out his son to gain power. He wasn't sorry that he had used Amanda, or that he'd been ripping his son's life apart, seam by seam.

Chase held strong, keeping me away from his father. I could've gotten a few cheap licks off on the old man, but Chase's words were ripping him to shreds far worse than any of my licks could. Besides, I needed to pee. I didn't need to add more chaos to an already volatile situation by pissing all over myself, while attempting to kick the ass of a sixty-something year old stroke victim who was criminally insane.

TK, yanked Amanda from the wall and marched her towards the steps.

"Where are you going with her?" James asked TK.

"I'm taking her to jail or the nut house, whichever will take her first. The gun you claimed was empty, *wasn't*." TK had the gun stuffed down the back of his pants. "She'll be charged with kidnapping and two counts of attempted murder. I'll be back for you. Mark Romero, can't save you this time." TK tapped the top of his left shoulder. "I have recorded you confessing to multiple crimes you've committed over the years."

TK's secret life was finally revealing itself. It was why he had access to so much more than I did and could get away with tricks of the trade that would have sent others to jail instantly.

"We'll have her out by tomorrow. And your little recording will be inadmissible. You're wasting your time," James said with confidence. He attempted to square his shoulders, but the right one hung uselessly low.

TK glared at me, projecting sorrow and pity, and damn me for still seeing him as a friend. I cut my eyes at him before me and Chase continued our journey toward the steps, leaving the group under the mountain of lies they'd built up.

Before our feet touched the first step, the light from above shined down and a shadowy figure started to march down. The figure looked imposing enough for Chase to shove me behind him. Had James hired someone to kill us? It wouldn't surprise me if he did.

When the face of the man came into view, I attempted to step around Chase's body, but he stopped me.

"Dad!" I called. He cast a smile in my direction, but his gaze turned menacing when it landed on James.

His eyes remained locked on James, but he spoke to TK.

"TK, let me have her and you take him. If I touch him, I'm going to kill him."

Once my father had Amanda, all eyes followed TK to James.

"Don't you dare touch me. You have nothing on me," James had the nerve to spit at TK.

"On the contrary," my father stated. "The recording I just heard and the evidence I have collected is enough to send you to prison for the rest of your life. I have evidence proving that you were a member of an illegal child pornography ring, of which, you sent an illegal video to my daughter to blackmail her. You are responsible for sending this young woman, who is no stranger to seeing the inside of a mental ward, to pick up my pregnant daughter with a loaded gun. I even found the man you hired to break your son's leg when he was in college."

James, for the first time, didn't have a snappy comeback as TK gripped him in a tight hold from the back.

"Lieutenant Governor Herbert Newcastle is being arrested as we speak. Illegal use of campaign funds and having an affair with a sixteen-year-old, just to name a few. I'll make sure you two are assigned to the same prison. And don't worry, I can guarantee you will be placed in the general population."

James' throat bobbed. It appeared he was in the midst of soiling his pants as his face had gone ghost white. His past sins had finally caught up to him.

My father reached out his hand to Chase, "Nice to meet you, Chase. Thank you for taking care of her." He glanced at me next. "I got your messages. Sorry, I wasn't early enough to stop you from being taken. You didn't think I would leave you hanging, did you?"

I shook my head.

"I'm sorry," he said, glancing at TK. He knew I wanted to kill him for lying to me all these years. "We'll talk about it, okay." I nodded and although I wanted to hang on to my anger, I knew that I had already forgiven him.

TK followed my father with Amanda, marching a limping James up the steps as he cried out for Chase. "Chase, help me, son. Don't let him take me to jail. I did this for you."

Chase and I were surrounded by people who assumed we couldn't make sound decisions or didn't have the capacity to take care of ourselves. I'd had a babysitter most of my life. No surprise I had trust issues and problems befriending people.

However crazy the situation was, the most amazing thing to come from the madness was Chase, and our little lemon. He was fluttering around in my belly like a little hummingbird, letting me know we were disturbing his rest.

Epilogue

Four months after my father revealed himself as the same controlling monster he had always been, Jax nudged me awake in the middle of the night. She had officially leased her apartments and moved in with me.

I was temporarily running Swift Capital, teaching Blake the ropes so he could take his rightful place. To my surprise, the job had a resoundingly positive effect on him as he appeared eager to prove my unspoken predictions about him wrong.

Thankfully, I had been smart with my earnings and investments, and could do whatever I wanted with the rest of my life.

My mother had arrived, months ago, with intentions of spending a few weeks with us. However, getting to know Jax and the joys of becoming a grandmother had kept her in place. She had quickly become obsessed over meeting her grandson, who she had felt numerous times, rolling around in Jax's belly demanding to be let out.

Jax's second call to me had me sitting up in bed, but her calming voice hadn't been alarming enough to keep me from dozing. Her voice sounded once more, sharper, and followed by a quick nudge to my side.

"Chase, I think it's time. My water broke."

I eased my feet over the edge of the bed, preparing to go and get her more water until my eyes focused and my brain pieced her words together. I noticed the large wet spot pooled under her and the worried expression on her face.

At the realization of what was happening, I jetted from the bed like a man on fire, snatching keys and the hospital bag we packed a month in advance. I assisted Jax to a standing position.

"I'm ready. Are you okay to walk? Do you need a new outfit? I'll get you one." My words were a bunch of rushed gibberish.

In her condition, Jax ended up calming me down. "I'm fine. First, help me to the bathroom to change, and please put something on before we leave the house. We don't need the doctors and nurses throwing dollars at you."

A glance down showed I was preparing to leave the house in nothing but my boxer briefs.

The last thing Jax was thinking about at this moment was how we had arrived here. However, it was heavy on my mind as I assisted her into the bathroom.

When Jax had walked into my board room, I was clueless about who she would be to me. The words my mother had imparted about allowing myself to be receptive when love called, inspired me to do one simple thing—listen. Not only with my ears, but with my heart and spirit.

Five hours later, the sight of my son's head being pulled through the long incision they had sliced across Jax's stomach had silenced me into a frozen state.

I knew the power of women, but I didn't understand the magnitude of what they were capable of doing. The ability to carry life and safely deliver it into the world. I would never fully understand the physical and emotional impact of the journey, but I was privileged to witness a part of it.

One of life's greatest miracles was unfolding in front of me. Knowing I was a part of creating it brought tears to my eyes as Jax's grip tightened around my hand. Even as my legs threatened to give, and shortness of breath made me lightheaded, my strength held as I was unwilling to miss a second of our life changing moment.

I was witness to the purity of love, experiencing the strength of a well-built connection, and a part of a bond tying us together forever. This was the moment we breathed life into our future.

Jax and I waited with bated breath, until our son's airway was cleared. The first shrieking cry raised goosebumps on my neck and arms. Jax and my eyes met before our lips turned into deep smiles filled with pride.

He was a six-pound-two-ounce, pink glob of wrinkly skin, who trembled with every strong wail he released. However, I had fallen unconditionally in love at first sight with Chase Alexander Taylorson, Jr.

End of Roots of the Wicked

Author's Note

My sincere thank you for choosing to read Roots of the Wicked.
I appreciate your support and time. Please leave a review letting
me and others know what you thought of the book. If you enjoyed it, please pass it along to your friends or anyone you think
would like it.

Other Titles by Keta Kendric

The Twisted Minds Series:

Twisted Minds #1
Twisted Hearts #2
Twisted Secrets #3
Twisted Obsession #4
Twisted Revelation #5
Twisted Deception # 6 (2024)

The Twisted Box Set

The Chaos Series:

Stand Alones:

Novellas:

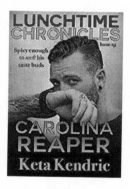

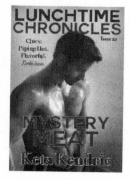

Paranormals:

Kindle Vella:

Audiobooks:

Connect on Social Media

Subscribe to my Newsletter or Paranormal Newsletter for exclusive updates on new releases, sneak peeks, and much more.

You can also follow me on:

Instagram:
https://instagram.com/ketakendric

TikTok:
https://www.tiktok.com/@ketakendric?

Bookbub:
https://www.bookbub.com/authors/keta-kendric

Goodreads:
https://www.goodreads.com/user/show/73387641-keta-kendric

Newsletter:
https://mailchi.mp/c5ed185fd868/httpsmailchimp

Facebook Page:
https://www.facebook.com/AuthorKetaKendric

Facebook Readers' Group:
https://www.facebook.com/groups/380642765697205/

Twitter:
https://twitter.com/AuthorKetaK

Pinterest:
https://www.pinterest.com/authorslist/

Made in the USA
Middletown, DE
26 September 2024

61083184R00243